ATRAMENTOUS

<u>BOOKS BY TIM FRANKOVICH</u>

<u>Heart of Fire</u>
Until All Curses Are Lifted
Until All Bonds Are Broken
Until All the Gods Return
Until All the Stars Fall

<u>Dragontek Lore</u>
Viridia
Incarnadine
Auric
Onyx
Amaranth
Atramentous

The Certainty of Blood

ATRAMENTOUS

DRAGONTEK LORE, BOOK 6

by Tim Frankovich

To Joshua and Will
I look forward to the moment they
realize this is here

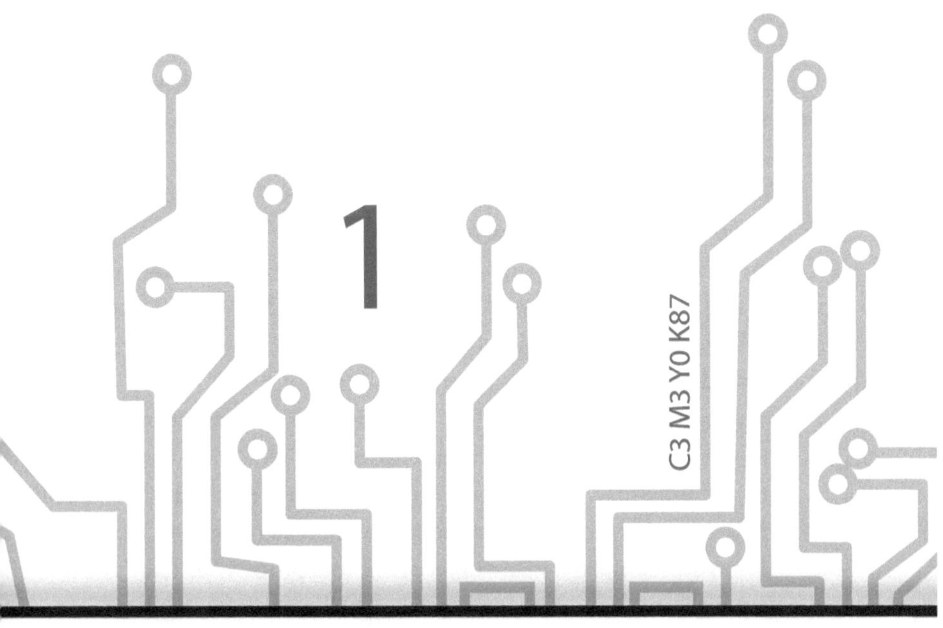

So I killed another dragon. Just me. I truly became a dragonslayer, something this world had never seen, as far as we knew. Yet only one day later, I was fleeing for my life because two other dragons showed up and claimed everything.

Five of us fled the city of Incarnadine. Six, if you counted the saber-toothed cat. And of course, one of the five was actually a dragon trapped in human form. Also, I could barely walk, so we "fled" at a pretty slow rate. It wasn't exactly a high point in my career as a rebel against the ruling dragons of our world.

I'd expected there to be seven of us escaping. But at the last minute, Marcus and Cerise Vermeil announced they weren't coming with us.

"We're not staying in this apartment either," Marcus said, as the rest of us loaded up all our gear. "We're going to go stay at a friend's house."

"Onyx doesn't know about this friend," Cerise added. "We should be safe there." She smiled sadly. "I just… I don't want to give birth out in the wilderness, Beryl. I'm not that strong."

"I think you're stronger than you think," I said, "but I won't argue with your decision."

"We'll be of more use to you here, keeping an eye on what the dragons do," Marcus put in.

"How will we contact you? Who's this friend?"

Marcus glanced at Amaranth, the dragon, who fumed nearby with arms folded. "I'll get in touch with you through Stacy," he said.

"Good thought."

"I'm not leaving either!" Amaranth announced. "I will not go on the run with you ridiculous humans."

"You heard Onyx call you a false god," I argued. "Are you going to walk up to him in your present shape and demand he take it back? He might call you a 'ridiculous human.'"

"I wouldn't be stuck in this form if not for you!"

"Come on, Amy," Caedan said. "You know it's the best chance you've got. And Beryl's the only one who can restore you."

For a fire dragon, Amaranth sure could turn on the icy glare. "You will not address me in so familiar a manner," she informed Caedan. "If I am to be stuck in your company, you will recognize me properly as Lady Rust."

"Very well, my lady." Caedan bowed. "Shall we flee for our lives?"

She came, under great protest. I wondered what this would mean in the long run. We couldn't trust her, of course, and her ability to breathe fire made her extremely dangerous. But on the other hand, she was an outcast now too. As long as we provided her safety and a possible way to strike back at Onyx, she would probably stick with us. Probably.

At first, she tried to get us to escape via her city, so she could pick up some things (and visit her source, I suspected). But that would mean we would have to cross one of the bridges, and those were guarded. We had no way of knowing how many guards might still remain loyal to their lady, and how many had already switched to the new power structure of Onyx and Atramentous.

We said farewell to the Vermeils with hugs and tears, and then set off toward the edge of the city. Once outside, we could jump on a train through to the Hub, at least. Or so we planned. In reality, I made it about a mile before Bice, watching me carefully, called a halt.

"This isn't going to work," he told the others. While he spoke, I leaned against a wall and tried to catch my breath. I'd been sending small boosts to my legs to keep me going, but every step agitated the stab wound in my side. Breathing was getting harder, and sweat stained my shirt in spite of the cool air.

Lainey knelt down to look at it. "He's bleeding again," she reported.

"He'll never be able to jump onto a moving train," Bice said, "and without the train, we're looking at days and days of walking. He can't do that either, in his condition."

I turned my head so that my right ear faced them. I still couldn't hear a thing with my left.

"Leave him," Amaranth said. "His weakness will be our downfall."

"He's the strongest one here." Caedan glared at her. "We're not leaving him behind."

"Besides, they want him most of all," Bice added. I didn't argue with him, but I suspected that wasn't true any more, since Onyx had given copies of Loden's notes to various scientists. I don't think my body held any more secrets worthwhile to the dragons.

Amaranth rolled her eyes. "Then let's buy tickets and take a ride," she suggested. "I'll purchase them myself."

"You don't think the Crimson Elite will be watching?" Bice asked.

"We just heard the black dragons talk about opening up travel between the cities," she answered. "We are just taking advantage of that. Why wouldn't they let a group of curious tourists try it out? For which city should I buy the tickets?"

"Viridia," I said. "It gets us the closest."

"Beryl will still have to jump off the train," Caedan pointed out.

"I'll manage," I said, pushing off the wall.

"At least then we won't be far from Hunter," Bice said.

"The train station is not far," Amaranth said. "This way." She set off without waiting for a response. We followed, but my injury kept us slow.

After two blocks of this, she lost patience. "I'll go on ahead and get the tickets then," she declared.

"Not by yourself," Caedan said. "I'll go with you."

"Suit yourself."

Bice took turns with Lainey supporting me as we followed at a much slower pace. "What will we do with Glacier?" Bice asked, glancing at the big cat following us.

"Are pets not allowed on the trains?" Lainey smiled. I couldn't be sure if she were genuinely asking, or trying to joke.

"I'm pretty sure they'll balk at a pet like that. It's going to be hard enough to get Beryl on with his chromark and scar. And hiding his injury."

"When the time comes, I'll boost everything long enough to walk normal," I promised.

"Glacier will be fine," Lainey said, along with something else I couldn't hear as she moved to my left side.

Caedan and Amaranth met us at the entrance to the train station. It felt weird to actually walk into one of them instead of sneaking around, like we usually did.

"Did you get enough tickets?" Bice asked.

"She bought an entire car," Caedan reported, pointing at Amaranth. "Told the counter we were throwing a party. A, um, wild party, from the sounds of it."

"I paid extra to ensure we are not disturbed," the dragon added, a smug look on her face. "We have only to get on board, and we will be left to our own devices."

"Great." I guess sometimes having a rich dragon-in-human-form could be helpful.

I took as deep of a breath as I could, sent boosts everywhere, and straightened up. The pain made my head spin, and stars appeared before my eyes. I blinked, sending more boosts, and the vertigo faded, but not the pain. "Lead the way," I instructed.

We followed Amaranth through the train station, laughing and talking. Only when we were halfway through did I think about Glacier. I looked back and didn't see her anywhere. Lainey said something, but she was on my left. Realizing it, she moved around me.

"I sent her around the building," she said. "I figure we'll let her into the train car when no one's looking."

I had no idea how Lainey could communicate something like that to a big cat. In my experience, cats didn't listen to people. Yet she quite often convinced Glacier to do things I never would have expected.

Going up the few steps into the train car almost destroyed me. Caedan practically pulled me up the last step and inside. I stretched out on the nearest set of seats and let myself relax… somewhat. I wouldn't feel safe until we were well on our way. I fully expected the Crimson Elite to burst into this train car and arrest us all. Or even worse, one of the black dragons to show up and rip it apart with us inside.

So when the train jerked to a start some time later, my gasp came not just from the sudden pain it caused me, but from surprise that this crazy plan seemed to be working.

We'd traveled much of The Circle on foot. We'd ridden on four-wheelers. I'd even flown a mission on a flying wing (I missed that thing). We'd been chased by soldiers, draconics, and dragons themselves.

Who would have ever thought we would make our biggest escape by buying tickets and getting on a train?

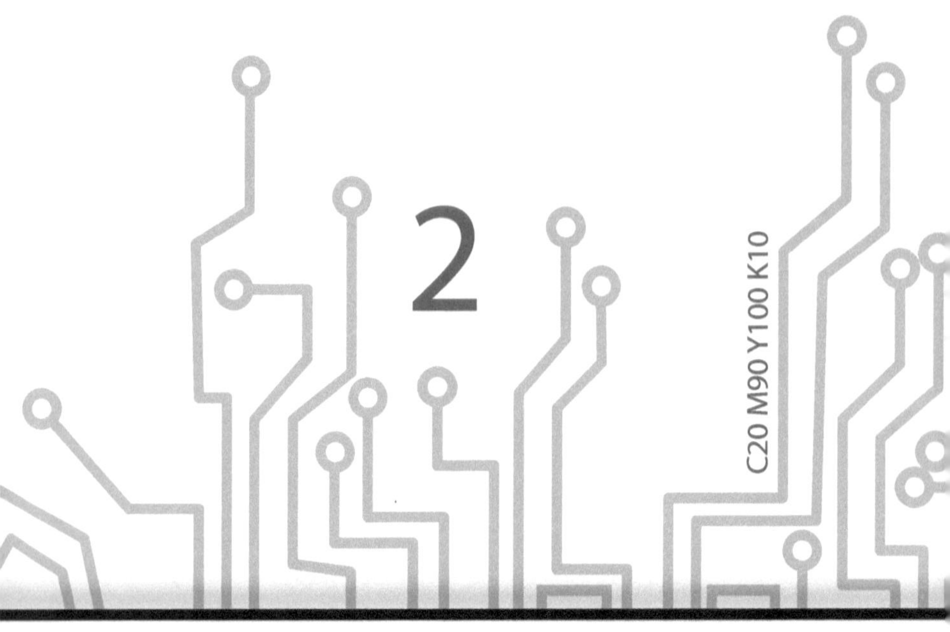

"Everyone may as well get some rest," Amaranth suggested. "We're going to be here for a few hours, at least. And since I bought the whole car for a private party, they won't be delivering any food or drinks."

"We'll be all right," Bice said. "We have some water, and we can eat when we get there."

"I hope your base of operations is sufficiently stocked then." The dragon queen sauntered to the back of the car and took a seat by herself.

Lainey crouched beside me and talked for a bit. But when Glacier became restless in the enclosed space, she went to deal with the cat for a while.

Caedan leaned over the back of the seat in front of me. "You're gonna be okay, right?"

"I'll make it," I said. My breaths were short and painful. But I only needed to hold on for a few hours. By this time tomorrow, Hunter would have examined me and done his magic. I hoped.

"Distract me from the pain," I told Caedan. "Tell me what you're thinking about."

"I'm trying to add stuff up in my head," he answered, shifting onto his knees to face me better. "I mean, all of the dragons teamed up to destroy Onyx three hundred years ago, right? So how is it he's now been able to convince two of them to join up with him?"

"I can hear you," Amaranth called.

"Then how about you answer it," Caedan said, looking back toward her. "Why did you team up with Onyx again, after what he did before?"

Amaranth got to her feet and came down the aisle. I could hear her shoes clicking on the metal floor. "Onyx is… highly persuasive," she explained. "When he first contacted me a few months ago, he apologized for his actions in the past. He claimed to have learned his lesson. We'd always been close, before… before his actions provoked the others. It was easy to fall back into that relationship."

"Relationship," Caedan repeated. "What kind of relationship are we talking here? Were you two lovers or what? Should we be expecting a baby dragon sometime?"

"Certainly not!" Amaranth's eyes flashed red. "We are siblings, all seven of us!"

"Then you really do have one mother," Bice observed.

"So Onyx—your brother—comes back from the dead, saying he's a changed dragon," Caedan said. "And you believed him."

"Much to my current shame, yes."

"Onyx told us that once Incarnadine was dead, he would convince you to side with him against the others," Bice said. "He claimed the two of you would rule all of The Circle."

"Yet now he's got Atramentous beside him instead," I added weakly.

"I had no such ambitions," Amaranth said, a coldness in her voice. "Whatever he told you, he lied."

"No surprise there," Caedan said. "Does he ever tell the truth?"

"Only when it suits his needs," Bice said. I couldn't see him, but I could picture him shaking his head. "He's a master at it too. I can't believe he deceived us for so long."

"In what way did he deceive you?" Amaranth asked.

After a moment of silence, Bice said, "Beryl? How much do you want to tell her?"

"Onyx convinced us he was a human rebel," I said, straining against the pain. "He helped come up with the plan to kill Caesious. Without his help, we never would have succeeded in that, or just about anything else after that."

"I see." She paused. "So, given that, do you find it so surprising that he was also able to deceive me? Or Atramentous?"

"Maybe," Caedan said with a grin. "But you're supposed to be these all-wise gods, aren't you? How can gods get deceived?"

Caedan actually flinched. Amaranth must have given him a serious glare.

"Gods can be deceived as well, especially by other gods," she answered.

"You know none of us believe you're gods, right?"

"You are all ignorant fools. I know that much."

"I was once a priest of Viridia," Bice said quietly. "And you are not gods."

"Yes, the Heretic. I am aware of your background."

"Then you can drop the god act," Caedan said. "None of us buy it."

"You will keep silence!" Amaranth's voice took on a different tone, one I'd heard before.

Caedan snapped his mouth shut and stared at her, grin gone.

"You need to stop that, Amaranth," I said.

"Stop what?"

"Your voice thing." I clenched my teeth for a moment to keep from crying out in pain. "You have some power in it. You've used it against me at least twice."

"Is that what it is?" Bice wondered. "That explains some things."

"Then why didn't she use it on Onyx?" Lainey asked.

"Onyx is… resistant to my power," the dragon admitted.

"That must be frustrating," I said.

"On the contrary." Amaranth came further down the aisle and stood where I could see her. "After hundreds of years of influencing weaker minds, I am fascinated by someone who can resist me." She looked down at me. "You're like him in that regard."

Lainey pushed past the dragon and knelt down beside me again. She lifted my shirt and checked my bandage.

"Amaranth," Bice chided. "You're forgetting something."

She rolled her eyes. "Fine. You may speak again."

Caedan gasped. "Fewmets! That was crazy!"

"Let me guess," I said. "You actually felt like you didn't want to speak."

"Yeah." He shook his head. "Wow. That's… I don't know what that is."

"She used it on me way back at the tower," I recalled. "Made me want to come see her. And then she tried it again when we met."

"To do what?" Lainey asked.

"To, uh, keep me from escaping. But I broke through it."

"And that is why you're fascinating," Amaranth said. I looked up and saw a sultry smile on her face. Great. Just what I needed.

"We need to talk about our next steps," Bice said. "We'll have to abandon the, uh, base, since Onyx knows where it is. I hope we'll have time to get everything out that we need. We may not have much choice."

"Onyx will not move against you right away," Amaranth agreed. "Having announced his intentions, he will first move against the biggest threat remaining: Auric."

"Should we warn him?" Lainey asked.

"Auric has spies in every city," Amaranth said with obvious disdain in her voice. Did she have something against Lainey or Auric? "I assure you: he already knows."

"Let's wait and see what Don and Lovat have found," I said, still struggling to speak. "Then we can make decisions."

Everywhere we turned, Onyx was the problem. We couldn't stay at the Achromatic Asylum, because he knew its location. The tower we'd lived in for a while? He built it. And his knowledge of the apartment was why we were fleeing Incarnadine now. He knew every place in Viridia. If he wasn't a factor, we had lots of options. With him as a factor... we didn't have much.

Amaranth returned to her place in the back of the car. A few minutes later, Caedan reported that she seemed to have fallen asleep.

"I'm really not sure about this," he whispered to me. "It was crazy enough bringing a dragon with us, but now? She can control us with her voice?"

"Yeah, it's a problem," I admitted. "I can break out of it, but she could make the rest of you do... whatever she wants."

"No, she can't," Bice said, joining us. How crazy did we look? The three of them crowded around the one guy lying across the seats, and whispering to avoid being heard by the one other occupant at the back of the car.

"What do you mean?"

"It's a matter of... eating," he answered. "Remember from the Books of Lore? The dragons feed off the energy from their sources. It's how they stay alive and use their powers. When Amaranth used the power—resomancy, for lack of a better word—to shield herself and you at the Flame, it drained her. That's why she slept so long afterwards. She hasn't been to her source since."

"So you think she'll use the voice power sparingly, to keep from draining herself further?" I guess it made sense.

"Then why'd she use it on me just now?" Caedan demanded.

"She's afraid and frustrated, and you were an irritant she just couldn't take any more," Bice explained. "And notice she's had to rest again. When we get a chance, we'll have a talk with her, and point out, since she doesn't know how long she'll be stuck as a human away from her source, she should take care how often and when she uses her powers."

"You think she'll listen?" Lainey asked, frowning.

Bice shrugged. "The dragons didn't get this far by being idiots. I think she'll listen to reason."

At that precise moment, one of the side windows shattered and a black-clad figure swung into the train car. The back door flew open, and several more charged in. The Sable Legion had found us.

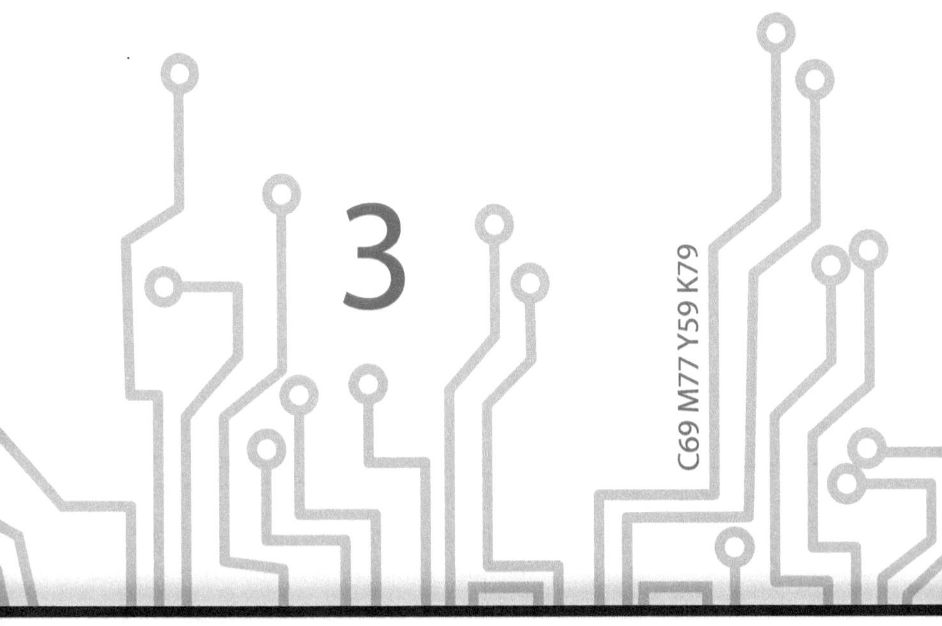

3

Two of the Legionnaires pounced on Amaranth. The one who'd smashed through the window—the leader, I assumed—lunged at Caedan with some kind of staff device.

"Leave this to us, Beryl," Lainey said in a hurry. She stood and yelled, "Glacier! Attack!"

I pushed myself up to try to see everything happening at once. Total chaos erupted in the train car.

Caedan whipped out his own weapon and fired. His projectile weapon's electrical charge did nothing against his attacker. The Sable Legion wore thicker and tougher armor than the other soldiers we were used to fighting.

Armor mattered not a bit to Glacier. The cat leaped out from her hiding place between the seats, tearing into the closest Legionnaire. He screamed as they fell onto another seat. The next one behind paused only briefly before stabbing at the big cat with another of those staves.

Closest to me, the leader of the Legionnaires managed to connect with Caedan. His staff had some sort of clamp on the end which caught hold of Caedan's left arm and held him in place. Caedan dropped one weapon and pulled out his baton instead.

Amaranth screeched. A loud boom followed her cry as Lainey fired her rifle at the Legionnaire stabbing at Glacier. As tough as their armor might be, it couldn't withstand bullets. Her target crumpled.

Another window shattered behind us. I tried to turn, but the pain slowed me. Yet another Legionnaire charged in, catching Lainey from behind and seizing hold of her rifle with one hand.

Caedan slumped, pretending to fall. His attacker stepped forward. Caedan lunged out with his baton, connecting hard with the attacker's knee. The leader of the Legionnaires fell in a tangle with Caedan outside my view.

I channeled a boost, trying to get to my feet to help Lainey. But Bice was already there, tackling her assailant from the side. He didn't accomplish much on his own, but he gave Lainey the opportunity to slam the butt of her rifle back against her enemy. He fell without a sound.

How many of the Sable Legion had entered the car? Two came through windows; one still fought on the floor with Caedan, while Bice and Lainey took the other down. But at least five had charged through the door. Two grabbed Amaranth, Lainey shot one, and the fourth still screamed from Glacier's attacks. Where was the fifth?

My answer came when something cold clamped down around my neck. "Back off!" a harsh voice shouted at the others. "Or this thing squeezes his head from his shoulders!"

From my limited vantage, I couldn't see the one holding me. Lainey and Bice took a step back. Caedan joined them, holding his baton, but the Legionnaire he'd been fighting did not get up.

The one who'd been screaming stopped. Glacier appeared in my peripheral vision, growling as she advanced. A sharp command from Lainey stopped her, but she didn't take her eyes from my attacker. The first two dragged Amaranth into my view as well, her hair disheveled from the struggle.

"It took the two of you to hold that one redhead?" my attacker asked. "She's hardly the biggest threat here."

"It appears your master failed to give you the full information necessary for your success," Amaranth said. "You clearly don't know who I am."

"You're all a bunch of rebels and heretics. And this one"—he shook the device holding my neck—"has cyb enhancements. That's all we needed to know." He paused. "Would have been nice to know about the size of that cat, though."

"Allow me to enlighten you regarding your errors," Amaranth

responded. She turned to her right and exhaled fire. The sight of the blaze emerging from this woman's mouth shocked everyone, I think. Flames consumed the Legionnaire as he screamed and tried to bat them out. The smell of burning flesh filled the train car. He staggered to the door and leaped out into the night air.

"Do the two of you require a further demonstration?" the dragon queen asked. The one holding her left arm let it go and ran after his companion. Amaranth smiled and took a step toward us.

"I'll kill him!" the final Legionnaire warned.

"Go right ahead. He means nothing to me. You, however, serve a despicable traitor. And that is something I find abhorrent." Flames erupted from her mouth again.

Screams came from behind me, along with more of the horrible smell. I heard scrambling and then nothing. I assumed he dove out the window through which he'd entered.

"Beryl, are you all right?" Bice came behind me and fumbled with something. The pressure around my neck disappeared.

"I'm fine," I assured him, though my side said otherwise.

Caedan stepped over one of the bodies. "What do we do with these guys?"

"Throw them out," Amaranth answered.

"I just knocked this one out. Maybe we should ask him some questions first?"

"What good would it do? They were clearly not given much information before being sent after us."

"She's right," Bice said. "This wasn't a serious attempt to capture us. It's just Onyx's way of letting us know that he knows we're running."

"But these guys are from Atramentous, right?" Caedan asked. "Sable something?"

"Sable Legion," I murmured, letting myself lie back down on the seats.

"It doesn't matter," Amaranth said. "Onyx likely gave them their orders."

"Come here, Glacier," Lainey said, then moved where I couldn't hear her.

"No," Bice answered whatever she asked. "I still think he won't come after us directly. At least not yet."

"He must deal with Auric," Amaranth said. "But these... human soldiers… Ugh. You there. Stop! Let me incinerate that one before you throw him out."

"I told you he's still alive!" Caedan exclaimed.

"He won't be for long."

"No!" Bice jumped up to join Caedan. This time, I swiveled my head to hear better. "You will not kill people while you are with us!"

"You dare to give me orders?"

"That's the deal, Lady Rust," Bice said firmly. "You agree to work with us in our way, or we throw you out with them."

"You think you possess the ability to do that?"

A loud click broke the silence that followed. "Yes," said Lainey. I couldn't see her, but I imagined her leveling the rifle at the dragon queen.

"You foolish girl. You join him in threatening me?"

"We all threaten you," Caedan said. "Go back to your seat and let us deal with things here."

She snarled something I couldn't make out. I heard her footsteps stomping toward the back of the train car. Caedan said something to Bice, and they worked together to get rid of the rest of the Legionnaires.

Lainey came to check on me a few moments later, and I assured her I hadn't been injured further. "I wish I'd been able to help."

"Sometimes you have to let others do the fighting, you know." She checked my bandages. "We're all part of this."

Pain made my breathing difficult again for a few moments. "If you'd been hurt…"

"I wasn't," she said. "None of us were."

Glacier poked her head around the side of the seat. Blood stained her saber-shaped fangs. I shuddered when I thought of what the Legionnaire had experienced.

"Glacier!' Lainey scolded. "Come here. Let me wipe that off."

"I know I've said it before." Caedan's voice came from behind me. "But I'm glad that cat is on our side."

"She has her own side," Lainey said. "We just happen to be going along with it."

"You mean it could change?"

"She's a wild animal." Lainey patted Glacier on the head. "As much as I want to believe she'll do anything for me, I know someday she may wander off and never come back."

Caedan let out a loud sigh. "We've got a dragon-lady who can take control of us and breathe fire, and a giant cat that might decide it's not on our side any more. I may never sleep at night again."

"Speak for yourself," I said. "I'm passing out right now."

"Well, sure. You've got—"

I never heard the rest.

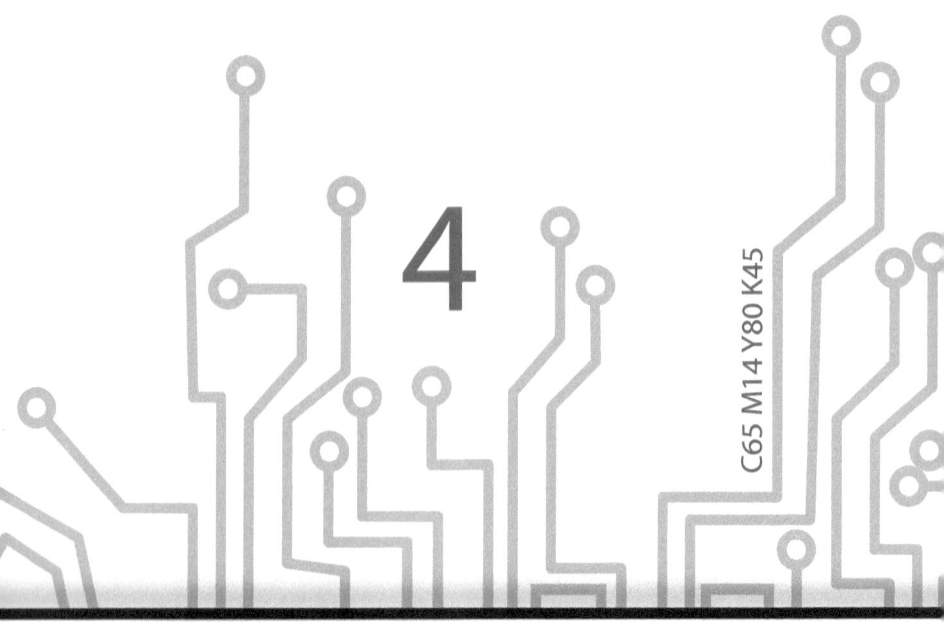

4

Hours later, we drew near our stop. Except, of course, the train wouldn't be stopping. We would have to jump. Fortunately, the train would be taking two long curves that would force it to slow down somewhat. Caedan knew the exact point where the train would be at its slowest.

"Are you going to make it?" Bice asked me as we stood near the door.

"I don't have much choice, do I? Can't go all the way to Viridia."

I knew it would hurt. I knew it would be bad. I braced myself for it. But even so, the intensity of the pain surprised me. When I jumped from the moving train, I boosted my legs as strong as I could to lessen the impact of the landing. But it didn't matter. The moment my feet struck the ground, pain exploded in my side, overwhelming my senses and my mind. I stumbled forward, rolled, and passed out.

I woke briefly and caught a glimpse of eyes looking down at me. I think they were Bice's. But I didn't stay conscious long enough to tell for sure.

My next moment of consciousness came some time later. I didn't see anything but the night sky this time. Voices argued around me.

"…should never have been allowed to travel!" I'm not sure, but I think that was Hunter's voice.

"We didn't have a choice. If we had stuck around, we'd all be dead or Onyx's slaves. At best." Definitely Bice.

"Sometimes you have to find creative…" The voices moved around toward my left side.

"If you're going to talk about me," I croaked, "at least stay on the right where I can hear you."

Bice came into view, followed by Hunter. "There is something wrong with his ear too?" Hunter asked.

"I hadn't gotten that far," Bice answered. "The side wound seemed a little more important." He disappeared from view, then came back with some water. I took a few swallows.

"…totally reckless," Hunter said, coming back around.

"You can't kill a dragon and not get hurt." It wasn't much of an excuse, but he made me feel defensive for some reason.

"Will he live?" Amaranth's voice intruded.

"Just back off, woman," Hunter said. "Let me do my job." He sighed. "All right. Let us get the board underneath him and lift him on to the four-wheeler. Caedan?"

Someone moved behind me, and then hands helped shift me as a piece of flat lumber slid under my body. "On three," Hunter said. "One. Two. Three!"

The sensation of movement almost sent me unconscious again. I rolled my head to the side and saw the others gathered around in the dark. I guess Lainey or Caedan had run to the Asylum and come back with Hunter and the four-wheeler. Good thinking.

Once they had the board on the back of the four-wheeler, they strapped it and me down. Caedan promised to drive slow and avoid the bumps. "Anyone else want to drive?" I suggested. Nobody laughed.

"Bice!" A sudden thought occurred to me as Caedan started the engine.

"What is it, Beryl?" He appeared by my side again.

"Don't let her in the workshop."

"Definitely."

With that, the four-wheeler started moving. I let myself rest for the trip to the Asylum. The pain wasn't too bad. I wondered if Hunter had given me something else…

And then I woke up inside Loden's workshop with the bright lights shining down on me. Kelly leaned over me this time. "What did you do now, Beryl?"

"Killed another dragon," I murmured.

"What did he say?" she asked someone else, looking up.

"He killed Incarnadine," Lainey answered. "All by himself."

"Wow. And who's the angry redhead outside?"

She moved around to my left, so I couldn't hear Lainey's answer. But I'm sure Kelly wasn't pleased by it. Hunter appeared in my view again. "I am giving you another sedative, Beryl," he said. "You absolutely have to sleep for a while. Your body can heal itself, but it needs to be left alone while it does."

"Whatever you…" I was out again.

Honestly, this cycle was getting old. Do something incredible, get hurt, spend days sleeping, repeat. And in this case, the serious injury didn't even come from an enemy.

When I woke up the next time, I felt well enough to get up and move around, at the least. As I sat up, I heard a feminine murmur coming from my left. "Lainey?" I turned my head to see (and hear better).

"I sent her to get some sleep herself," Kelly said. "Chance and I took over watching you sleep."

Chance? I pushed myself up on my elbow, wincing a little. There he was. The little guy toddled around the workshop, staring at everything with his huge eyes. "I swear he's grown six inches since we left."

"It might be that much." Kelly leaned forward and waved at the draconic child. "He grows like a weed and eats like a horse."

I sat up and looked around. The workshop looked sparser than usual. "Some stuff's been moved," I observed.

"We're packing up. Getting ready to evacuate this place as soon as you can move." Kelly stood up. "Which I guess is now, huh?"

I gingerly slid off the table on to my feet. The weight shifting caused some pain, but it wasn't too bad. "Then Don and Lovat are back?"

Chance came back, arms outstretched. Kelly picked him up and grunted. "You're already getting too heavy for this." She turned to me. "Yeah, they came back before you did. They've seen you, but I guess you haven't seen them. They found us a new place. Don says it's perfect, much better than this one."

I raised my eyebrows. "Then I'm looking forward to seeing it."

With slow steps, I made my way out of the workshop and through the cave. The sight that met my eyes when I emerged amazed me. Everywhere I looked, I saw people engaged in busy work: packing bags up, loading equipment onto a trailer attached to the four-wheeler. Wait… when did we get a trailer?

In our time at Incarnadine, I'd almost forgotten how big our team had grown. Besides little Chance, we had fifteen people milling about here. There were Caedan's recruits (whose names I still struggled to remember), the ex-prisoners Hunter, Fern, and Basil, our original team, and…

"We are wasting our time!"

Oh yes. Her.

Amaranth spotted me and stalked in my direction. She waved toward the trailer. "What good is all of this stuff going to be when Onyx and Atramentous descend on this place in a storm of fury?"

"You said yourself they wouldn't move against us right away," I said. "Won't they go after Auric first?"

"I said that two days ago! These people have done practically nothing in that time, except debate over what to bring along from your forbidden cavern, and—oh." She stopped her rant to stare past me. Kelly came out, holding Chance. "The child," Amaranth murmured.

"My child," Kelly corrected.

"Fascinating. Never before, to my knowledge, has a draconic child been raised by humans." She drew herself up. "You realize, of course, that he will come of age within months. If his sire is not available to connect with him, I don't know what will happen."

"Maybe he'll have a normal life then," Kelly said.

"Normal by your definition? Doubtful. He will be recovering the memories of three or four previous lifetimes, all at once. One can hardly call that normal."

"We'll take care of him," I said. But a thought occurred to me. "No one's ever said it for sure. Can Onyx sense his child's presence? Can he find us through Chance?"

Amaranth snorted. "We can sense our children, yes. But not at a great distance, and not with specificity. He will know, in general, in what direction this one travels, but nothing more than that. If he were to engage in a serious search, however…" She paused. "He will find us."

By now, the others had noticed my appearance. Lovat ran to meet me.

He paused a step away. "Hunter says not to hug you," he declared.

I reached out and ruffled his hair. "Yeah, that might hurt. Thanks. Did you get taller while I was gone?"

He put his own hand on his head. "Did I?"

Kelly pointed to his feet. "His pants are too short. But I think they already were when we left the tower."

"This domesticity is both galling and banal. Will we be leaving soon?" Amaranth crossed her arms and waited.

"I don't know. Bice, will we be leaving soon?" I asked as he approached.

"We were just waiting on you to wake up," he said. "If Hunter checks you out, you can ride on the four-wheeler with Caedan."

"How far is this new place?"

"It's about a day's hike west of Auric," Don said, joining us. "Big place. Safe too."

"Good to hear. And good to see you."

"All right!" Caedan called out. "He's up. Let's get the last of what we need from the workshop and head out! The sooner we leave, the sooner we get to our new home!"

Home. We'd had several in the past year. To me, none of them were home… and all of them were. It depended on these people around me. Wherever they were, that was my home.

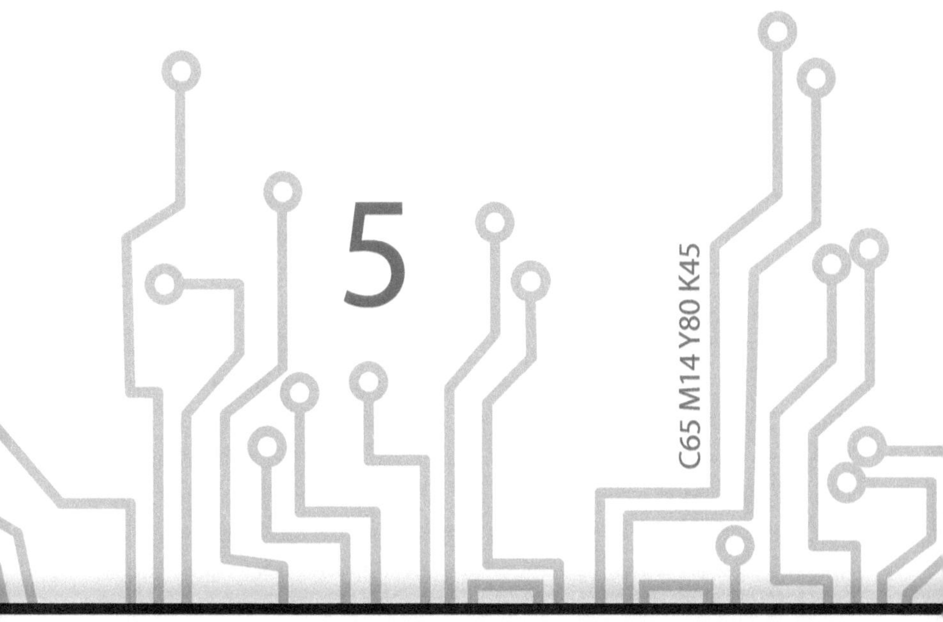

Riding on the slow-moving four-wheeler was a strange experience. The others had agreed that for the first day, at least, we would all travel together, which meant the four-wheeler couldn't go faster than the slowest walker.

"Why don't we just take the four-wheeler and trailer on ahead, and then come back for everyone else?" I suggested to Caedan.

"We might do that tomorrow," he replied. "But for today, we wanted to make sure you could handle the travel all right."

"I'm not dying," I grumbled.

I looked back at the trailer, piled high with our remaining food and fuel, Carl's old equipment, our personal belongings, and whatever had been deemed important from Loden's workshop. We'd left behind a lot of his stuff, sealed off, for now. I'd come back for it when I could. Anything from Loden might be valuable.

"Where did the trailer come from, anyway?" I asked.

"Don appropriated it from a construction crew near the Hub." Caedan chuckled at the thought. "Just drove the four-wheeler in, hooked it up, and drove off. They were too busy to even notice."

Without it, I don't know what we would have done. Everyone was already carrying packs of stuff that didn't fit on the trailer as it was. We would probably have had to take several trips, loading down the four-wheeler as best we could. And given the location of this new base, they would be long trips.

We traveled almost due north, bearing a little to the northwest eventually. The air wasn't especially warm, but after spending time in Incarnadine, I enjoyed it. The cold weather had gotten to me more than I liked to admit.

We made leisurely progress. I'll admit to some anxiety over the size of our group. When only three or four of us walked through the open spaces together, I rarely worried we'd be confronted. But with this many people, someone might take notice. To my relief, we encountered no soldiers or other dangers.

Sleeping outside again wasn't the best, and I woke up stiff and sore. But at breakfast, I insisted that we speed ahead with the four-wheeler. "It makes the most sense," I argued. "Caedan and I can get there, and he can come back with the trailer faster than all of us can walk together."

"Lovat can go with you," Don suggested. That also made sense. Caedan knew the general directions, but only Lovat and Don had been there.

Kelly and Chance were also persuaded to climb on to the trailer. I was a little concerned about the towing power of the four-wheeler, but Caedan insisted it could handle all the weight and then some. "This baby's tough," he claimed.

We left the others behind and pushed ahead much faster. Despite Caedan's assurances, I could tell the four-wheeler didn't appreciate all the weight. The engine growled at a harsher tone than usual, especially when traveling uphill.

"He can't hear on that side!" Caedan called back.

What? Apparently, someone tried to talk to me. I turned as Lovat's head appeared on my right. "Miss Kelly wants to know how you're doing."

"Tell her I'm fine."

Around lunchtime, we approached the large river I'd seen only from a train window. Once again, the size and power of it awed me. How could water move so fast? We would have no way of getting across it if not for the railroad bridge. We looked long and hard to make sure no trains were coming before crossing the bridge and the tracks leading from the Hub to Auric. I watched them run on toward the northeast and wondered what might be happening in the golden city now.

I didn't have to wonder for long. Less than an hour past lunch, Lovat grabbed my shoulder from behind and shouted, "Dragon!"

Caedan put on the brakes, and we all looked where Lovat pointed. Sure enough, I could spy a dark shape in the sky to the southwest. As we looked, a second one appeared. "Both dragons!" Caedan shouted some words I didn't recognize, but the intent was clear. Fewmets.

"Let's get under cover!" Kelly called. "Maybe they haven't seen us."

Caedan gunned the engine and aimed for some nearby woods. I didn't see enough room to drive in among them, but Caedan pulled up alongside, getting as close to the trees as possible. The others scrambled down, while I followed more slowly. We hid among the trees and waited.

I glanced over at Chance in Kelly's arms. His eyes looked even larger than usual. Did he sense the approaching presence of his father? Could Onyx sense his child's presence?

With a rush of wind that shook the trees and rained leaves on us, the dragons swept overhead. They ignored us and continued on their route. We stepped out from the trees and watched their shapes shrink as they kept going.

"They're on their way to Auric," Caedan said, stating the obvious.

"We need to follow them," I said, turning back to the others.

"What?" Kelly exclaimed. "You want to go after the black dragons that want to kill us?"

"No. But we need to see what happens. We just need to get close enough for me to zoom in and watch."

"What difference does it make?"

"Auric has helped us," I pointed out.

"He also tried to destroy Caesious," Caedan said, meaning the city. "He's still a dragon, Beryl."

"But if he fights back strong enough, maybe he'll take out one of the others. We need to know about it. Our future plans depend on knowing about it." I pressed my case. "We can unhook the trailer and just take the four-wheeler. Just the two of us. Then we'll come right back."

Caedan wanted to do it. I could tell. I turned back to Kelly. "We need to know what happens, Kelly."

"What if they destroy the whole city, like the Blasted Lands?" She held Chance tighter.

"We're not going to stay," I argued. "And if they do, maybe we can rescue some people as they run away."

"How?" Caedan asked. "The four-wheeler can't hold a crowd."

"We can guide them away. Come on! We need to move, and now!"

"Fine. We'll wait here." Kelly didn't look pleased about it. "But you come straight back once you've gotten a good look!"

"As soon as we can tell what's happening," I assured her. Behind me, Caedan unhooked the trailer. "Lovat, you keep Kelly and Chance safe, all right?"

"No problem," he answered with a mock salute.

"If Bice catches up to us before you get back, he's not going to be happy," Kelly pointed out.

"It won't take that long," I promised.

With a hand from Caedan, I climbed back onto the four-wheeler, disguising the pain from Kelly's watchful eyes. I gave her a wave, and we shot off toward the northeast.

"Follow the train tracks!" I shouted to Caedan.

"I know!"

Now Caedan really made the four-wheeler fly. We shot across the countryside, up and down hills and through plains. About an hour later, I spotted the smoke in the distance. I pointed it out to Caedan. He took us to the top of the highest hill around, and we dismounted.

"What do you see?" he asked, staring toward the black cloud, much closer than we'd expected.

I triggered a boost toward my eyes and focused. Like binoculars, they zoomed in toward the city of Auric. I took a sharp intake of breath at the sight.

The black dragons circled back and forth above the city, releasing bursts of acidic fire every so often. Smoke rose from at least a dozen spots, but most from a large structure in the dead center of the city. Auric's headquarters, I assumed. But his resting place was underground. Surely the black dragons knew that. Maybe it lay beneath that burning building.

"This is bad," Caedan murmured. "Are they destroying the whole city?"

"I don't think so." I looked as close as I could. "I think they're targeting specific spots. Maybe where Auric's draconics live? Or his soldiers?"

Both dragons converged on the central spot again. They poured their acidic wrath down upon it, burning through anything and everything. If Auric were hiding beneath it, he wouldn't be able to avoid the destruction. I expected any moment to see the golden dragon burst up out of the devastation and attack one of the other two.

But it didn't happen. Nothing else happened. Strange. Was Auric already dead? Had he fled the city in the last couple of days, once he knew about Onyx and Atramentous? Where would he have gone?

"Something's coming," Caedan said.

I allowed my vision to return to normal and looked where he pointed. Something small kicked up a plume of dust, coming in our general direction from the city. "Another four-wheeler?" I wondered.

"Why don't you take a closer look?"

Oh. Right. I zoomed in on the dust plume. Sure enough, I saw a small motorized vehicle, but it looked as if it only had three wheels instead of four. As it drew closer, I could tell there were two men riding. The driver wore goggles and a helmet, so I could see little of his face. The other kept his head turned, watching the city behind them. When at last he glanced forward, I staggered back a step.

I'd seen him before. The second man was Ciaru, the human form of the dragon Auric.

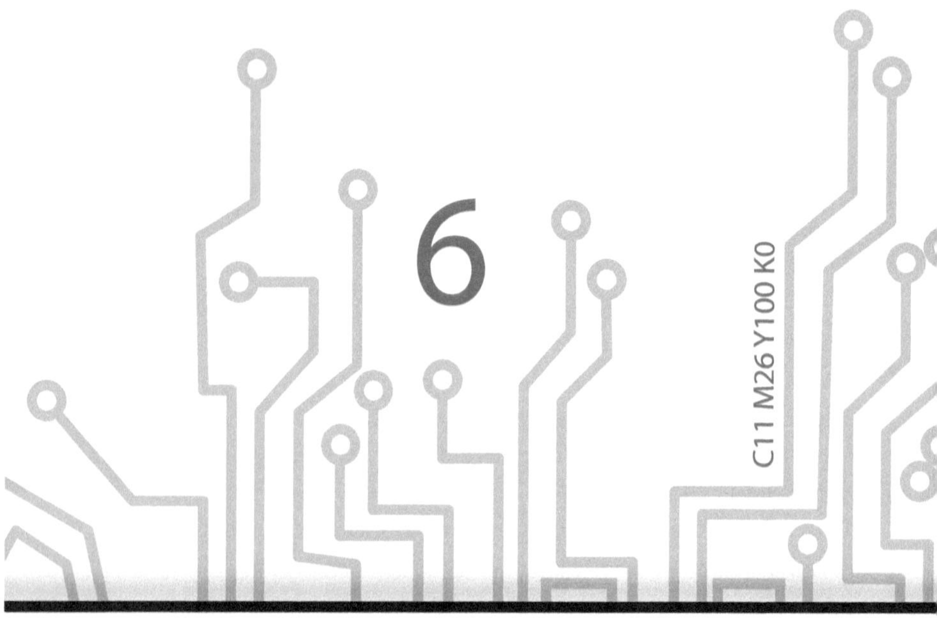

6

"What do you see?" Caedan asked.

My vision snapped back to normal. "It's Auric."

"I know it's Auric, but—" Caedan blinked. "Wait. You mean that's Auric himself down there?"

I nodded. "On a three-wheeler."

"Really? Huh. That's kind of cool. More maneuverable, I guess." Caedan literally slapped himself, before going on: "You're sure about this? Auric in human form?"

"Yeah." I started walking down the hill.

"Wait, wait. Where are you going?"

"I'm going to talk to him."

Caedan caught up with me. "Beryl! Why do you want to talk? We can kill him! Isn't that our goal?"

I pointed at the black dragons. "Those two will destroy everything! And they have help from outside The Circle! If we're going to stand a chance at even surviving this, we need all the help we can get!"

"He tried to destroy Caesious," Caedan growled. His face grew hard, reminding me of the first time we met, when he worked for the blue priests as a soldier himself. "He's the reason Peri is dead. You haven't forgotten Peri, have you?"

"No, of course I haven't." I glared at him. "I will never forget him. Or the moment he sacrificed himself. How could you ask that?"

Caedan pointed. "Because he's the cause of it! Peri would still be alive if not for him!" His jaw tightened.

I closed my eyes and took a deep breath. "You're right. And we won't ever forget it. But for the moment, we need to focus on the black dragons. We will get justice for Peri. I promise."

Caedan's jaw worked for a moment, and then he nodded. "I'll hold you to that."

I agreed and resumed walking. Caedan followed, muttering, "Kelly's not going to like this. Or Bice. Or you-know-who with the red hair… Hey!" He grabbed my shirt tale and tugged it down. "At least keep your bandages hidden. Don't show weakness, you know."

As we neared the bottom of the hill, I lifted my hand and waved at the approaching vehicle. After a moment, it altered course and came directly toward us. The three-wheeler stopped a few yards away, and the driver stepped off. He removed his helmet and examined us, before glancing back at his passenger.

"Captain Tawn," I said, recognizing his stern face. "You know who I am, and I know who's riding with you."

Ciaru dismounted, moving forward with the familiar stoop to his stride. As before, he wore black gloves and simple clothes trimmed in gold. The human forms of the dragons raised so many questions. Did they choose them early in their lives and get stuck with them? Could they alter them at all? Onyx, of course, appeared as a very young man. Amaranth appeared young as well, and, if I admitted it, amazingly beautiful. Auric, though… he seemed much older, like a man in his late forties or early fifties, even though he didn't have any gray hair.

"Now that's a serious mustache," Caedan whispered.

"Well, I suppose I shouldn't be too surprised," Ciaru observed. "I am somewhat disappointed, however. You seem to have killed the wrong dragon."

"It's a long story," I replied. "I see you've abandoned your people to save your own life."

"It's the best way to save the most lives," he countered. "Were I to stay and fight, who knows how many would be killed in the conflict?"

"People are dying right now," Caedan pointed out.

"The most lives," the dragon repeated. "I told you this before.

Sometimes, the few must be sacrificed for the sake of the many."

"Whatever you say." I took another look at the black dragons. One of them was settling down into the city, perhaps looking for Auric's body. "So what is your contingency plan? Where will you go?"

"I have options," he said. "None of them involved you, I will admit. Your presence here raises other possibilities."

"I told you before, but now I know for sure. The purple robes from outside are working with Onyx." I was gratified to see Ciaru's long eyebrows raise a bit. Maybe his spies didn't see everything, after all.

"The eyes of Auric see all," Captain Tawn inserted.

"It appears that we share common enemies," Ciaru said without acknowledging the captain. "What do you propose, Beryl Godslayer?"

I rolled my eyes. "If you have to give me a title, just say Dragonslayer. After everything that's happened, you can't possibly think we still believe any of you are gods."

Captain Tawn stiffened even more at that statement, if possible. He was already pretty stiff.

"It depends on your definitions, I suppose. Still, what do you intend?"

"We're on our way to a safe place," I said, pointing my thumb over my shoulder. "Do you want to join us and work together?"

Caedan made a disapproving noise.

"You intrigue me. Perhaps…"

"We don't need them, my lord," Captain Tawn said brusquely.

"Oh? Is my most loyal Sentinel now giving orders to me?"

"Of course not, sir."

"Then let us proceed." Ciaru looked at us. "I assume you have your own means of conveyance?"

"Huh?"

"A vehicle?"

"Oh, right."

Caedan fetched the four-wheeler, and I joined him, doing my best not to show my injuries. Ciaru stood watching the city. He shook his head. "My children are dying, and there is nothing I could or can do to stop it."

I remembered Taizong Gold, the draconic. That one had listened to Protogonus Blue. I couldn't help feeling a little bit of sorrow myself, for what might have been.

Caedan gunned the engine. We led the way back to where we'd left the others with the trailer. And that led to another debate.

"No. No way," Kelly said, after pulling me in amongst the trees. "Bad enough you brought Amaranth back. But two dragons?"

"Everything's changed," I argued, glancing over my shoulder to make sure we were far enough away. I didn't want Auric to know about Amaranth just yet. "With the purple robes involved, we don't know what we're up against now, but it's terrifying."

"We would if Lainey would just tell us."

"Don't blame her. She's been through a lot!"

"I know, I know. Sorry. But…" She looked past me and held Chance tighter. "I'm scared, Beryl. We can't trust them."

"I don't trust them. Look, Amaranth is trapped in human form, and—" I stopped, because Ciaru strode directly toward us.

"I could hear some of your argument," he announced. "Not all, but enough." He looked at Kelly and Chance. "You are a remarkable woman, trying to raise a dragon's child as your own. You are to be commended, though I do not know if you will be successful."

"We'll see about that," she answered, her eyes narrowed.

Ciaru reached into a pocket and produced what looked like the same disk I'd used on Amaranth. "Perhaps your friend here has told you what this device can do?"

Kelly's eyes darted between us. "It traps you in human form, right?"

"Yes. And only the person who activates it can deactivate it." He offered it to Kelly. "Will you do the honors?"

She shifted Chance and took the disk. "You're… placing your life in my hands?"

"If it is the only way we can work together, then yes." He turned and pulled his ponytail out of the way, uncovering the back of his neck.

Kelly looked at me. I had no idea what to say. Before I could think of anything, she stepped forward and slapped the disk onto Ciaru's neck. He winced a little bit, then stepped away.

"It is done. Will you trust me now?"

Kelly bit her lip, no doubt wondering if this was some kind of trick. I wondered, myself. "All right," she said at last. "For now."

"Excellent. Shall we proceed?"

Caedan reattached the trailer. A few moments later, we were on our way again. Lovat crawled up to talk with me again.

"Is that guy really the gold dragon?"

"Yeah. Yeah, he is. So I've got a job for you, man."

"What is it?"

"Keep an eye on him. And the other guy. Captain Tawn." I glanced across at the three-wheeler. "Don't spy on them all the time, and don't make it obvious. But let me know if they do anything unusual."

"You got it, Beryl."

I smiled at him. "I know I can count on you."

About an hour later, Kelly pointed out the two black dragons behind us, heading back toward the west. I guess they were satisfied with their work in Auric, or they'd given up searching for the gold dragon. Amaranth's revelation that the dragons were all siblings made Onyx's actions so much worse. He'd murdered one of his brothers, arranged the murder of a second, and now tried to kill a third. How twisted did someone have to be to kill their own family members?

We spent another night under the stars. Ciaru and Tawn kept to themselves that evening, and we didn't bother them. I had little sympathy for dragons, but it couldn't be easy to go on the run like this after a thousand years of unlimited power.

The next morning, we set out again as soon as daylight arrived. Lovat hung on to the side of the four-wheeler, discussing the directions with Caedan. At mid-morning, we came to a stop. Captain Tawn brought the three-wheeler up beside us.

"There," Lovat said, pointing. "That hill up there. It's under the hill."

Ciaru looked and started laughing. Caedan scowled at him. I turned so as to hear better. "What's so funny?"

"That's the location of your safe place?" he asked.

"Yeah. What of it?"

Ciaru laughed again. "I built that."

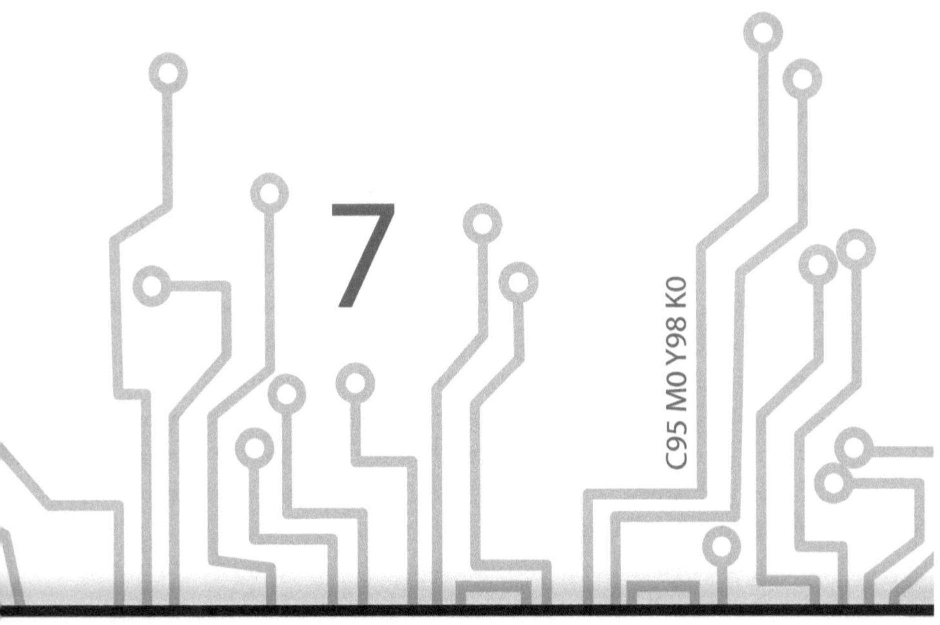

7

Ciaru continued to laugh.

"What do you mean, you built it?" Caedan demanded.

The dragon calmed himself. "We were heading that direction already. I had this place constructed two hundred years ago, as a last-ditch shelter for myself and those most loyal."

"You were expecting to be overthrown two hundred years ago?" I couldn't believe that.

"Not exactly. But I reasoned that if all of us could be united against Onyx, which we were, then what if the others all united against me? I made many such preparations against every contingency I could conceive. The escape tunnel Captain Tawn and I used, for example. This vehicle." He suddenly leveled a piercing look straight at me. "And others."

For a brief moment, Auric terrified me. Someone who made plans against remote, outrageous possibilities, hundreds of years in advance, was either supremely paranoid or supremely intelligent… or both. I didn't like the way he looked at me.

"No way a dragon built it," Lovat grumbled.

"I'm sure humans did it under his instruction," I said. "And now they're all dead, so he's the only one who knew about it."

"What about his draconics?" Caedan called back. "Should we be expecting them to show up next?"

"Maybe. If any of them survived." That could get complicated. Auric and one human soldier would be greatly outnumbered by our band. But if draconics started showing up, we would be the ones outnumbered. Not a good thought.

As we approached the hill, an odd feeling swept over me. Ever since the day we left Viridia and spent our first night outside, I'd grown to love the outdoors so much more than city life. Kelly talked all the time about living in a city again once this was all over. I didn't want that again. I wanted to live out here. And in that moment… I wanted to live on that hill. It was perfect. Gentle slopes dotted with trees led to a wide-open top. Plenty of room for a small cabin or house. Not too far from the mountains, but not too close either. And far from the cities. I figured we must be halfway between Auric and Amaranth.

"To the right," Lovat told Caedan. "That's where Don found it. We started up the hill to get a good look, and he found it."

"Found what?"

"You'll see." Lovat grinned.

Caedan followed his directions. We ascended about halfway up the hill to a more level area where we stopped the vehicles. We dismounted, and Lovat led us in amongst a small grove of maple trees, oddly enough. Hidden by the trees and some rock formations, we saw a pair of metal doors built into the side of the hill at an angle. Captain Tawn and Caedan each took hold of one of the doors and pulled them open. Stairs led down into the hill.

"It has lights, but we couldn't get them on," Lovat said. "We used—"

Ciaru stepped down into the opening and lights illuminated the stairs in front of him. I couldn't help but notice that he now carried that strange orb again. "They are coded to my presence," he explained. "I can adjust that, of course, so they don't go off every time I go for a walk."

"That would be helpful," Kelly mumbled.

Ciaru started down the stairs, talking as he went. We followed him, though I could tell Lovat was annoyed he didn't get to explain the place. "You'll find living quarters for at least thirty people. More than enough for this small group."

"We have more coming," I said.

"Really? Well, I hope it's not more than thirty or it might get tight."

"Thirty beds inside the hill?" Caedan murmured. "That's crazy."

The dragon stopped at the bottom of the stairs, where hallways branched right and left. "The living quarters are on the left," he explained. "To the right, you'll find a fully-equipped kitchen, along with a well-stocked pantry." He looked at Lovat. "I'm assuming you couldn't get that open."

"No," Lovat said sulkily.

"It's coded to me also. Beyond that, are some storage rooms, a laboratory, a medical room, and a gathering hall." He chuckled. "Some of my followers wanted it to be a throne room, but I decided on something more practical."

"How magnanimous," Kelly said.

"Anything else we should know about?" I asked.

"Not especially."

"What about weapons?" Caedan demanded.

"Excuse me?"

"You don't expect me to believe you built this place as a secret hidey-hole and didn't stock any weapons in it, do you?"

Ciaru smiled. "No, of course not. One of the storage rooms is an armory."

"Now we're talking."

"All right," I cut off the conversation. "We can all explore later. Right now, let's get the trailer unloaded so you can head back for the others."

"You're not unloading anything," Kelly said. "As our leader, you should explore this place. Lovat, show him the rest. Let us handle the heavy stuff."

Clever. Getting me out of the work without talking about my injury. I'm not sure Ciaru didn't see through it, but he nodded and returned to the surface with Caedan and Tawn. Kelly went to choose quarters for herself and Chance, where she could put him down to nap while she helped.

"Come on," Lovat told me, gesturing to the right.

I followed him down the hall, amazed at the construction. The walls were solid concrete. Regularly-spaced fluorescent lights illuminated our path. I also spotted a couple of air vents of some kind between the lights on the ceiling.

"Here's the kitchen," Lovat announced, stepping into a room without a door. I stopped in the doorway and stared. The kitchen was easily big enough for five or six people to work on individual projects, whether cooking or preparing or washing....

The pantry and storage rooms would be locked, at least for the moment. "Where's the gathering hall?"

Lovat pointed toward the end of the hallway. "Also path through the back of the kitchen," he explained. I checked it out and found three large tables, each with a dozen chairs. One smaller round table stood apart from the others, with a single chair.

"This is incredible," I said. "Compared to where we've been, this is pure luxury."

I also checked in on the medical room, as Ciaru called it. I was surprised to see what looked like a fully-equipped operating room from a hospital. I hoped we'd never need to use it, but with the way I did things… I'd be on that stretcher sooner rather than later.

"Come see the beds," Lovat suggested.

We passed by the stairs where the others were carrying in supplies. Even Ciaru appeared to be helping. I wouldn't have expected that.

"Four beds inna room," Lovat said. He opened a door and flicked a light switch. "See?"

I stepped in for a quick look. The rooms were small, but two bunk beds sat against the opposite walls. Each possessed a thin mattress and nothing else. Couldn't expect more, I suppose. The beds themselves were larger than I'd expected. Longer too. Maybe they were intended for draconics as well as humans? Beside the exit, another door led to the right. "What's that? A closet?"

"No. Better." Lovat grinned and stood aside to let me see for myself.

The door led to a narrow bathroom connected to the next bedroom. Two sinks, mirrors, a toilet, and a shower. "Luxury," I repeated. I turned the faucet on one of the sinks and watched water pour out. "Pure luxury."

We returned to find the hall filled with our supplies. Caedan set down one final package, some of Carl's equipment. "I'll head back now, and get the others. Should be back sometime tomorrow." He glanced up the stairs. "Will you be okay here? A dragon and a soldier. And you're not in the best shape…"

"There won't be a fight," I assured him. "We'll be here when you all get back."

"All right." He leaned across the pile of supplies and pointed at Lovat. "I'm counting on you, okay? Keep this guy safe."

"Ya, I got it."

Caedan chuckled and trotted back up the stairs, passing Kelly, carrying a pair of sleeping bags. She tossed them on the pile. "Some place, huh?"

"Best we've seen," I replied. "Even beats the tower."

"Anything beats the tower." She shivered.

Ciaru and Tawn descended with the last two bags. It occurred to me that with the dragon and captain's arrival, we would have every chromark color represented except black. Seemed fitting.

"All right, let's figure out where this stuff goes," I suggested. "Auric, if you'd be so kind as to open those other doors, we can clear out this hallway, and then get some rest."

He nodded. "Of course. But in this form, please call me Ciaru. It feels more appropriate. I would prefer not to remind your people on a constant basis of the presence of a dragon among them."

"Gonna be hard not to," Kelly muttered. She picked up the sleeping bags again and started toward the bedrooms. "Two of them," she mouthed to me as she passed, shaking her head.

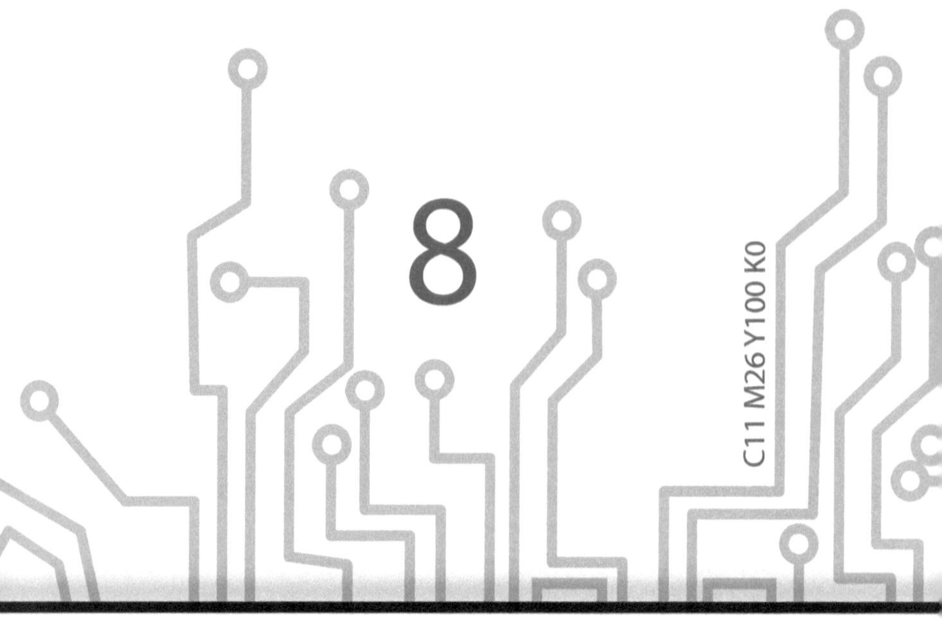

8

With Ciaru and Tawn's help, we moved our supplies around to the proper locations. We stashed our meager food stores in the pantry, but we probably needn't have bothered. The pantry, once the dragon opened it, had enough food to feed an army for a month or more. Even with Chance and Glacier's growing eating habits, we should have plenty.

"Do you dragons even need to eat in human form?" Kelly asked.

"We don't have a need for it," Ciaru said. He took a candy bar from the pantry shelf and unwrapped it. "But we enjoy the tastes. It is one of the pleasures of being human." He took a bite, closed his eyes, and chewed slowly.

Kelly rolled her eyes. We left him there and moved on to the laboratory, where Tawn was just setting down a box full of Loden's equipment. "What is all this stuff?" he asked.

"I'm not entirely sure about a lot of it," I said. "And I don't see much reason to tell you about the rest."

He studied me for a moment. The captain of the Aurelian Sentinels wore dark clothes beneath a few pieces of the usual golden armor: a breastplate, knee pads, and some kind of forearm guards. The gold chromark might not have even been visible on his skin if not for the narrow black outline.

"Make no mistake," he said. "I am here to serve my god, Auric. We may work together for a time, but his will is the only thing that matters to me."

"Oh, we won't forget it," Kelly replied.

"For now, we have common enemies," I said. "Onyx and Atramentous. And the purple robes."

"Yes, so you have said." He looked to Kelly. "You are the one who placed the disk on his neck?"

"That's me."

He gave a short nod. "Then you can be sure that I will do everything in my power to protect you above the rest. You are the chosen of the god."

"Chosen for what?"

He cocked his head. "For the highest of honors. It is all that matters." He pushed past us, seeking out his master.

"What was that supposed to mean?" Kelly wondered.

"I don't know. But he knows you're the only one who can restore Auric to dragon form. That makes you pretty important."

"And you trapped Amaranth."

"Yep." I grinned. "Guess we're both honored."

"I don't need honor. I'd better check on my baby."

After all the travel and excitement, I needed a nap. I chose a bedroom at random and stretched out on one of the mattresses. My side ached, but it didn't take long to get to sleep.

When I woke up, I found Lovat sitting on the bunk across from me. "Hey, bud. What's up?" I sat up and stretched without thinking. The sudden pain in my side reminded me not to do that.

"Keeping you safe."

Right. Caedan's instructions. I yawned and got to my feet. "What are our guests up to? And what time is it?"

"Dunno what time. The soldier is in the kitchen. The dragon disappeared."

"Disappeared?" I blinked. "He left?"

Lovat shrugged. "Can't find him. So I came to watch you."

"Right." I headed toward the kitchen, Lovat close behind. Tawn sat on a tall stool, munching on something. "Where's Ciaru?" I asked.

"I believe he is meditating alone," the captain responded, "not that his movements are any concern of yours."

"They are of great concern of mine," I countered. "If he walks out of this place and somehow draws the attention of Onyx, it's my problem too."

"Then you have no problem." Ciaru strode into the kitchen from the back hallway leading to the gathering hall. I turned so as to hear him better. "I will not leave this place without informing you."

"Where were you?" Lovat asked, narrowing his eyes and staring at the dragon.

"As my loyal Sentinel told you, I needed solitude. I sought out the dark corner of one of the storage rooms to meditate on my fall from grace."

Lovat glared. Clearly, he didn't think it possible for the dragon to have hidden from him.

"What did your meditation tell you?" I asked.

Ciaru turned his placid eyes toward me. "Meditation is an end unto itself. It calms me, clears my mind, and prepares me for what is to come."

"What is to come?"

"Change. Too much change. And as the black dragons unite with purple allies, we must all stand together against them."

"Why?"

"You wish to see your people free? Under that combination, they will be the furthest from free they have ever been." He paused for effect. "Those who live through the coming upheaval, that is."

"Upheaval? What do you mean?" I felt stupid asking so many questions, but he wouldn't keep talking if I didn't.

"Upheaval always comes with times of change. You've seen some of it already: the deaths of dragons, the destruction of landmarks, the killing of my people. This is only the beginning."

"Uh-huh." I settled myself onto another stool, wincing a little. "So what do you think our next move should be?"

He studied me a moment. "What did you do with the disk I gave you?"

"I had to use it on Amaranth." I saw no need to hide the truth from him.

"Is she alive?"

"Yes. On her way here, in fact." May as well lay it all out.

Ciaru perked up. "Ah, then we have more power than I thought. This is good."

"There's something else you need to know about Onyx. He's been augmenting himself, trying to replicate my cyb abilities."

He nodded. "This I suspected. It will make him difficult to defeat, but ironic, considering the purpose of your enhancements."

"Excuse me?"

"So we have yourself, a handful of other humans, and two dragons, both trapped in human form. Not much of an army."

"But what did you mean—"

"If you and your lady friend free us from these disks at the right time, the two of us may be able to overcome Onyx. But not if Atramentous is with him. Perhaps he should be our first target."

"Target, sir?" Tawn asked.

"This is war now, Captain Tawn. And not like the pretend war the rest of the dragons recently engaged in. Onyx and Atramentous have attacked us and killed many. We must respond."

"What about their allies?" I asked.

"All the more reason we must act quickly. If they become more involved, it will prove more difficult."

"I don't understand these allies, sir," Tawn said. "Who are they, exactly?"

Ciaru closed his eyes. "They come from outside The Circle, and they are not to be underestimated. That is all you need know now. When the time comes to face them, I will tell you what you need to know."

"You talk a lot," Lovat said, "but don't say much." He grabbed a snack bar from the counter and left the room.

"What is the purpose of that child?" Ciaru asked.

"He's a member of my team. That is all you need know now." Hey, I used his own words against him. Points for me.

Ciaru nodded. "Very well. You have achieved some surprising results, so I suppose I should not question the makeup of your companions."

"I'm still trying to understand," Tawn said. "Are we planning to kill Atramentous?"

"Sure," I said. "Why not?"

"That's impossible. The dragons are immortal."

I snorted. "This may be news to you, but three dragons are dead now."

His stern look almost made me back down, but I persisted: "I killed Incarnadine just a few days ago."

"You?"

"Drove a sword up through his brain."

"I find that highly unlikely."

"It doesn't change the truth."

Ciaru raised a hand. "I am inclined to believe him, good Captain. His abilities are… impressive."

"Fine." Tawn continued to stare at me with a set jaw. "Then he can kill Atramentous too."

"Precisely what I was thinking."

"Wait, wait, wait." I held up my hands. "Killing Incarnadine took a specific plan, and I took advantage of an unexpected weakness. We don't have anything similar for Atramentous."

"Then we will have to come up with one." Ciaru smiled. "With two dragons helping you plan, don't you think the odds of your success have significantly improved?"

I didn't know what to say to that. But thinking of dead dragons did make me remember something else: "One thing does puzzle me. Viridia would still be alive if you hadn't told me where to find his power source. Why did you do that?"

"I told you at the time. It was a test, to see if you could set aside your need for vengeance."

"You gave up the life of one of your dragon brothers… to test me?" I shook my head. "Why? How could that possibly be of more value to you?"

Ciaru stared at me for a moment. "I cannot give you an answer you will understand at this time. You will have to accept that a thousand years of ruling here has taught me the value of long-term plans that unfold slowly."

I snorted. I shouldn't have expected a straight answer.

"Besides," he added, turning away, "I never got along with Viridia, anyway."

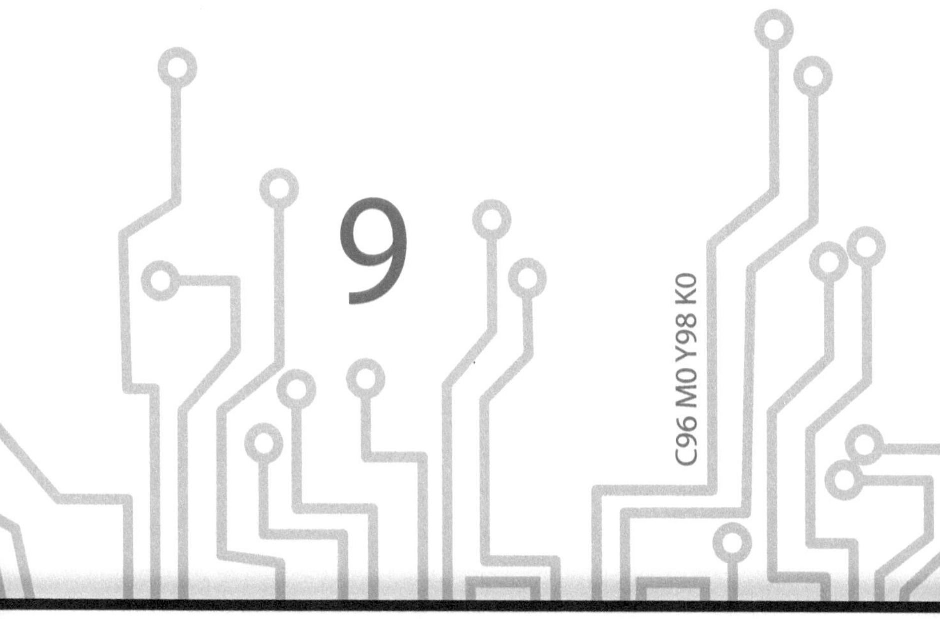

9

I'm not sure how the others slept that night, but I did all right. Lovat, still serious about his instructions from Caedan, slept in the same room with me. Kelly and Chance had their own room. I don't know where Tawn and Ciaru slept, and didn't much care.

The next morning, we were delighted with the breakfast options available in the pantry. We settled on bacon and eggs, which all of us enjoyed. After the past year of living frugally, never knowing whether we'd have enough later, it felt wrong to eat without consideration of days to come. But Lovat, Kelly, and Chance showed no hesitation, and I soon agreed. It was delicious.

I walked through the lab, moving some of Loden's equipment around to make more sense. I set the spare cyb hands and eyes off to one side, hoping I would never need them.

Carl's equipment drew my attention. I'd never had much chance to examine it. During his time with us in Viridia, he kept it all to himself. Then we'd brought it to the Asylum but promptly left it there to go to the tower. It sat in Loden's lab ever since.

The largest piece, a box-shaped metallic thing a couple of feet long and about a foot high and wide, intrigued me the most. Several dials and switches covered the front of it, while a thick wire connected it to a small device which fit easily into my hand. The grid on one side reminded me of the talkers a little. Carl always seemed to be setting this down whenever we entered the hut in Viridia. Could it be some kind of communication device? Hadn't Lainey suggested that once?

"Beryl!" Lovat's voice echoed through the hall. I set down Carl's device and stepped out to meet him. He pointed up. "Caedan's comin' back!"

I followed him back down the hall and up the stairs. I still experienced a few pains in my side from the climb, but I could handle it. Outside, we found Kelly and Chance already enjoying the open air.

"The hideout is fantastic," Kelly said, "but I hope we don't have to hide in it too much of the time. It's so nice out here."

I had to agree. "I want to live here someday," I told her.

Her eyes darted to the open stairway. "We already are."

"No." I pointed to the top of the hill. "I want a house. Up there. When this is all over."

Kelly glanced up toward the summit and frowned. "It's a nice thought, Beryl. I don't know if you'll be able to just retire, though. If we live through it all, people will look to you as a leader. I've told you this, remember?"

"But what about what I want? Maybe I don't want to be a leader any more."

"Hey!" Lovat interrupted. "They're coming!"

We turned to see where he pointed. The four-wheeler chugged up to the base of the hill and came to a stop. The rest of our clan dismounted from the trailer and began climbing toward us. I couldn't help but notice that Amaranth—Lady Rust, that is—had ridden on the four-wheeler behind Caedan rather than sit with all the others.

I stepped forward and lifted my hand. Bice raised his in return. And for a moment, that odd feeling swept over me again. It was like I'd experienced this before. No, that wasn't right. Like I was going to experience it again. Someday. How… odd.

"Caedan praised this place to the max," Bice said as he drew near. "Don only shrugged and agreed. So now I'm eager to see it."

I took his hand and gave him a short hug, protecting my side. We turned, and I saw two figures watching us from not far away. "Oh, we have two other guests," I said.

"Caedan said we did, but he was vague on who—" Bice broke off, then chuckled. "Well, no wonder. Captain! What circumstances bring us together again?"

Tawn greeted him with a stiff bow. "As always, I serve my god," he answered.

Bice turned to Ciaru. "Then you must be—"

"I knew it!" Lady Rust charged into our gathering. "Ha! I knew you'd escape. You're far too smart to let Onyx catch you. When we saw the smoke rising from your city, I knew you couldn't be there."

"Greetings, sister," Ciaru replied. "I am pleased that we can work together again, though not so pleased with the circumstances."

"Circumstances! Is that how you describe the complete upending of everything we've built for a thousand years?"

The rest of the clan gathered near us, watching the confrontation between the two dragons. Lainey slipped up beside me. I smiled and put my arm around her, though I had to turn a little awkwardly to keep my one good ear facing the conversation.

"We will overcome this challenge in time," Ciaru said calmly, "as we have all others before it."

"Tell that to Caesious, Viridia, and Incarnadine!" she ranted. "Or have you forgotten?"

"I have not forgotten. I mourned each of them greatly."

Lady Rust put her fists on her hips, glaring at her brother. "You mourned. Well, I suppose that makes it all okay then. You sit there in your golden city, never deigning to join us for gatherings for centuries, then try to order us to stop fighting, and now... now..." She sputtered to a stop.

"Should we air all our grievances in front of the humans?"

"I got news for you," Caedan put in. "You're part of the humans now."

Lady Rust put a hand to the disk on the back of her neck. Her mouth and eyes widened. "You! This is your handiwork, isn't it? This is just the kind of technology you've always tinkered with. You did this to me!"

Ciaru lifted his ponytail and turned his head to show the disk on his own neck. "I provided it to Beryl here, yes. But it is not my handiwork, but that of someone quite... extraordinary."

That piqued my interest. "Maybe we should retrieve your scientist from the city to join us," I suggested. "We could use someone like that."

"He is—" Before Ciaru could finish his sentence, Lady Rust flew at him, trying to claw at his face with her nails. Captain Tawn stepped in and grabbed her wrists. They struggled for a moment before Ciaru intervened. "Let her go, Captain. And sister: this is not the kind of behavior I expect from you. Come. Let us reason together alone for a while."

She glared at him, but nodded. Tawn led the way for the two dragons to head below. I turned around and looked over the rest of our crowd. They stood around, some smiling, some confused.

"Hey, everyone. Welcome to our new home. You're going to be… impressed. Lovat, would you do the honors?"

He stepped forward with a big grin and waved his hand toward the base entrance. One by one, the others followed him, carrying their own backpacks and such. The whole team was back together again, and what a team it was now. In addition to a pair of dragons, we had a baby draconic, people from Viridia and Caesious, Captain Tawn from Auric, Lainey and—

"Mrow?" Glacier pushed up behind me and knocked me off balance. I would have fallen if not for Lainey catching my arm. Stupid cat.

"She's hungry," Lainey said. "Should I go hunting with her?"

"You won't need to. Wait until you see the pantry."

"We have a pantry?"

"Come on. I'll give you a personal tour."

Glacier balked at descending beneath the ground again, maybe because she'd gotten used to enjoying the great outdoors. Lainey let her run free while we headed down the stairs. At the bottom, we found happy chaos. All of the team members went back and forth, exclaiming and admiring the new rooms and amenities.

Before I could show Lainey anything, Hunter pushed his way past two of Caedan's guys and waved at us. "Beryl! Have you seen the medical facilities?"

"Sure. What do you think? Look good?"

"Good? It is fantastic!" He leaned against the hallway wall to let Fern and Kelly go by. "I could not ask for anything more. It is probably better equipped than some hospitals!"

"Then let's check out Beryl's side injury again," Lainey suggested.

"Absolutely. But we can do much more than that." Hunter smiled. "How would you like me to fix your face again?"

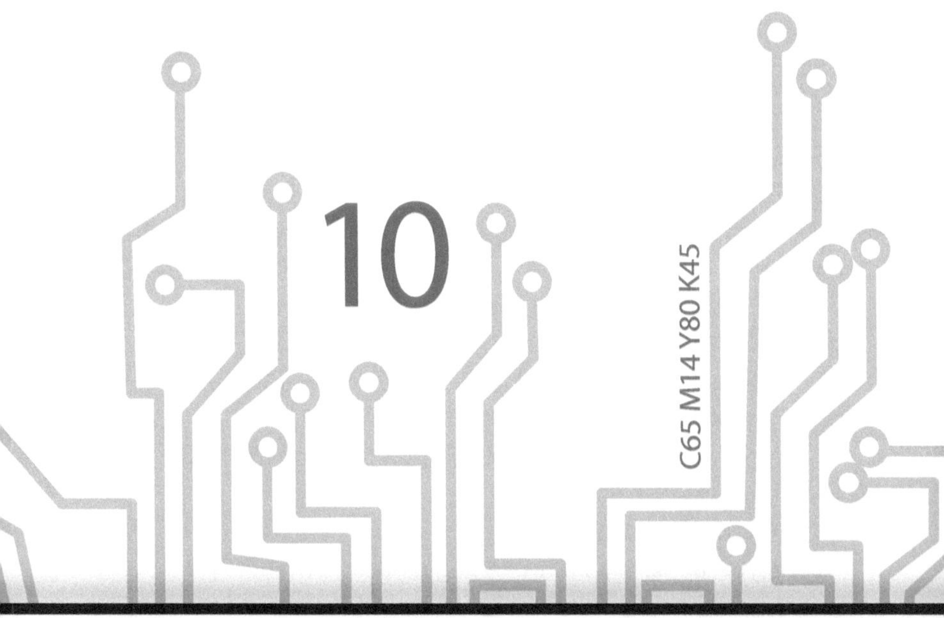

At first, I hesitated. Hunter's proposal, though appealing, would put me out of commission for a day or two. With all the turmoil going on, I didn't think it smart. But then he pointed out now would be the best time, since I was still recovering from the side injury.

"You are not going to be charging into battle any time soon as it is," he insisted. "Let me do this for you."

I conceded, but not without insisting on first having a meeting that included Bice, Caedan, Lainey, and Kelly. We assembled in the gathering hall, where we closed both doors for temporary privacy. The other four sat down at one of the tables. I stood at the end and watched Hunter approach.

"What is this all about?" he asked.

I glanced at the others, then decided to launch right into it. "Why didn't you tell me about my heart?"

"What about it?"

Bice pulled out the papers. "We have the rest of Loden's notes now. We know what the two of you did."

"Do you? Because I do not fully understand it myself."

"Why didn't you tell me?" I repeated.

Hunter sighed and took a seat. "You had just learned so much with the rest of the notes," he said. "I did not want to overwhelm you—"

I slammed my palm down on the table, though it hurt my side. "No! That's no excuse. You withheld important information!"

"How?"

"How what?"

"How is it important information? How does it change your life in any substantive way to know this?"

"It… it does. That's all. I mean, how can I know my capabilities if I don't know how they work?"

"You practice." He pointed at me. "Did not you discover on your own that you could send a boost to your heart?"

"Yes, because I was desperate! I'd rather know things before that happens!"

"What are we talking about?" Kelly asked.

"Beryl's got a dragon heart," Caedan said.

"No, no. Not… precisely," Hunter replied. "We grew him a new heart, and—"

"You grew it?"

While Hunter explained about the genetic manipulation, using bigger words than Cerise, I sat down at the head of the table and waited. I didn't know what to think.

"But why?" Kelly asked when he finished. "Why give him a heart like that?"

"Think about what Beryl does on a regular basis," Hunter went on. "He strains his body to the absolute limits. And then collapses. We have all seen it. His body has trouble handling it. An ordinary human heart would never be able to handle that kind of stress. He would be dead in months. At best."

"So his heart is stronger," Lainey said.

"Much stronger, far stronger. And that helps with the battery thing."

"The what?" I asked.

Hunter wrinkled his brow. "I know we talked about this."

"No. No, we didn't."

He closed his eyes and lowered his head a moment. "I am sorry. Sometimes, I genuinely forget who I have told things to." He lifted his head again. "Your boosts. The energy you use. It comes from within you. This is why there is a limit. While you are resting, you are storing up energy, like a human battery. It's thermoelectricity. Are you sure we did not talk about this? I distinctly remember the conversation."

"It wasn't with me," I said. "I'd remember that." Who else had he been talking to?

"After your operation, your body needed a couple of years to get acclimated to all of these changes," he explained. "I am sure you had a very difficult time of recovery, learning to walk again, and so on."

I did. Bice had been there to help, or I might have given up.

"But then it started storing energy. As long as you were not exerting yourself, using boosts on a regular basis, it kept storing it up. That is why you have been able to do so much in the past year. You had a lot stored up. And then you have had at least some rest in between major events."

"Are you saying I'll run out of energy at some point?"

"You already have, a few times. That is why you have had to sleep so much." He folded his hands together. "There is a law of diminishing returns here, Beryl. The more often you do this, the faster you burn your energy out. If you do not get enough rest in between times, you will not charge up as much, and you will run out faster."

I didn't like the sound of that.

"You knew all this, and didn't tell him," Caedan said. "That's not okay."

"I agree," Kelly added. "Why keep this to yourself?"

Hunter spread his hands. "I genuinely thought we had this conversation already. No, I did not tell him about the dragon genetic material. I did not think it necessary. I do not tell every one of my patients every single detail of the work I do."

"It's not the same thing," Bice said. "Beryl is not just any patient, and you know that."

"What else have you kept hidden?" I wanted to know. "I mean, you never mentioned Loden's assistant until Bice remembered him. So what else are we missing?"

Hunter's mouth hung open. "Why are you attacking me? I have done nothing but help you since you freed me from the pit!"

"My best friend turned out to be a dragon in disguise," I growled. "I have trust issues."

"I am not a dragon!"

"We know that much," Caedan put in. "They're all accounted for."

"Unless there are more dragons we don't know about," Kelly said.

Caedan gave her a horrified look. "Don't even think things like that!"

"Listen. Loden was the most secretive man I have ever met!" Hunter exclaimed. "He told me only what I needed to know. I was honored to work with him: he was a genius! But he kept secrets from me. Lots of them."

"That—" I began.

"I already told you I never met his assistant," Hunter barged on. "I know he had one, but other people also came into the lab from time to time. At least one of them was a representative from his patron, I think. I overheard them talking about money a couple of times."

"Patron?" Bice exclaimed. "Why would he need a patron? He was working for the city!"

Hunter pointed off in the distance. "You remember how full that old lab in the cave was, yes? Do you think the city paid for all of that? Do you think Loden paid for it?"

"You're saying someone else was supporting Loden's work into fortek?" I asked.

"Into what?"

"Forbidden technology. None of the tech we found in his lab was sanctioned by Viridia."

"Some of it, for certain," Hunter agreed. "I mean, nothing he did with you was sanctioned. He hid it all, by pretending he was using you to help the draconic."

Troilus Green. I wouldn't forget that.

"Someone was paying him, supporting him," Bice mused. "I wonder who. And why."

"Sort of how Lady Rust was supporting the rebels?" Caedan suggested. "Only maybe for real? Some rich person who wanted to strike a blow against the dragons?"

"Maybe…" I considered it. Something didn't add up, though.

"No, no, no." Kelly shook her head. "None of you are thinking straight."

"What do you mean?"

Kelly pointed at me. "What does filling Beryl with cyb parts do against the dragons?"

"What?" I wrinkled my brow. "I wouldn't have been able to do any of what we've done over the past year without it."

She shook her head. "But it doesn't make sense. No one could plan for what you've done. No one could plan for you to lead Incarnadine into the tower, or climb into his broken eye socket."

"Well, no, but—"

"For that matter, what part of Loden's tech was created for fighting the dragons at all?"

"He built a whole train for it," Caedan pointed out.

"Besides that. The last thing he did. Everything else. What about it? Cyb hands and eyes. The flying thing. The talkers. The stuff we don't understand yet. What part of any of it has anything to do with the dragons?"

"What are you saying, Kelly?"

She waved her hands. "I don't know. I just don't think it's as simple as Loden wanting to overthrow the dragons and building stuff to fight them. Everything we've done fighting them has been improvisation. None of it was planned!"

"Then what was Loden—or more specifically, Loden's patron—working toward?" Bice wondered.

"We'll ask him when we find him," I said.

"Or her," Caedan added.

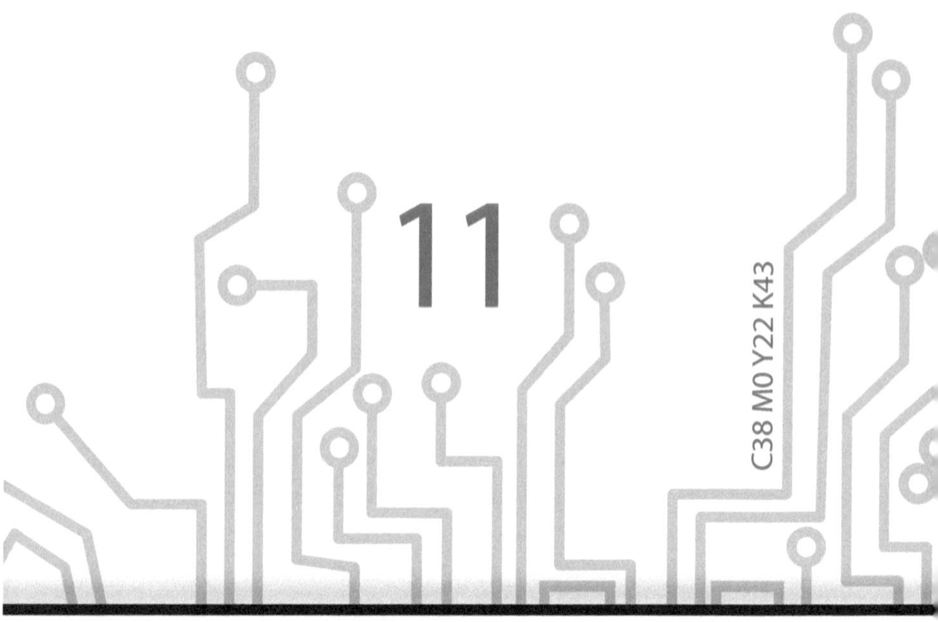

I looked around the table at the others. Hunter and Caedan looked confused, Bice thoughtful, Lainey stunned, and Kelly… she'd thought through this more than we had. She looked confident, but…

"We're missing something," she said. "Something really important."

"Yeah. If Beryl wasn't built to fight the dragons," Caedan said, "then what was he built to fight?"

"Who says he was built to fight anything?" Bice asked, looking up. "Maybe we should take Loden at his word there. He did what he did to save Beryl's life."

I thought back to Loden's story, the one he'd told us back in Viridia at the start of all of this. How he'd worked in the Emerald Ascendancy for years, discovering greater and greater things, some of which he hid from the draconics. He'd only turned to studying the dragons and their weaknesses after my accident, according to him.

"He did not need to go as far as he did," Hunter said quietly. "We could have saved Beryl without giving him so many abilities." He paused. "But that is what Loden wanted. To this day, I do not know why."

We sat in silence for a few minutes. Finally, Kelly spoke up again: "As I understand it, you wanted to question Hunter to see whether you trusted him enough to work on you again. What do you think now?"

Hunter's eyes widened. "Really? I just wanted to help repair his face!

And check on his side."

"But if you were still lying about your time with Loden, we needed to know," I said. "You didn't tell me everything, and that still bothers me."

"I am sorry," he said, looking straight at me. "No more excuses. I was wrong not to tell you everything."

"Fair enough. When do you want to go to work?"

He got to his feet. "Give me the rest of today to get acquainted with the equipment. And after a good night's rest in a real bed... we can start tomorrow."

"Good," Caedan said. "Then Beryl can stop being the king of ugly."

"Yeah, wouldn't want him challenging you for that title," Kelly said.

Caedan clutched his chest. "Ow! I'm hit!"

Bice said something, but I only heard a murmur since my head was turned the wrong way. I looked back at him. "What?"

Everyone laughed.

"He was asking Hunter if he could fix your hearing," Caedan said.

"What is wrong with your hearing?" Hunter asked.

I pointed at my left ear and explained what had happened.

"We can do some tests and see if we can determine how much damage is done. It may come back on its own over time. Or it may require another surgery."

"Ugh." I stood up. "If there's nothing else, I guess we're done here."

"We're not going to talk about the two dragons?" Kelly asked.

"Not right now. Everyone's still settling in here. Let's wait a day or two, then have a general meeting. Humans only."

We left the gathering hall. I was amused to discover most of the rest of the team had assembled in the kitchen. Fern seemed to have taken charge there and had Caedan's four assistants taking inventory of the pantry. I learned Don and Basil were working to camouflage the vehicles outside. Lovat wandered from room to room. The dragons and Captain Tawn were nowhere to be found.

"He's got a secret room," Lovat declared to Bice and me near the stairs.

"You think so?"

The boy nodded, scowling. "They're not in any of the other rooms."

"It makes sense," Bice observed. "If he really did build this place for himself, he'd have his own bedroom somewhere, at least. He wouldn't be sleeping in the group bedrooms with all his minions."

"But he keeps messing with our stuff," Lovat complained.

I looked down at him. "What do you mean?"

Lovat pointed down the hall. "The new lab. He's messing with stuff in there."

"Have you seen him?" Bice asked.

Lovat shook his head. "No. But someone is. Stuff's moved around when I check it."

"Could be anyone, then." I had to admit I was impressed. Lovat could tell someone had been moving equipment around in the lab? I probably couldn't tell if someone had moved my own stuff, let alone all that stuff I didn't understand.

"Why anyone?" Lovat folded his arms. "They all seen it before, back at Asylum."

"So you think it must be Ciaru," Bice said.

"Or Tawn," I added. "Or Amaranth for that matter. Lady Rust. Whatever. Could be any of them."

No one answered me.

"I found something that looks fun," Lovat said suddenly.

"What do you mean by 'fun'?" Caedan asked as he entered the kitchen.

"It looks fun," the boy repeated.

I chuckled. "All right. Show me."

Caedan joined the two of us in a short walk to the lab. Lovat led the way to a table in the back where a lot of Loden's old tech had been stacked. He picked something out and held it up. It looked somewhat like Lainey's rifle, but with an impressive metal claw-like thing at the end. Four claws extended out in opposite directions before curving down, back toward the rest of the device.

"Where did you find that?" Caedan exclaimed.

"You know what it is?" I asked.

Caedan took it from Lovat's hands and cradled it like a weapon. "We could have used this back at the tower! Or any other time we had to climb stuff."

"What is it?"

"It's a launcher for this." He pointed at the claw thing, and traced a finger down to a large spool of thin cable. "The Cerulean Corps were experimenting with something like this."

"So it's a projectile weapon?"

"Not a weapon. It's for climbing. You launch the claw somewhere where it can hook on, and it takes the rope with it. Then you can climb." He pointed to a type of handle near the other end. "Here is the triggering mechanism."

I looked it over. "You're right. This would have come in handy. I don't think it would have helped me climb into the pit, but certainly other times." I paused. "How did we not find it before?"

Lovat shrugged. "You don't know how to look."

I laughed. "And you do?"

"Found that, didn't I?"

"Maybe I should put you in charge of all the tech." I took the claw launcher from Caedan and looked it over. It was surprisingly lighter than I expected. It even had a strap for carrying it over the shoulder, again like the rifle. "Seriously. This does not look like Loden's tech work."

"Maybe it was already here," Caedan suggested. "It came from Auric?"

"That makes more sense." I set the launcher down and smiled at Lovat. "You let me know if you find anything else that looks fun!"

"Right." At least, that's what I think he said. He'd moved to my left side. So annoying!

"I need some sleep."

Something shook me awake. I sent a boost to all my limbs before my eyes even opened. Lovat looked down at me. "Beryl!"

"What is it, buddy?" I licked my teeth. Why was my mouth so dry? Yuck.

"Someone's in the lab," Lovat said. "Snooping around."

I sat up. "You couldn't tell who?"

"Came to get you first."

"Right, right." I got to my feet and followed him out into the hallway. Save for dim hall lights, everything inside the base was dark and quiet. I didn't ask what Lovat had been doing awake. He had his own sleep patterns.

In my bare feet, it was easy to move without sound on the smooth flooring. At least, it wasn't too cold. We passed the stairs and approached the other rooms. I saw a brief flash of light from a doorway ahead. Someone was definitely in the lab with a flashlight. Lovat pointed, and I nodded.

I moved carefully into position just outside the door. At least the lab didn't have another exit. We had the spy trapped. I motioned for Lovat to put his hands on the door. Then I counted with my fingers: 3… 2… 1.

Lovat threw open the door. I flipped on the light switch. A figure stood bent over some equipment at one of the tables. Shoulders slumped, the figure turned around.

Lainey?

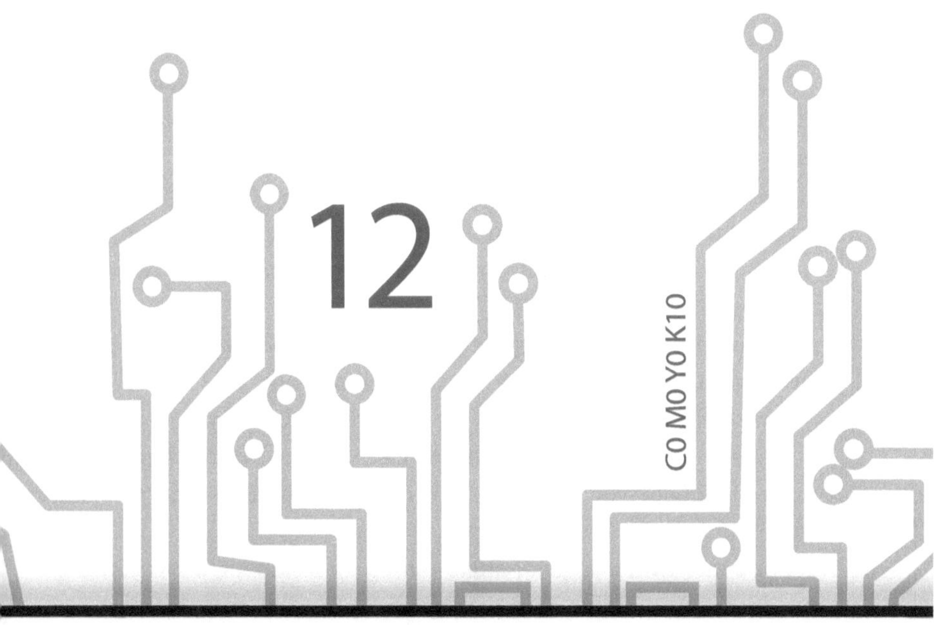

"Lainey? What are you doing?"

She sighed and turned off her flashlight. As she stepped to the side, I saw the equipment she'd been examining: her father's. "If you wanted to look at that, you only had to ask," I said. "Why the secrecy?"

"It's something Caedan said this morning," she answered, not meeting my eyes.

"What did he say?"

"He wondered what you were built to fight."

"Yeah, that doesn't—"

Lainey held up a familiar container. "Remember this?"

"Sure. We brought it from Incarnadine. It—"

"You tore this piece of cloth from one of the purple robes, Beryl." She kept interrupting me. "No one's ever done something like that."

"What are you trying to say?"

"I think you were built to fight them." Her face tightened.

I blinked. "What?"

"They use cybernetics. You are cybernetics!" Lainey shook the container. She was almost in tears. "They play with genetics. Your heart was genetically modified! You can touch them! You can hurt them!"

"Lainey…"

"I'm serious!"

"I've never seen the purple robes," Lovat complained. I glanced at him and realized he was right. He'd never been around when we encountered them.

I walked around one of the tables toward Lainey. She bit her lip, lifted the container again, then set it on the table beside her father's equipment.

"Let's… let's assume you're right for a moment," I said. "What were you going to do in here?"

She pointed at the nearest device. "I told you he talked into it sometimes. I thought… I thought if I could get it to work…"

"You want to contact them?" My eyes widened. "Why?"

"I don't know. Maybe I could threaten them. Maybe they want to know more about you." She choked up. "Maybe they'll send my father back."

For a moment, a surge of anger pulsed up inside me. How could she even think about telling them about me? How was that different from Rick? But my rational side pushed it back down. Of course it was different. Rick betrayed me for his own power. Lainey… she just wanted her father back. How could I blame her for that?

"Come here," I said, reaching out. She fell into my arms, sobbing, and saying something about being sorry. I think. She landed on my left shoulder, so I couldn't hear her very well.

My eyes met Lovat's, and he rolled his. I knew what he was thinking: girls. At his age, he was a long way from understanding them. Then again, was I any closer?

I let Lainey cry a little bit, then pulled her away from my shoulder to look in her face. "I promise you," I said. "We'll go try to find your father when everything is done here."

"When will that be?" she whispered, then hiccuped. She pulled up her shirt collar and wiped her eyes.

"I don't know. But if you'd told me when this all began that we'd have three dragons dead in such a short time… I'd never have believed it." I tried to smile for her. "The world is changing so fast, faster than I ever thought possible. Look, I don't know anything about these purple robe guys, or whether I can fight them much. Maybe my enhancements were built to take them on, or maybe it's a coincidence. I don't know. But we'll try. As soon as we can."

As I walked with Lainey back through the lab's door, two thoughts wrestled for my attention:

One - we really needed a new tech person. Someone needed to figure out Carl's equipment, not to mention Loden's. Even though I didn't trust Ciaru—and some of the others trusted him even less—he might know some things, or know someone who would. He'd mentioned a scientist, the one who'd designed the inhibitor disks. I needed to talk to him about it.

Two - Lainey's theory was disturbing. Too much of it made sense. But if true, it implied even stranger things. Loden would have known about the purple robes and their capabilities. And he would have wanted a way to fight them. Yet he never mentioned anything like that to any of us. His focus had always been on the dragons. Had he known they would come afterwards? Had he planned to deal with the dragons himself, and built me for the next stage of the battle?

"Built me." Those two words shook me up. I'd had plenty of conversations with Bice over whether I was still human. But to think of it that way… that everything about me had been especially designed for a singular purpose… it messed with my head.

Loden cared about me. I knew this. I mourned his death unlike any other in my life. He didn't treat me like a weapon. He treated me like a son. So I could reject the idea that he'd given me all of these powers just to use me against either the dragons or the purple robes. But were the two ideas completely exclusive? Could he have cared about me and still planned to use me? Or at least, ask me to help? Planned a purpose for me? I guess it could make sense that way.

I escorted Lainey back to her bedroom, then returned to the one I shared with Lovat. Fatigue dragged at me, but I lay awake at least another hour, chasing those same two thoughts around.

In the morning, I met Hunter in the medical room. He'd recruited Fern as his assistant again, and they both looked like they were prepared for anything. Fern directed me to climb onto the operating bed or whatever it was called.

"So what's the procedure here?" I asked.

"Let us start by looking at your side," Hunter said. "I am a little concerned that you have not been resting it as much as you should."

With Fern's help, I removed my shirt. "How do you rest a side?"

"You rest your whole body. You do not go walking across The Circle."

"I haven't been—"

"You know what I mean. The good news is: you will be asleep during this procedure, so I can at least force you to rest for a few hours." Hunter unwrapped the bandages and discarded them. "While I examine this, tell me what you want done with your face."

"What I want done? Um, I want the acid scar gone, I guess. What do you mean?"

"He means your chromark," Fern explained. "He's going to give you new skin on one side of your face. He could do the same on the other."

"But I don't need new skin on that side."

"I can replace that skin," Hunter repeated. His fingers pressed on a spot on my side and I jerked from the pain. "You can have a clean face completely, if that is what you want."

"I would not have a chromark?"

"If you like." Hunter stepped back and let Fern begin wrapping me with a new bandage. "I cannot change what is there, but I could remove it. I can do wonders with skin, but not tattoos. I am not an artist."

"Yes, you are," Fern said. "Just not that kind of artist."

I thought for a moment. "It's tempting, but... no. I had Jaden give me this chromark for a reason, and that reason still exists."

"Noted." Hunter moved to a small stand full of tools and sorted through them. "I guess we can get started. Fern, the anesthetic?"

A few moments later, I was out.

Waking up from anesthesia is always weird. It didn't help that Hunter had to cover up one of my eyes with the bandages while the new skin around my eye healed. So when Lovat tried to shake me awake, I could only open one eye... slowly.

"Whath goin' on?" I mumbled. My mouth felt like someone had shoved it full of cotton balls.

"Beryl! Wake up! Emergency!" Lovat's voice cracked in the middle of his words.

"Wha?"

Lainey's face appeared over mine. "You need to get up as fast as you can, Beryl. It's urgent."

I blinked a few times, then swung my legs out to sit up. I came up, careful not to bang my head on the upper bunk, but when I did, my consciousness spun. "Whoa." I would have fallen right back on the bed if Lainey hadn't caught me.

"I know you're fighting the drugs," she said, "but we need you right now." She patted my face, a little harder than might be necessary.

"What is it?" I managed. "What's wrong?"

"It's Caedan," she told me.

"He tried to kill the dragon!" Lovat exclaimed.

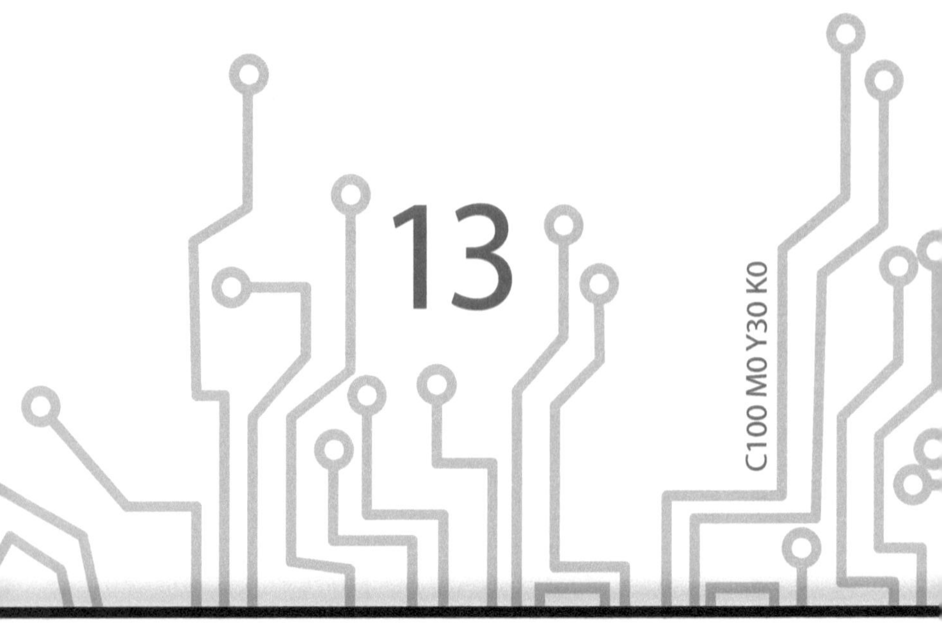

13

Caedan did what? I struggled to my feet, trying to clear my head. "Water," I murmured.

Lovat dashed out of the room and returned only a few moments later with a bowl full of water. "All I could find."

I took the bowl, drank a few swallows, then splashed the rest of it onto my face to wake me up. Except half my face was bandaged. I really wasn't thinking straight. The water helped, but Hunter would be annoyed at the wet bandages.

"Where is he?" I asked.

Lovat pointed out the door. The three of us exited and made our way to the kitchen. I took everything in with my unbandaged eye.

Caedan, his face pale, sat against the refrigerator, holding his right arm with his left hand. Blood seeped out all around his fingers. He glared up at Captain Tawn, who stood above him, holding a long knife aimed at Caedan's head. Another bloody knife lay on the ground a few feet away. Ciaru stood on the opposite side of the room, holding back the blood from a wound in his left shoulder. Lady Rust stood beside him.

"Find Hunter," I told Lovat. I stepped further into the kitchen. "What happened here?"

"Your man attacked my god," Captain Tawn reported. "His life is forfeit."

"We waited as a courtesy to you," Lady Rust snapped. I had to turn my head to hear her. Hunter hadn't done anything with my hearing yet. "Now that you're here, that's done. Execute him, Tawn."

"Wait!" I lunged forward.

"He does not take orders from my sister," Ciaru said. "Stay your hand, Captain. Until I give the order."

Lady Rust harrumphed and folded her arms.

I reached up to rub my eyes, forgetting the bandages again. I rubbed the uncovered one. "Caedan, did you attack him?"

"Of course I did." He turned toward me, but the anger on his face remained. "Peri is dead because of him! He tried to kill everyone in Caesious!"

"Ah," Ciaru said. "A blood debt. I see."

"No, you don't," I said. "Peri was our friend. He died stopping your bomb from reaching the city. Caedan's not wrong about that." I looked down at him. "But I told you we needed him for now."

"Yeah, well. That's why I waited until you were asleep."

"Caedan…" I ran a hand through my hair and massaged my scalp, still fighting the anesthetic.

"He has confessed," Lady Rust stated. "What more do we need?"

"Shut up, Amy," Caedan growled.

"You will address me as Lady Rust!"

"Ciaru, please have Captain Tawn step back," I said.

"Why would I do that?"

"We have an alliance here. If you kill my friend, it's over." I turned to look directly at him. "And I will kill you."

"He broke the alliance already!" Lady Rust insisted. "He must pay!"

"Sister, please," Ciaru said. "Beryl, a blasphemous attack against a god cannot be simply overlooked."

"Are you proclaiming yourself the sole arbiter of justice here?"

"When it comes to situations such as this, perhaps I am."

"It can't work that way."

"I repeat: he assaulted a god."

"Gods can't be hurt by a human assault!"

"This is a trifle. It is the act itself that is the problem."

Lovat and Hunter burst into the room.

"Do you need medical assistance?" I asked the dragon.

"No. As I said: a trifle."

"See to Caedan," I told Hunter.

He started forward, but Captain Tawn shifted to block his path. "Excuse me?" Hunter said.

"Are you denying him medical help?" I asked.

"By our law, he deserves to die," Ciaru replied.

"Your law doesn't rule here!" I fought against the fuzziness in my head. "You said you understood why he did it. You've also been trying to tell me how you're different from the other dragons."

Lady Rust snorted.

"Prove it! Show mercy."

Ciaru hesitated. "We cannot simply let this go by without some consequence. Or would you have us live by no law at all?"

"Look, Caedan's an idiot, but he had reason. You did try to kill his city. And no, we don't have any specific laws here. That's a problem, clearly. We should get together and discuss it. But for now, I'm asking you directly. Please. Let it go." I took a step toward Ciaru.

The dragon took a deep breath and let it out. "Captain Tawn," he said at last. "Sheath your weapon and stand back."

"Outrageous!" Lady Rust grumbled.

Tawn obeyed. Hunter knelt beside Caedan and took his arm. "Oh, this is bad. He has lost a lot of blood."

"Get him to your med room," I said. "Lainey, help him."

I picked up the fallen knife, then turned to Ciaru. "Thank you."

He stared at me with an impassive face. "I allow this. This once. Should anything else like this happen, there will be justice. My justice."

"We'll talk about it later."

He gave a slight nod of his head. "That seems to be your solution to many things. If you continue to wait until later on everything, it will eventually create a disaster." He turned and left the room, followed by Tawn and Lady Rust.

"Don't like him," Lovat muttered.

"Yeah, I don't blame you."

I hurried to the med room, to find Hunter sewing up Caedan's arm. I'd seen the inside of a dragon's eye socket, but the sight of him giving stitches still gave me a quesy feeling. Caedan remained conscious, and not in a good mood. He glared at me.

"What were you thinking?" I demanded.

"Oh, I don't know," he shot back. "Maybe I was thinking of killing a dragon. You know: the whole purpose of our rebellion!"

"That's not—"

"I told you! I told you when Peri died!"

"Stay still!" Hunter warned.

"I told you I was on board," Caedan went on. "That I bought into everything you believed. Kill the dragons. Save the humans. So that's what I'm trying to do."

"Everything's changed, and you know it," I said. "We're not just dragon assassins."

"Why not? We have two of them here. We kill them, and we're down to only two remaining."

"But one of those two is Onyx, and we need help to defeat him. Plus, he's got help from outside. I hate it too, but right now, we need Auric and Amaranth."

"We need Auric," Lainey added. "Can't say we need Amaranth."

I shot her a look, then turned back to Caedan. "Our tactics have to change. They always had to change. We weren't going to kill every dragon with a train like the first one."

"We're working with the enemy, Beryl."

"We've trapped them in human form!" I argued. "If they step too far out of line, I'll kill them myself. They can't match my abilities."

"They have abilities of their own," he growled. "Have you forgotten her voice?"

"I haven't forgotten." I threw my arms out, but the dizziness from the motion forced me to lean against the wall. "Why won't you trust me? Have I been that wrong so far?"

He locked eyes with me. "Peri's dead."

"And because of that, you won't trust me? I told you that was his choice. I tried to stop him!"

"Auric did that. I don't trust you as long as he's here and alive."

That hurt.

"My ultimate goal has not changed. Come on, Caedan. You were there when Amaranth offered us half of The Circle. Did we accept that? No! We want everyone free. Everyone." I leaned in. "And that doesn't happen as long as the dragons are around."

Caedan lowered his head and didn't answer.

"Done," Hunter announced, straightening up. "We'll bandage that up and let it heal. Be careful with it."

"Beryl, what did you do to your bandages?" Fern asked. "They look horrible!"

"He splashed water on his face," Lainey said, and giggled a little.

"I wasn't thinking," I grumbled, giving her a half-frown.

"That's my line," Caedan said. I looked back at him. He looked at the stitches on his arm, then back at me, and smiled a little. "I sometimes feel like we're in competition to see who can do the craziest thing without thinking it through."

"If you'd succeeded today, you might have won," I said. I shook my head. "Seriously, man, if you had killed him… Tawn would have killed you. Or Lady Rust. They wouldn't have waited for me, either."

"I know. But maybe it would have been worth it." His smile got a little larger. "You killed a dragon by yourself. I need to catch up."

"Sit down," Fern ordered me. "I have to replace your bandages again."

I sighed and took a seat beside Caedan. "I haven't had many friends my age," I told him quietly. "I lost Rick. I don't want to lose you too."

He took a deep breath. "I'll wait. For now." His smile this time wasn't quite happy. "But don't make me wait too long."

Ciaru's eyes darted around the lab. "You wanted me to look at these things?"

"Yeah. You seem to have some tech knowledge," I said. "Maybe you can figure something out that we can't. Our last tech girl worked for Onyx. And we lost the guy who built most of this." After dealing with Caedan and getting some breakfast, I'd decided to move on to the next challenge right away.

Auric ran his own cybernetic hand along the fingers of another cyb hand sitting on one of the tables. "Your friend Loden, correct?"

"Uh, yeah. How'd you know?" The skin of my face itched enormously under the new bandages Fern had applied. She said that was a good thing. I saw no sign of Ciaru's injury or any effects of it. He'd insisted the dragons didn't heal any faster than ordinary humans, so he must be simply hiding it.

"You've spoken about him frequently. Based on what was done to you, he was quite the genius. If I am accurate in my observations, much of this tech is his. I see a few items from my own labs." That explained the grapple launcher. Ciaru took a step and pointed at a different table. "But that equipment appears different from the rest. I suspect it is not mine or his."

"It's not. And that's really the main reason I asked you in here." I walked over to the table. "This stuff belonged to Lainey's father. He brought it from outside The Circle. I want to know what it is."

Ciaru bent over the equipment and turned his head back and forth, eyeing it from each direction. "I will help you, but I require something in return."

I braced myself. "What do you want?"

He lifted his head and looked straight at me. "What were Caesious's last words? You still haven't told me."

I saw no reason to keep that a secret any longer. "He said, 'The Circle will fall. Auric.' That's all."

Ciaru nodded, as if he understood perfectly. He returned to examining Carl's equipment.

"What does that mean to you?" I asked.

"It means that Caesious, in his dying moments, realized that I have been right all along." He tapped the surface of the device with a gloved finger.

"Right about what?"

"Everything important."

I rolled my eyes, and decided to re-focus on the present. "You mentioned a scientist," I reminded him. "The one who built the disk thing on your neck. Could we retrieve him from your city?"

Ciaru straightened and pulled off his gloves. "He's dead. And I do not know how many of my other scientists may have survived the black dragons' attack. I am naturally anxious about the fate of everyone in my city, but for now, I believe it prudent to wait for word to reach me."

"You're expecting someone then?"

"I am hoping." He tapped Carl's largest device with a metal fingernail. "This appears to be a communications device of some kind."

"That's what we were thinking." My eyebrows went up. Maybe this wasn't a waste of time. "Lainey remembers seeing her father talking into it. But he never did it while we were around. Since then, no one's used it." I paused. "We tried, but couldn't get it to do anything." In addition to Lainey's attempt, I had messed with it myself a little bit when no one was watching.

"Communications technology has been forbidden for humans."

"Half of my body is fortek. We left that rule behind long ago."

"Fortek?"

"Forbidden tech."

The dragon glanced at me. "Yes, of course. I suppose it is, along with almost everything in this room." He turned back to the device. "Curious. It has no wire to connect it to power. That implies some other sort of power source. A battery, perhaps?"

"If you say so."

"I do." He turned the device around and looked at the back. "Here. Probably behind this panel. Do you have any tools?"

"Uh, there's a box of them over there." I pointed.

Ciaru sorted through the box's contents and removed a screwdriver. As he bent over the device again, he asked, "Tell me: what is the nature of your agreement with Amaranth?"

"Didn't she tell you?"

"Yes, but I prefer to hear both sides of a story, whenever possible."

"In exchange for removing the disk, she promised to tell me the history of the dragons and anything else I wanted to know."

"But she hasn't yet, has she?"

"No."

Ciaru removed a panel from the device. "Perhaps she is not so anxious to have it removed then."

"She complains all the time. But you don't."

He lifted his gaze to me. "I agreed to this condition for the sake of our temporary alliance, in order to make your companions more comfortable. However, it has opened me up to unexpected attack. This leads me to question whether my sacrifice was appropriate."

"It won't happen again. I've talked to Caedan. I'll also talk to everyone else, just to be sure."

"From my testing of you, I now have a reasonable grasp of your morality, I believe." Ciaru bent down to look inside the device. "I am convinced you are sincere in your statements. But I do worry about your ability to enforce your morality on the rest of your tribe."

"They'll listen to me, or they'll leave."

"And so it begins."

I blinked. "What?"

He reached inside the machine and removed something. "As I thought, a battery of some kind. I believe it is dead, but if we can find another one, or something similar, perhaps this can be used again." He looked up. "And you have taken your first step toward becoming one of us."

My jaw dropped. "What does that mean?"

"You just said that you would tell your people what to do, and you threatened to enforce it with exile if they didn't agree. How do you think we began our rule over these cities, save with something similar?"

"I don't—it's not the same!"

"It's the beginning. You start by enforcing something you know to be right. Preventing them from doing wrong. And then you realize: you have power. You can make people behave in a specific way, because you're the strongest." He moved to a nearby box and poked through its contents. "And once you realize that, you begin to force them to behave in ways you believe to be right, or not do things you believe would be bad for them. You do it all because you care about them, of course. You may make a show of seeking wise counsel, but ultimately, the decision is all yours." He looked up at me. "Because you have the power. And that makes you right."

I closed my eyes and shook my head. "No, that can't be right. Power doesn't determine what's right. It can't."

"Why not? I have more power than everyone in my city put together. Therefore, I make the rules. Who can stop me?"

"We're going to stop you." I clenched my fist.

"So that you can make the rules? You have more power than any other human. Will that make you right?"

"No! We work together. I won't force my will on others."

"So what happens if you tell your friends not to attack me or my sister, and they all disagree? Will you bow to their will, or will you enforce yours?"

"That's not going to happen. They're good people. Enough of them will agree."

"So majority rules, then."

I narrowed my eyes. "Maybe. Is that wrong?"

Ciaru almost laughed. "It's just another variation of power making the rules. The majority, by definition, is greater than the minority, so they can enforce their will." He sorted through a few items he'd pulled from the box. "The only reasonable system, then, is for one leader, a leader with wisdom and understanding, who knows what is right, to lead everyone else."

"And you dragons have all the wisdom and understanding, I suppose."

"Not all of us, no. But I am convinced enough in my leadership to believe I am doing what is right for my people." He opened his palm toward me. "As do you."

"It's not the same!"

"Very well. Explain it to me." Ciaru picked up something from the sorted items and returned to the original device.

"I'm not an expert on this. I never even wanted to be a leader."

"You're not an expert on how people should be led." He bent down and peered into the open panel. "And yet you seek to overthrow the current leaders. How is this stance logical?"

"I know what's wrong. I know the difference between freedom and slavery."

"You know what's wrong," he repeated. "Once again, it comes down to your personal belief about morality, which you seek to enforce on everyone else." He looked up. "How are we different again?"

I don't know if I'd ever felt so frustrated in my life. "You twist words back and forth!" I took a breath. "Let me put it this way. You're dragons, not humans. My goal is to get you out of the picture and let humans decide for themselves. When that happens, I'll get out of the way. I have no desire to rule over them once the job is done."

"And what if a large number of them decide they want a dragon to rule over them?"

"Then—then at least they'll have made the decision for themselves!"

He gazed at me over that ridiculous mustache. "How do you know that hasn't already happened? Perhaps not in Viridia, but in my city, for example?"

I stared back. "I don't believe you."

He shrugged. "You're welcome to believe what you like." He fiddled with something behind the panel, then turned the entire device around. "I believe, myself, that I may have fixed this device." He flipped a switch. A hum and a crackle came from Carl's device. It worked.

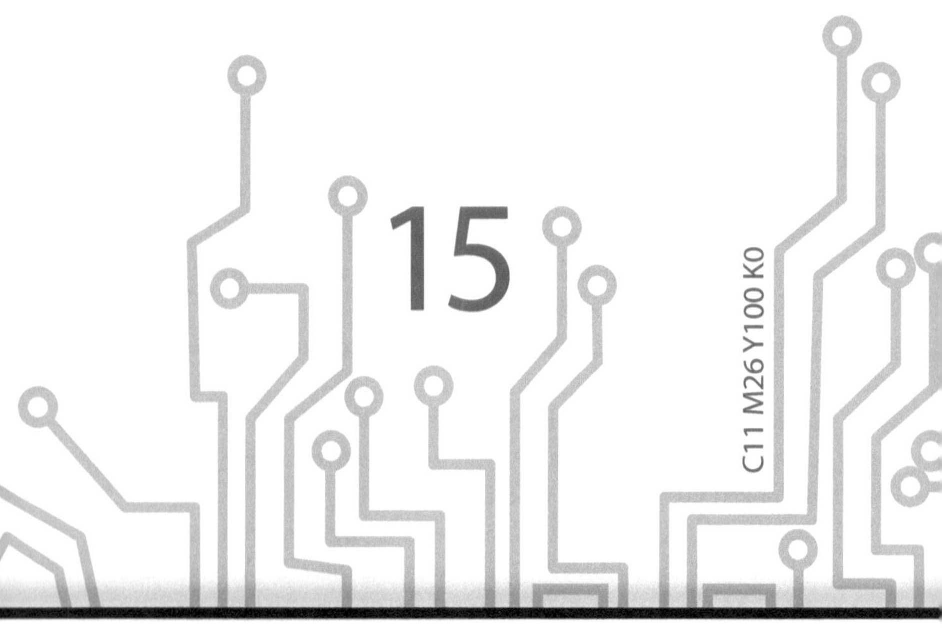

15

I walked around the table next to Ciaru and stared down at the communications device. A green light shone from one side, while another series of colored lights fluctuated up and down.

"What does it mean?" I asked.

Ciaru cocked his head. "I'm not entirely certain, but I believe this"—he pointed at the fluctuating lights—"indicates the strength of a signal. That is, whether it can have enough strength to receive or transmit sound waves."

"The signal doesn't look very strong then." The line of lights looked to be about a dozen tall, but only the first four were lighting up, and that inconsistently.

"We are underground. I imagine it would work better outside, or at least nearer to the surface."

"Curious." I reached to rub my face, but had to stop myself for the bandages again. "Carl used it in a cave when I first met him, but it was in the side of the mountain. And then he used it in a house in Viridia."

"Tell me about this Carl," Ciaru said. "What type of man was he? What became of him?"

"The purple robes took him, right in front of us." I didn't see any reason not to tell him the truth. "From our time together, he seemed like a good man. A good father. Very smart."

"But not on the same level as Loden?"

"No, he wasn't a tech guy." I gestured at the device in front of us. "I mean, he used stuff like this, obviously. And he understood more than I do, which isn't very hard. But he didn't create stuff, at least not that I knew about."

"Indeed. This device doesn't appear too complicated." Ciaru pointed. "This is the microphone you speak into."

"Like our talkers."

Ciaru glanced at me, but didn't respond to that. "I imagine you turn this dial to find the right frequency, and once you have a signal, you can speak into the microphone and be heard." He looked to the side of the device. "I'm not entirely certain where the incoming sound would come out. The speakers must be inside." He flipped the main switch and the lights went out. "I only found the one extra battery, so we shouldn't waste it."

"Let's carry it outside and see if it works," I suggested.

"Whom do you wish to contact with it?"

I scratched the top of my head above the bandages. It didn't help with the itching underneath them. "Lainey thinks we can contact those outside The Circle. Maybe even get Carl back."

"I do not see how that would be advantageous."

"We need information. This base is great, but we're blind here. We need to find out what's happening elsewhere. Maybe by talking with these other people, we might learn something."

Ciaru lowered his head for a moment. "Perhaps… perhaps it is time I showed you something."

Now he had my attention. "What do you mean?"

"Please. Wait here." He left the lab. While I waited for his return, I looked at Carl's device and considered the possibilities. Should I tell Lainey we got it working again? She would want to try it out as soon as possible. I'd wanted to try it myself before showing her, but maybe that wasn't the best course.

My face continued to itch under the bandages. I wanted to see Hunter's work, but I would have to be patient for now. The itching meant healing, or so they told me. "Scratch somewhere else," Fern advised. I tried that. It didn't help.

A few minutes later, Ciaru returned, holding the mysterious orb I'd always seen with him. He set it on the table where I took a closer look. The surfaces of the different panels appeared cloudy, as they usually did, but multicolored lights flashed around them.

"Do not ask me to explain this technology," Ciaru warned. "It was built by someone much smarter than myself. And what I do know, I do not wish to share."

I nodded, trying to contain my curiosity.

"Only my hands will activate it." He placed both of his cyb hands on the orb and moved his fingers about to precise positions, connecting with each side apart from the main panels. The lights accelerated in their movements, and the panels cleared up, becoming almost transparent.

"We should check on Atramentous first." Ciaru moved his right hand on the side of the orb. The transparency shifted, forming images. I stepped closer to see better.

Within the top panel, I looked down on the city of Atramentous from high above. Ciaru adjusted something with his left hand, and the view zoomed in closer. "It is made possible by—"

"Cameras very high in the sky," I interrupted. "Can you see all of the cities?"

"Yes." He tilted his head. "How did you know that?"

"Onyx had something similar in his tower. We used it for a while. We could see all of the cities except Viridia. I assumed it was because his power source was gone."

Ciaru's expression was hard to read. "He had an orb?"

"No, it wasn't an orb. There were these boxes on the wall." I tried to explain how the room in the tower had looked before I smashed it.

Ciaru pointed to the orb. "Look closely. Would you say this is the same view?"

I peered into the orb. "I think so... can you show me another city? Amaranth?"

He rotated the orb to a different panel, revealing the city of Amaranth, just as I'd watched it from the tower. "It's the same view," I confirmed.

Ciaru let go of the orb and the view faded, becoming cloudy again. He paced away, hands behind his back.

"I'm guessing this is a problem?" I asked.

"If Onyx had these views..." He paused, probably deliberating over how much to tell me. "If he can do this, it means he's stealing it from me. The cameras are mine."

"He couldn't have his own cameras?"

Ciaru shook his head, agitated. "It's not possible. I would know."

"Well, I mean… he didn't exactly steal it, right? You still have it."

"He had the same views from the same cameras. It's a different kind of stealing." He pointed a metal finger. "And it raises a very disturbing point."

"What's that?"

"If Onyx can do this, either he has become a tech genius in his years as a human, or he's had help from someone else."

"Like the purple robes."

"It certainly gives credence to your suggestion they're working together."

"Suggestion? We all saw it! They were there when Onyx and Atramentous announced their new power structure!"

Ciaru stopped pacing. "They were?"

I pointed over my shoulder. "Ask any of us who were there. Lainey. Caedan. Bice. Fewmets, ask Lady Rust! She saw them." I looked down at the orb. "I guess you weren't watching with this then."

"I cannot watch everywhere at once! I spend most of my time watching over my own people."

I picked up the orb. It weighed less than I expected. "Are you sure this only works with your hands?" I asked. "I've got this cybernetic hand now, you know." I tried touching it where he had.

"It's more than that." He sighed and returned. "There are sensors in my hands that connect to it."

I handed it back. "If you say so." Like I knew what "sensors" were…

"The orb has other purposes, that are… specifically tied to me." He activated it again and rotated the panels until he looked down on a city partially obscured by smoke. I stepped in to get a better look.

"Auric?"

He nodded. "The damage is… significant, but not as extensive as I'd feared. I've been watching the repair work."

I studied Ciaru as he gazed down. Now that I considered it, I could see the bags under his eyes. He hadn't been sleeping much. Had he really been watching his city the whole time when he wasn't around us? Did he actually care about his people? This dragon still confused me, in so many ways.

"Do you still feel you did the right thing in escaping?" I asked after a moment.

Ciaru nodded. "As we discussed earlier, everything I do is for the greater good. I can see it much more than anyone else, so it is only proper for me to make the decisions." He adjusted the view on the orb. "In this case, I sacrificed a few to save the most."

"But not sacrificing yourself, of course."

He looked up with furrowed brow. "What good would that do?"

"It might have saved everyone in your city if you'd just flown out to face the dragons yourself."

"But then I would not be around to plan for their defeat, a defeat that will save even more people."

"So it's all about the balancing act for you? One life versus two lives. A thousand lives versus ten thousand."

"Yes." Ciaru deactivated the orb. "It's the most logical method I can find."

"It's not always about logic, you know." I patted my heart. "What about love?"

He gave me a skeptical look from the side. "It is love that motivates me to make these decisions." He sighed. "You'll understand one day. As your power grows, and theirs diminishes… as they age, and you don't… you'll feel yourself growing distant from them. You'll see them, not as individuals, but as numbers. Numbers to balance."

I didn't answer him. I couldn't think the way he described. Not ever.

And yet I was terrified he might be right.

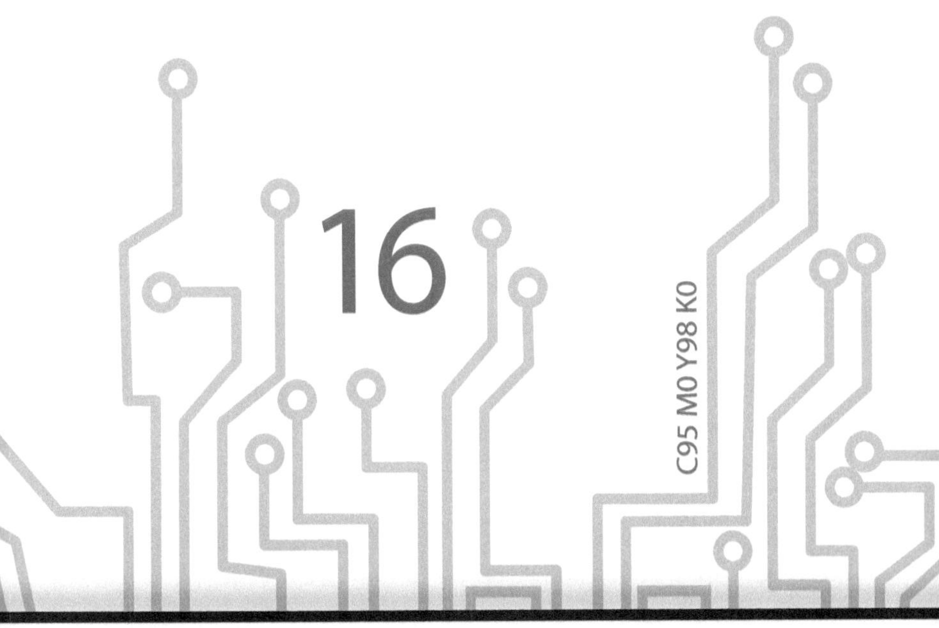

16

Ciaru and I did agree we should have a general meeting. Considering everyone was right there, in the base, you'd think getting everyone together would be easy. But some people were napping, taking showers, outside working on the vehicles… It ended up taking almost half an hour to get everyone into the conference room.

I looked around the tables. We'd met like this just yesterday morning, even though it seemed much longer. The only difference now was the presence of Ciaru, Lady Rust, and Captain Tawn. The three of them sat at a separate table from the rest of the team.

"All right. I'm glad that everyone is settling in to the new base…" I began.

"But we need action!" Turq exclaimed.

I almost took a step back. Definitely not the person I expected to interrupt.

Turq waved his arms. "I mean, this place is great! I love it! But we can't just sit around and play like we've got our own little city all to ourselves. Shouldn't we be doing something?"

"Yes. Yes, we should. Now that we're safe here, we can—"

"Safe?" Fern interrupted. "Is that why we had to give Caedan stitches?"

"He attacked my lord," Tawn said in an overloud voice.

Several other voices chimed in. I raised my hands until they finally quieted. It took far too long.

"We're in this together for now," I said forcefully. "We have some un-likely allies, but we're going to work together for our mutual goal."

"I thought our goal was to kill dragons," Don said.

"Our goal is freedom. For now, we work with these two." I looked toward Ciaru and Lady Rust. "But we will never forget who they are or what they've done."

"Are we going after Onyx then?" Cobalt asked.

"We will deal with Onyx. But it may be wiser to take down Atramen-tous first. We think he's more vulnerable."

"When is a dragon vulnerable?" Hunter asked. "Except when they are human…"

"You need to know something." I hadn't planned on revealing this to everyone just yet, but enough people already knew. "Onyx has had en-hancements, like mine."

That got everyone quiet.

"I'm not going to hide things from you. It's bad. Very bad." I pointed at the dragons. "The fact that we have two dragons here with us shouldn't anger you. It should terrify you! Because it means we're up against some-thing that has driven them from power already! Yes, they're in human form right now. But if they turned back into dragons and tried to fight Onyx, they'd lose. And they know it. That's why they're here. Because we're their only hope as well."

I put both hands on the table and leaned in. I'm sure I looked some-what ridiculous with the bandages over half my face still, but I didn't care. I'd never tried to look like anything other than what I was.

"Onyx and Atramentous have help from outside The Circle. These… strangers in the purple robes are powerful. We don't know how to stop them. We don't even know why they're here or what they want!"

More than one pair of eyes turned to look at Lainey.

"But we know they're our enemies. And we'll fight them. Right now, our number one need is for information."

"We used to get a lot," Kelly pointed out.

"Right. We need someone to visit Viridia again."

"You mean St—" Saxe began.

"Don't use names," I cut him off. "Not everyone here knows about our information network."

Kelly smiled at the words "information network."

"The only problem now is that we are much further away from Viridia. Even with the vehicles, it's a long trip."

"And we don't have a ton of fuel," Caedan added. "We used a lot of what we had left just getting here."

"There is more fuel in a separate bunker outside," Ciaru said. "It should be more than sufficient for a lengthy period."

I turned to him. "Any more secrets you want to share with us about this place?"

He folded his hands together. "None that come to mind. I do, however, have an easier method for your travel concerns. We use the trains."

"We've done some of that. It's a risky move, but—"

"I can eliminate most of the risk," the dragon declared. "Three miles from my city is a stand where farmers often load their supplies. If anyone is waiting at that stand, the train will stop. I can provide passes that will allow you on board without any questions… as long as Captain Tawn goes along."

"That could work, at least for most of the journey there," I said.

"We can't show up at the Viridian station," Bice said. "We'd have to jump off before we got there."

"Getting used to that," Caedan put in. "Shouldn't be a problem."

"But what about the return trip?" I asked.

"We'd have to stow away, most likely," Caedan said. "Otherwise, it's gonna be a long walk."

"If you are on a train at any time, and you show the passes I give you," Ciaru said, "no one will question your presence."

"That's handy," Royal mumbled.

"All right. Then who's going?" It physically hurt me to say the next words: "It can't be me. My… doctor says I need more time to recover. Don? You and Lovat again?"

The miner nodded. "We can do it."

"I'll go too," Basil spoke up. I'd forgotten he was there.

"Do you want any of us to go?" Saxe asked. "I mean, it's the chromark thing…"

"No, that should be sufficient for now." I pointed to Don. "Find out everything you can from our contacts, and hurry back. Especially see if there's any word about the purple robes. I'm curious to know if they're showing up more publicly, like they did at Incarnadine."

"They're hidden everywhere," Lady Rust stated. I'm surprised she contributed at all. "They've always been undercover throughout The Circle. But we could never find them all."

"Yeah. I know exactly where one is," I replied. "In Viridia."

"What?"

"Why didn't you mention this before?"

"Where?"

"At the time, I didn't know who they were," I answered when the questions stopped. "But I found one of the robes hidden in a police locker. Someone in the Viridian Guard is one of them, and I know how to find him."

"Then maybe we should go after him right away," Caedan exclaimed. "Why wait?"

"We don't know enough yet," I reminded him. "That's what Don and the others will find out. We don't act until we have information."

Bice chuckled. I didn't blame him. Look at me trying to be all responsible and careful.

"So do the rest of us just sit here and wait for them to get back?" Turq asked.

"We'll be getting ready. We need to be prepared for anything. We don't know what our next move will be until they get back. We may go straight back to Viridia. We might move on Atramentous. Or something entirely unexpected. Thanks to Ciaru over here, it won't take as long as I'd feared. But make no mistake: we're seeing this through to the end. Onyx will fall."

After answering a few more questions, I moved on to the issue of behavior in our home. I didn't want to call them laws, because I didn't want us to start thinking of ourselves as our own city, at least not for very long. I got some pushback from a number of people as we discussed.

"Can we at least agree that no one should harm another person here?" I asked.

"Define 'person,'" Caedan suggested. I gave him what I thought was an annoyed look, but who knows how I appeared with the bandages?

"It is a good thought," Bice said. I noticed that he kept his gaze down, not looking at anyone in particular as he spoke. "When there was just a handful of us, such measures weren't necessary. But as our company has grown, we have… growing pains. That's normal. People are different. They have conflicts. But it's how we handle those conflicts that determines what kind of people we will be."

"It seems like a simple enough rule," Hunter said. "I do not see any problem."

"And what happens when someone breaks the rule?" Tawn asked, probably at the prompting of Ciaru.

"Anyone who breaks the rule is not welcome here," I declared.

"That's it? Some kind of exile?" The captain folded his arms.

"For any kind of infraction?" Cobalt asked. "I mean, it's the same thing if you punch someone or if you kill them?"

"I think we can determine the consequences at the time," Bice suggested.

"Who will?" Lady Rust demanded.

"The entire group," I cut in. "We'll handle it when it happens. And that's enough for now. As Turq said at the start, we need some action! Let's get things moving!"

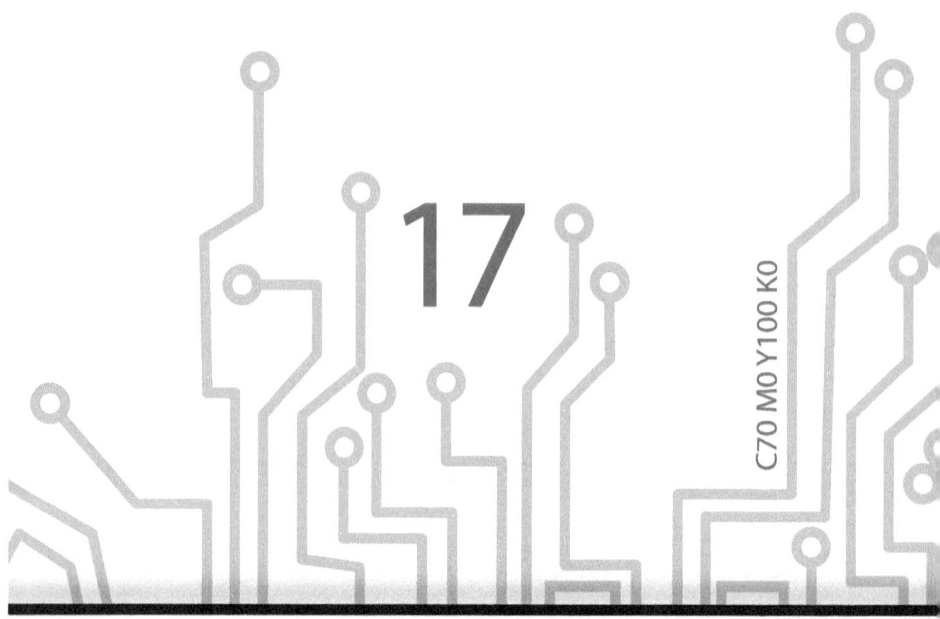

The next two days were mind-numbing. Don, Lovat, Basil & Tawn left in the early morning. After that, despite my words about getting ready and being prepared, the rest of us had to sit around and wait most of the time.

Caedan got his four guys busy doing inventory of everything in the base. Unfortunately, Ciaru refused to let him into the armory after his earlier attack. I argued that we needed to know what we had in order to make plans, but Ciaru countered that he would be perfectly willing to provide what we needed… when we needed it. If Lovat were around, I could have had him spy on them, or try to find another way into the armory. I didn't think anyone else could handle that job.

On the second day, Hunter removed the bandages from my face while I sat on a stool in the med room. Fern held up a mirror, and I studied myself. I'd gotten so used to the scars from Onyx's acid, I almost didn't recognize the man in the mirror. I turned back and forth, comparing the new skin to the old, the huge chromark to the bare side of the face. I put my hand up to touch it.

"Careful," Hunter warned. "It will still be sensitive for a couple of days, at least."

"Cool," Lainey said. "I'll admit it now: you were ugly."

I chuckled and took the mirror from Fern's hands. "It's… almost perfect."

"I think the new skin might be a touch lighter than the skin around it," Hunter said. "It is hard to get an exact match."

Glacier pushed between Lainey and Hunter and plopped herself down on my feet for some reason.

I looked at Hunter. "You offered to change the other side too. Can you do this for other people? Just to get rid of their chromarks, I mean?"

He frowned. "I suppose so. I mean, it's kind of a complicated process, but I guess I could, now that we have what I need here."

"I want to offer this to everyone," I said in a rush. "Everyone."

Fern's eyes widened. "No chromarks… wow…"

"It will take a lot of work, dependent on skin color and other factors," Hunter mused. "The only thing that would slow it down is, well, me. I do not think I can do more than one of these procedures every few days."

"That's fine. That's great."

"Not everyone will want it, Beryl," Fern broke in.

"Why not?" Lainey asked.

"When you've had something your entire life, it's not always easy to let it go," Kelly's mom explained.

"Even if it's a symbol of oppression?"

"Even then."

"No, she's right," I said, looking at the mirror again. "Some people might not be ready for it." I almost said I wanted to do it myself, but… not yet. I still liked the symbolism of my multi-colored mark.

"I'll take your word for it." Lainey didn't look convinced.

When I walked out of the med room, and began to encounter the others, I explained the idea. The reactions ranged from amazement and awe, to excitement and eagerness to try it themselves… and some skepticism. Ciaru didn't comment. Lady Rust snorted and turned away.

After a still-painful walk up the stairs, I found Kelly and Chance outside. To my surprise, she turned me down immediately when I offered the process to her.

"This is how Chance knows me," she said, gesturing to her face. "I don't think I should make such a drastic change while he's still so small."

Chance, hearing his name, looked down at us from the crest of the hill. Kelly waved to him. He resumed digging in the dirt for something.

"I haven't asked in a few days," I said. "Anything new with him?"

"Say what you mean, Beryl. No, he hasn't started remembering previous lives in service to Onyx." Kelly started up the hill toward the child.

"I'm just trying to keep up with everything." I followed her up the slope. "We still don't know what will happen, or when."

"Auric said it would happen within months," she replied. "When it happens, it happens. We'll deal with it."

We reached the top and watched Chance playing for a while. Though he was only a few months old, he behaved more like a young child. He was far more advanced than seemed normal.

"He's growing so fast," I said. "Not at all like… babies I remember."

Kelly sat down in the dirt beside him. "We know nothing about draconic life cycles except what Protogonus Blue told us." She helped Chance dig a trench. "But he's my son, and I'll take care of him."

"Of course. I trust you." I smiled. "And unlike our other guests, at least we don't have to worry about him trying to kill us in our sleep or something."

"Kill!" Chance exclaimed.

Kelly threw up her hands. "Oh great! That's his first word? Way to go, Beryl."

"Really? That was his first word?" I crouched down beside them. "Chance, man. You gotta do better than that. How about 'Mom'? Can you say 'Mom'?"

The small draconic with the huge eyes looked up at me. "Kill," he repeated.

Kelly threw dirt at me. "This is your fault!"

"How is it my fault?"

"You're the one who used that word!"

"I didn't know he'd repeat it! I didn't know he could say anything!" I knew she was teasing, but I couldn't help defending myself.

"Idiot." Kelly pushed me, and I lost my balance. I sat in the dirt with a thump.

"I'iot," Chance repeated.

"You taught him that one!"

Kelly laughed with me. It made me remember old times. Listen to me. "Old times." Like a year ago was so long.

"Hey, look!"

I turned in the direction Kelly pointed and saw a small cloud of dust in the distance. With a thought, I zoomed my cybernetic eyes in closer. "It's the four-wheeler," I reported. "They're coming back."

I took a step down, but Kelly caught my arm. "You can wait for them to get here. Don't rush it." She pointed to my side. "You're still healing."

"Did Hunter recruit you?"

"Haha." She shaded her eyes to look toward the approaching vehicle. "They can't all fit on the one four-wheeler, can they?"

"No. It looks like there's only three. Lovat's hanging on the side."

When the team left, Saxe had gone with them to drive the other vehicle. After dropping them off at the railroad, he'd brought it back, leaving them only the four-wheeler. We'd figured when they got back, we could make an extra trip to pick up half the team. I hadn't expected three of them to ride together. They'd left only one person behind?

As the vehicle drew closer, Lovat waved excitedly. I recognized Captain Tawn driving. The third passenger would be Don or Basil. They were halfway up the hill before I could tell Don for sure. Kelly and I descended a few feet to meet them near the entrance to the base.

The four-wheeler came to a stop. Lovat jumped off and ran to meet us. He gave both of us a hug before noticing my face. His eye widened. "Hue." He jumped up and threw his arms around me again.

Don approached a good deal slower, while Captain Tawn drove the four-wheeler off toward the hidden shelter we'd made for it. I furrowed my brow and looked at Don.

"Where's he going? Don't we need to go pick up Basil?"

Don shook his head and didn't look at me. "No. We lost him."

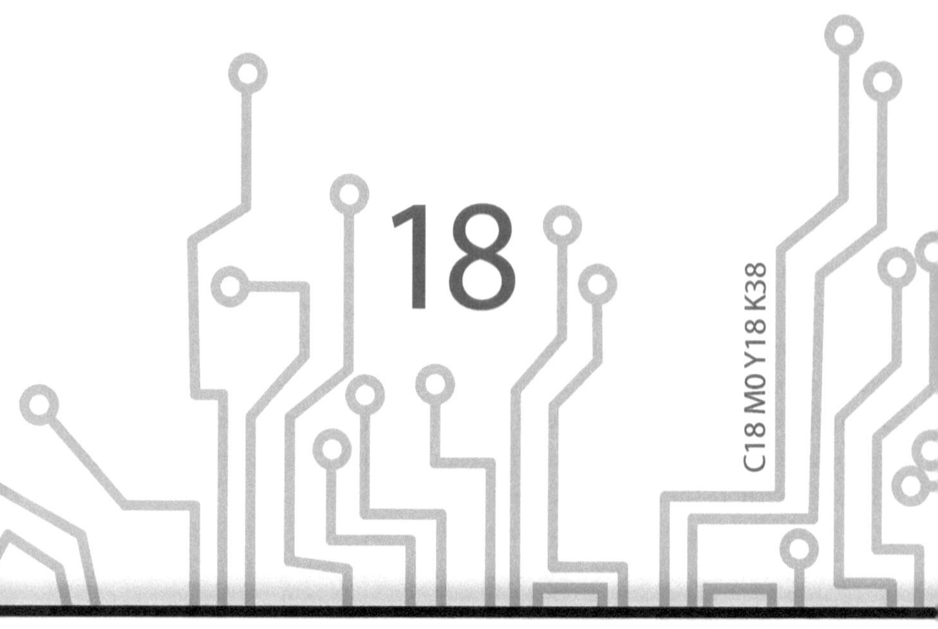

"Lost him? What does that mean?" Kelly exclaimed.

"We don't know, exactly," Don answered, his face down.

"He didn't come back," Lovat said. "I looked, but couldn't find him."

"Wait, wait." I held up a hand. "Start over. How'd he get separated from you?"

"Before we met with Stacy," Don said, still not looking up. "He said he wanted to check on a friend. I thought he'd be all right. But he didn't come back."

"I looked," Lovat repeated.

"I believe you. You found no sign of him?"

Lovat shook his head.

"If the Guard got him," Don began, "I don't know—" He lifted his eyes and stopped at the sight of my face.

"Yes, no scars any more. You can lose your chromark too, if you want. I'll tell you more later." I took a deep breath. "This could be really bad. If he tells them about our base... well, at least we're a long way from Viridia, I guess."

"He might not have been caught," Kelly said. "He may have just... left."

"What do you mean?"

"I never spent much time around him." She bent and picked up

Chance as he toddled up next to her. "But he... made me a little uncomfortable. I don't know why. Maybe he never really believed in the cause."

"I never took the time to get to know him very well," I berated myself. "I should have made the time."

"What did we know about him, anyway? I know he helped you in the prison break..."

I shook my head. "My fault. I should have made the time." I clenched my fist. "I'll talk to Cobalt and the others. They had more time with him than anyone."

"Worst case scenario. He told the Viridian Guard everything he knows," Kelly said. "What does that mean to us?"

I tried to think. "Viridia may or may not be under the black dragons' control yet. It depends on what Troilus Green is doing, I suppose."

"But if the draconic knows about us, would he come after us? All this way?"

"Too far," Lovat muttered.

"Maybe? As long as we aren't bothering him, he might leave us alone." A worse thought occurred to me. "Or... he might trade information about us to Onyx in return for continued rule over his city. Or even the purple robes. Stacy said someone had seen them together."

"Worst case," Don said.

I sighed. "We'll need to bring the others in on this." I clapped Don on the shoulder. "You didn't do anything wrong, Don. It's my fault if it's anyone's."

He shrugged.

"So you saw Stacy?" Kelly asked.

"Yeah. She's good."

I hadn't talked with Stacy since before we went to Incarnadine again. I'm sure she'd gotten at least as much information from Don as she gave him, if not more. That's how she worked. I'd suggested he not tell her about our dragon guests, but I suspected she'd pull it out of him anyway.

Don didn't like talking in front of people, so I let him tell me everything he learned from Stacy first. Then we headed below and gathered up Bice, Caedan, and Lainey in the conference room. First, we talked about Basil again, just to fill the others in. After debating his motives for a few minutes, I decided to move on.

I stood up, took a deep breath, and told them what else Don had reported: "We're going to have to stay hidden for a while."

"What do you mean?" Caedan asked.

"Stacy says things are bad out there. Troilus Green has not submitted to the black dragons, but that doesn't mean Viridia is any safer. Things are worse than ever. The Guard is cracking down hard on people."

"Isn't that more reason for us to get involved?" Bice said.

"Troilus Green is blaming it all on us. It's telling everyone that we created a dangerous terrorist group that's killing people and stuff. There have even been some attacks attributed to us."

"We haven't even been there!"

"I know. And Stacy knows nothing about them either. Troilus Green probably had some Guard members do it, to fire things up. It's like… they're trying to turn people against us, but they're making themselves hated at the same time for their crackdowns. It's a mess."

"Is Stacy going to be all right?" Kelly asked Don.

He nodded. "She's safe. They don't know about her."

"What about the other cities?" Bice asked.

"They're not much better." I sighed and took a seat. "Onyx and Atramentous are basically doing the same kind of thing everywhere. They're using what's left of each city's police force, combined with a bunch of new recruits, and working to control everyone more than ever before."

"What about the purple robes?" Lainey asked.

"Whatever their involvement, they're staying out of sight. Stacy doesn't have any reports of them being seen, and her people know to keep an eye out." I scratched a little bit of the new skin on my face. "Apparently, their big appearance in Incarnadine was a one time event."

"I can't help but wonder if it was done for us," Bice said. "And the other dragons."

"To intimidate us?" Caedan asked.

"To let us know they were behind this, yes."

"So we're backing down? We're letting it happen?"

"No! I just…" I took a deep breath. "I hate this. I really do. I want to get in there and do stuff now, now, now. But… we can't. We're not in any shape to do it just yet."

"You mean you're not in any shape to do it," Bice said quietly.

"That's a big part of it, yes," I admitted. "I don't like risking everyone else, when I'm the one who can handle the risks better than anyone else."

"This isn't a one-man operation, Beryl," Kelly said.

"I know, I know. And I value each and everyone here for what they can do. But… what can we do right now? Stacy thinks we should hide out and wait for a few weeks, to see if things calm down. I think she might be right. That'll give me time to fully heal, according to Hunter. And he can do the chromark removal for anyone who wants it. That actually makes us more flexible, because we can use the stage makeup for fake chromarks better when there isn't another one underneath."

"We can still run some operations," Caedan argued. "We can spy out Atramentous, for one thing."

"We'll do what we can," I said. "But nothing big. Not yet."

"Our guests are going to grow impatient, maybe even sooner than the rest of us," Bice pointed out.

"Should we care?" Kelly asked.

"They're still very dangerous, even in their current form," Bice replied.

"I think Auric can wait," I said, thinking it through. "He seems to be the most patient of all the dragons. But Amaranth may be a problem, especially if she wants to follow through on the agreement."

"What was that?" Kelly hadn't been with us.

"She promised to tell us the history of the dragons, and anything else we wanted to know, in exchange for removing the disk," I explained.

"Don't forget how she offered us half The Circle too," Caedan added. "She said we could have three cities."

"But we never agreed to any of it." Bice raised a finger. "She made multiple offers, but we never said yes." He looked at me. "Unless you did so when I wasn't listening?"

"No." I shook my head. "I guess it wasn't an actual agreement. I just kept thinking about it so much. It seemed like a good deal at the time, especially after she dropped that bit about her mother."

"Yeah, what's up with that?" Caedan chuckled. "Now I can't get the idea out of my head that the seven dragons were rebellious teenagers who ran away from their mom."

"Whatever the case, we can't take those disks off," Kelly said. "Can you imagine if one of them got angry at us after that? Boom. Full-size dragon. Annnnd we're all dead."

"Yeah." I sighed. "But it worries me. A lot. I mean, let's face it. They're a lot smarter than we are. You don't rule for a thousand years without intelligence. Amaranth was even funding her own rebels so she could control them! If we don't keep them happy, and they start plotting against us… they'll win."

"And we're all dead," Kelly repeated.

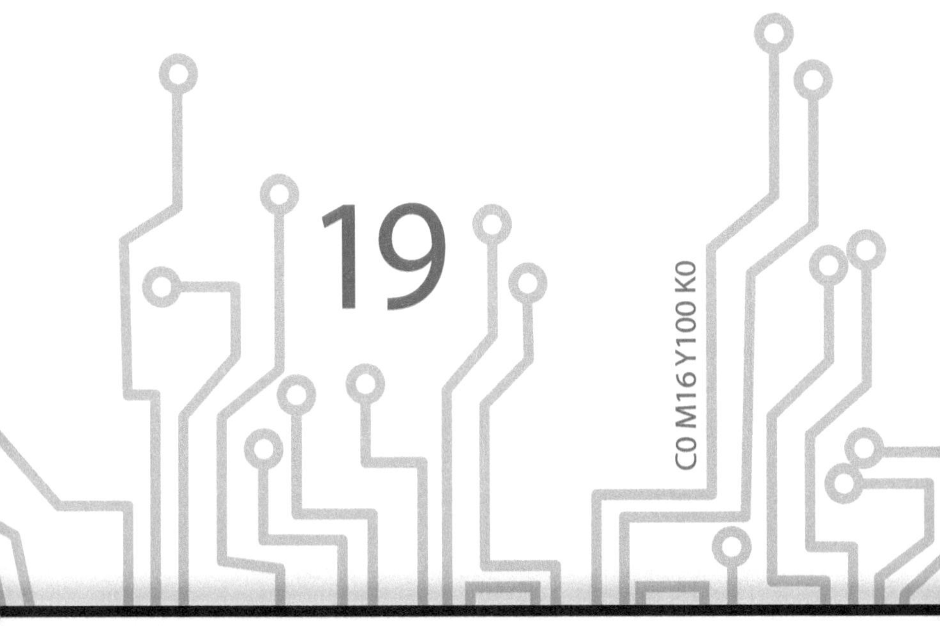

"Lovat!" I called. "You in here?"

In response, the boy crawled out from under one of the other tables. Laughs and gasps came from the others.

"Did anyone else know he was in here?" I asked. None of them had. "He's getting really good at it. And now his main job is going to be spying on the dragons. For one, I'm tired of them disappearing. I want to know where that secret room is."

"It's right over there," Lovat said, pointing at the back hallway.

"What?"

"I saw them go in this morning. There's a secret door about halfway between here and the kitchen."

I laughed. It felt good. I hadn't expected that at all. "Great job, man. Now we just need to figure out how to spy on them inside there."

"Apparently, we've got weeks in which to figure it out," Caedan muttered.

"I know you and the guys are going to hate this," I said. "So how about you take a couple of them at a time on scouting missions to the edges of Amaranth and Auric? Just to see if you can spy anything going on."

He nodded. "I guess that'll keep us busy for a while. We should probably keep an eye on the Hub too."

"Do it."

Cobalt burst into the room. "Caedan! Uh… Beryl! We've got a problem!"

We all waited. "You've got our attention," Bice prompted.

"Oh, right. Um." He pointed up. "There's a draconic at the top of the stairs."

Boosts hit my legs as I lunged out of the chair. I was through the door before anyone else could stand up, raced down the hall and came to a sliding stop at the base of the stairs. I looked up.

The dark silhouette at the top took a few steps down into our lighting, resolving itself into the familiar shape of Taizong Gold. Except… the draconic looked as if it had come through a war. Bloody gashes and burns covered much of its body, and its cybernetic left hand and forearm hung in tattered wires and circuitry.

"Beryl," it rumbled. "Why am I not surprised?"

"I guess I just show up everywhere." I took a couple of steps up toward it. I didn't have my sword with me, but if we had to fight, I could hold this thing off long enough for the others to show up with their weapons.

"Where is my Lord Auric?" The draconic made no further moves to descend.

Hearing several others run up behind me, I called, "Can someone go knock on his lordship's door and let him know he has a visitor?"

I took another step up. "You don't look so good. Were you the only draconic survivor of the black dragons' attack?"

"I do not know." Was I imagining it, or did the monster sway on its feet? "Until I drew near this place, I couldn't even be sure my lord survived."

"Taizong!" Ciaru's voice rang out behind me. The dragon pushed past, followed by Captain Tawn. As they drew near, the draconic fell to one knee. Ciaru placed a hand on its shoulder. "Well done, my child."

Lovat squeezed around behind me and stood a step higher so he could watch.

"Did anyone follow you?" Tawn asked, moving past them to stare outside.

"No." Taizong Gold shook its head. "I am alone, in all ways."

"Come." Ciaru offered his own shoulder for support to the much larger draconic. "I will tend your wounds, as I have done before. You can rest in safety here. Tawn! Your assistance, please."

The two men did what they could to help the draconic down the rest of the stairs. I moved to the side to allow them to pass. Caedan stepped up behind me. "Are you sure this is a good idea?" he whispered.

"No. But what can we do? Tell the dragon to kick out his wounded child?"

"Works for me."

I waited until they were closer. "Will you be returning to your own room?" I asked. "Do you need our medical doctor's assistance? He has some… experience with draconics."

"Thank you, but it will not be necessary," Ciaru replied. "I will care for him myself."

Across the hall, my eyes met Lainey's. Did she have tears in them? I mean, I wasn't going to kick Taizong Gold out, like Caedan wanted, but tears? Really? For a monster? And then I remembered Protogonus Blue.

"Ciaru," I said as they reached the bottom of the steps. He turned a quick look to me. "Is this one just a number?"

He paused and closed his eyes. "I could answer you with how his value is greater than most others, both strategically and tactically, but…" He shook his head and moved on. "No. He is not just a number."

I put my hand on Lovat beside me. "Neither is this one."

Ciaru favored Lovat with a quick glance, but kept going. We waited until the three of them had passed on through the kitchen.

"I hope that secret room of theirs is pretty big," Caedan observed. "Its population keeps growing."

The next two weeks went by surprisingly fast, but I hated every minute of it.

Taizong Gold remained in Ciaru's hidden room and never re-emerged. Amaranth also rarely came out.

Caedan and his crew ran the scouting missions, but uncovered very little. We learned more from Auric's orb about the movements of the black dragons… or black dragon, anyway. We saw Onyx travel back and forth from city to city, except for Atramentous and Viridia. But Atramentous himself never seemed to come out of his pit. He hadn't come out when we'd watched from Onyx's tower either, come to think of it.

Fern, Turq, and Cobalt opted to undergo Hunter's chromark removal.

Caedan agreed to, but then changed his mind. "Not until Caesious is free," he declared. I didn't see the connection, but let him make his own choice.

Chance continued to grow at an astounding rate. By the end of the two weeks, he could talk in complete sentences, and must have gained another two or three inches in height.

The most dramatic change came from Glacier. She hit a growth spurt, I suppose, and became truly frightening in size. One evening, as the stars were coming out, I sat outside with Lainey. Glacier bounded past us and stood silhouetted at the top of the hill.

"She's already the size of her mother," I pointed out.

"Isn't it incredible?" Lainey lay back on the hillside. She held up her hand to block out the moon, while she rolled her head side-to-side to watch the stars.

"It's terrifying. Those fangs are enormous."

"She's a big kitten."

I put my hands behind my head and lay back beside her. "Some of the others are really scared of her now," I said. "It was one thing when she was just a big cat, but now she's bigger than anyone. Well, except the draconic, I guess."

"She won't hurt anyone," Lainey assured me. "I know my Glacier."

"I hope you're right."

I turned my head to watch Lainey while she watched the sky. Ciaru's words about living on while my friends grew old bothered me. Would I see Lainey change? Would I stay the same? Would she leave me in time? Most frightening of all, would I ever reach a point where I looked at her and the others as just numbers? I'd debated the idea with Ciaru three or four times now, each time emphasizing the importance of each life. But would I always believe that? Would Lainey always be this important to me?

Our relationship wasn't progressing, despite the downtime. I couldn't blame Lainey. Not entirely, anyway. I mean, she seemed content with the way things stood. She didn't push me to go further or do anything different. In some ways, I appreciated that. Part of me wanted more. But I didn't want to push either. I couldn't decide whether I was afraid, or whether I just didn't know what I wanted.

I guess I didn't know whether I deserved a real relationship anymore. No, not "deserved." That's wrong. Almost no one ever got what they deserved... and that was probably a good thing. Maybe what I meant was that I wasn't sure I wanted to deal with the hazards of a more serious relationship. I could die on any of these missions. It was a miracle—no, a whole series of miracles—that I was still alive now. And Lainey might die. Was it worth it to get serious with that hanging over us?

I glanced over at her face as it looked up. Sure, it was worth it. Absolutely. But… I don't know. Maybe the fear of betrayal still held me back too much.

A shadow appeared, blocking out part of my view of the stars. "Who's that?"

"Your presence is requested down below," said the voice of Captain Tawn.

I scrambled to my feet, squinting to make out the Captain in the dark. "What's going on?"

"Viridia is up to something."

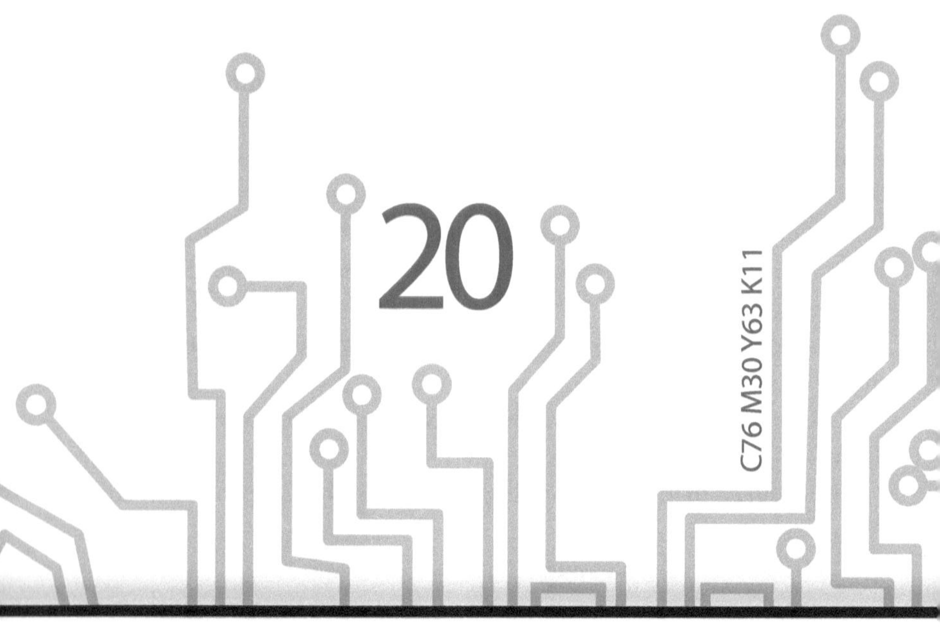

20

I found Ciaru in the laboratory, standing over his orb. Lainey, Glacier, and Tawn followed me. The cat immediately went to a corner and stretched out. Once upon a time, that didn't matter. Now… she blocked multiple paths between tables. I had to step over one of her legs.

"What's up with Viridia?" I asked.

Ciaru beckoned and pointed to his orb. "Come see for yourself." He stood to the side to allow me a clear view. I looked down at the streets of the city I'd known for most of my life. Seeing it from this angle was strange, but as I studied it, I started to recognize specific locations.

"What am I looking for?"

"It seems that Viridia—or Troilus Green, depending on how we wish to refer to him now—is engaging in some form of urban renewal. Or rather, urban destruction." Ciaru pointed to a specific area. "He's been tearing down some buildings here and there, but leaving all the others intact around them. I confess to bafflement as to his motives."

"Viridia almost never tore anything down," I recalled. "That's why we had so many empty places all over town. When he wanted something new, he would just add to the city." I peered closer. "I'm not sure… oh, now I see."

Sure enough, I looked down at the ruins of a large building, perhaps apartments or something similar. And as Ciaru observed, all of the buildings around it were untouched. Something seemed familiar about the location, but it took me a while to figure it out. I leaned to the left and then right, trying to get a different angle.

"It's… my apartment building," I said at last, convinced. "I used to live there."

Ciaru nodded as if he expected the answer. "And what about this one?" He stepped in, adjusted the view on the orb, and stepped back again.

This one confused me at first. It was a much smaller building. In fact, it looked like they had destroyed one unit out of a line of shops. I couldn't figure it out. Then a suspicion occurred to me. "Can I see it in relation to the other one?"

Ciaru adjusted the view, and I looked again. My eyes traced a path from the ruins of the apartment building, down several blocks, a turn, then a few blocks more… a path I had walked so many times. "The bike shop. It's the bicycle shop where I used to work."

I looked up at the dragon. "He's deliberately tearing down places that are associated with me. Why?"

Ciaru folded his cyb hands together. "It could be for several reasons. It might be sheer spite, to destroy anything that might mean anything to you, his enemy. It could be in punishment for anyone who may have assisted you, or was suspected of assisting you. Or…" He paused, glanced away, then looked back. "He could be simply trying to get your attention."

I looked back at the orb. "I don't know. He doesn't know me very well, I guess. Neither of these places really mean much to me. I had no desire to see them again."

"They are not the only ones." He reached toward the orb. "If you will allow me…?"

I nodded. While he worked with the orb, I sent Lainey to bring in Kelly and Lovat. I might need their help in identifying locations, especially if some of them turned out to be associated with someone other than me.

With all of us gathered around the orb, Ciaru pointed out the next location he'd spotted. This one wasn't hard. "The shrine," Lovat said before I could. We'd known Troilus Green had used it for himself for a while. Even so, it was odd to see it now reduced to a smoldering ruin. That one had to be spite.

Ciaru showed us two more locations that none of us recognized. I was starting to wonder if we'd been wrong. Maybe this wasn't connected to me somehow. "One more," the dragon declared, stepping away from the orb a final time.

I looked down at the ruins of another building, larger than the bike shop, but not quite the size of my apartment building. I frowned. The location didn't look familiar at all. I tried looking from each angle. Nothing. I shook my head. "Don't get this one either. You two?"

Kelly peered at the view. "Something vaguely familiar, but I can't place it…"

"It's the theater," Lovat said.

"What?"

"The Citrine. The theater where we meet Stacy."

I met Kelly's eyes. The fear on her face mirrored mine. "Stacy. He's got her!" she exclaimed.

"We don't know that," I cautioned. "Lovat and I were seen behind this place once, so maybe that's it. Maybe she's all right."

Kelly put both hands over her mouth and stared down at the orb. "You know I'm right, Beryl. You felt it. He's got Stacy. He's tearing these places up to get your attention and bring you back."

"No." I didn't believe it. I couldn't believe it. If Stacy had been captured, everything was in jeopardy. Everything.

"Who is this Stacy?" Ciaru asked.

"The, uh, head of our intelligence network," I said. "It's how we know so much."

"And I assume she knows all about you?"

"Everything."

Ciaru shook his head. "Foolish. For one person to know so much. I agree with the lady here. Troilus Green has your friend, and is calling for you to come."

My hands shook. For over a year, Stacy had worked hard to stay separate from our work, but kept gathering information for us. She knew everything about us and had contacts in every city. All of them would be in danger now if Troilus Green got that information from her. Stacy was strong; she wouldn't reveal anything willingly or easily. But how long could she hold out against the draconic and its interrogation methods?

"Do you know how long it's been?" I asked. "I mean, can you tell when the building was torn down?"

"To determine how long your friend has been in captivity? A wise thought. Unfortunately, it is difficult to tell." He frowned and toyed with the end of his mustache. "I have not been observing Viridia so closely every day, so I do not know when this was begun. I don't recall seeing the destruction a week ago, so I suspect it's been since then. One of the other ruins still smoldered, showing it to be recent. This one does not. But it seems likely they were all done in a relatively short time frame…"

"So it hasn't been long," I concluded. Good. We had a chance.

"Unfortunately, if Viridia is indeed sending you a message, we have no way of sending one back to him," Ciaru mused.

"Maybe we do."

"Excuse me?"

I left the orb and strode to the next table. "We're taking this outside." I picked up Carl's communication device.

"But it doesn't work," Lainey protested. "I—we've tried to use it."

"Ciaru fixed it."

In a few minutes, I'd carried the device up the stairs and out. For good measure, I took it to the very top of the hill, trailed by the others. Lainey knelt beside me as I straightened it out, making sure it was level.

"Are you sure about this?" she whispered. "We don't know their connection to… to Viridia."

"If we can shake them up, it's all to our benefit," I answered. I smiled at her. "Either way, we're going to see what happens."

I flipped the power switch. As before, the green light shone from one side. To my delight, when I turned the dial, the line of lights showing the power of a signal now ascended to at least eight. The ninth light wavered on and off. Much better than inside the bunker. "I think we've got something here."

"It seems strong enough," Ciaru confirmed.

I glanced up at Kelly and Lovat standing above us, eyes wide. I looked back to Lainey, reached out, and squeezed her hand. "Here goes." I picked up the microphone (as Ciaru called it), and pressed the button the side. "Hello. Can anyone hear me?"

I released the button and waited. A brief burst of static came from within the device, but nothing more. I tried again, with equal results. Ciaru suggested changing the frequency. I turned the dial, losing the eight lights. I rotated it until a new burst of lights erupted. This time, nine lit up solid, with a tenth one flashing.

"Can anyone hear me?" I spoke again. "I'm looking for Troilus Green in Viridia."

The static grew stronger for a moment in response, and then a cold voice spoke from within the device: "Beryl Godslayer. You reach beyond your grasp."

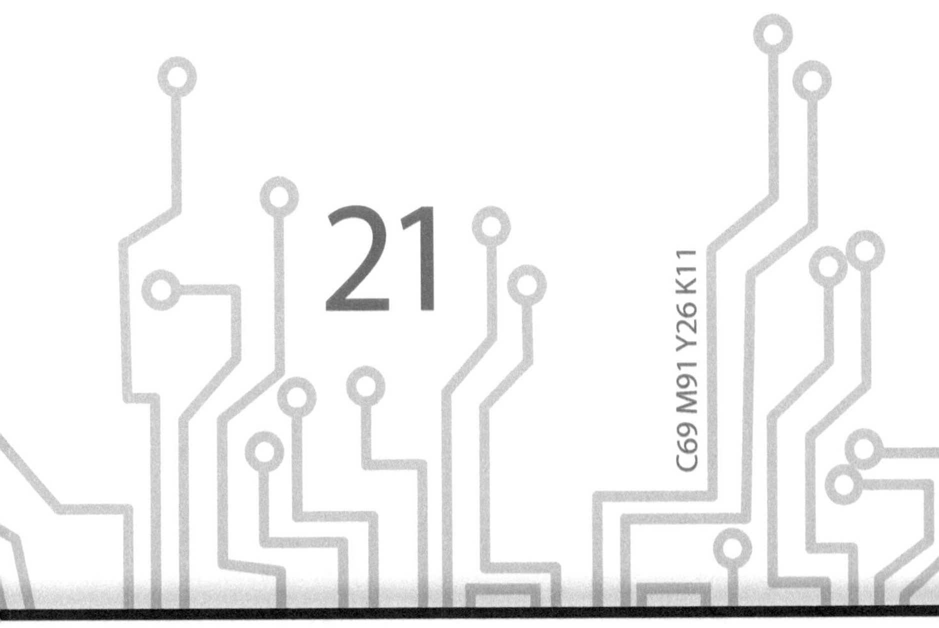

If I hadn't been kneeling on the ground, I might have staggered back a step. I know Kelly did. I exchanged looks with Lainey, whose eyes looked ready to explode from her face. "Who is this?" I asked.

For a moment, no sound came from the device. Then: "You know who we are. Why do you toy with technology beyond your understanding?"

"Why do you interfere with events in The Circle?" I shot back.

"All that happens with the children of Chroma is our concern."

I looked up at Ciaru. He folded his arms and stared off into the distance. Chroma. Amaranth said she was the mother of the dragons.

"Are you helping Onyx?" I demanded. "Are we enemies?"

"We do not have to be enemies, so long as you stay within your place."

"You didn't answer. Are you working with Onyx? Or Troilus Green?"

"We do not explain ourselves."

I frowned. "Where is Carl Roberts? Why did you take him?"

"This conversation will not be a productive use of our time. Or yours."

"Wait! Tell Troilus Green I got his message, and I'm coming for him!"

"We do not deliver messages. Farewell, Beryl Godslayer. Should we speak with you again, it will be on our terms, not yours."

"Oh yeah? Well, I'll come after you too! Once the dragons are all dead here, I'll come for your Chroma. Do you hear me?"

I heard nothing but static. I adjusted the dial and tried several more times. No more voices came from the device.

"I guess we're done sitting around," Kelly observed.

I stood up. "No doubt. Get Bice and Caedan. Let's put together a plan."

"What about Atramentous?" Ciaru asked. "Was he not our next target?"

"Stacy comes first," I said. "Maybe we'll go after him next."

"Might I suggest combining the missions?"

I raised my eyebrows. "You have a way to kill him?"

"I believe I do."

"Come share it with us, then."

Once Bice and Caedan were informed of the developments, they gathered with us in the conference room. Lovat disappeared somewhere along the way. I considered whether to call any of the others in, but decided to stick with the core team for now.

Ciaru entered the room, followed by Captain Tawn, who carried a large sealed chest. Ciaru pointed to the table, and Tawn obediently placed the chest down. He stood over it protectively.

"What's this?" Caedan asked.

Ciaru toyed with his orb. "Atramentous is actually the most vulnerable of all the dragons, when you know the facts."

"How so?" I asked. "Was he badly injured in the fight with Incarnadine?"

"No, nothing so simple." Ciaru set the orb down beside the chest. He placed a hand over his heart. "You may have noticed cybernetic work on the black dragon's chest."

I had, but hadn't thought much of it. The cyb parts were small and difficult to see. Most people probably hadn't noticed. But Incarnadine's cyb eye ended up being his weak spot. Why hadn't I considered it more?

"It is more than outward enhancements," Ciaru went on. "Atramentous's heart is defective. The cybernetic parts keep him alive."

"So if we can shut those down, we shut him down!" Caedan made a fist, but thankfully didn't pound the table.

Ciaru nodded.

"Forgive me," Bice said, "but I don't see how this makes things any easier. Is shutting down dragon cybernetics somehow easier than killing a dragon by other means?"

"It is if you have one of these." Ciaru gestured to the chest. Tawn removed a lock and flipped the lid open.

I stood to get a better view at the interior. Inside the chest, a metallic object rested on custom padding. The object, about a foot in length, was somewhat cylindrical with tapered ends. I could see several buttons, colored lights, and some sort of flat panel on one side, but I couldn't grasp any function to it.

"Is it an explosive device?" Lainey wondered.

"Of a sort," Ciaru replied. "In some ways, this is the most dangerous weapon ever invented within The Circle."

"More dangerous than the one you tried to use on Caesious?" Caedan asked, brows lowered.

"It depends on what it's used for," Ciaru answered calmly. "The device you reference creates great destruction, but a dragon would probably live through it." He laid a hand on the side of the box. "Atramentous would not live through this."

"That little thing?" Bice shook his head.

"This device creates an electromagnetic pulse," Ciaru explained. "I understand that most of you will have no idea what I mean by those words, so I will explain it simply: it shuts down anything electronic."

My mind immediately saw the possibilities. If set off within a city, the device could shut down all electricity, but if set off near Atramentous, it would shut down his heart. I took a couple of steps toward the chest, gazing at the device.

"How close does it need to be?" I asked.

"Very close." Ciaru folded his hands together and sighed. "Unfortunately, to have a wider range, the device would need to be far larger. This one was intended only as an experiment, but it is all we have now."

"How close?" Caedan repeated.

"It would need to be set off within a few feet of the dragon."

I nodded. Of course. And only one person could get it that close. "Guess it's up to me then."

Ciaru turned to me. "I said it would need to be that close to the dragon, because it needs to be strong enough to affect his massive cybernetics. However, it will still affect other, smaller electronic and cybernetic devices within a larger range. Perhaps a hundred yards."

"You're saying the blast would kill Beryl, also," Lainey said.

Ciaru tilted his head. "It would… shut down his cybernetics. And since the primary implant is in his brain…"

He didn't need to say anything else. Everyone fell silent. Bice lowered his head.

"How much of a timer does it have?" Caedan asked. "Could Beryl place it and run away in time?"

"There is the difficulty," Ciaru said. "We can rig a timer, but… it may be that stealth is more required here than power. If Atramentous saw you, he would not stay still."

"I can do it!" Lovat's voice rang out.

"Lovat?" We all looked around. "Where are you?" I asked.

Ten feet away, an air vent cover in the ceiling swung open. A pair of feet dangled out, and then Lovat dropped through the air onto another table.

Ciaru chuckled, as if he'd already known.

"I'm impressed," I told Lovat. "But I'm not sending you next to a dragon."

"You already have!" he protested, pointing at Ciaru. The dragon raised his eyebrows in bemusement.

"That's not the same thing! He's in human form!"

Lovat, still kneeling on the table, folded his arms and glared at me. "Still dangerous."

"Everything we do is dangerous, but I'm not sending you into that kind of danger. I've been that close to a dragon before. It's terrifying. He could kill you with a flinch!"

"Every method of delivering this device is fraught with peril," Ciaru said. "There is no easy way."

"I'll do it," I said. "I'll figure out a way."

"I can do it," Lovat argued.

"I want you with me," I told him. "You'll be there. Just not… doing that."

"It won't be just the two of you," Kelly said. "I'm going too. Stacy's my friend."

"Same here," Lainey added.

This time Caedan did hit the table with his fist "We're all going."

I turned back to them. "You can go with me to Viridia. But Lovat and I go on alone to Atramentous. First we rescue Stacy, and then we get rid of another dragon."

"So we're finally going to deal with Troilus Green, or Viridia, or whatever he is?" Kelly asked.

"He's taunted me. He wants me. He's going to get me."

"Are we just charging in?" Caedan asked. "You usually have at least a bit more of a plan."

"We'll figure it out on the way. Since we don't know how long Stacy's been a prisoner, we need to hurry. We won't charge in, but once we know where they're holding her, we'll move fast. We can't afford to wait."

Bice lifted his head. "I hate to ask, but what about the purple robes?"

"They're going to help us," I said. "They just don't know it yet."

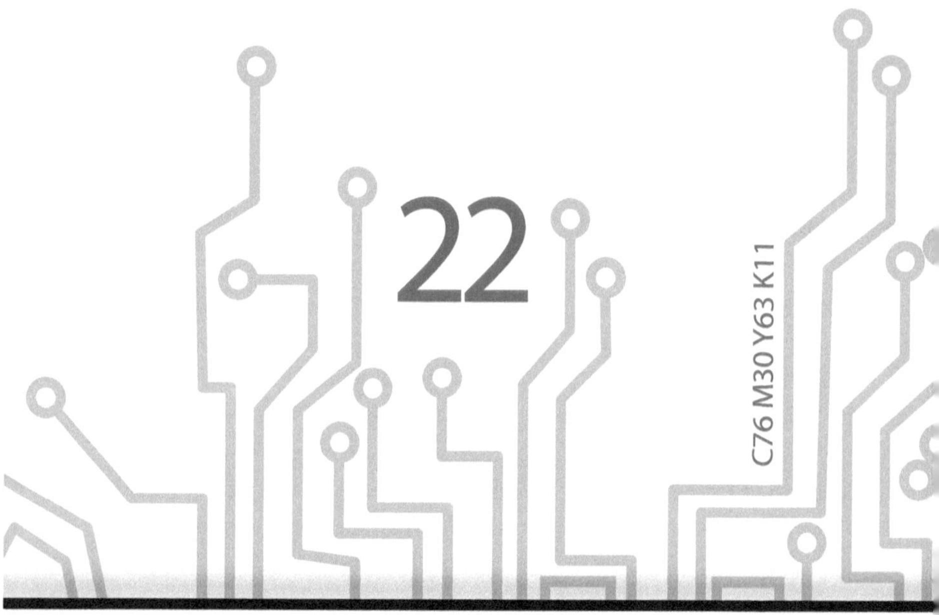

To coordinate with the trains, we planned our departure for early the next morning. Without telling anyone else, Caedan and I met with Cobalt and Turq in the laboratory the night before we left. Caedan explained our mission, and then let me talk.

"We might need backup on this one," I told them. "I don't want to be caught completely out of contact with our base way up here. So I want the two of you to take the four-wheeler across The Circle and set up where we can find you if we have to."

Cobalt and Turq looked at each other with wide eyes. "You got it," Cobalt said. "Where do you want us?"

"Set up midway between Viridia and Atramentous, on the north side of the railroad tracks," I said. "Each day, you'll keep an eye out. If we need you, we'll come to you. If you don't hear from us in a week's time, come back home."

Caedan gave them a list of equipment and supplies to take along and warned them about traveling. "You've been on trips with me enough that you know what to do now," he said. "I'm counting on you."

"We all are," I added.

As they left the room, Caedan went to find Saxe and Royal. I browsed the boxes of tech we'd brought from Loden's lab. My eyes wandered to the box containing a pile of batons. Dusk said they delivered some kind of electrical charge, but not enough to take someone down, like the Viridian Guard's shockspears. I took three of them to pack in my bag. Extra weapons might come in handy at any time, even if they weren't the best. I added the claw launcher too. I didn't foresee any climbing, but I think every other time we needed to climb had been unforeseen anyway.

Saxe and Royal entered, along with Caedan and Bice. Once together, Caedan explained we were entrusting the safety of our home to them.

"I don't anticipate any trouble from the dragons," I added, "but go to Bice with any concerns you have, anything you see out of the ordinary."

In this way, we'd given everyone a job of some kind. I hoped we made them feel a part of the team.

Lovat came to me in our bedroom that night with more information. "I've been able to hear some of the talking in the secret room," he reported.

"By crawling through the vents?" His reveal during the earlier meeting had been on purpose, both to let Ciaru know what he'd been doing, and to prove to me what he could do. This kid was getting smarter.

"Yeah." He put together a small backpack for the next day. "They don't say much of anything interesting. Amy gripes a lot about the disks and what they've lost."

"Amy. Did Caedan teach you to call her that?" I checked the contents of my own pack and chuckled.

"Yah. Anyway, I think I heard something important, but I can't be sure."

"Tell me."

He glanced around, as if someone else might be listening to us. "I think Ciaru's disk is fake."

"What?"

"He said something that made it sound like he could turn back into a dragon whenever he wanted."

I considered that. It didn't surprise me, really. Auric was very different from the other dragons, but when he'd offered the disk to Kelly, it had seemed too convenient. But if he was lying about that, what else could he be lying about? All of a sudden, leaving the base with him here didn't seem so safe.

"Also, he knew I listened."

"What?" I looked up from my pack.

Lovat shrugged. "When none of the others were around, he talked to me."

"Did you answer him?"

"No!" Lovat's look said, "How could you think I would be that stupid?"

"What kinds of things did he say?"

He shrugged again. "Just talking. Said he didn't care if I listened to them. Said I was clever."

"He's right there." I grinned. "You are clever. And getting cleverer... uh, more clever."

Lovat snorted, then stretched out on his bed. "Guess so. Clever enough to get near a dragon. Near enough to kill one."

"Yeah, you're still not getting that job."

Everyone gathered to see us off in the morning. We'd gotten up early to get fake chromarks applied to those who needed it, but as the sun rose over the mountains, we prepared to set out.

I couldn't help overhearing Kelly saying goodbye to Chance. "Mommy will be back in a few days. Be good for Grandma, okay?"

"Why?" Chance asked.

"I have to go help a friend," Kelly explained. "You'll have plenty of fun without me."

I knew that Kelly and Fern's relationship had been strained at their first reunion. Fern had been adamantly opposed to the birth of the draconic baby. But I guess they'd worked all that out between them over the past few months. They'd been sharing a room since we'd come to the new base, anyway.

"Should the child have any difficulties, I will be here to help," Lady Rust announced.

Kelly glared at her. "You stay away from Chance!"

"I'm only offering my assistance..."

"And I'm only telling you to stay away!"

Lady Rust rolled her eyes and walked away. I wondered why she'd even bothered to come out. She hadn't been seen outside the secret room for days.

I walked over to Lainey. "We'll be waiting for you," I told her. Since Glacier couldn't possibly ride the train as a passenger, she'd be taking Tawn's three-wheeler and traveling separately from the rest of us.

"You never know," she said with a grin. "Maybe your train will break down, and I'll get there first."

"With our luck, I wouldn't be at all surprised." I gave her a long hug and a quick kiss. No sense dragging it out when we'd see each other again very soon.

We set out hiking toward the train station, while Lainey drove off almost due south with Glacier bounding along beside her. She would get far ahead of us at first, but fall way behind once we got on the train.

That ended up being a surreal experience. With the passes Ciaru gave us, the people working the train paid us every deference. They even brought us a meal while we traveled. No one even looked twice at us, which felt… weird.

It was well into the night when we finally left the train, a couple of miles from Viridia. We gathered at a lone oak tree on a hill, one of the only obvious landmarks in the area. We laid out sleeping bags on the side of the hill facing the city. I sat and watched the lights, memories dancing through my head. The other three soon joined me.

"What's the plan?" Caedan asked.

"In the morning, I want you and Kelly to stay here and wait for Lainey."

Kelly opened her mouth to protest, but I hurried on: "I'll take Lovat, and we'll do a scouting mission, see what we can learn. It'll work better with just the two of us."

Caedan made a grumbling noise, but didn't argue.

"We'll try to find Jaden," I said. "If he's all right, it means Stacy hasn't been forced to give away too much yet."

"And if he's not?" Kelly asked.

"Then we see what we can find out elsewhere."

"How?" Caedan asked. "I mean, without Stacy, who's going to tell us anything?"

"We may have to force someone." I hated the thought of it, but servants of the dragon, human or not, were still my enemies. "Maybe a Viridian Guard new recruit again. That's worked before."

"What about that Pit?" Kelly asked. "Could they have taken Stacy there?"

"I don't think so. She's too valuable. If she's anywhere, it's probably the

Emerald Ascendancy. Or maybe one of the Guard stations, if we're lucky."

Caedan stood and stretched. "At least the nights are warmer now. Let's get some sleep. Big day tomorrow."

Kelly and Lovat agreed and got up. I stayed seated, watching the city. Somewhere among those lights, Stacy was being held, probably being hurt. Because she helped us. In my mind, I saw her: tied up somewhere, with Troilus Green leering over her.

"No more," I whispered. This time, I would make sure Troilus Green was dead. I'd cut that draconic head off if that's what it took. Or burn the whole body. My imagination bounced through several other gruesome possibilities.

I ran down a list of everyone I knew still within the city. Jaden was my top hope; if Stacy hadn't given him up yet, he might know something. Thinking of him reminded me of Olive. Who knew where her loyalties had bounced to by now? She seemed to follow the crowd. Plus, she wasn't very knowledgeable about things outside her own theater world. Still, she might know something about Stacy.

Lovat might know a few other people. He seemed to have a few friends or at least allies, back when he was alone and hiding from the Viridian Guard. And then I remembered. One other person was in the city, who knew an awful lot about us. And might know even more about what was going on… since it might actually be his fault.

Basil.

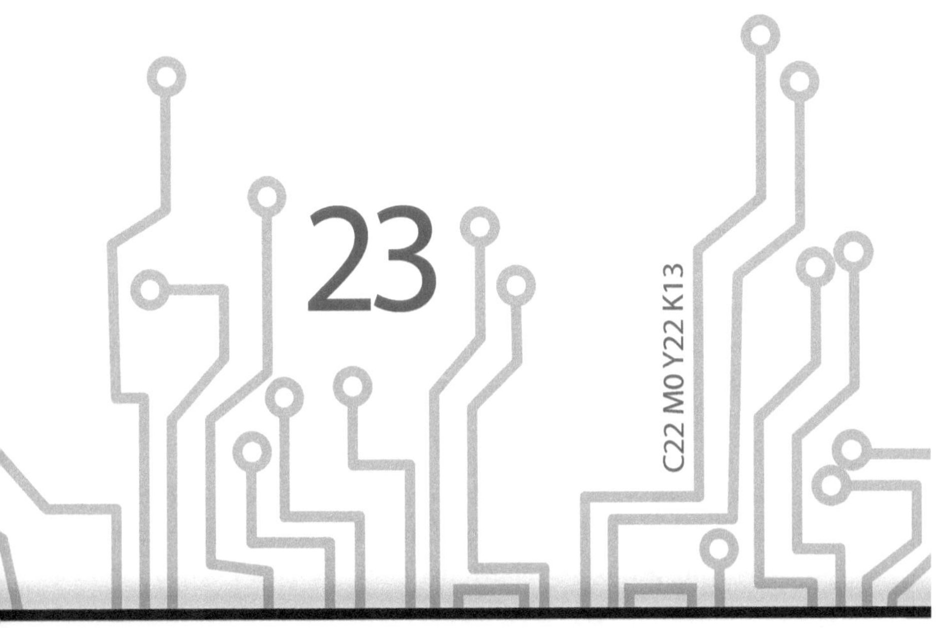

"Why didn't we think about Basil?" I asked the other three the next morning.

"You mean he's why Stacy's in trouble?" Caedan asked.

"Right. How else could Troilus Green have found out? I think Basil is a traitor… or he was caught and gave up information to save himself."

"I completely forgot about him, to be honest," Caedan admitted. "He's always just been there in the background, since he came along."

"That's because you're a guy," Kelly said.

"What's that supposed to mean?"

"Basil made all of us uncomfortable. The women, that is." Kelly sighed. "It's not something I can easily explain."

"What? Did he do something to you?" I demanded. "Or Lainey? Or—"

"No. I told you I can't explain it easily. He just…" She bit her lip. "This is going to sound stupid, but it's the best I can do. He stood too close. He looked too much. He made us… a little scared, to be honest."

"Why didn't you say anything?" I asked. "Do they other girls feel this way?"

"Yes, we talked about it among ourselves." She shrugged. "But if I'd told you this, what would you have done?"

"Had a talk with him, at least! Tell him to stop doing those things."

"Wait," Caedan interrupted. "Is this why Sapphire left?"

Sapphire had been one of Caedan's recruits. She'd stayed with the other guys from Caesious while we were at the tower rescuing Kelly. And Basil had stayed too.

"I never met her," Kelly said. "But from what I've observed, I'd guess so."

"Fewmets," Caedan muttered. I felt the same way.

"Look," Kelly went on, "if I'd told you these things, without the context of him maybe being a traitor, would you have taken it seriously?"

"I hope I would."

"Do you know that you would?"

I paused. "No," I admitted. "I don't. If you'd told me he stood too close and looked too much, I guess I don't know how I would have reacted."

"That's my point." She shook her head. "It doesn't matter now. He's gone."

I ran my hands through my hair and held the back of my neck. "We have got to find a better way of… of checking out the people who join us. You'd think I'd have learned that from Rick."

No one said anything for a moment. Then Lovat looked up at me. "Are we going to the city or what?"

"Yeah. We're going." Lovat's face looked so wrong with a fake chromark, but we needed to blend in.

I reluctantly left my sword behind. I wouldn't be able to walk through the city carrying it without attracting attention. In the past, that might have been all right, when my reputation was at its highest. Now, with what Troilus Green had been up to, I had to be careful about showing my face, let alone a weapon.

Lovat and I entered the city near the railroad station. In the early morning, we didn't see many people on the streets. The few we saw appeared more… frightened than ever before. No one looked each other in the face, or greeted anyone else.

We made our way first to the ruins of the Citrine. I don't know what I expected to find there, but I wanted to see it for myself. I smelled it before I saw it: the odor of a smoldering wood fire struck my nostrils a block away.

The destruction was complete. The Citrine had been a wooden structure, which made it ideal for burning once they'd torn it down. Or maybe they'd just burned it. Either way, ashes and partially-burned timber remained in a huge pile where the theater once stood.

I'd never been a big fan of the whole theater industry, but I knew many Viridians were. It provided entertainment, an escape from their otherwise mundane or miserable lives. Troilus Green didn't care about any of that. He'd torn down an entire theater just to send me a message. I shouldn't be astonished at the cruelty, knowing all the other atrocities committed by the dragons, but it still pained me to see.

Lovat shoved a half-burnt beam with his foot. "Nothin' here," he observed.

"Yeah. You know the theater Jaden works at?"

"Sure."

I took another look around. Something bothered me about this. If the destruction had been meant to summon me, why wasn't anyone here watching to see if I showed up? I felt a chill run down my back, and spun around. Nothing. In that moment, I'd been sure I'd see a purple robe in my peripheral vision.

"What was that for?" Lovat asked.

"Thought I heard something. Let's go."

Lovat led the way. I still marveled at his ability to remember all the streets of Viridia and make his way through them to any destination.

Technically, Jaden had been in danger from the moment he stepped back into Viridia. He was a deserter from the Viridian Guard, and if anyone recognized him from that time in his life, he'd be arrested and thrown into prison… or the Virescent Pit, if it was open again. By living and working in the theater, he avoided being seen most of the time—I mean, as long as he stayed in the background and not on the stage itself, I suppose. If Stacy had been broken, she would have told them about Jaden for sure. Unfortunately, I couldn't remember if Basil and Jaden had ever met. I didn't think so.

My heart sank when we reached the second theater. A huge padlock hung on the front doors, and green ribbons stretched across the entire front, marking it as closed by the Viridian Guard. Not a good sign.

We moved around to the back. A smaller lock hung on this door, but I snapped it off easily with my cyb hand. Lovat and I slipped inside. I let my eyes adjust to the dark before trying to find anything. From what I could tell, the hallway and storage areas looked as they had the last time I'd been here. Nothing seemed to be destroyed or ransacked. Maybe it had been closed for a different reason. Or maybe they'd marked it for destruction, but hadn't gotten to that job yet.

"Over here," Lovat said. He pointed toward a door leading off from one of the hallways. I remembered it: Jaden's tiny living quarters were behind the door.

We were far enough away from any windows now, so Lovat flicked on a flashlight. I licked my lips and pushed Jaden's door open, almost trembling over what I might find. My mind imagined his dead body lying on the floor. Or maybe I'd find nothing here, but when we went out to the stage, we'd find both Jaden and Olive hanging from the rafters as a warning. I wouldn't put anything past Troilus Green.

Lovat shined the flashlight around the small room. Bed. Chair. Stacy Moss poster. Barely enough room to turn around. Everything looked just the same, if a little messier. No Jaden. I didn't know whether to be relieved or not. If he wasn't here, he was probably in custody. He had nowhere else to go.

I turned to go, but Lovat put out a hand. He lifted a finger to his lips, then pointed at the bed. I checked it, then looked back at him, eyebrows raised. He dropped to the floor and aimed the light underneath the bed.

"Ow! Hey! All right, all right. I'm coming out!" Jaden crawled out from the bed, shielding his eyes against the light. He got to his feet, wavering a little, and finally looked at me. "Beryl? I almost didn't recognize you without your fancy mark."

"Jaden." I let out a breath I'd been holding. He appeared healthy, at least, even if his clothes and hair were disheveled. He looked as if he hadn't been taking care of himself for days. "Am I glad to see you. Are you all right? What happened here?"

"The Viridian Guard happened." He sat down on the bed. "They showed up about a week ago, and told us they were shutting down the theater. We all had to leave, while they locked it up. I snuck back in later, and"—he waved at the room—"I've been hiding in here ever since. Well, except for sneaking out to buy food and stuff." He shrugged. "And now I'm out of money. I'll run out of food in a couple of days. Not sure what I'll do after that."

"You should come back with us," I said. "We've got a new place, and plenty of room. And food." I glanced at the darkened hallway. "You're not safe here. Once we rescue Stacy, we should all get out of this city."

His eyes widened a little. "Rescue Stacy?"

"That's why we're here."

Jaden swallowed and looked at his feet. "You haven't heard, then. I think it's too late."

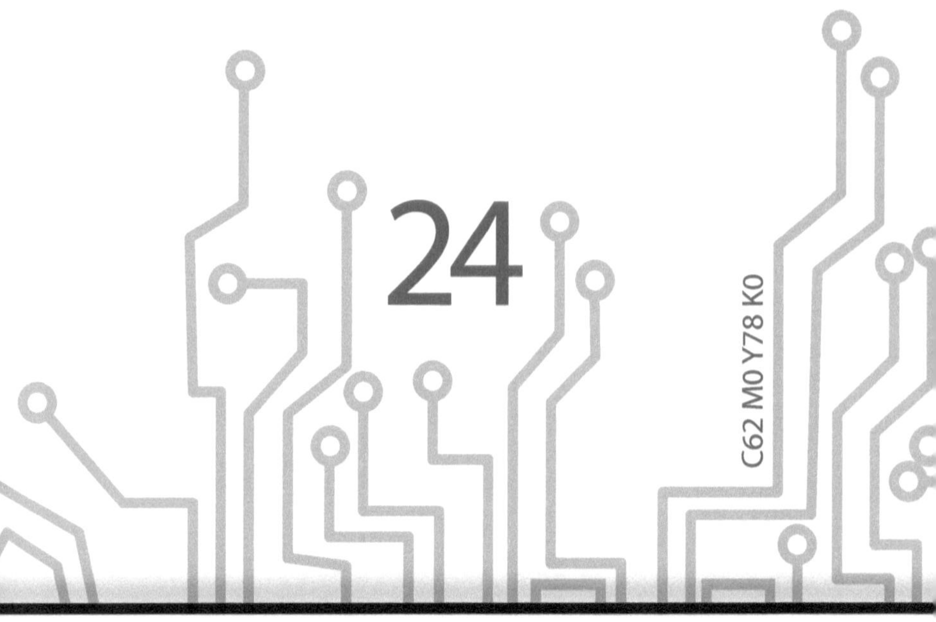

"What do you mean?" I demanded.

Jaden rubbed the scruff on his chin. "They took Stacy about, I don't know, around two weeks ago, I think. They've since been putting up posters and handing out flyers and everything, all telling about how she's been fomenting rebellion against Viridia, being a part of terrorist actions and so forth."

I nodded. Pretty much expected that much.

"They even drove around the city with her tied up in the back of one of the trucks, where everybody could see her, calling her a war criminal and enemy of the people and stuff." He hesitated. "And then, two days ago, they, uh, mounted her on a big pole, and she's been up there ever since."

"What do you mean by 'mounted'?"

"They just tied her up there. I mean, she was alive when they did it, but she's been up there for two days now with no food or anything. It might be too late to save her."

"Where is she?" Whether I meant to do it consciously or not, small boosts of energy ran through all of my limbs.

"It's, um, in the ruins of where you used to have your base. That temple place?"

Of course. The place where Troilus Green and I had met multiple times. Where he and Bice had fought with resomancy. Fewmets. I should have brought Bice for this. We had no one else who could use that power. Why did I always think of these things too late?

"We gon' save her?" Lovat asked.

"No question about it. Jaden, have you seen Basil in the past couple of weeks?"

He frowned. "Isn't he one of the guys we rescued from the Pit?"

"Yeah, you remember him?"

"We didn't really get to know each other. I met him at the Pit that day, and then you guys left the city. I haven't seen him since then. Why?"

"He might be the one who told them about Stacy." I stepped through the door. "Find whatever you want to keep. Let's get out of here, and meet up with the others."

Jaden didn't have much to bring along. Like most of us, he'd lost most of his possessions in the course of things. He stuffed a bag with a few food and clothing items and followed us out. With Lovat leading, we left the city and returned to the lone oak tree. Lainey hadn't arrived yet. Kelly and Caedan, tired of waiting, griped at me for not reporting in with the talker. We explained everything we'd learned.

Caedan picked up his baton. "Let's go get her."

"It's a trap," I said. "We all know it. Troilus Green wants me to come rescue her. They'll all be waiting for us." I shook my head. "Right out in the open too. No way to sneak in or anything."

"Do we know that for sure?" Kelly asked.

"Let me go scope it out," Caedan suggested. "I'll find out how many they've got watching."

I considered it. "We do need more information before acting." I sucked air in through my teeth. "Okay. Lovat, take Caedan there. You guys find out everything you can, but stay out of sight, and don't try to rescue Stacy on your own. Got it?"

"Got it." Caedan clapped Lovat on the back. "Let's go, little man."

"Wait." I held out a hand. "Once you're done, meet us at… um…." I tried to think of a familiar, but safe location.

"You want us to take the talker?" Caedan asked.

"No, I want Jaden to keep it, in case we need to call for Lainey's help. And Kelly and I will have a different mission."

"How about the market?" Lovat suggested.

I knew the one he meant; we'd been chased through it before. "Sure.

That'll work."

"What are we going to be doing?" Kelly wanted to know.

"Like I said: we need information. I've got a couple of other places I want to scout."

Jaden was more than happy to stay behind and wait for Lainey. The rest of us re-entered the city and split up in our separate directions.

"Where to?' Kelly asked.

"The Guard station," I said. "I'm going to try to find the purple robe spy."

This area of town I knew. I'd spent years walking through these streets. And this Guard station… I'd been taken here after meeting Rick. I first met Troilus Green here. Rick was held here, before Loden and I came to rescue him.

"I'm kind of surprised they didn't tear this place down too," I said as we watched the station from a block away.

"Guess they still need it," Kelly replied. "Plus it might send the wrong message. Destroying a theater? Sure. Destroying a Guard station?"

We took a narrow alley to the back of the station. I'd snuck in before, but that had been after dark, when the place was almost empty. This was a lot riskier.

"Stay here, and be ready to run," I told Kelly.

"What are you going to do?"

"I just want to find the name of the spy, and I'll be right back."

She nodded. "Good luck."

I made my way to the back door of the station and waited, listening. At first, I heard some people talking, but soon those voices faded. I assumed they'd moved further away, but couldn't be sure. Why hadn't Loden given me boosted hearing? Was that even a thing?

The door wasn't even locked this time. I turned the knob slowly, and eased it open. I stepped into the locker room I'd searched before. I paused, listening again. Voices continued, down the hall somewhere. Not close.

Now. Was it the fourth or fifth locker? If I remembered right, I needed to check the fifth. I popped it open with my cyb hand and looked through the contents. As before, I saw a pile of ordinary clothes… but no purple robe this time. Had I been wrong about the number? I opened the fourth locker to be sure. No, it held a shrine to Viridia at the top. I remembered that. The fifth one had held the robe. I returned to it and looked everything over.

On the outside of the locker door, I saw only a last name: Pine. How could I find out more? I needed a way to identify him or find him outside this place. I searched every inch of the locker, but found nothing else helpful.

I stepped to the doorway leading into the hall. The voice sounded even further away. I peeked out into a long hall that might have stretched all the way to the front of the building. I didn't see anyone, even when I zoomed my vision to check all the way to the end, making sure no one stood in a doorway about to step out or anything. As I returned my sight to normal, I noticed a map on the opposite wall, several feet down from where I stood.

Keeping my eyes and ears peeled, I took a few steps to get a better look. The map showed this area of the city of Viridia, divided into five color-coded sections. Each section held a pair of names—magnetic labels, I guessed. I skimmed them until I found the one I wanted: Pine, paired with someone named Harrison. His section of the city lay a few blocks east of the station. I took one more look around, then retraced my steps to exit the building and rejoin Kelly.

"East," I told her. "We're looking for two Viridian Guard on patrol. One of them is our spy."

"All right, but we can't spend too long on this." Kelly picked up her pace to keep up with me. "Stacy needs us."

"I haven't forgotten."

I led the way through several turns, going back and forth through the section of the city I'd seen marked. When I didn't want to see a Viridian Guard patrol, they were everywhere. Now that I was trying to find one…

"What are you going to do when we find them?" Kelly wanted to know.

"Get the one we want and ask him a few questions."

"Right. Well, there they are." She pointed ahead of us on the sidewalk. Two of the Viridian Guard walked side-by-side away from us, about a block ahead. Neither wore a helmet, at least.

"Harrison!" I shouted.

The taller of the two turned around at once, followed by his shorter companion. They both squinted against the afternoon sun to see me. I walked faster as I approached. "Harrison!" I repeated.

"Do I know you?" he asked, still trying to make out my face.

"Fewmets." The shorter one whipped out his shockspear. "That's Beryl the terrorist!"

Harrison's eyes widened, as he grabbed for his shockspear too. "Viridia's looking everywhere for him! Let's take him down!"

"Are you kidding? You know he has enhancements! We can't take him by ourselves!"

"Do you want to run for help while I hold him off?"

Were they seriously going to debate what to do while I kept getting closer? I shrugged, boosted my legs, and charged.

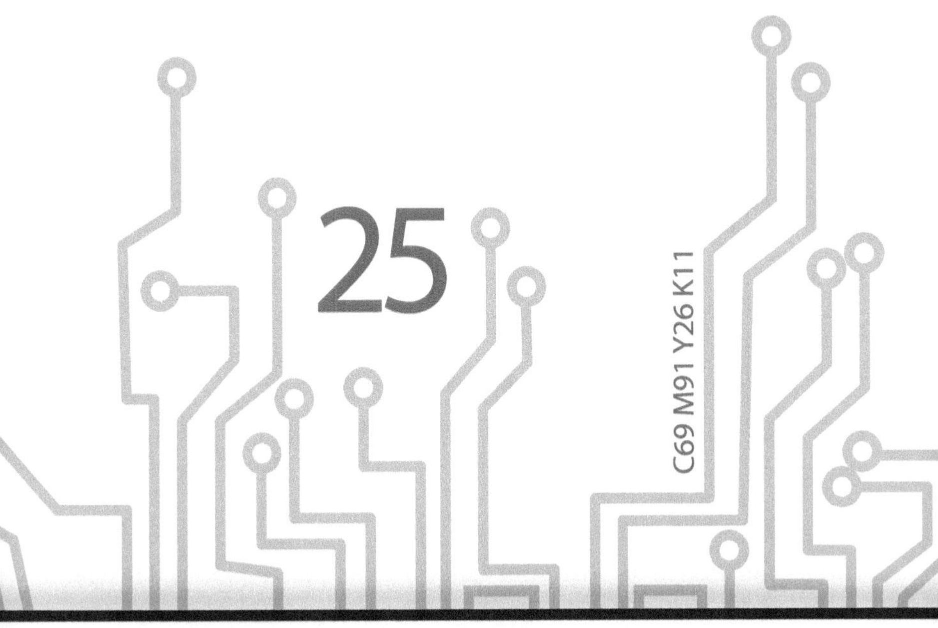

25

I lunged forward, catching the two Guards unaware, even though they'd been watching me the whole time. I grabbed Harrison's shockspear with my cyb hand, seized the front of his uniform, and slammed him up against the concrete wall beside the sidewalk. While he staggered, trying to recover, I smacked Pine's shockspear to the side, then tapped him on the side of the neck with Harrison's spear. He fell flat on the sidewalk, shaking. I turned and smacked Harrison's head against the wall again. This time, he fell unconscious.

Kelly caught up. "I forget how fast you can move." She looked over the two fallen Guards. "Which one do you need?"

I pointed at Pine, who continued to shake from the shock. "This one. Let's get him off the street somewhere."

Kelly put her hands on her hips. "And the other one? You realize as soon as he gets back to the station, everyone will know you're back in town. They'll double the number of guards around Stacy!"

I did not think this through.

"All right. I guess we'll have to hide him and tie him up too."

"Got any rope?"

Why did everything have to be so complicated?

It took some annoying work, but we managed to get Harrison tied up and stashed in an empty building. I figured he'd be able to work his way free in a few hours, giving us the time we needed. I hope. We took Pine to a different building—like I've said, Viridia has no shortage of empty buildings—where I removed his Guard uniform before tying him up. By then, he'd long since recovered from the electrical shock.

"Viridia will deal with you!" he growled.

I crouched in front of him and smiled. "Come on. We both know you don't really work for Viridia." I glanced up at Kelly. "What was the name? Oh, right." I looked back at him. "You work for Chroma."

His brow furrowed. "What do you mean by that?"

I picked up the shockspear and tapped it on my cyb hand. "You know what I mean. It's all about that purple robe you had stashed in your locker."

"I wear green."

"Sure you do… while you're here. But outside The Circle, and, I guess, when you need to do other stuff here, you wear purple." I leaned in a little closer. "But you're not wearing it now, so no vanishing on us like your buddies."

He stared back at me, mouth slightly ajar, brow still furrowed. "I have no idea what you're talking about."

I sighed. "Why do they have to be this way?"

"We don't have time for this," Kelly grumbled. She grabbed the shockspear from me, flicked the power switch, and tapped Pine on the chest. He went into another seizure.

I shook my head. "Now I have to wait until he can talk again."

"It doesn't take long." Kelly leveled the spear and pointed it right at the prisoner's nose. "Hey! The next shock comes in through your nose. And the one after that will come through an even more sensitive spot. Got it?"

"I don't… know what… you want," he managed to say as the effects faded.

"Tell me what the connection is between your boss and Troilus Green," I suggested.

"Isn't it obvious?"

"No. Tell me."

"That information is not for you, Beryl Godslayer." The spectral voice came from behind me.

I leaped to my feet and spun around. A purple robe, its frayed edges waving in non-existent wind, stood seven feet away. As usual, I couldn't make out a face within the hood.

Kelly gasped. This was the first time she'd seen one of them.

"So you know when one of your people is in danger, huh?" I took a step toward the newcomer. "How does that work? Some crazy tech, I guess. They wear something that sends out a signal of some kind?"

"Our technology is far beyond you. Release him."

"You haven't given me a reason to." I remembered something from our last encounter. "And if your tech is beyond us, how come you didn't know about the tech I used on Amaranth?"

"Release him. Or suffer the loss of another of your comrades."

"That's pathetic!" I took another step closer. "You're scared of me, so the best you can do is threaten someone else?"

"We do not fear you. You serve a purpose here in this valley. When you no longer serve that purpose, we will remove you."

I felt a breeze now. Indoors. Did they take wind with them everywhere? Why? Just to create the effects around their robes?

"Kelly. Shock the prisoner again." The grunts behind me confirmed her action.

"Why do you do this?" the robe asked.

"To remind you who's in charge here. You're trying to threaten my friends. I have one of your friends right here." I held up the second shock-spear. "I could spin around and kill him in seconds, faster than even you can move."

"So you believe."

"So. I. Know." With each word, I took another step. Only about three feet separated us now. The wind blew harder, whipping through my hair.

"What do you hope to accomplish through this?"

"You already know that. I'm after information. I want to know why you're here and what you're up to. What are you doing with Troilus Green? With Onyx? Where is Carl Roberts? Shall I go on?" I braced myself, preparing my boosts.

"We do not dispense information. Continue your fight against the dragons, and we will leave you alone."

"What if I finish off the dragons here and come after yours? What if I decide to take on Chroma?"

The robe didn't answer me. I don't think he liked me invoking the name of their mother dragon. And I'd had enough of this pointless conversation. I let the boosts flow and lunged forward.

"Beryl!" Kelly shouted. "There's another one!"

It was too late to change my action. I charged into the purple robe, cyb hand extended. This time, I knew what to do. The robe itself flowed around me, but the cyb hand could grasp it. Icy air struck my skin, as the robe enveloped me. I groped forward until I felt something solid, and then I slammed the shockspear into that spot.

The spear penetrated into something, and I triggered the electrical charge. Around me, the robe fluttered violently in all directions. Maybe I had disrupted its cybernetic components. I hoped so, anyway. I released my grasp on whatever I'd caught, and instead grabbed at the spot where I suspected the head to be. My hand caught hold of something, and I yanked as hard as I can.

Amongst the billowing flow of purple, a face appeared: a human face without a chromark. A hairless male glared back at me. A spot of blood stood out at the corner of his lips.

Kelly screamed.

I turned, still holding on to the hood or face mask or whatever I'd caught. A second purple robe stood next to Kelly. Long strands of the robe itself wrapped around her, pinning her arms to her sides. My mind, racing from my accelerated movements and boosts, focused on what that meant: they could choose to make their robes interact with other physical things. It wasn't always insubstantial.

None of that mattered in the moment. They had Kelly. The shockspear lay on the ground. Pine pulled himself into a seated position, smiling at the turn of events.

"Release him," intoned the new robe.

"Release her!" I shot back. "I've already got a spear in this guy's side." I pointed at a growing stain on the floor. "He's bleeding pretty bad. You don't have long to save him."

The robe suddenly seemed to flow away from Kelly and toward me. The wind picked up, and I shivered in the icy blast. The air warped my vision, so I couldn't see precisely what was happening. I tightened my grip on my captive.

For a few moments, I could see nothing but purple. The robes flowed around me, and I couldn't tell where one ended and the other began. I lost sight of the face. And then all of it folded in on itself. The warping effect grew stronger. With a loud tearing sound, both of them vanished, leaving me holding at least half of one of the robes. The shockspear clattered onto the floor and rolled in the pool of blood.

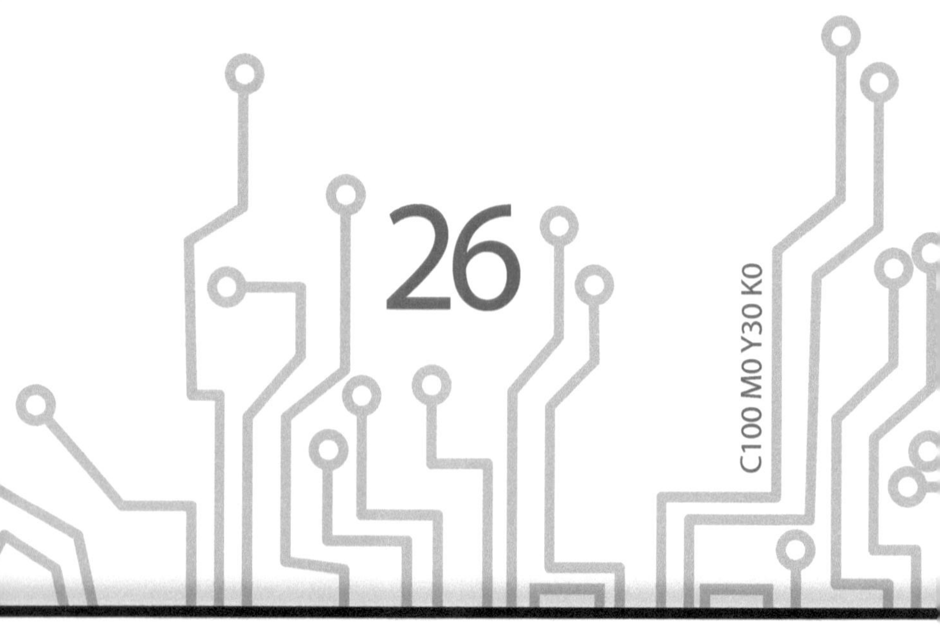

"That was the freakiest thing I have ever seen!" Kelly exclaimed. She shook all over and wrapped her arms around herself.

"Are you all right?" I hurried over to her.

"I'm fine. I'm fine. Just… so weird!" She motioned me back.

I looked down at Pine. "Well. Looks like they left you behind, buddy." I held up the remains of the purple robe. "And I got a souvenir."

He stared at me. "They'll be back. They won't leave me with you for long."

"Maybe so." I picked up the shockspear again, and crouched down. "But that still means we have time to get back to the questions I want answered."

"Nothing's changed," he insisted, his eyes watching the blood dripping from the spear. "I'm still not telling you anything."

I pushed the spear forward and let some of the blood drip on his face. "You sure about that?"

"You're not a killer," he hedged. "We've watched you. You wouldn't kill a prisoner."

I let the spear point rest against his cheek. "You haven't been watching long enough, I guess. Last year, I killed one of the priest guards here in Viridia. Drove my sword right through him. Did you watch that?"

"He did it to save a friend," Kelly added. "And you people just threatened all of his friends."

"So why are you here?" I repeated.

Pine eyed me and the spear for a moment. "Chroma naturally wishes to know what is happening here with her children," he said.

"That would explain watching things. But you're not just watching any more. You're involved. Why?"

"Since the death of Caesious, things have changed. The balance was thrown off." He lowered his eyes, seeming resigned for some reason. Did he feel guilty for telling me things? Or was he upset for being left behind?

"You don't seem to be helping restore the balance," I observed. "In fact, you're backing Onyx, who's created the most chaos of all."

He looked back up at me. "Onyx is willing to submit."

"Submit? To who? Chroma? Is she trying to take control of The Circle now?"

He didn't answer.

"He asked you a question," Kelly said, stepping closer.

"No," he said at last. "I've said too much already."

Kelly looked at me. "What do you think? Shock him again?"

I grimaced. "Nah. He's not going to say anything else. At least not without a lot of persuasion."

"I bet if we introduced him to Glacier, he'd talk." Kelly chuckled.

"Yeah, but we'd have to get him out of the city, and that wouldn't be easy." I sighed. "Let's just gag him and leave him here, like his buddy."

Kelly nodded and proceeded to gag the prisoner. When did she get so good at that? It was kind of scary.

I held up the torn purple robe and looked it over, turning it back and forth. "I wonder if Ciaru can do something with this."

"He does have two cyb hands," Kelly answered. "Maybe he can work with it." She reached out and let the material flow over her hand. "I can't even grab it."

"It's not going to be easy to carry around."

"Why can't we just stuff it in one of our packs?"

Sometimes, I really did not think. With Kelly's help, I shoved the robe into my backpack. It took some work, but we got it all inside and zipped the pack up.

"We've wasted enough time. Let's go meet the others," Kelly suggested, heading for the door.

I followed her. "I don't think it was a complete waste. We got some information." I flexed my hand. "And the purple robes might be a little bit more afraid of me now."

"All we learned is that Onyx is willing to 'submit,' whatever that means."

We left the building and headed down the street in the direction of the market. "Let's think about it." I held up a finger. "With the chaos we've created here, nothing is stable. So Chroma decides to step in and take control over her wayward children."

"Thinking about dragons as rebellious teenagers is still funny."

"Maybe. Or maybe it's deeper than that. We don't know yet. The point is, if she's coming back, maybe the other dragons weren't so happy about it. Maybe that's why Amaranth made those comments about her mother."

"But Onyx is okay with it? I don't know. He seems like the one least likely to support someone else taking over."

"Not if she offered him more power." I waved my hand as we kept walking. "Look, he wanted revenge on all the other dragons. But now Chroma comes along and tells him she needs to step in and control this place. But maybe she offers him control, under her, once the other dragons are gone."

"Then why work with Atramentous?"

I shrugged. "He'll betray him eventually. It's what he does." I paused. "Or maybe he's counting on us dealing with him, like we've been planning to do."

"You think we're playing right into his hands?"

"I don't know. And I still don't know how Troilus Green fits into all this!"

"It won't matter if we kill him, will it?"

I set my jaw. "It won't matter at all. Because that's what we're going to do."

We reached the market a few minutes later and blended right in with the people walking about and shopping. I caught a glimpse of Lovat getting a sandwich from a cart. I think I remembered the cart's owner helping us during one of our escapes, but I couldn't remember his name. The bearded man nodded to me as we approached, then looked away quickly as if he didn't want to be noticed.

Caedan turned around as we reached them, a sandwich in his hand also. "Hey, there you are. Have fun?"

"Let's keep walking," I suggested. As we continued on our way, I gave them a quick summary of what Kelly and I had been doing. "What's the situation with Stacy?"

Caedan shook his head. "Not good. They've got her hanging by her arms from a big pole right in the center of the ruins. She doesn't look good at all."

"Guards?"

"At least six out in the open, spaced out around the place. No way to sneak past any of them." He took another bite of his sandwich. "And that's just what we could see," he added with his mouth full.

"No draconic?" I asked, glancing at Lovat.

"No," he said. "But I think someone else is watching from a house across the street. Couldn't get a good look at them."

"Six in the open. More watching. More sure to come the moment we're spotted," I summed up. "Not looking so good."

"Is it, though?" Caedan finished off his sandwich and wiped his hands on his pants.

"What do you mean?"

"Maybe it's time for a show of force." He pointed vaguely in the direction we needed to go. "Look, this is the only place where we can do something crazy and probably not have to worry about a dragon showing up. That limited us before, right? Not an issue now."

"We can't take on the entire Viridian Guard," Kelly said.

"Maybe not all of them, no. But it won't be all of them." Caedan pointed at me. "I mean, Beryl could handle those six all by himself, am I right?"

"Maybe…"

"Bring in Lainey with her rifle. She could take out several more on her own. Then add her crazy teeth cat." He shrugged. "The rest of us could do a little more. All I'm saying is… we have more power than we tend to think."

"You know Troilus Green will show up."

"So Lainey shoots him, and then you cut his stinking head off." Caedan pointed at the people milling through the market. "We know some of the populace is on our side, even if they've now been scared into submission. Something big and dramatic might wake them back up. Maybe we can overthrow all of Viridia's remnants with something like this."

I looked to Kelly. "If Bice were here, he'd be the voice of caution. Can you take his place here?"

"I don't know." She pushed her hair back. "He's... kind of making sense."

"Kind of?" Caedan repeated.

"I don't see everyone rising up," Kelly said. "But I do think we might be able to rescue Stacy with a decisive attack."

"You're both crazy." I threw up my hands. "Let's go meet with Jaden and Lainey. Maybe she can talk some sense into you."

"You want me to be right, and you know it," Caedan said, pointing at me.

I couldn't tell him he was wrong... because he wasn't.

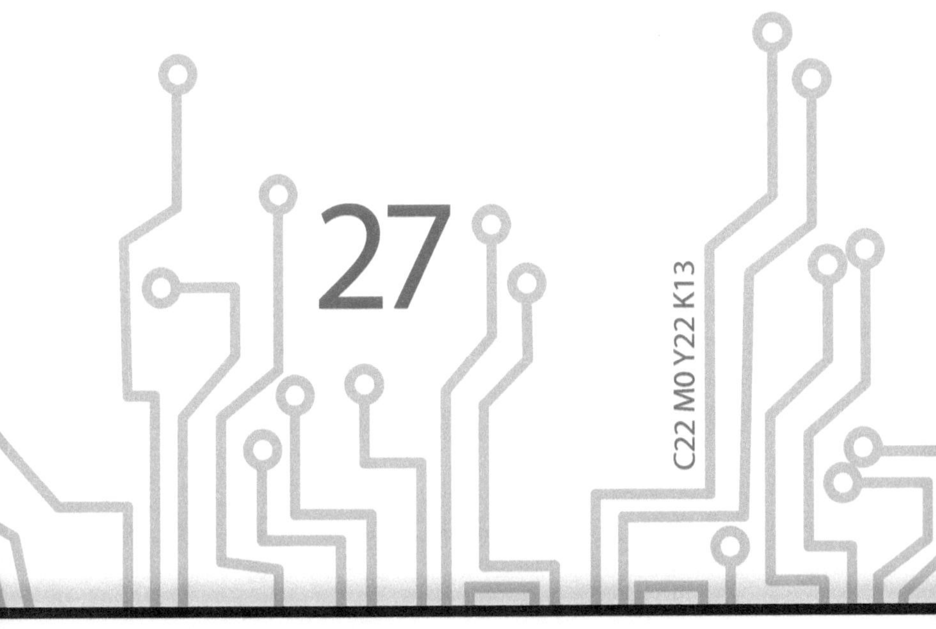

I pulled out the talker and checked in with Jaden. "Has Lainey arrived yet?"

"Yes! And you didn't tell me how big her cat got! That thing's terrifying!"

I chuckled. "All right. Stay put. We're coming to you."

"Beryl," another voice said over the talker. "So good to hear your voice again."

I almost dropped the device. Troilus Green! How…? Then I remembered: he'd killed Mason, who'd had one of the talkers with him. Good thing we hadn't been using them much here, if he'd been listening in.

"Wait. Who's that?" Jaden asked.

"What do you want, draconic?" I demanded.

"I want many things. But for now, all I want is you. And an end to your blasphemous rebellion."

"And I want you dead. Guess we don't always get what we want."

"Ah, but I do have something you want. I think. Wait." A pause. "Yes, she's still alive. I wasn't sure. I don't suppose you'd want her if she were dead already. But I have been wrong on rare occasions. Maybe you do have uses for a corpse."

"I'm coming for you." I gripped the talker tighter. "No more of this. I am going to take you down. This is the day you die."

"How confident you are in your arrogance. I'll be waiting. You know where to find me."

I clicked off the talker and looked up at the others. "Let's go."

We found Lainey with Jaden at our meeting tree. It didn't take long to fill her in on what we'd learned so far.

"Caedan is right," she declared.

"What?" I looked around the group. "Is this some kind of joke? Are you all in on it? I'm the one who's supposed to be suggesting crazy things, and you all talk me out of it. Not the other way around!"

"Sometimes, the crazy thing to do is the right thing to do," Caedan said.

"That was… somewhat profound," I admitted.

"I think you're all crazy," Jaden put in. "You're threatening Viridia himself!"

"It's okay," Kelly told him. "We don't expect you to come. Someone's got to guard our stuff here, anyway."

I gave an exaggerated sigh. "All right. Everyone gear up. If we're doing this, I want everyone armed with some kind of weapon."

"I don't have a weapon," Kelly said.

"I've got you covered." I opened my pack, took out one of the batons, and tossed it to her.

She looked over it with a critical eye. "What is this? Just some kind of club?"

I showed her where to hold it to find the hidden button. "It generates an electrical charge, though not much of one. It's probably better as a club." I took the second one of the batons and stuck it in my pocket as backup. Might be handy if I didn't want to actually kill someone with my sword.

"What about me?" Lovat asked.

I handed him the third baton. "I don't expect the two of you to do any fighting, if you can help it," I told them. "Your job is to get Stacy down."

Caedan and Lainey each had their own weapons. And Glacier pretty much was a weapon. I looked over each one of the team. "I guess we're ready. But let's be smart about this. We'll get Lainey in position to shoot at stuff before we make our attack."

"She should be at an angle to see the front of that house Lovat noticed," Caedan said. "So she can see anything that comes out of it."

"Right." I took a deep breath. "Well, let's go. No use wasting any more time.”

"Wait." Lainey tossed me a wet cloth. "Get rid of the fake chromarks."

She had a good point. I cleaned up the makeup, exposing my multi-colored mark. Caedan did the same, showing his blue. Lovat cleaned his off and smiled defiantly.

The five of us started toward the city, followed by Glacier. Kelly looked us over. "This is crazy," she admitted. "He knows we're coming, and we're going to be noticed as soon as we start walking down the street like this."

"Guess we may as well make the most of it then," I said. "Everyone look impressive."

I'm not sure if that made any difference. I mean, we already looked somewhat impressive, what with the weapons… and the giant cat with enormous fangs. We got plenty of stares as we walked down the streets. A small crowd gathered, following us from a distance. I considered making some kind of speech to them, promising the end of the dragon's reign, but I didn't want to waste any more time.

As we drew closer to our destination, I tried to think through everything that could happen. "Caedan, take Lainey and help her find the best spot, then come back to us. Lainey, take Glacier with you."

"Shouldn't she go with you?"

"No. Once you start shooting, you'll be a target. You'll need protection."

Lainey shrugged and agreed. "But if you get in too much trouble, Glacier is coming."

"I don't doubt it."

The three of them peeled off and hurried away. I slowed our progress to allow Caedan time to come back. I needn't have worried. He rejoined us a few minutes before we reached the ruins of the shrine.

I don't know what I had expected to see. Troilus Green had destroyed several of the buildings around the shrine the last time we'd been here. One of them fell over into the shrine, crushing Bice's old cabin. I'd even seen the destruction now from above, using Auric's orb. The thought of it made me glance up. Was he watching us now? Hardly a cloud floated in the sky. If he were watching, he'd be able to see everything.

Knowing what I did about the destruction still didn't prepare me for the actuality. We stopped at the edge of the debris. Not only had they torn down what remained of the shrine, uprooted all the trees, ripped apart the sidewalks and walls… they'd shoved some of the debris from the other buildings into the remains of the shrine. Here and there, a few small pieces of wall remained standing. One shredded tree still rose above it all, a devastated reminder of what had once been.

Not far from the tree stood a single post, about eight to ten feet tall. Stacy hung against it, her hands bound by chains connected to the top. Anger flooded into me at the sight of her still body. If she were dead, nothing would stop me from tearing down the Emerald Ascendancy and ripping Troilus Green apart.

Hadn't Caedan mentioned Viridian Guard stationed around the ruins? In answer to my thought, he pointed. "There. The Guards have pulled back. They must want us to come closer." A dozen or so soldiers milled about on the opposite side.

"Can they be any more obvious about it?" Kelly muttered.

I glanced back at the substantial crowd that now watched us. "Then let's see what happens next." I stepped into the ruins, heading toward Stacy. The other three followed.

"At last we come to it." I knew the voice, almost as well as I knew my own by now. I turned to watch the reptilian form of Troilus Green stride toward us from the left, its dark green robe fluttering in a slight breeze. It spread its arms wide. "My enemy. My surprisingly human foe. You've come, as I always knew you would."

"Get Stacy down," I told the others. I glared at the draconic. "I told you I would come for you."

"Yes." The beast lowered its head, revealing the metal plate where Rick had stabbed it. "This will be the final confrontation between Viridia and Beryl, the resistance fighter."

"And this time, I'll make sure you're dead." I drew my sword and tossed the scabbard to the ground. "Cutting off your head completely should work, don't you think?"

Troilus Green chuckled. "Did you honestly believe that I would face you in single combat? That I would give you even a remote chance of victory or escape?" The jade scaled head shook back and forth. "No. This is the end."

Viridian Guard troops poured out of the streets and surrounded the ruins of the shrine completely. I counted at least thirty. To my right, nearest the post, another green draconic stepped from among the Guards and approached. I spun to see a third one coming from the opposite direction. Three draconics. Thirty soldiers. The odds were piling up.

"Now," Troilus Green said, taking a step toward me. His sickly-sweet odor drifted over us. "Will you watch as we tear your friends apart first? Or will you surrender and let them live, while we tear you apart?" The cruel jaws spread in a kind of grin. "Either way, your life ends today."

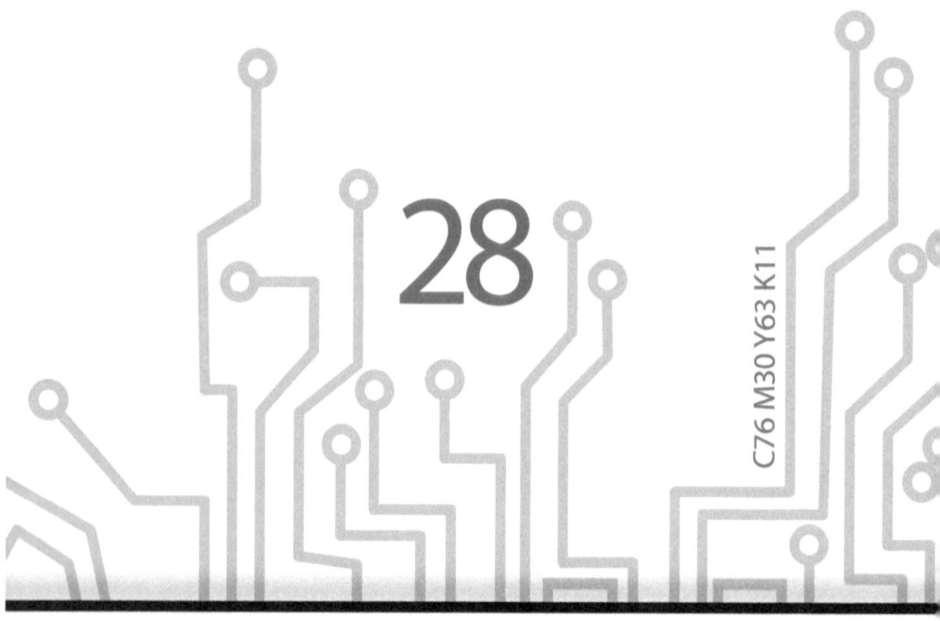

Caedan stepped apart from Kelly and Lovat, his weapons at ready. "What's the plan, Beryl?" he called.

My mind raced, helped along by a short boost I sent its way, just in case. "Can you hold one of them off for a few minutes?"

"Maybe. I—"

The loud crack of Lainey's rifle echoed across the ruins. The draconic nearest to Caedan and the others stumbled backward, and fell.

"Guard!" Troilus Green shouted, pointing. "Find who did that! She'll be in that direction!"

"Bad news for them," I muttered. I might not want to kill the human members of the Viridian Guard, but I doubted any of us would be able to hold Glacier back if she thought Lainey was threatened. A few moments later, my thoughts were confirmed by a tremendous roar. I'll admit it: I didn't know Glacier could be that loud. I wouldn't want to be those Guards right now.

I wondered again if Auric were watching us via his orb. Did he have others watching with him? Would he allow Bice to see what was happening? Or stick to his own, like Amaranth?

I advanced toward Troilus Green, trying to keep my focus on him, but also keeping track of everything else around us. It looked like Kelly and Lovat were getting Stacy down. Caedan circled around behind me, no doubt planning to engage the third draconic.

"Scamandrius!" Troilus Green called. "The other one is of no consequence. Only Beryl matters."

Scamandrius. I'd seen that one before, when I'd been in Viridia's lair. At the time, he'd seemed like a superior to Troilus, but everything was different now, what with Troilus claiming to be Viridia. None of it mattered at the moment. I needed to end this as fast as possible.

Boosting everything, I charged Troilus Green, sword at my side. Its chest was armored, so I knew stabbing it would be pointless. I needed to go for the head, which raised another problem: the draconic was over a foot taller than me. As I neared it, the sickly-sweet smell of decay increased.

I jumped and tried to slash across its jade-scaled face. To my surprise, not only did it move fast enough to counter my boosted strike, a series of metal spikes erupted from its forearm. My sword threw off sparks as it impacted them.

"I've had a few improvements since our last fight." The draconic swung its other hand around in a blur. The cyb-tipped claws tore at me, narrowly missing my chest. I dodged backward, not an easy task among the ruins.

Troilus Green yelled one of those weird words again—what was up with the "magic" words, anyway?—and threw up a palm toward me. I'd been expecting it from the beginning, and instantly sent a boost to my heart. The sensation like a rush of electricity swept over me, even as the draconic's force wave threw up all of the debris around us. I'd stopped it from impacting me, but I couldn't stop the bricks and branches from striking me. I kept the boosts going to make me faster, dodging as much as I could. But I'd be feeling the bruises from that attack later.

The reborn draconic possessed a wide range of abilities I needed to remember. In addition to the cyb enhancements, it could spit venom and wield the resomancy as just demonstrated. I worried most about the voice power it had used on me in the Emerald Ascendancy. Carl had saved me that time. I didn't know if I could resist it alone.

Again, I took a quick glance at the others. Stacy no longer hung on the pole. But Caedan looked to be having trouble with Scamandrius Green. Even though he was a skilled fighter, he couldn't move anywhere near as fast as I could. The draconic's size and power would be too much for him alone.

I feinted toward Troilus, then kicked off to my left and rushed

Scamandrius. Neither of them expected the move. My sword sliced cleanly through the second draconic's left thigh. Blood erupted from a huge gash. It stumbled, and Caedan took advantage. He leaped in and smashed it in the face with his baton.

I swung back toward my primary target. At least I'd given Caedan more of a chance. Except I paid for it. Troilus Green caught up and punched me with a huge right swing. I tried to spin, but the punch still caught me in the ribs. I flew back several feet and rolled into a tree trunk. I fought to regain my breath, but at least kept a grip on my sword.

Another one of Lainey's shots rang out, but I didn't see anyone hit. I'm sure she was doing the best she could, as Guards tried to get at her. And we were moving so fast out here, and so close together, it probably didn't give her very many clear possibilities.

"Come, oh fearsome enemy," Troilus Green called, its arms spread again. "Surely you aren't giving up already."

I got to my feet slower than I needed to. That pose. The loud voice. The crowds. Troilus Green wanted a show. It wanted theatricality. It wanted-ed to defeat me in front of all these people. Fine. I'd give them the best show of their lives. I took a deep breath and steadied myself.

"Do I need to come to you?" my enemy demanded, taking a step toward me.

I sent boosts to everything: both arms, both legs, my brain, my heart, and everything in between. And then I did it again. The energy inside me built to a crescendo. I felt like I would explode from it.

I charged. When I fought others while boosted, they moved in slow motion. Troilus Green, faster than anyone else I'd fought, moved at a more normal pace, even as I moved as fast as I possibly could. I didn't gain much of a speed advantage. But at the very least, it made me its equal.

As my sword ricocheted off some of the forearm spikes, the draconic spat at me. Most of it missed me, but a single drop of venom struck my upper arm. It burned, though not as bad as Onyx's acid.

I kept moving and attacking, spinning around Troilus Green. I struck at it from every side. A couple of my blows connected, cutting short gashes through its robe and into its tough skin. Its claws connected with me once, cutting long but shallow lacerations across my left side.

Caedan seemed to be holding his own. At least he didn't appear to be in dire need. Stacy lay on the ground with Kelly kneeling over her. Lovat stood beside them, his eyes wide and riveted on my fight with the draconic. Another rifle shot rang out. Troilus Green winced as Lainey's bullet struck its metallic chest. "That is becoming annoying," it growled.

"Aim for the head, Lainey!" I wanted to shout. She probably wouldn't be able to hear me.

I grabbed up a piece of piping and threw it. Troilus Green batted it out of the air. But I took advantage of the distraction to change my tactics. I lunged in down low. My sword slashed across the beast's ankle... and struck metal again.

"You cut me there once before!" It grabbed at the back of my shirt. The claws ripped through the fabric, but seized hold. I boosted my legs further to give me enough traction to break free. I left the remains of the shirt hanging from its claws.

"Enough of this." Its eyes began to glow.

Fewmets. I felt again the utter sickness within, and the horrible drain on my muscles. I resisted, boosting them against this dragon power.

"Fall!" the evil creature bellowed in that voice stronger, deeper and greater than its usual rasp. My brain refused the command, insisting that I attack. Attack now! But my body listened to the voice instead of me. I collapsed into the debris, like a puppet without strings.

No, no, no. I fought back, boosting everything I could think of, trying to find a way to break through this mental poison. Nausea and fear washed over me. Though I lay on the ground, I felt frozen. I couldn't even shift my hip to avoid a broken brick poking into my side.

Troilus Green strode toward me. Its eyes continued to glow. I could almost feel its gloating. What could I do? I had no power against a god.

"Leave him alone!"

To my horror, Lovat charged across the ruins. He smacked Troilus Green with the baton I'd given him, accomplishing no more than if someone struck me with a toothpick.

Troilus Green backhanded him.

Lovat flew through the air, slammed into one of the still-standing walls of brick, fell to the ground, and stopped moving.

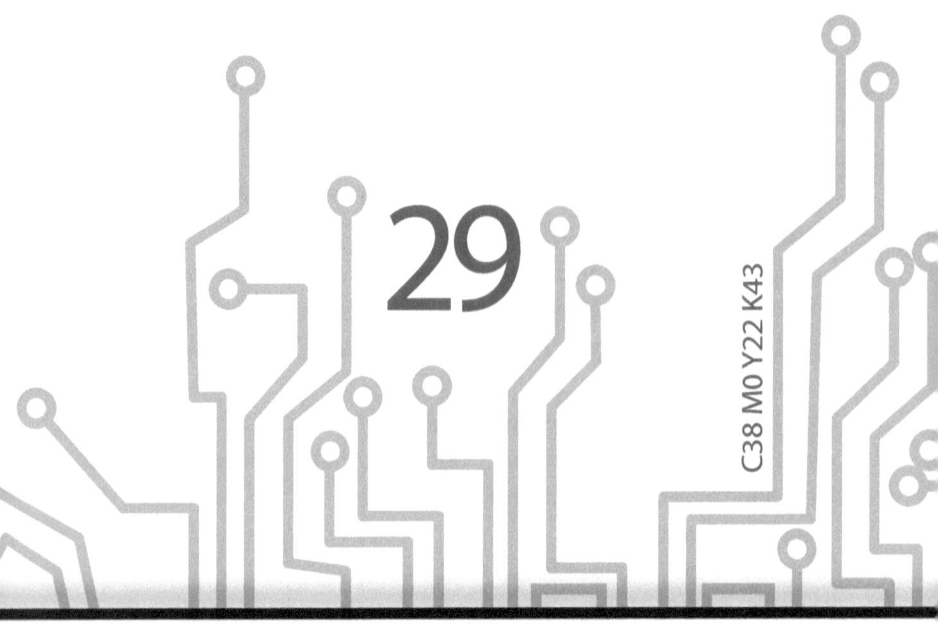

29

"Noooo!" It took a moment to realize I was the one screaming. Some-how, the emotion and force of it broke me free of the draconic's control. I staggered to my feet.

The wall above Lovat wavered and began to topple toward him. I dropped my sword and ran. I dove over his body just as the bricks fell. They cascaded around and atop me, striking every inch of my back. But none of them struck the small body beneath me.

As the dust cleared, I stared down at him. Was he breathing? Was he still alive?

"How apropos," Troilus Green called. "A falling wall. Just like the one that sent us both to the hospital so long ago, Beryl."

I shifted, throwing broken bricks off my back, boosting myself just to keep moving. Pain blossomed from the back of my head down to my an-kles. I ignored it, and pushed Lovat's hair out of his face. I leaned in close. He was breathing!

"Does the child live?"

I looked up at the draconic, trembling. "If he dies—"

"You'll what?" Troilus Green spread one hand outward. "Look around you, Beryl. I've won."

Caedan scrambled up next to me, staring wide-eyed down at Lovat. Scamandrius Green joined its brother.

"If you want the child to live… surrender. Now."

I looked back at Lovat. I couldn't even guess how bad his injuries might be. Someone his size, struck by that monster, and then hitting the wall… he clung to life. But for how long? I could see massive bruising forming on all of his exposed skin. Blood trickled from somewhere, but not too much… I hoped.

The explosive sound of Lainey's rifle pierced my ears again. Scamandrius Green staggered and fell, catching itself on its hands. Blood poured from a gaping wound in its back. Troilus Green turned to see.

In the next moment, Glacier leaped out of nowhere, crashing into the draconic with a blood-curdling snarl. An eruption of claws, teeth, fur, and scales followed. The draconic was still much larger than the cat, but her sheer ferocity gave her a chance.

I didn't have time to watch the fight. Too much was happening at once. Lainey stepped up next to Scamandrius Green and put the barrel of her rifle against its head. "Move and you lose your brain," she said. Caedan traded places with Kelly. She knelt beside Lovat and looked him over.

"Beryl, this is bad. I don't… I don't see how he can survive."

I didn't want to hear that. I couldn't accept that.

"Get my sword," I growled. "I'm going to need it."

Kelly scrambled away.

"Lovat," I whispered. "It's all right. It's going to be all right." I didn't know if he could hear me.

Troilus Green managed to seize hold of Glacier and threw her a dozen feet away, not far from us. The cat twisted in the air and landed on her feet. With a snarl, she crouched, ready to pounce again.

"Glacier!" Lainey snapped. "Wait."

Glacier snarled again, but obeyed. She kept her crouch, her eyes never leaving Troilus Green.

The draconic wiped blood from a wound on its shoulder. "Fascinating creature. Your control of it is impressive."

"Let us go, or I blow your friend's head off," Lainey replied.

Troilus Green pointed at me. "And what of the child? Wherever it is you are hiding yourselves now, you cannot possibly get him there in time to save his life. Are you abandoning him?"

I glared up at him. "His life is infinitely more valuable than yours."

"Then surrender." It reached a claw up and tapped the back of its own skull. "His body is shattered, much as yours was that day. The only thing likely to save him is a cybernetic implant like yours."

I glanced at Lovat. It might be true. It was also true that we couldn't get him back to the base soon enough. How much was his life worth?

"We can save him," Troilus Green repeated. "You know my scientists have made a breakthrough in this area. We can do for him what was done for you."

"No. He can't."

I turned and saw Stacy being held up by Caedan. "His scientists have come a long way," she said, her voice barely audible. "But none of them are capable of that kind of operation. Not yet."

Caedan brought Stacy near us and lowered her to the ground beside me. I gave her a half-hearted smile. She looked at Lovat, her eyes wet behind the bruising on her face.

"We're willing to try," Troilus Green shot back. "He doesn't have a chance otherwise."

I rested my hand against Lovat's chest, feeling its movement. What could I do? To save him, I would have to surrender. In essence, I would be sacrificing the rest of our lives for his. I had no right to do that for the others. But to give up myself? That I could do. I took a breath and opened my mouth to say as much.

"Beryl Godslayer!"

How did they do it? How did these purple robes manage their timing? And where—?

"You were warned, but you persisted in interfering." The ethereal voice seemed to come from everywhere.

I turned at a gust of wind. The purple robe appeared directly behind Kelly. Frayed lengths of cloth extended outward in either direction.

"What is this?" Troilus Green demanded.

"You attacked us and took one of us captive. Now this one will be taken." The lengths of cloth moved, wrapping themselves toward Kelly.

"Beryl?" Her voice sounded uncertain, but she acted nonetheless. She swung my sword at the figure within the robe. Purple cloth closed around it and yanked it from her grasp.

"Kelly!" I leaped to my feet, but they were too far away. Even as I sent boosts to my legs, I knew I could not reach her in time. Caedan was closer, but he couldn't move fast enough.

The robe enfolded around her. The wind blew harder. The air warped around them.

And then the frayed edge of the robe burst out in every direction, snapping like whips. The wind and warping vanished. The robe fell down around its owner like ordinary cloth.

Kelly stood before him, holding the baton I'd given her. It crackled with electricity as she released the button.

The man within the robe held up his palms. "What? How did you do that?" His voice sounded normal now.

Kelly swung the baton as hard as she could, smacking the man in the head. He wavered a moment and collapsed.

For a moment, no one moved.

"How was this accomplished?" Troilus Green cried, taking a step in her direction.

"Stay back!" Lainey warned.

Glacier growled and inched forward.

The baton. We'd found an entire box of them in Loden's laboratory. The electrical charge they generated wouldn't harm a human… but apparently, it hit just the right frequency or whatever to disrupt the purple robe's cybernetic workings! The implications stunned me. Loden had been working on ways to fight them! Maybe the same applied to me after all!

Caedan ran to Kelly. He nudged the purple robe with foot to be sure he was out.

Lovat moaned, just loud enough for me to hear. I turned back to him at once. "Lovat?" I reached toward him again, but Stacy put a hand out to stop me.

"Beryl, he's dying," she whispered. "He doesn't have long."

I stood, knowing what I had to do.

"Troilus Green, I will surrender myself to you in exchange for medical treatment for him." I pointed at Lovat. "But you have to let everyone else leave peacefully."

"No bleaking way that happens," Caedan exclaimed.

"Beryl, no!" Lainey said at the same time.

"I have to save him." I looked around to each of them. "I can't let him die."

"They can't save him," Stacy insisted. "They don't have the capability. We need—"

Troilus Green remained staring at Kelly. "Your terms are not accept-able," it said.

"Need I remind you about my gun here?" Lainey demanded.

Troilus Green turned to look at me, but pointed at Kelly. "I need that as well."

"What?"

"You must share the secret of defeating them with me."

I couldn't believe what I was hearing.

Troilus Green lowered its head in a slight bow. "In this, we are on the same side."

I looked down at Lovat one more time. Maybe they couldn't save him. But I knew we couldn't. Didn't I have to at least give him a chance to live? I owed him that much. I opened my mouth to answer.

And once again, I was interrupted.

This time, a dragon showed up.

30

Auric the golden, in all his majesty, descended from the clouds directly toward us. The wind from his wings struck us all with far more force than the breeze created by the purple robe. I'd never seen him flying before now. He wove across the sky, descending toward us in a sinuous motion, almost like a serpent who moved through the sky instead of the dirt.

Lovat had been right. The disk on Auric's neck was fake. He'd never been trapped in human form after all. At the moment, I couldn't be angry at him. I could only stare along with everyone else.

He came to an awkward landing in the ruins, scattering debris from his impact. He shuffled a little, struggling to regain his balance on only three legs. His fourth—his front left cyb hand—was held aloft and kept from striking the ground. Once settled, he lowered it down.

"What are you doing here?" Troilus Green cried.

Auric opened his hand, and a human tumbled out. He struggled back to his feet and wavered, before turning to glare up at the dragon. "Never do that again!"

"Hunter?" Caedan exclaimed, running to him.

Hunter turned around. "Caedan? What—?" He stared around at everything. "We are in Viridia?"

"Over here!" Kelly shouted, waving as she ran up beside me again.

"Save the child," Auric intoned. He turned his head toward Troilus

Green. "You will do everything they ask in assistance."

"Of-of course," the draconic answered. I'd never seen a draconic look intimidated, but I'm pretty sure that's what we all saw now.

I stood and stepped back as Hunter dropped down beside Lovat. "What happened?"

Kelly told him in rapid words as I stepped further back and looked up at Auric. He had been watching. He'd seen Lovat injured. He knew how bad it was, and brought Hunter. I looked up with my mouth hanging open. This dragon… risked his own life… to save a human boy.

"Thank you," I said. I didn't know what else to do.

Auric dipped his massive head in a nod. "An individual. Not a number."

"What about this one?" Lainey asked, still holding the rifle at Scamandrius Green.

"Hang on," I told her.

"Get the medics in here!" Hunter shouted. "We need transport to the hospital!"

"Do it," Troilus Green said, gesturing to the nearest Viridian Guard. It stepped closer. "What is this, brother? Why are you helping these rebels?"

Auric deigned Troilus with a haughty stare. "This is all as it needs to be, if we are to defeat—" He broke off, and his head jerked upward, scanning the sky.

"What is it?"

Two things happened at once. First, a massive gust of wind struck us all again. Unprepared, I staggered a step back. Second, a black dragon appeared literally out of thin air and slammed into Auric.

"Atramentous!" Troilus Green screamed. "Wait!"

As the crowd—both Viridian Guard and civilians—tried to escape out of the way, the two dragons tumbled through and smashed into one of the smaller buildings outside the ruins. Atramentous reared up, then slammed back down with both front legs clawing at Auric.

My brain struggled to comprehend. Of course Atramentous had seen Auric in flight: that much I understood. But how… how did he appear out of nowhere like that? My thoughts flashed back to the time I'd lost sight of him in the air. Could the black dragon turn himself invisible? Disappear and reappear at will? All this time, I'd considered him the least important of the dragons. When we watched the cities from the tower, we'd almost never seen him. I'd assumed it was because he was a loner, hiding in his pit, or something like that. Instead, he might have been coming and going the whole time, and we never saw.

One of Auric's cybernetic hands slashed across Atramentous's snout, slinging dragon blood across the ruins. The black dragon fell back. The gold dragon shot into the sky.

Caedan stepped up beside me. "What do we do?"

I watched as the black dragon roared and took off, his wings doing more damage to the structures still standing nearby. People screamed and ran. "I don't know. What can we do?"

"The weapon Auric gave you. What about that?"

My eyes sought out the chest area as Atramentous flew over us, pursuing Auric higher. I caught a glimpse of some metallic scales, but the real cyb parts were inside. "It's back at our camp," I said, grinding my teeth. But even if it were here, how could we possibly use it right now? Even I couldn't get near two dragons in a full-blown death duel.

"Two stretchers!" I heard Hunter yelling. "I have two patients here, you idiots!"

Even as he flew up, Atramentous faded from view. I blinked and squinted. He'd completely vanished! Auric twisted around in mid-air, trying to watch every direction at once.

Atramentous re-appeared a split-second before tearing into Auric again. The impact sent both of them careening across the sky. I thought they might crash into more buildings, but Auric pulled free at the last minute. Both dragons swept up again. Auric managed to wrap himself around Atramentous and attack him from above. His cyb claws tore holes through both of the black dragon's wings. Flames burst from his mouth and enveloped his foe. Atramentous screamed, a horrific sound that echoed across the city.

"Beryl..." Lainey tried to get my attention again.

I tore my eyes away from the dragons and looked back. "I don't know." I watched the medics loading Lovat and Stacy onto stretchers, then turned to Troilus Green. "Are you listening to Auric? Or do we need to keep going with the threats back and forth?"

The draconic shook its head. "No. You need not surrender. Your man will have complete access to the finest medical facilities we can offer." It held up a claw. "But. You must share with me how you defeated the agent of Chroma."

I glanced at the others and nodded. "We can do that."

Lainey lowered her rifle. Scamandrius Green got to its feet and staggered away. Lainey called Glacier to her side. The cat came reluctantly, growling at the draconics.

As one, we turned our eyes back to the sky.

The dragons rocketed past us, wrapped around each other, clawing and biting. Acid from Atramentous spilled down, sizzling as it struck the ground and debris not far away.

Lainey aimed her rifle and followed their passage. She sighed and lowered it again. "I don't think I could do any kind of real damage to something that big."

I agreed. We could never match the level of ferocity, size, and power on display here. The only way we humans could hope to do anything to the dragons was through technology or luck. When dragons fought, we could do nothing but watch... Except I had done something when Onyx and Viridia fought. I'd destroyed Viridia's source, weakening him. If only we knew where Atramentous hid his source!

The black dragon's damaged wings, now glowing red for some reason, did not appear to be slowing him down much. Both of them bled from multiple wounds. Some of them looked enormous to me. Would they end up killing each other? Auric roared in pain as Atramentous ripped off one side of his strange mustache-like growth.

"What's with the black one's tail?" Lainey asked, coming up beside me.

"His tail?" I looked closer. In the few times I'd caught a glimpse of Atramentous, I'd never noticed his tail, but now I saw it. The end of his tail was entirely metallic, over a dozen feet of gleaming chrome tapering to a sharp point.

"They're coming back this way!" Caedan exclaimed.

All of us moved away from the center of the ruins, though I didn't know whether it would matter. The dragons weren't aiming for this spot as far as I could tell, but they tore at each other in the air as they spiraled in our direction.

Atramentous smashed into the ground on his back. His wings swept through a massive range, destroying even more of the surroundings. The pole where Stacy had been hung and the single tree were shredded. We all ducked, but the wings didn't reach our location.

Auric landed on top of him with another crash. The gold dragon's head twisted up, then shot down, jaws wide. With the most savage noise I'd ever heard, he ripped a chunk out of the black dragon's chest. I wanted to close my eyes to the violence, but I couldn't stop watching.

Auric spit out the chunk of flesh. Fire shot from his mouth at the wound he'd created. Atramentous screamed again, so loud I clapped my hands over my ears to shield them.

And then it all went wrong. Atramentous, larger in body than Auric, forced the other dragon off by sheet power. In moments, their positions reversed. The black dragon slammed his bulk on top of the writhing gold dragon, holding him down by his weight.

"No, no." I started forward, but Caedan grabbed me.

That tail. Atramentous whipped his tail around over his own shoulder. He seized it with both front hands and thrust it down like a spear.

Auric's death scream was the most horrifying sound I'd ever heard in my life.

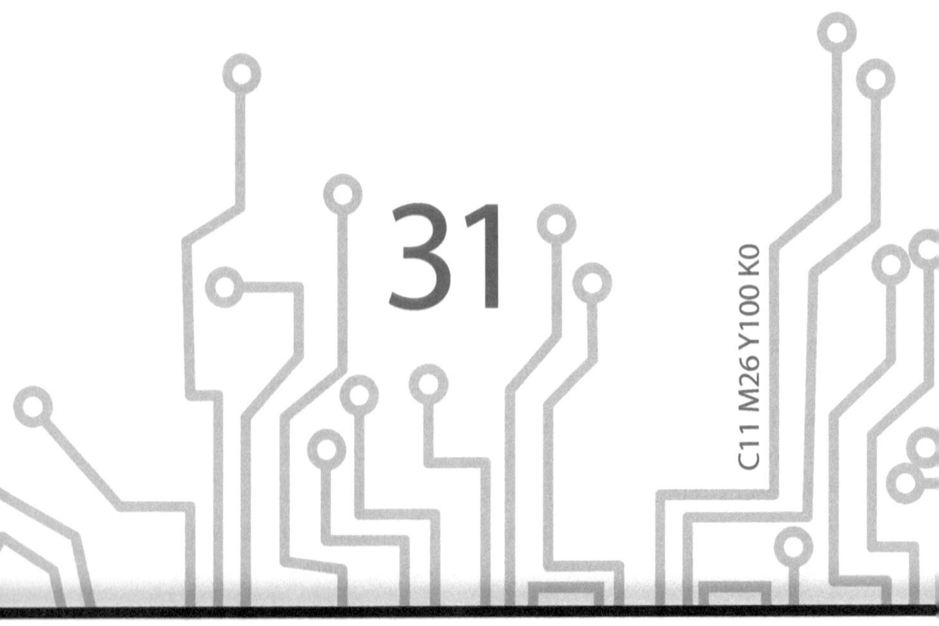

31

Atramentous did not stay to gloat. In fact, throughout the battle, I'd never heard a word from him. He yanked his tail spike free with a gush of dragon blood, gathered himself and shot into the air. A few moments later, he faded from sight, disappearing as he'd come. He'd suffered horrific wounds and no doubt didn't want to stick around to keep anyone from taking advantage of it.

But Auric… the one dragon who'd talked with me almost like an equal, the one who'd treated his people with a different level of care than the others, the one who'd risked everything for the life of one small boy… if he weren't already dead, he lay dying.

I shook free of Caedan's grasp and ran forward. The ruins about me now smoked and sizzled from dragon fire, acid, and blood. The fight we'd been engaged in only minutes before now seemed so tiny and inconsequential compared to the fury we'd just witnessed.

I slowed as I neared Auric's head. I circled around to see his eyes. They were still open, but his breath came in wheezing gasps.

"The child…" he whispered.

"Hunter's taken him to the hospital," I said mechanically. "If anyone can save him, he can." I shook my head. "You… you…"

"Learned… from you… Beryl Dragonslayer…"

Why did my heart ache so much? He was a dragon, one of the enemies

I'd sworn to destroy, wasn't he?

"Tell Tawn…" His eyes slipped closed.

"Yes? Tell him what?" I stepped near, heedless of my own safety.

"Contingency… two…" Auric lifted his head slightly, drawing in a massive amount of air through his nose. And then his head collapsed as he exhaled a tremendous blast right at me.

Energy flooded my body. A wave of heat swept over me and through me. I gasped and took a step backward. My entire body felt almost on fire, but without pain. In fact, the pain from all of the bruises and cuts I'd received in the battle faded away. The injuries remained, but I didn't feel them. Back in the city of Auric, the dragon had invigorated me along with the entire population. But now? I swear I felt like the energy dispersed among hundreds of thousands of people that night had all been injected into me.

I lifted my right hand and stared at it. I fully expected to see beams of light exploding from my fingers or something, but it looked normal. I stepped forward, again expecting to launch myself into the air, but nothing special happened. The power filled me, but wasn't coming out… at least not yet.

I trickled a tiny boost to my hand and made a fist. My fingers locked into place faster than my eyes could see. I released the fist and went back and forth a few times. I couldn't demonstrate it, but I could feel amazing strength in that grip.

Was this what Hunter meant about being a human battery? What had he called it? Thermoelectricity? Auric's breath supercharged me, filling me with more power than I'd ever had before. How far could I take this? The implications were enormous.

I looked back up at the dragon. Blue. Green. Red. Gold. Four dragons dead. Only three remained. Our quest to transform The Circle had taken some strange turns, but… in some ways, we were closer to victory than ever before.

But maybe… maybe losing Auric was a disaster, not a stepping stone to success. He'd been allied with us against the black dragons and the purple robes. I couldn't help but feel we'd lost something very important today. Would his people mourn him? Many of them would, I suspected, and not in the same way as the priests of Viridia had mourned at his death.

Caedan, Kelly, and Lainey caught up to me. Glacier bounded up and sniffed at Auric's head. She emitted a short yowl and paced back and forth. Finally, she sat on her hind legs and cocked her head, staring at the fallen dragon.

"Are you all right?" Lainey put a gentle hand on my forearm.

"I'm more than all right," I answered, my eyes still fixed on Auric.

"What does that mean?" Kelly asked.

I blinked and tore my gaze away. "It's… hard to explain." I noticed Troilus Green in the distance, watching us. "Listen, I'd better head to the hospital. But I don't trust these green draconics. I want the rest of you outside the city. Meet up with Jaden and wait until you hear from me."

Kelly started to say something, but closed her eyes and shook her head instead. She sighed. "I want to come with you, but you're right. You have the talker. Let us know about Lovat and Stacy as soon as you can."

"I will," I promised. I turned to Lainey. "Are you all right? I couldn't see what happened with you and Glacier at first."

She shrugged. "I'm fine. Glacier's a bit cut up, especially from fighting the draconic, but she'll be all right." She glanced at the saber-toothed cat, who'd resumed pacing in front of Auric. "I think I need to get her away from here, though."

I gave her a quick hug, worried that I might accidentally squeeze her in half. Every move I made felt that way: like I would explode from the power within me.

Kelly handed me my sword and its scabbard. I slung it on my back, which felt weird without a shirt. I left my friends there and strode across the ruins to face Troilus Green again. As I approached, I pointed back at Auric. "What will you do with the body?"

"When Onyx destroyed my… previous body, we had to burn it," the draconic said. "Everything except the skull, that is. We cleaned it up. It is mounted in a special shrine within the Ascendancy now." After a moment's pause, it added, "We can do the same here. We will contact his people to hear their desires. If it is within our power to grant, we will."

"All right." I took one last look at Auric, then squared my shoulders. "Take me to the hospital. I need to see what is happening."

"Of course." Troilus Green nodded. "But we did not take the child to the usual hospitals. We took him directly to the Emerald Ascendancy. Only there do we have the means to save him. And now, thanks to the arrival of your doctor, we have the ability."

"Right." I stared up at the draconic's face. "I don't trust you. Not a bit. You want that information about the robes? My friends and I walk out of here unharmed once Lovat's recovered. And then I'll tell you."

Troilus Green scowled. "It may be too late by then." It gestured and we both walked to the edge of the ruins where a truck waited.

"What do you mean?"

"The forces of Chroma are on the move. With Auric gone and Amaranth missing, I alone am left to resist them and the black dragons." We climbed on to the open back area of the truck. Troilus Green signaled the driver, and we started out. A large crowd watched us go. I wondered about the optics of the situation. What would they think seeing the two of us together now?

"I had been trying to forge a neutral path," the draconic went on. "Making myself appear as if I would serve them, while also working toward my own ends. However, with today's actions, they will no longer believe in my neutrality."

"We were the ones who took down the purple robe," I said. "Maybe they won't hold you accountable for that."

Troilus Green smiled, his vicious teeth curving upward. "Yes, but I took him prisoner. Once you have seen to your wounded child, would you care to join me in interrogating him?"

I shuddered. I remembered well how intimidating this draconic could be in questioning someone suspicious. How much more terrifying would he be against a clear enemy? I'm not sure I wanted to see that. Still, the possibility of gaining new information intrigued me. "I'll consider it."

The draconic looked away. "You say you do not trust me, though I gave my word to Auric. How shall I trust you then?"

"You don't have any reason not to trust me."

"Do I not?" The green-flecked black eyes turned back to me. "You have sworn to kill the dragons of The Circle." The draconic's head lowered in a mock bow. "And I am a dragon."

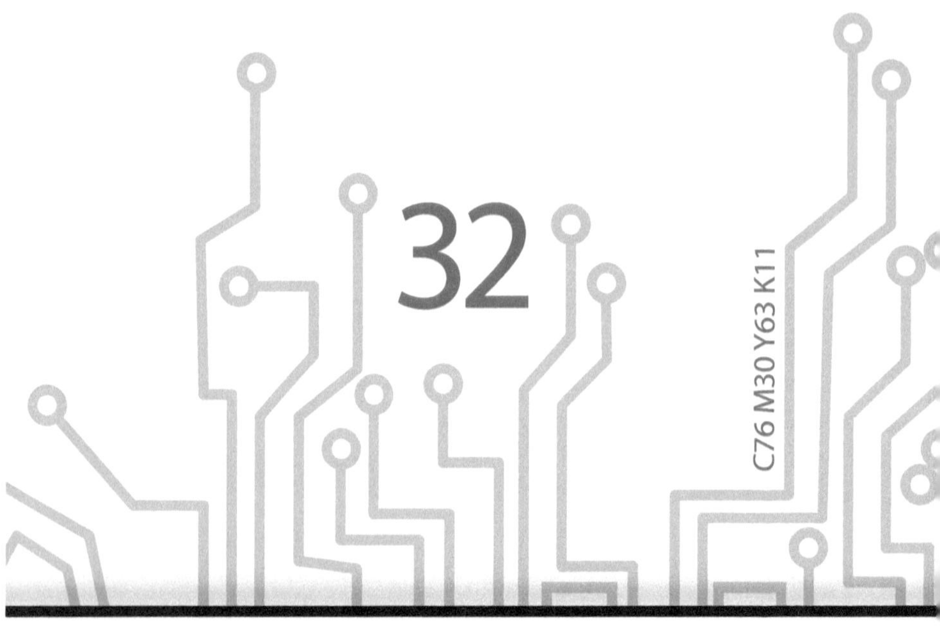

32

For a moment, I was tempted. With the infusion of power from Auric, I could trigger boosts, whip out my sword, and stab Troilus Green through the eye before he could react. He would have no chance. And why shouldn't I? I'd wanted to do it for so long. But if I did, it might put Lovat, Stacy, and Hunter in jeopardy.

"I've kept my promises," I said. "As long as my friends are treated right, you don't need to fear me."

The draconic snorted. "Thank you. I was trembling."

We rode in silence for another minute before I thought of something else to ask. "What does Chroma want, anyway? Why are the purple robes really here?"

"It is somewhat of a conundrum," Troilus Green admitted. "For centuries, she did not interfere with us. We never saw any sign that she even knew what we had done here. And then, four years ago, her agents began to make appearances."

"What have they done? Have they asked for anything?"

The draconic stared down the street behind the truck as we rolled along. "At first, they came as diplomats. They sought us out and only wanted to know how things were going. They inquired as to our successes, our economy, and so on. And naturally, we told them…"

"You bragged," I finished. "You couldn't resist."

A short nod. "Arrogance is, perhaps, a fault we are somewhat suscep-tible to."

My turn to snort.

Troilus Green sighed. "I suspect, however, that seeing our greatness only inspired greed on Chroma's part: greed for all that we've achieved here."

I frowned and wrinkled my brow. "But… isn't Chroma the mother of the dragons? Why would she want to take from you?"

"Familial relationships differ throughout this world's various species. Perhaps a human mother would not have the same ambitions or desires. I do not know."

I pointed at it. "That's the problem right there. You—if you really are Viridia—have been ruling over humans for a thousand years, and yet you don't even understand something as simple as a mother's love?"

"Why should I concern myself with human relationships? You're born. You reproduce. Or not. And you die. We have watched millions of you follow this cycle. To us, it appears no different from any of the other crea-tures who populate this world. Should I examine the family dynamic of the sheep we raise outside the cities?"

I closed my eyes and took a deep breath through my nose. I would not let him antagonize me. But the thoughts persisted. My sword was right there. And all of this power made me feel… invincible.

The truck slowed and came to a stop. I opened my eyes as Troilus Green leaped to the ground, robe fluttering. I followed him down before looking up. The Emerald Ascendancy loomed before us in all its magnifi-cence. "Ah. Here again," I muttered.

"That's right. You have been inside before." Troilus Green strode up the stairs toward the main entrance.

"More times than you know," I replied as I followed.

It gave me a sharp look before continuing. The Viridian Guard held the doors open for both of us. I have to admit I tensed up as I walked past them. Somehow, none of this felt real. I was walking into the Emerald Ascendancy alongside Troilus Green. Never in my wildest dreams could I have imagined this… even after two dragons came to live with us.

As we headed to the elevators, Troilus Green picked up the previous conversation. "Before long, the agents of Chroma were no longer willing just to ask questions. They made demands. They spied on us."

"They infiltrated your Viridian Guard."

It stopped before the elevator doors and looked at me. "You know this?"

"I talked with one earlier today. I discovered his presence within your Guard months ago." I shrugged, trying to make it seem like nothing.

Troilus Green nodded. "You will identify him for me later."

The elevator opened and we stepped inside. "So once they gathered information, they decided they wanted everything?" I prompted.

"So it would appear. Weeks ago, they informed us of the death of Incarnadine, and the new rule of the black dragons."

"I was there too." Yes, it was unnecessary, but I couldn't help myself. I wanted to irritate this monster. Part of me hoped it would lose patience and attack, giving me the excuse to kill it.

"You have traveled widely since our first encounter. Tell me, how long have you been working with Auric?"

"We first met around six months ago," I estimated. I honestly couldn't remember in the moment.

"Hmp. What was his connection to Onyx, then?"

"None. Onyx and Atramentous attacked his city."

"So I have heard. That does not preclude earlier involvement. If Onyx has shown us anything, it is the depths of betrayal."

"You can say that again," I muttered as the elevator doors slid open.

Troilus Green led the way down one of the familiar halls of the Ascendancy. I didn't think I'd visited this particular floor before. The elevator said eleven. I confirmed my thoughts when we came to a set of wide windows allowing for a view into several medical operating rooms. I would have remembered this.

Hunter and several other masked doctors huddled around a table where Lovat lay still. He looked so small. I put my hand against the glass and leaned closer. Hunter looked up to see us. He said something to one of the other doctors and came out. Pulling his mask down, he took a deep breath.

"What's happening?" I asked.

"We are working on setting all the broken bones… and there are a lot of them. We are keeping him alive, at least." He eyed Troilus Green warily. "Beyond that, I cannot promise. They have an experimental implant, based on yours. I am not ready to resort to that, but… it is close. He might not survive without it." He paused. "And he might not survive the implantation process."

"I did," I pointed out. "And my injuries were more severe."

"You were older than he is. And we had Loden." He sighed and shook his head. "I do not know if I can trust these cyberneticists. Even if he lives through the procedure, it may not work."

"Are you always this negative about your patients' prognosis?" Troilus Green asked.

"I am when a draconic tries to kill a child." Hunter glared at the monster beside me.

"What about Stacy?" I asked quickly.

"She will recover. She is severely dehydrated and malnourished, in addition to being covered in bruises and contusions." He pointed beyond us. "She is sleeping in a room down the hall. If you want to talk to her, it may be a while. I gave her a sedative while the IV works to restore her fluids." He looked me over. "What about you? I see blood."

I hadn't considered my own appearance. I looked down at my shirtless chest, covered in dirt, grime, and blood. "Just a few bruises and small cuts," I said. "I'll be all right."

"Turn around."

I obeyed, and Hunter grunted. "Your back is a collection of massive bruises. It looks worse than Stacy's. How are you still standing?"

"I feel fine." I shrugged. I felt better than fine. Auric's infusion drove away any sensation of pain. I wondered how long it would last. For now, though, I figured it best to keep that a secret. Let Troilus Green think me injured and worn out. It would give me an advantage if needed.

I glanced at the draconic, who carried its own share of injuries. "You might want to check this one over, though," I added. "Might need some help."

Troilus Green scowled.

"I will let you know if anything changes with Lovat," Hunter said. He hurried back into the operating room.

I took out my talker. "I need to update my people." I held the device up. "And I'm going to need back the one you took when you killed Mason. I haven't forgotten that."

"Nor have I forgotten how you killed Caesious and started all of this." The draconic spun and moved down the hall to speak with a waiting Guard.

I flicked the talker on. "Anyone there?"

Lainey answered right away. "Beryl! Are you all right?"

"I'm fine." I updated her on Lovat and Stacy's status.

"What do you want us to do?"

"For now, sit tight. But don't let your guard down." I watched my un-willing host down the hall. "Troilus Green promised Auric, but... I can't trust it."

"Of course."

We exchanged a few more words, then disconnected. Seeing me put the talker away, Troilus Green returned. "Your friends would be welcome and safe within these walls."

"You know I won't agree to that."

The draconic scratched at the edge of the cybernetic plate on its head. "As you wish. Shall we see to our prisoner now?"

"Why not?"

"We've taken him to the most secure location we have." We started back to the elevator.

"You have a dungeon below this or something?"

"No." It gave me an odd look. "My own lair."

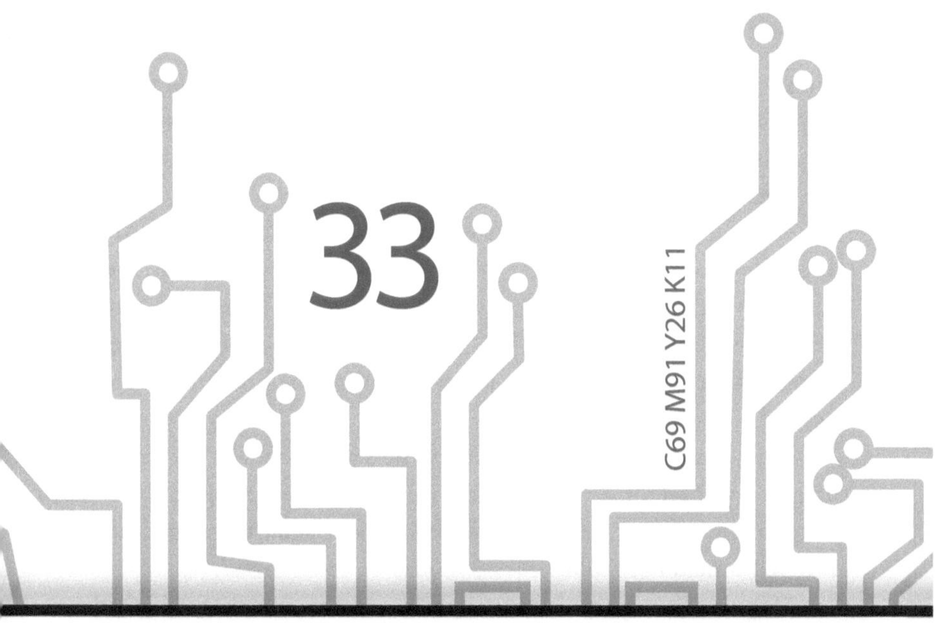

I wondered if it meant its lair as a dragon, or something new. After a series of halls and stairs, we entered a familiar elevator decorated in garish green shades. I remembered this one. Built for draconics, not humans, everything about it was a little bit taller and larger than normal. When Troilus Green pushed the button for the lowest floor, I knew where we were going: the former dwelling place of Viridia, the green dragon.

"This isn't where you keep all your prisoners," I said. "Worried they'll come for this one?"

"It's the most secure location."

"Secure? It's got a wide open entrance from above!"

The draconic spared me a glance. "It's secure."

Another thought occurred to me. "What about your other important prisoners? Where do you keep them? Where's Dusk?"

"Dusk?"

"The woman from Atramentous that you captured."

"Ah. That one. He asked for her return. I had little choice at the time."

For someone who claimed to be a dragon, Troilus Green didn't seem to have much sway with the other dragons. Something to keep in mind.

When the elevator stopped, we walked down the hall to the final door. I let the draconic open it without revealing I'd been here as well. I cast a quick glance to see if they'd repaired the damage Carl and I did to the lock.

They'd patched it up, but the repairs were obvious, as if done in a hurry. We stepped out into the vast cavern where I'd nearly died from Viridia's poison. Now that I'd seen Auric's cave, this one didn't seem as impressive, except in one regard: something new.

All of the spotlights and mirrors in the cave had been adjusted to aim at one spot in the exact center. Mounted on a massive pedestal, the white skull of Viridia gleamed, reflecting the light in all directions. I suppose it might have been blinding… but I think the power roiling around inside of me affected my eyesight, or let me adjust to the brightness faster than normal.

For a moment, I let myself enjoy the sight. This was the skull of the dragon I'd hated for so long. No one would ever see him again. Not in this form, anyway. Then I shivered. Without the dragon to provide heat, the cave felt unnaturally cold.

"So… you're saying that's your skull. Or was your skull?" I asked.

"We've been over this." Troilus Green shot me a look. "I am Viridia in every way that truly matters. The only difference is this body."

"Kind of a big difference, you know."

"Only to those who think the physical is all that exists."

I wanted to counter that I'd never seen anything non-physical, but… the resomancy destroyed that argument. Not to mention I'd admitted to Bice that I hoped some kind of spirit or life existed after the death of our physical bodies. Maybe there was more to life, or maybe there wasn't. I couldn't decide which side I wanted to be on.

As we walked nearer, I noticed the prisoner. A bald man hung suspended within the open jaws of Viridia's skull. Cords stretched all four of his limbs outward. He'd been stripped of the remains of his purple robe, and wore nothing more than an undergarment. His chin hung down. The closer we got, the more bruises I could see on his pale skin. A single Viridian Guard stood nearby, shockspear at ready.

"What are you going to do when more of them show up to take him back?" I asked.

"They could not possibly know where he is." The draconic stopped walking and looked down at me.

"I don't know. They seem to know an awful lot of things they shouldn't know."

"If they track each other, it is through the robes. And after your friend deactivated this one, we took the robe to our lab, not here."

I shrugged as we started walking again. I didn't trust any of this.

"Is he awake?" Troilus Green called.

The Guard tapped the prisoner with his spear without an electrical charge. The hanging man flinched. "Yes, sire," the Guard answered.

The draconic stopped and looked up. I did the same, though the weirdness of the situation kept bugging me. I hated that so many people were seeing me side-by-side with this monster.

"The mighty Viridia stands before you now," Troilus Green proclaimed. "Prepare yourself to answer my questions!"

The prisoner's chin lifted from his chest. "The mighty Viridia seems a lot smaller than was previously reported," he said in a gravely voice.

I stifled a laugh.

Troilus Green reached up with one of its cybernetic claws and cut a short gash across the prisoner's stomach. He tensed up, but didn't make any sound.

"Without your robe, you are completely helpless. Why prolong your torment? Tell me: what does Chroma plan with the black dragons?"

"Why don't you ask them?" The prisoner coughed, before adding, "Aren't you all brothers?"

I struggled against liking this guy. He'd tried to kidnap Kelly, I reminded myself.

"We have lived apart from Chroma all this time," the draconic went on. "Why try to change things now?"

The prisoner's steel-gray eyes shifted to look at me. "Him."

Troilus Green didn't react. "Cease from your attempts at humor. This human could not be the cause of something so monumental."

"He killed Caesious. Changed everything." He nodded to me. "Beryl Godslayer."

"They're not gods," I answered automatically.

"No, you're right," he agreed, to my surprise. "But Chroma is."

"Chroma is a dragon, and we've proven dragons can be killed. They can't be gods."

"Chroma is so much more than that." He paused, wincing as a shudder ran through his body from pain or the cold or both. I shivered again myself. "She is... glorious beyond our understanding. Her power cannot be measured."

"What color is she? Purple?" I don't know why I asked, but the question popped into my head.

"Color?" His brow furrowed. "I don't… what do you mean?"

"You've never seen her, have you?" Troilus Green asked in an almost hushed voice.

"I have never… been worthy enough to lay my eyes on her magnificence."

Troilus Green snorted. "What nonsense."

I wanted to slap back at him with reminders of some of his own religion's nonsense, but the topic bothered me. "Wait. What difference does that make? Don't you have images? Paintings? Statues?"

"It is forbidden to make images of the almighty Chroma."

Fewmets. This almost made the priests of Viridia sound sane.

"What's your name?" I tried.

"I gave up my name when I entered Chroma's service."

"Right… but people still have to call you something, don't they?"

"I am number four hundred thirty-eight."

"You're a number. That's not very convenient." At the same time, I almost took a step back. Over four hundred of these guys? If they all showed up at once, how could we possibly stand against them, even with Loden's weapons?

"This is pointless." Troilus Green punched the prisoner in the stomach and left him gasping for air. "You speak of Chroma's power! Where is it then? Where is the evidence of her power? Why would she let you be captured and treated like this if she is all powerful?"

"I am… tested…"

"You think she's letting this happen to you?" I exclaimed. "To test you?"

"I am… zealot…"

"Zealot? Is that the name for your band of purple robed numbers?"

"He means he's a fanatic for his worship and service to Chroma," Troilus Green said. "Although, it's as good a name for them as any."

It's a step above calling them the "purple robed numbers," I supposed.

I winced as Troilus Green reached up and cut a gash across the zealot's forehead. The blood flowed down into his eyes. "What good is that going to do?" I demanded. "If he's a religious fanatic, he's not going to tell us anything."

"Perhaps not." The draconic looked down and smiled at me. "Or perhaps his devotion has its limits. I, for one, intend to find out."

"I don't have to watch this." I turned on my heel and took a step.

"Beryl Godslayer!" The prisoner's voice rang out louder than he'd been talking so far. I turned back to look at him. He struggled for a moment to regain his breath after his exclamation. "You… started all of this, and now… you dare ally yourself with this… abomination?"

"We're not allies." My eyes narrowed.

"You wish to know what is coming? What Chroma is going to do?" The zealot pulled at his bounds, stretching his arms tight and arching his body. Every muscle in his body looked tense, strained to its limit. He jerked his head upward and cried out: "Look to the west! The towering shield will guard no more! Chroma, light of the world, brings her light to those in darkness! The Circle. The Circle… will fall!"

His body slumped, going limp. His head fell to his chest. Blood trickled from his forehead and dripped from his nose and chin, spattering on the dragon's lower jaw.

Troilus Green reached up and grasped the zealot's chin. He lifted the head up and turned it from side to side before releasing it again. He shook his own head and looked back at me. "He's dead."

34

"Fewmets!"

Troilus Green looked at me. Someday, maybe I'd figure out the draconic expressions. I couldn't tell if it was aghast or amused at my language choices.

"You said yourself we wouldn't gain anything more from him. Why so upset?"

I pointed at the dead zealot. "They took someone I want back. I was hoping to talk them into making a trade: their man for ours."

"A hostage exchange." The draconic nodded. "Perhaps we can still accomplish that. Where can I find the agent you mentioned within the Viridian Guard?"

I hesitated, but couldn't see any reason not to reveal it. "His name is Pine, and he's at station number four."

Troilus Green spoke with the remaining Guard and sent him running. "We'll seize him, if he hasn't already fled."

I almost didn't hear. My thoughts were busy with the zealot's last words. "What do you suppose he meant?" I looked back at the dead prisoner.

"Fanatical nonsense. It may not mean anything."

"I don't know." The west side of The Circle would be the side running from the red cities down past Caesious, all the way to Atramentous, a very long stretch. Could "the towering shield" be the mountains themselves?

Had Chroma found a way through? No, that didn't make sense. Of course there was a way through. Otherwise, Lainey and her father wouldn't have come, not to mention the purple robes—or zealots, as I now thought of them.

"If the mountains don't guard us any more, then… what?" I looked to Troilus Green. "You once told me you'd seen beyond The Circle. Have you been there?"

"In one of my earlier lives, I climbed the mountains." The draconic's voice came slower than usual. "When there weren't so many of you humans to control, I had more free time. I'd heard the stories from Viridia, but wanted to see with my own eyes. I found a narrow pass between two of the peaks and stepped through to the other side."

"What did you see?"

"It was… not much different from what I saw on our side of the mountains. Plains. Hills. Cities."

"Dragons?"

"I saw no dragons that day."

"But you say you're Viridia too," I pressed. "Do you remember seeing all of it… before you came here?"

Troilus Green lowered its head. "We were so very young when we came here, seeking the power beneath the ground."

Something about that nagged at the back of my thoughts.

"How well do you remember the first five years of your life?" the draconic went on, lifting its head to look at me. "I am over a thousand years old. If an eighty-year-old human cannot remember much of the first five years… by comparison that is over sixty of your years for us."

"You can't remember the first sixty years of your life?"

"I am not saying that. I am saying that those early memories are vague and… not very clear. It was so long ago." It looked up at the skull again. "Caesious commissioned his priests to write a record of those days. I didn't see the point at the time. It would be helpful to have that record now."

Oh. "You mean the Cerulean Books of Lore?"

Once again, the black eyes turned on me.

"Right. So… I stole them. But Incarnadine destroyed the first and oldest one, so I didn't get to read that."

Troilus Green snorted. "You seem to have been everywhere."

"Auric was going to tell me more about it, but now he's dead. And

Am—" I broke off.

"Amaranth? You know where she is hiding?"

"I… think I'd like to go back to see how the patients are doing by now."

The draconic ground its teeth together. The sound assaulted my ears like fingernails on a chalkboard. Ouch. Troilus Green stalked to the door, which opened automatically for it. We didn't talk during the elevator ride and walk back to the medical facilities.

Seeing us, Hunter emerged from the operating room. "It is not good," he said at once. "We are going to have to try the implant."

"Do you have everything you need?" Troilus Green asked.

"Your people jump to obey my every request. I am assuming it is because they are that terrified of you." He shrugged. "For now, it makes things efficient, anyway."

"What are his odds?" I asked.

"Not good at all." Hunter hesitated. "I told you he might not survive the operation. I cannot even say he has a 50-50 chance." He sighed. "At least I got a good night's sleep before being yanked up by a dragon and flown here inside a metal fist. This is going to be grueling."

"How long?"

"Six hours at the minimum. And he will be in mortal danger for every minute of it."

I swallowed. "Then we'll stay out of your way."

Hunter nodded and headed back inside. I took another look at the small figure lying on the bed inside. "He can't die," I whispered.

"The boy is stronger than most," Troilus Green said. "I think your doctor is overly pessimistic."

"You shut your mouth," I snarled. "You did this to him."

Troilus Green did not answer for a moment. "I suggest you go see your other friend. I will leave you now. I have other work I must do."

"Fine. Go oppress someone else." I marched down the hall in the direction Hunter had indicated. It took me a few minutes, but I found Stacy's room and slipped in. Her bruised face and arms provided a stark contrast to the bright white sheets. She stirred when I entered, but didn't open her eyes.

I settled into the only chair in the room. When I rested against the chair's back, my own bruises made their presence known… but still not as painful as it should have been. Auric's final gift continued to work on me. If things were normal, I should be completely collapsing into the chair, exhausted. Instead, I wondered if I'd ever need sleep again.

"The Circle will fall," I muttered. The last words of Caesious had been echoed by the zealot. Did they both mean the same thing?

"It better," Stacy murmured. "After all of this."

"I didn't know you were awake!" I got to my feet and approached her bed.

"I'm not. Not really." She kept her eyes closed, and her voice sounded a little slurred. "I'm not alive either."

I stopped beside her. "Stacy, I'm… I'm so sorry…"

"Shut up."

"Oh. Um, okay. Sorry."

She yawned and then whimpered. Opening her mouth wide had to hurt with all those bruises. "Knew what I was gettin' into," she mumbled. "Not y'r fault."

"But it is. I got betrayed again. And you suffered because of it." Saying the words reminded me of Basil. I needed to track him down and… what? Something. I don't know.

"You can read people's thoughts then?"

"Uh, no…"

She cracked one eye open a little bit to look at me. "Then it's not y'r fault. Shut up. And find a shirt."

I smiled. "Right. It's, uh, good to hear your voice. Get your rest. I'll make sure you're safe."

She made a little snort and closed her eye. "Y' can't even keep yourself safe…"

"Sometimes I do all right." I stepped back. "Go to sleep."

"Wait."

I leaned back.

"Still with Lainey?"

I laughed out loud. "Yes. We're good."

She nodded her head a tiny bit. I waited to see if she had anything else to say, but nothing more came. I went back to my chair.

Even with everything happening, and her own injuries, Stacy still wanted the personal gossip. She would make it through this, I was sure, but she wouldn't be the same. She couldn't go back to acting, not unless we won and everyone became free. She also wouldn't be able to spy for us any more. Of course, at the rate things were accelerating, espionage might not be as important any more. We needed spies outside The Circle now. Although now that I thought about it, there were things we still didn't know. Where was Onyx, for instance? We'd last seen him attacking the city of Auric, but he hadn't shown up since. Auric hadn't seen him through the orb for quite a while either.

The talker buzzed at my waist. I stepped back out into the hallway before answering it. "What's happening?"

Kelly's tense voice answered me: "Beryl! They're here! The purple robes are here!"

I froze. How had they known? How— Why bother asking? They knew way too much

"How many?" I hurried down the hall, calculating how long it would take to get outside the city. If I boosted myself and ran the whole way… it would still take far too long.

"Six," Kelly answered. "No, seven. I didn't see that one. They're surrounding us, but not moving closer… yet."

Weapons. Kelly still had the baton she'd used against the last one, but… I'd only brought three of those with us. Lovat had taken one, so no telling where it might be now. And the third… hung from the right side of my belt.

If I couldn't get there in time to help, and they didn't have enough weapons… only one other thought occurred to me. "Tell them I want to talk to them!"

"What?"

"Tell them Beryl Godslayer wants to speak with them! If they agree, give them the talker."

"Okay. Hang on."

The talker went silent. I paced back and forth in the hall. Three times, I started down the stairs. Every time, I came back up. I couldn't abandon Lovat and Stacy to Troilus Green, even with Auric's instructions. But neither could I abandon my other friends to the zealots.

At last, the talker crackled again. "You have become tiresome, Beryl Godslayer."

"You were tiresome by the second time I saw one of you," I countered. "What do you want now?"

"You took one of ours. Twice. And you still hold one. We will be taking your friends now."

"Those friends, with their special weapons, are why we captured one of yours! You don't stand a chance against them."

"Then I suppose we'll find out if that's true."

"Besides," I added in a hurry, "you took one of my friends first! You started all of this."

"We did not."

"Then where is Carl Roberts?"

A long pause followed the question. I guess they hadn't considered that. Finally: "Roberts belonged to us from the beginning. We merely took him back."

"He was my friend and the father of my best friend, and you took him away! Return him, and then we can talk about your man."

"You wish to do a prisoner exchange?"

"It's something to consider." How long I could keep them from learning their man was dead? That might be tricky.

"We would need assurances."

"Well, you're not getting any." I let that sink in a moment, before adding, "Think about it. You know we took down one of your men and captured him. And it wasn't me that did it. In fact, it was the girl who handed you this device. Any one of my people can now do the same thing. You can't assault them, and you can't assault Viridia looking for your man. So you have to make a deal."

"You underestimate us."

"Maybe I do. I guess it depends on how much you want to risk."

Another long silence followed. I wondered if this zealot was making the decisions himself, or discussing it with the others.

"Such a trade would have to take place at a neutral location. Not in or near this city."

"Not in or near one of the black dragon-controlled cities, either."

"As I said: a neutral spot."

"Fine." I smiled to myself. "How about… on the west side of The Circle. We were going to be heading that way soon, anyway."

The silence lasted even longer this time. I could only imagine what he might be thinking. Did I learn something from their man already, or was my reference to the west side a coincidence? I didn't wait for him to respond.

"Make it about halfway between Caesious and Incarnadine."

Again, silence. Now I second-guessed myself. Had I gone too far? What if I'd just named the exact spot where they were doing whatever it is they were doing? Or were they plotting a way to ambush me? I mean, I was plotting a way to get Carl back without giving them what they wanted. And of course, I couldn't give them what they wanted. But they didn't know that.

"Your terms are acceptable," the zealot said at last. "The timing is the only question remaining. As you might imagine, we are most anxious to recover our companion as soon as possible. How soon can you arrive at the designated location?"

That was an issue. We could ride the trains to the Hub, but even from there, it was a very long walk to the mountains. But a crazy idea popped into my head, and I grinned. This might be fun.

"Four days," I said. "We'll be there in four days, probably the evening."

"We will be waiting."

"Just in case," I said quickly, "my plan for travel doesn't work out, it may take a while longer. But we will leave tomorrow."

"We will be waiting."

"Good. Return the talker to my friend."

I waited until I heard Kelly's voice again: "Beryl? What was that?"

"Are they still there?"

"Yes, they… oh, wait. They're…"

"What? Vanishing?"

"Yes! I mean, I know the one we fought disappeared, but this… Wow."

"Good. They won't bother you again. At least I don't think they will." I considered the situation for a few moments. "I need to work some details out, but I need everyone ready to move tomorrow. Some of us will be going on a trip, and some staying here."

"What kind of trip?"

"I'll tell you in the morning. Like I said, I need to work something out with the green one here."

"Okay. Anything new with the others?"

I told her what I knew about Lovat and Stacy, then promised to talk again in the morning. "Say goodnight to Lainey for me."

"Will do." Pause. "Caedan wants to know why you didn't want to say goodnight to him."

"Give him a zap with your stick. Talk to you in the morning."

I hung the talker back on my belt and took a deep breath. Now I just needed to persuade Troilus Green to give me a truck.

"What would you need a truck for?" At my request, the draconic pulled himself away from a conference with some dour-looking men in suits.

"I'm going to investigate the west side of The Circle. I'll need to take a train to the Hub, and then use a truck the rest of the way."

"Why not take the train to Caesious, then follow the track north to Incarnadine?"

I thought about it. "That would work, as long as I could disembark halfway. I could still use the truck after that."

"Why? How close to the mountains do you need to go? For that matter, why even leave the train? You can get a good look at the west mountains from the train as you go north."

"For one"—I ticked off my fingers—"I don't want to go anywhere near Incarnadine right now, because Onyx might be there. And two, I need a closer look. I think Chroma might be working on a way through the mountains."

"Why? Her agents are already here, and if she wants to come herself…" Troilus Green trailed off and cocked its head to one side. "Hmmm. Even I had difficulty surmounting the highest peaks. Perhaps in her old age, she cannot do so any more."

"If I weren't around, wouldn't you be sending someone else to scout it out?"

"Possibly. It wasn't high on my current list of priorities." It glanced toward the group of men. "Very well. I will arrange to have a truck loaded on a flatcar, and provide authorization for your journey."

"I already have that from Auric, but thanks." I turned to leave.

"You will be leaving the wounded here then?"

I stopped and looked back. "Yes. And someone will be here to guard them and let me know if anything happens while I'm gone."

"I gave my word to Auric. I will not break it."

I didn't find that very comforting. But another thought occurred to me.

"Oh, while I'm at it, I also need the body of the zealot."

"Whatever for?"

"This is one where you'll need to trust me." I left it at that and walked away.

On my way back to the medical area, I glanced outside. To my surprise, the sun was setting. I didn't feel a bit tired, but at some point, I should rest. I didn't know when I would have an opportunity to do so again.

I stepped into the elevator and pressed the button for the medical floor. The doors slid toward each other, but a gloved hand stopped them at the last minute. One of the Viridian Guard joined me and stood with hands behind his back, staring straight ahead. The doors closed again, and the elevator began rising.

Lost in my own thoughts, I almost didn't hear when the Guard spoke in a whisper:

"He's lying to you."

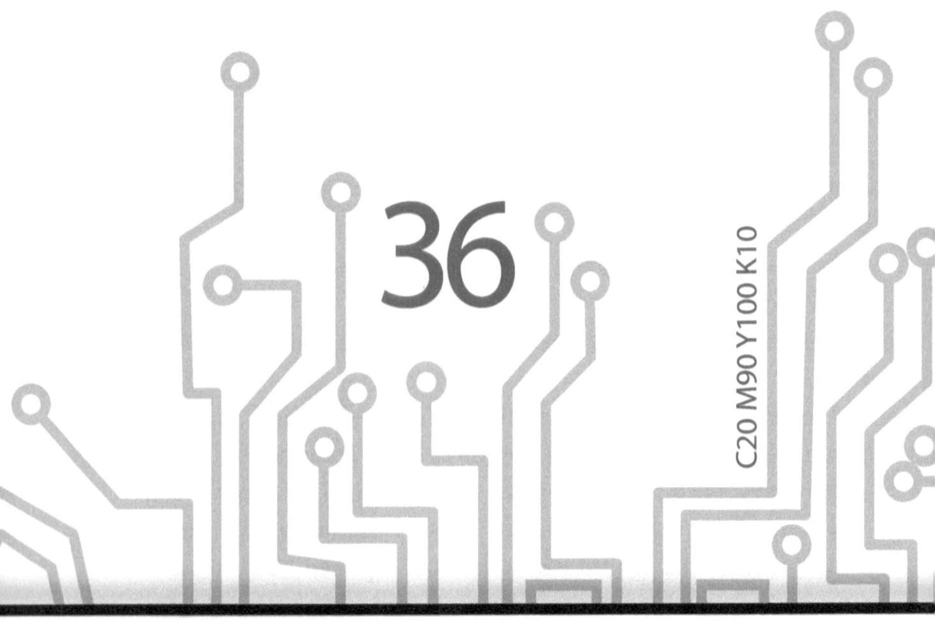

"What?" I looked at the guard, but he hadn't moved.

"Don't look at me," he whispered, his mouth barely moving. "Camera might be watching."

I glanced around the elevator, but didn't see any cameras. I returned my gaze to the moving digital numbers. "Why are you telling me this?"

"Some of us know the truth, even within the Guard. We serve that thing, but only because we have to."

"Okay, so what is he lying about?"

"I don't know exactly."

I rolled my eyes. "That does me no good."

"I'm just trying to warn you. What you do with it is up to you."

The elevator was almost to my floor.

"Look, I don't trust Troilus Green any more than I can throw him." I paused. Could I throw him? With enough boosts, maybe... Wow, my brain got sidetracked. "But I, uh, need more than just a warning that he's lying. I already know that."

The Guard took a deep breath. The elevator came to a stop.

"He's planning something with the kid. That's all I know."

The elevator doors slid open.

"I have to take a trip," I said as I started to step out. "I'll have someone here on guard, but it may not be enough. If you're serious about the truth, then you may have to help if something happens."

He didn't answer me. As the doors slid closed again, I added: "Depends on how brave you are, I guess."

I ran my hand through my hair and shook my head. How many others out there were like that Guard? Believing in our cause, but not willing to do anything about it? What would it take to make them rise up? I would have thought seeing Viridia with his head torn off would do it, but here we were. The more things changed, the more they stayed the same.

I found a chair in one of the unoccupied rooms and dragged it into the hallway outside the operating room. I didn't want to see the details of what Hunter was doing to Lovat, but I wanted to be near. I settled into the chair to wait.

I watched the slow movements of the people on the other side of the window. Not the most exciting view I'd had for a while. My eyes drooped.

"Finally!"

I blinked and jerked my head to the side. Lady Rust—Amaranth—stood beside me, wearing the light red dress she'd worn when I visited her home. Before I could process the scene, she sat on my lap and put her hands on my shoulders. "I thought you'd never fall asleep," she complained. The sultry smile on her face didn't seem to match her words.

"I'm asleep?"

She rolled her eyes. "Of course you are. I didn't warp clear across The Circle just to be with you."

Her warmth rolled over me. "Um, I don't—what's happening?"

"You're dreaming, idiot. Has no one told you we can communicate through dreams?"

Huh. Until this moment, I don't think I'd actually believed Dusk when she said Onyx appeared to her in dreams. "Oh. Right." Dusk also said her dreams of Onyx were... erotic. I swallowed.

Lady Rust leaned in closer, her chest brushing against mine. "I'm here because I need to know what's happening. Where is Auric?"

"I—he—um, it's... you're making it really hard to talk..."

She sighed and pulled back a little. "You're not cheating on your precious girlfriend if it's a dream, you know."

Somehow, I didn't think she'd see it that way. "Yeah, uh, everything went wrong here. Auric is dead."

She stood up abruptly. I started to relax, but she adjusted her dress and sat down on my lap again, straddling me. Why hadn't I gotten up too? Could I even move in this dream? She put her hands on either side of my face. "Tell me everything."

I swallowed again and told the story as best as I could. She showed no emotion at my description of Auric's death.

"He told me to tell Captain Tawn 'contingency two.' Can you pass that on for me?"

"Of course." She frowned. "Do you still have the device to use against Atramentous?"

"Yes. I'll go after him right after this trip to the west."

"Hmmm." She shifted again. Her face was right in front of mine. Fewmets. This was simultaneously exciting and intensely uncomfortable.

"You're the only dragon left that's not working with the zealots from outside," I said, trying to divert my own attention. "You should probably, um, stay hidden there. For now."

"Of course." She leaned in all the way and whispered. The warm air of her breath brushed against my ear. "It's not too late, you know, to change your mind about me. When all this is over, I can be a great help to you." She lowered her voice deeper in her throat. "Imagine what we can do together."

It was hard enough controlling my imagination right this minute.

Another hand shook my shoulder. "Beryl?"

I came instantly awake and jumped to my feet. I could move now!

"Whoa, whoa." Hunter backed up, palms out. "It is me."

"What did—how—" I shook my head and blinked several times. What a bizarre feeling. I'd been asleep, but came fully awake faster than I could ever remember doing. Auric's parting power surge still flowed through my body, waiting to be used. How had I even slept? And had that really been Amaranth? I paced a few steps and shook my head.

Hunter waited until I gained control of myself. "I figured you would want an update before I went to sleep myself."

"Yes, of course." I looked to the operating room. "How is he?"

"For now, he is alive." Hunter let out a breath, and his shoulders slumped. "I have done all I can."

I watched the small form on the table. "It's going to be a long process." My thoughts went back to my own recovery. "I know it's only been hours, but how soon do you think we can move him? I want him back at our place with Bice. I don't trust anyone here."

"It will be a while." Hunter shook his head. "I cannot take him away from the cyberneticists here until we are sure it is working. And for that, he has to be conscious and able to move."

"All right. Go get some sleep." I paused. "And… thank you, Hunter. He'd be dead without you."

"He would be dead without Auric." Hunter turned to go. "At least I can tell people I flew with a dragon…"

I didn't want to think too hard about Auric. If I did, I'd have to resolve my feelings, and I still wasn't sure whether to grieve or rejoice.

I found a clock to check the time. I'd slept for around three hours. Still a long way to go until morning. I paced the hall, trying to think through every potential problem. I needed to protect Stacy and Lovat. I needed to check on this threat from the west. I needed to kill the two black dragons and Troilus Green. I needed to decide what to do about Amaranth. This whole thing started with "let's kill all the dragons." I missed those days. Everything had been so simple: the dragons were bad, and we were good. How had it gotten so complicated?

At some point, I slept in the chair again. As far as I could tell, I didn't dream this time. I wasn't sure if I were relieved or disappointed. When I woke, I slipped into the operating room to take a look at Lovat. He lay face down on the table. I crouched down to look beneath at his face, exposed through a padded opening in the table. His face appeared as a combination of paleness and dark bruises. So much of the rest of his body was encased in casts. A bundle of wires emerged from the back of his head at the base.

I wanted to throw up. Though my implant gave me so many abilities, I never wanted anyone else to go through what I'd been through to get it. Lovat always wanted to be like me… but not like this. Not like this.

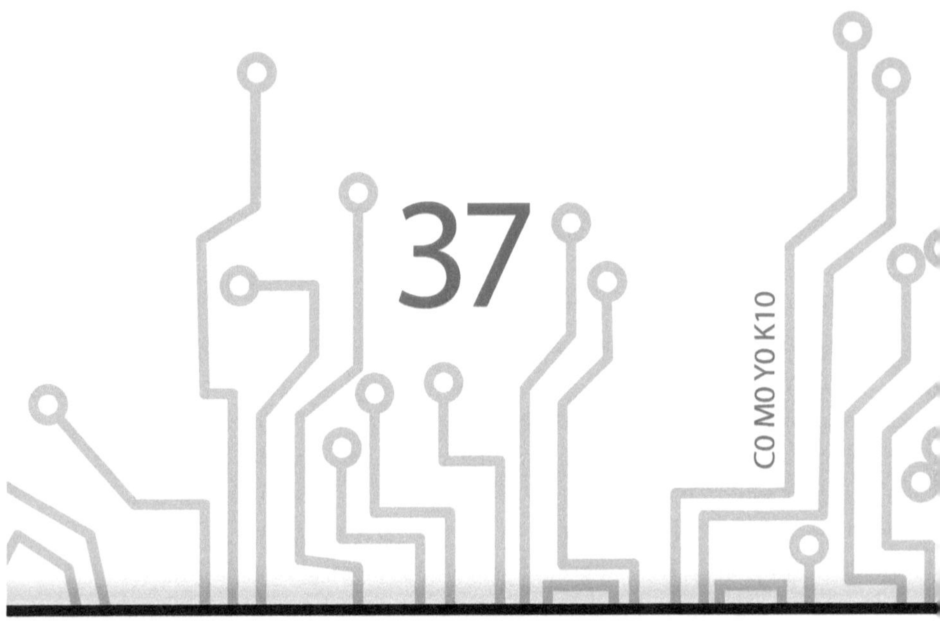

I left the room and called the others. Caedan answered, his voice a bit groggy. I'd probably woken him, but I didn't care. Enough waiting.

"Here's the plan. I want you and Kelly here, as soon as you can, to guard Stacy and Lovat. We can't trust Troilus Green, no matter what it promised Auric."

"Can do. What are you going to do?"

"Have Lainey and Jaden meet me at the train station. Yes, I know Jaden will freak out, but I need him. Tell him he'll get to drive a truck."

"Lucky," Caedan muttered before passing the messages on.

"No one should bother them before I get there, but if they do, tell Lainey to tell them Troilus Green approved their presence."

"With Glacier there, I don't think anyone will be brave enough to ask any questions."

"Good point."

We discussed a few more details before ending the conversation. I checked on Lovat, but found him unchanged from the night before. I gave his shoulder a gentle squeeze and hurried on to visit Stacy. She was awake and eating breakfast.

"Feeling any better?"

She cocked her head and an eyebrow. "Some of us take time to heal, Beryl. It's going to be a while before I even feel human again."

I updated her on the plan and promised to send Kelly as soon as she arrived. She responded by asking more awkward questions about my relationship with Lainey. I managed to avoid straight answers and said goodbye.

I paced the hallway until Caedan and Kelly showed up. We made sure they were recognized by the Viridian Guard, and then I gave them a quick tour of the floor where they'd be staying. "Stacy's waiting in that room for you," I told Kelly, pointing at the right door. Fortunately, Hunter emerged while we were talking, and I filled him in as well.

After giving them as much information as I could, I left the Emerald Ascendancy. I considered requesting a ride to the train station, but decided against it. I could use the exercise, since I would be riding on trains for so long. Besides, it gave me the opportunity to walk the streets of Viridia without fear. While I wanted to enjoy the experience, it only reminded me of how no one else could do the same yet. I developed a sour mood by the time I reached the station.

When I reached my destination, it didn't take long to spot Lainey and Jaden. It's hard to go unnoticed in an urban environment when a giant white-furred saber-toothed cat stands beside you. But someone else also stood with them: a tall draconic. Even though its robe hid the freshly-treated wound on its back, I recognized Scamandrius Green.

"What are you doing here?" I demanded.

The draconic turned to me with deliberate slowness before smiling.

"I am going with you."

"That wasn't part of the deal!" I glanced at the other two, making sure they were all right. Lainey looked unperturbed, as usual, but Jaden's wide eyes showed his fear.

"Nevertheless, it is what will happen now." The draconic shifted awkwardly. "I am not comfortable with this arrangement, but as always, I follow the word of my lord and master."

"Really." I tapped my fingers on my thigh. "I remember when Troilus Green reported to you. I watched it happen once."

"Regardless of the past, he is now Viridia. I do not question his orders." Scamandrius Green pointed at a train waiting on the next track over. "The truck and the body have been loaded. I go where they go. Shall we board at this time?"

"You go on ahead. I need to speak with my people."

The draconic gave a short nod, then moved away. I noticed it walked with a slight limp, thanks to the injury I'd given it the day before. I turned to the others. Lainey almost knocked me over with a sudden embrace.

"Hey, I'm happy to see you too." I couldn't hold on to the bad mood with her in my arms.

Glacier uttered a short yowl that I took for a greeting. Jaden took a deep breath and shook his head. "Man, I thought we were going to have to fight that thing." He pointed after the draconic. "What are we going to do?"

I pulled my face away from Lainey's shoulder. "I guess it won't matter in the long run. We're coming back here after this trip anyway. Let it spy on us."

"I'm not worried about it spying," Jaden said. "I don't want to be killed and eaten!"

I gestured. "Have you seen what condition it's in? I could take it down easy. So could Glacier. It almost seems like Troilus Green sent it along as a punishment for failing yesterday."

"That doesn't make me any less nervous."

"So… where are we going?" Lainey asked.

"Let's talk in the train."

"Okay. Here's your bag."

I picked up the large duffel bag she indicated. I hadn't told her to bring this along, but I'm glad she did. This trip might take us to different places than we planned. The contents of the bag might prove useful along the way.

I took a quick look at the truck on the flatbed and made sure the body of the zealot had been loaded in the back. Scamandrius Green led us to a passenger car, then left us alone, to my relief. I didn't want that thing listening in to our conversations.

"All right, let me explain what's happening…" As the train started up, I filled Lainey and Jaden in on everything I'd seen and heard. When I was done, I turned to Lainey. "Does this make any sense? Do you think they could be forcing a new way through the mountains somehow?"

"Anything's possible," she said slowly. "When my father and I came, the journey through the mountain pass was extremely difficult and dangerous. They certainly couldn't bring many people through that way."

"But could they make it easier somehow? Cut a tunnel through the mountains, maybe?"

"I just don't know."

I tried to imagine what kind of power could cut through a mountain. Some kind of enormous drill, perhaps? Or maybe they could use explosives, like those Auric had used to threaten the other cities. Onyx had destroyed them and heavily damaged the Hub. Unless he kept one or more of them for himself… With that thought came another: did more of those explosives exist? If so, who controlled them now, with Auric gone? I would need to talk to Taizong Gold and Captain Tawn about it, once we were able to return to our base.

We'd used these train cars multiple times before, but never with so few. Jaden found a place by himself up near the front of the car. I think he fell asleep within the first hour of the trip. Glacier stretched out in the aisle, blocking any traffic, even if we'd wanted to walk around. Lainey and I sat close together near the back. I enjoyed the warmth of her presence, but… she wasn't as warm as Lady Rust had been in the dream. Was that good or bad?

"You're tense," Lainey observed. She squeezed my forearm. "It's like you're about to explode."

"I feel that way." I told her about Auric's final gift. "It's like he fully charged up my battery."

"That's so cool. So no matter what we run into, you'll have the energy you need, right?"

"It feels like it."

She smiled. "And maybe not have to sleep for two days afterward?"

"That would be nice." I chuckled.

"Do you really think we can get my father back?"

"We're going to try. Unfortunately, I'm sure the zealots are expecting us to return their man alive. I'm just hoping Carl is there, and we can rescue him anyway."

"So you're going to double-cross them."

"Sort of. I never said he was dead or alive."

"I kind of think they're expecting alive."

"Yeah, well… nobody really gets what they want."

Lainey snuggled in closer. "You've got me, don't you?"

She had a point. I leaned in and kissed her. Lady Rust's face as she sat on my lap popped into my mind, and I pushed it away. Lainey was real.

Lainey was human. And I loved her.

A few minutes later, I tried to shift my position and ran into one of the seat's arms. "Why can't we ever find a comfortable place together?" I grumbled.

"Someday," Lainey promised, "we'll find somewhere comfortable."

"And then what?"

Her eyes twinkled. "You'll have to wait and see."

I swear: even with all the power roiling around inside me, my heart skipped a beat or two.

"I don't deserve you," I said.

"What do any of us deserve?" Lainey shrugged. "If we only got what we deserve, I think the world would be far more miserable than it already is."

That was not a pleasant thought.

There's not a lot more to tell about the trip. Both Jaden and Lainey showed interest when we traveled through the Hub, and both stayed glued to the windows as we passed through Caesious. I didn't blame them. Out of all the cities I'd seen so far, this one might be the most beautiful, with its river, bridges, and blue spotlights. Certainly, it topped Viridia's concrete. We stopped briefly at the train station in the blue city, reminding me of when I met Caedan. I pointed out the waiting room where we'd fought.

"How did you convince him to join you?" Jaden asked, having never heard the story.

"I took him hostage."

Jaden snorted. "At least you gave me a choice. Sort of."

A low rumble shook the car. A bigger train must have passed us.

"I wish I'd had more time to visit Caesious before now," I said.

"Why is that?" Lainey asked.

"We've found more friends from this city than any other, except Viridia. I guess that makes me want to know it better. You know, to see where Caedan and Peri and Cobalt and the others all grew up."

Moments later, our car started moving again, changing direction and heading around the outskirts of Caesious toward the north. We had just crossed the river again, leaving the city, when Scamandrius Green crossed into our car. Glacier stood and growled.

The draconic lifted its hands, palms out. "I just came to tell you the engineer has orders to stop in the approximate center point between the cities. Is that accurate?"

"Yeah, that's fine," I answered. "Anything else we need to know?"

It paused. "Did you feel the train shake back at the station?"

"Sure. It wasn't much."

"Some Cerulean Corps troops informed me that the earth has been shaking like that several times a day for the past week."

"Earthquakes?" Lainey asked.

Scamandrius Green nodded.

That didn't sound good. I'd heard about earthquakes during my Learning Years, but they were supposed to be ultra-rare events. No one could remember one within The Circle, that I knew. But if anyone had a long memory… "Has that happened before?" I asked the draconic. "Do you remember earthquakes in The Circle during any of your lifetimes?"

"I do not."

No way this could be a coincidence.

"If I'd had more time at our stop," the draconic continued, "I would have consulted with their scientists. No doubt they've been able to determine the epicenter of these quakes."

I had no doubt, either. The epicenter would be exactly where we were going. Chroma was up to something.

"I can almost see a road," Jaden said from behind the steering wheel, "if I squint and use my imagination."

"Whatever helps you get us there," I answered. I kept my eyes on the rear view mirror most of the time. Scamandrius Green, Lainey, and Glacier all rode in the back of the truck. I didn't like the arrangement, but nothing else would have worked. Neither the draconic nor the cat could sit in the cab, and we couldn't leave the two of them together without someone to keep Glacier calm. She really didn't like draconics. And I guess I was starting to like cats, after all.

After Lainey rolled her eyes at me multiple times, I finally turned my attention ahead. Though we still had miles to go, the mountains loomed large in our view. "The towering shield," I muttered.

"What's that?"

"Something our dead friend in the back said. 'The towering shield will guard no more.'"

"You think he meant the mountains? How can someone bring down a mountain?"

"They wouldn't need to bring it down. Just make a path through it."

Jaden wrinkled his brow. I had to remind myself that he hadn't seen everything I'd seen, like the explosions that killed Peri and destroyed Viridia's source. He didn't know the power that technology could bring to bear.

The truck jostled as it went over uneven ground. Jaden cursed and swung the wheel to the left. "Forget what I said about a road," he grumbled.

"Just do your best. No one's blaming you for the rough ride."

We fell silent and drove on. Jaden did his best, dodging as much of the difficult terrain as he could, but sometimes we hit some pretty rough spots. I had no idea if the truck were built strong enough to handle this. What did I know about trucks?

The mountains drew nearer. This particular part of the range looked much steeper to me, at least for the lower parts. I guess it did make it seem more like a shield, or a wall.

The truck came to an abrupt halt. I almost smacked my head against the windshield. "Jaden! What was that for?"

Jaden lifted one hand from the wheel and pointed. "I think we're here."

I looked off to the left where he indicated. A small hill rose up a couple hundred yards away, part of the growing elevation leading to the mountains. A single figure in a purple robe stood at the top of the hill, strips of cloth waving outward in the wind.

"Get us closer."

"Closer?"

"I don't want to have to carry that body any further than I have to. Do you?"

Jaden rolled his eyes and released the brake. He drove to the foot of the hill and came to a stop. "I, uh, I'll wait here while you guys talk, right?"

"Sure. No problem."

I got out and joined the others as they dismounted from the back of the truck. "What is your plan?" Scamandrius Green asked.

"I'm going to talk to him."

"Clever. They'll never see that coming."

A draconic with a dry wit? What next? I slipped the shockstick—not sure when I started calling it that—out and held it loosely in my right hand.

"Be ready," I told Lainey. She nodded, holding her rifle.

I climbed the hill, calling ahead, "Here we are! Are you the same one I talked to before?"

"I am. Where is my compatriot?"

"Your friend? He's back there in the truck. Where is Carl Roberts?"

"He is here." The zealot stepped to one side, revealing a second purple robe behind him. This one's robe and its strips were bound up together like a wrapped present or something. As I took a few steps closer, the bindings came loose, like a bunch of worms or snakes wiggling apart from each other. The figure in the robe stepped back, and Lainey's father stumbled into view, seemingly out of nowhere.

"Dad!" Lainey started up the hill behind me. I wanted her to hold back, but I couldn't really force her. Not when this was happening.

"Here he is," the first zealot said. "Now where is our man?"

"I told you. He's in the truck." I stopped a few feet away from them.

"There is only one person in your truck: the driver. And he is not ours."

"Look closer. There's a box in the back." I activated the shockstick, feeling a light vibration run through it along with its electrical charge.

"Beryl," Carl said, his voice somewhat hoarse, "I don't know what you're doing, but don't try to be smart with these guys. You don't know."

"We've learned a lot more since you've been gone, Carl. Leave this to me."

Lainey caught up to me. She started to move on toward her father, but the first zealot held up a hand to stop her. "Wait. What are you trying to do here? Why a box?"

"You didn't specify what condition your man had to be in," I answered. "I did the best I could with what the draconic left me. You know what Troilus Green is like, right?"

I imagined the zealot's eyes narrowing under his purple hood. "What condition is he in?"

I pointed with the shockstick. "See for yourself. He's all yours." I ran through several maneuvers in my head. Could I zap the first one and get to the second before he did anything to Carl? Could I move fast enough to take them both down? I channeled a few boosts to prepare my muscles.

"Lainey. It's so good to see you," Carl whispered. "Are you all right? Is—" His eyes widened as the saber-toothed white cat sauntered up beside her. "Is that Glacier?"

"She's grown—"

"Quiet!" the zealot snapped. "Beryl Godslayer! This is not what we agreed to."

"You haven't even looked—"

"He's dead!" That voice came from behind me. I swung around and saw a third zealot standing in the back of the truck, robe waving in the wind. Scamandrius Green stood watching. I could only imagine what Jaden was thinking.

"Enough. You failed to uphold your end of the bargain," the first zealot declared.

I spun back and lifted the shockstick. "I brought him here. It's not my fault he's dead. He screamed something about your dragon and then just died. We're taking Carl now."

"We are aware of your capabilities."

Another purple robe warped into view beside the first two. And then another. And another.

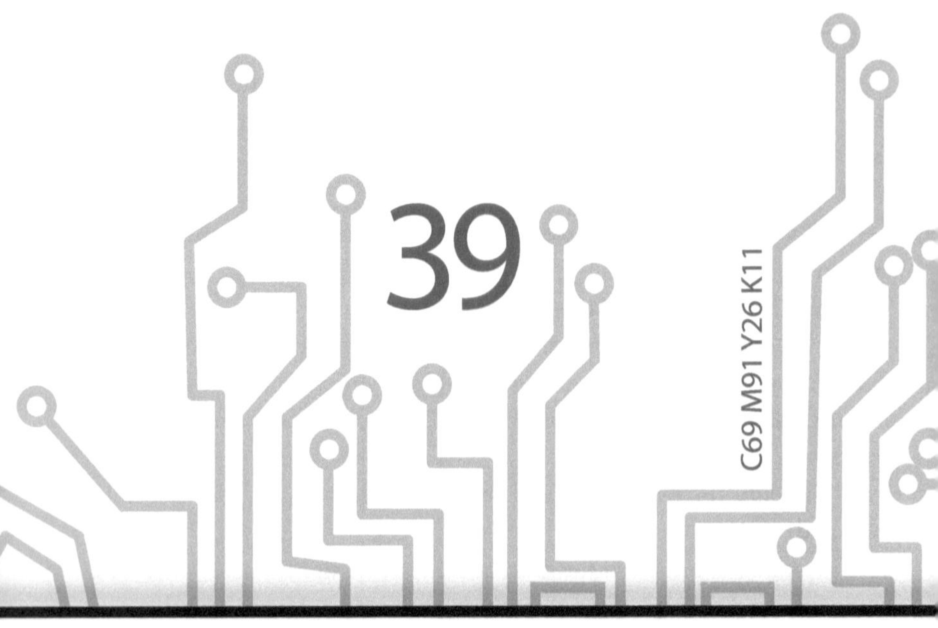

39

I attacked. I hoped it was the last thing they were expecting. I stabbed at the first zealot with the shockstick even as I sent boosts into both legs. With the extra speed, I reached the second one before he could react. Cold air rushed about me, but I ignored it. I seized the zealot with my cyb hand and zapped it with the shockstick as well. The purple robe collapsed harmlessly into normal cloth-shape.

Lainey shouted something, and Glacier roared. I knew they would be unable to affect the purple robes, but maybe they could distract them long enough for me to attack. The zealots didn't seem to carry any weapons. Other than their vanishing and the cold wind, what could they do to us?

They could vanish with Carl again. Or even Lainey.

Two of the zealots came at me from either side, even before I turned completely away from the one I'd zapped. Amidst all the flowing and writhing purple, I couldn't see what was happening to the others.

Carl shouted something that sounded painful.

Ice cold air whipped against my exposed skin.

Something struck my shoulder, a blunt impact. I lashed out with my shockstick, but didn't strike anything in return.

"Dad!" Lainey yelled.

A ferocious growl, but not from Glacier. Scamandrius Green?

I triggered the shockstick over and over, but couldn't seem to connect.

Another impact hit my lower back, and I stumbled.

Lainey shrieked.

I boosted everything, feeling power rush through me from Auric's last breath. I spun in a circle, swinging wildly. I don't know if the shock got anyone, but the stick itself struck something hard enough to knock it from my grasp. At the same time, part of my view opened up as one of the zealots lost his balance and tumbled down the hill.

Glacier pounced on that one, but couldn't seize hold of the malleable robe. The cat yowled in frustration.

"This is a pointless fight," one of the zealots said.

"We're at war!" I shouted.

The second zealot pulled away from me, restoring my vision. Two of them faced me, their robes fully intact and moving about. I saw no sign of the two I'd shocked. I spun quickly to see everything else:

A third zealot held Carl with arms of purple cloth.

Lainey glared at him, holding her left arm with her right hand. Where was her rifle?

Glacier moved behind Lainey, eyes on the nearest zealot.

Scamandrius Green threw the body of another zealot from the back of the truck. It struck the ground, unmoving. I saw a lot of blood.

"We did not intend a war with you," the zealot told me. "You could have continued your path without fighting us."

"You declared war on me the moment you took one of my friends!" I pointed at Carl.

"He belongs to us."

"No one belongs to anyone else. We're free."

"Freedom is a deception."

The wind picked up, blowing against me.

"Are you going to run away again?" I demanded.

"When next we meet, it will not go well for you." The air warped around the speaker. "We have avoided the use of weaponry against you and your people before now. That will end."

"You're cowards! You strike against others, but refuse to fight me directly!"

"The one who uses his capabilities to their maximum benefit is no coward." The speaker's robe folded in on itself as he vanished away. The air warped around the second one.

"Dad!" Lainey shouted.

I spun back around to see the air moving around Carl and his captor as well. I lunged forward with my cyb hand outstretched.

"Lainey!" Carl shouted as they began to fade. "Tell him! Tell him everything!"

I caught hold of purple cloth. A tearing sound assaulted my ears along with the wind and icy air. Carl and the zealot disappeared. I stumbled to a stop, holding a large piece of the zealot's torn robe.

For a moment, Lainey and I stared at each other, neither moving.

The door to the truck opened and Jaden leaned out. "Now what?" he called.

With twilight deepening, we made a campsite next to the truck. Scamandrius Green disposed of the two bodies: the one from the truck, and the one he'd somehow managed to kill. He didn't say anything about it, and I didn't ask. I didn't want the details for all that blood.

Lainey's upper arm appeared burned or something. She described how one of the purple strands had wrapped around her, followed by the most intense cold she'd ever experienced. "It's an ice burn," she said. I treated it and bandaged it with what little knowledge I possessed.

"He said tell you everything," she whispered while I wrapped the bandage around her arm. "Now?"

I shook my head. "Tomorrow. It's been a long day, and we need sleep."

We ate a few snacks from the truck's storage, and stretched out our sleeping bags. I suppose a guard would have been smart, but I didn't worry about it. Glacier would be enough.

After such intense usage of my boosts, I would ordinarily be very tired by now. But like the previous night, I felt full of energy. The power I'd received from Auric did not seem diminished in any way. I'd be surprised if I slept at all.

She invaded my dreams again. I opened my eyes to find Lady Rust lying beside me in a pink nightgown. She traced imaginary shapes on my chest with her fingernail. As in the previous dream, I couldn't seem to move as much as I'd like.

"Why are you here?" I demanded.

"Your talker things don't work over long distances. This is the best way we can communicate."

"We don't need to communicate."

She made a face of pretend outrage and tsk'ed at me. "Now, now. Don't you want your friends to know what's happening? Your man Bice is very concerned, since I told him about the boy. He's considering traveling to Viridia himself."

"Tell him to wait. I'll bring Lovat to him as soon as he can be moved."

Lady Rust shifted her weight, pressing against me. "I told Captain Tawn your message. He says he has something for you." She narrowed her eyes. "Maybe I have something for you too."

I closed my eyes. Then I opened them again, because closing your eyes while dreaming made no logical sense. "I need you to stay out of my dreams, Amaranth."

"In this form, I prefer Lady Rust, as you well know." She sat back on her knees. "Have you reached the mountains yet?"

I told her about our encounter with the zealots. While I talked, she shifted her legs out to the side and leaned on one hand next to my knee.

"We'll return in a few days," I added at the end, "so you can stop doing this."

"But your dreams are so intriguing. Men's dreams always are. They're so rarely… coherent."

That much was true. My dreams, when I could remember them, almost never made any sense.

"You never dream about your supposed girlfriend, for example."

"So what?"

"Just an observation. There is one face that shows up in your dreams a lot though." She gestured in the air, amidst a sudden swirl of smoke. "Who is this?" A face coalesced within the smoke: a young man with a green chromark.

"He's not one of your little band of rebels," Lady Rust went on, "and it's not Onyx's human form. A family member, perhaps?"

"It's none of your business." I knew the face, of course. It was the temple guard I'd killed while trying to rescue Bice. The sight of him, so clear and distinct, overwhelmed me.

"Are you sure?" Lady Rust leaned over my chest again. The smoke-face moved with her, floating only a few inches away. The guard's eyes stared into mine. His expression became pleading, as if he wanted to beg me for something. I groaned.

"Beryl?"

I jerked awake, and saw Lainey leaning over me, her hand on my shoulder. "Are you all right? You were moaning."

I sat up and ran my hands through my hair while I tried to control a sudden trembling. "It's okay. I'm all right."

"It doesn't look like it."

"It's Amaranth. Lady Rust. She keeps showing up in my dreams."

Lainey side-eyed me. "You were moaning while dreaming about Amaranth?"

My own eyes widened. "Oh. No. No, no, no! I mean she's talking to me in my dreams. The dragons can communicate that way."

"You've never mentioned it before." She folded her arms across her chest.

I groaned and put my face in my hands. "It's not like that, Lainey. She's asking how our missions are going."

"And that makes you moan."

I lifted my face. "Is there anything I can say that will make this sound less awkward?"

"Nothing comes to mind." Lainey climbed back into her own sleeping bag.

"I wish nothing would come to mine." I paused. "While I'm sleeping, that is."

"Go back to bed, Beryl." Lainey rolled and faced away from me.

I hate dragons.

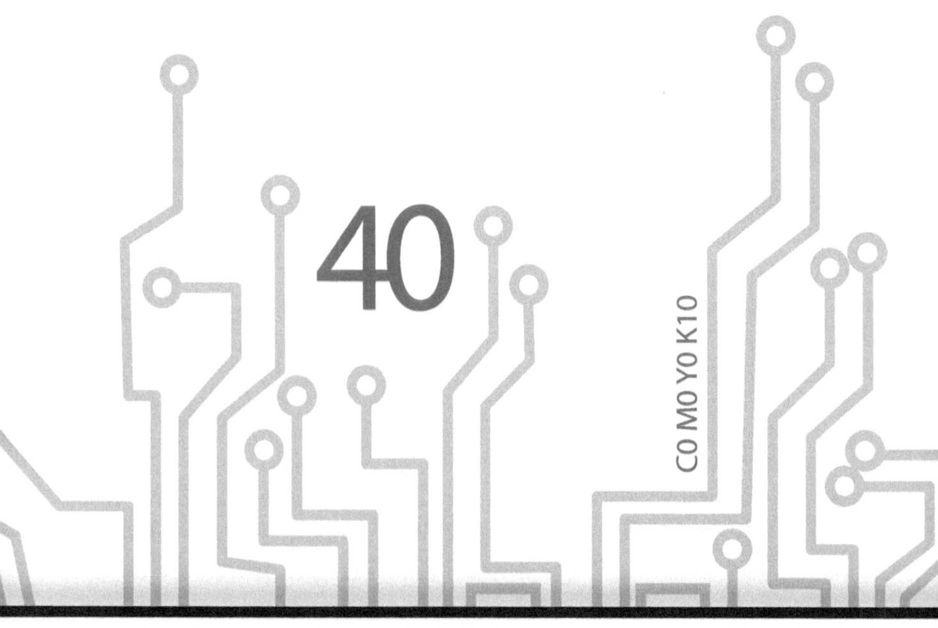

The next morning, Lainey did not seem her usual cheerful self. I told myself she'd just lost her father again, so it would be expected. But the dream conversation couldn't have helped.

"Do we head back to the train tracks?" Jaden asked.

"Not yet. Let's get closer to the mountains."

Scamandrius Green looked toward the towering wall of rock. "I see nothing unusual."

"Maybe you're not looking close enough." I was in no mood to deal with a draconic. I briefly considered stabbing it here and now, then telling Troilus Green that the zealots did it. But maybe not. My friends were still inside Viridia, within his power.

We loaded up, and Jaden obediently drove us straight toward the mountains. He did his best to dodge the uneven ground again, but the truck would not get us more than a mile or two closer. The earth sloped upward, dotted here and there with outcroppings and other rocks.

It wasn't long before Jaden brought the truck to a stop. "I don't think we can get any closer."

"We'll walk from here then." I picked up my pack from the floor and reached for the door handle.

"Maybe I should stay with the truck. Just in case," Jaden suggested.

I stopped. "What happened to you, Jaden?"

"What do you mean?"

"You were in the Viridian Guard." I pointed at him. "When we first met, you were fighting us. You were our prisoner, but you kept defiantly shouting your loyalty to Viridia. You acted like a soldier with no fear. But now… what happened? You're scared of everything."

Jaden didn't look at me, but his fingers on the steering wheel flexed back and forth. "I thought you were going to kill me that day. I had nothing to lose."

I waited.

"I just… being a soldier only got me hurt. Working with you got me nowhere. Everyone got excited, feeling hopeful when the dragon died. I thought things were about to change. But Viridia is worse off than it ever was. We accomplished nothing. And all we're doing now is running from one danger to another." He sighed. "I'm tired of it. I don't see hope any more."

"I understand."

Jaden blinked and looked at me. "You do?"

I nodded. "How do you think I felt when my friend—my best friend!—turned into a dragon and destroyed everything I'd worked for? When other friends died, disappeared, and were kidnapped? I lost all my hope."

"Then why are we doing this now?" He finally took his hands off the wheel. "You have a secret hideout. Why don't we all just go hide there and live away from everything?"

"Because hope returned." I glanced back at Lainey as she climbed out of the rear of the truck. "It's not a lot of hope, but it's there. Four dragons are dead, Jaden! Four! Could you even have imagined that a couple of years ago?"

"Yeah, but… now we've got these purple guys, and they're from outside, where things are worse?"

"Worse in some ways. Better in others. Look: I get it. It would be easy to go hide from everything. We could have our own little world, and pretend nothing else mattered." I shook my head and reached for the door handle again. "But we would know. We would know it's a lie. And I don't know about you, but that would eat me up inside. I couldn't live like that, knowing other people were in trouble, and I could do something about it."

I opened the door. "Don't stay with the truck, Jaden. Come with us. Let's be free: free from the dragons, and free from fear."

He shook his own head in response. "When did you get so good at speeches?"

I shrugged as I climbed out. "They made me be the leader. I had no choice."

"No choice at what?" Lainey asked.

"No choice in loving you," I answered. Actually, I didn't. I thought of it a couple minutes later. Instead, I said something like, "Gotta go on foot now."

One instant after my feet hit the ground, it shook. We heard a rumble, distant but distinct. The shaking of the ground was definitely stronger than it had been back at the city. We were getting closer to the epicenter.

After a little more hesitation, Jaden joined us. Scamandrius Green brought up the rear as we walked on toward the mountains. The draconic said little. Glacier moved around us, in front and behind, never staying long in one position.

"So…" I said to Lainey after a few minutes. "Tell me everything?"

She sighed. "That was before I knew you were talking to dragons in your sleep."

"Come on! I have no control over that."

"Are you sure about that?"

"Lainey…" What else could I say? Just when I thought I was starting to understand women, this happened.

"Fine." Her tone said "not fine." She went on: "Whatever. What should I tell you?"

"Um… he said everything?"

"You know I grew up in a city outside your Circle. In some ways, we're way ahead of you in technology."

I pointed at the rifle. "Knew that much."

"But in other ways, we're way behind." She glanced at me. "I'd never even heard about cybernetics until I came here."

I wrinkled my brow. "But the purple robes use it."

"Yeah, but we didn't know that."

"Who are they? The zealots?"

"They're the priests of Chroma. They enforce her will."

"Chroma. She really exists? The mother of the other dragons?"

"I didn't know she was a mother, either."

"Is she the only dragon on the outside?"

"As far as I know. I never saw a dragon until my father and I came here." She paused while I helped her over a larger rock. "No, not even Chroma. No one sees her, except the priests."

I started to ask a question, but she went on without waiting for me: "After my mother died, my father was hired by the priests. He was always somewhat of a traveler. Loved to camp out in the wilderness. I guess that's why they selected him. His job was to investigate the valley inside these mountains and report back to them."

"So they didn't know what was going on in here."

"No. How could they?" She looked back at the draconic following us. "If what you've been taught is true, then my best guess is that the dragons you know came here a thousand years ago, and she didn't know it. I don't know if they came to get away from her, or what."

Caedan's description of the dragons as "rebellious teenagers" popped into my head, but I didn't repeat it.

"I don't know why Chroma didn't go looking for them," Lainey went on. "None of it makes any sense to me."

"Maybe dragons don't care about each other the way we do," I suggested.

"Maybe."

"Carl—" I broke off for a moment, thinking about my words. "Carl told me your people were in a struggle for freedom too. Did he mean against Chroma and her priests?"

Lainey nodded. "I don't know much about it. I mean, I guess we're sort of freer than your people in Viridia, but not by much. The purple priests are always watching. And if anyone steps out of line, does something—or even says something—that's not approved, they show up and take them away."

"Like they did with your father."

"Twice now." She kept walking and didn't speak for a while. I had more questions, but I didn't want to upset her any more than she already was. Even so, she wasn't telling me much in the way of new information. No one had spelled it out like this, but I had surmised a lot of this myself.

"The priests are all the same," Lainey said abruptly.

"What do you mean?"

"Haven't you noticed they look alike?" She shot me another glance. "I mentioned it once already, when your friends were talking about genetics."

"The priests are messing with genetics?"

"They want to purify humanity," she answered. "Make everyone per-fect."

That didn't sound so bad to me.

"Of course, their definition of 'perfect' means 'all the same.'"

"What do you mean?"

Lainey stopped walking and looked at me. "They're all the same," she repeated. "All of them."

I shook my head. "I still don't understand. How are they the same?"

"They used genetics. I don't know how it works." She swallowed and watched Glacier bound off one rock onto another, before turning back to me. "They are all the same man. Every one of them."

"How is that possible?" Jaden demanded. I guess he'd been listening to us.

Lainey shrugged. "They all look like the high priest. I've seen him before, when he gave speeches. I'm guessing he's the first, and the others are all copies of him."

"You can't make copies of people!"

"I don't understand it," she said. "I'm just telling you what I see." She looked at me. "What you've seen now too."

I did have to admit: the zealots I'd seen face-to-face did look identical. It was… disconcerting.

Scamandrius Green caught up to us. "What are we doing here?" it asked. "I don't see anything unusual ahead of us."

I looked ahead. We were hitting the area where going on would mean some climbing instead of just walking. Some of the slopes ahead grew much steeper. The mountains truly began right about here. But as the draconic said, nothing looked out of the ordinary.

"What were we expecting to see?" Jaden asked.

"I don't know." I shook my head. "Something… like maybe a partial tunnel, I guess."

"This was a fool's errand," Scamandrius Green declared. "Let us return to Viridia."

"But we felt the ground shake less than an hour ago," I protested. "Something is going on!"

"If so, it is not something we can see or investigate here." The draconic turned to go back to the truck.

"Where's Glacier?" Lainey asked, looking around.

"She was just here…" I joined her in scanning the rocks and clefts around us.

"She must be behind some rocks," Jaden offered.

"Glacier!" Lainey's shout echoed off the rock walls ahead of us. "Glacier!"

"She's here somewhere," I said, but Lainey started forward again. "Lainey, wait!"

She ignored me and kept moving. "Glacier!"

"There!" Jaden exclaimed, pointing.

We all looked, ahead and to the right, as Glacier emerged into view. She looked back at us for a moment, then turned and vanished again.

"Glacier!" Lainey headed in that direction.

I sighed and looked at the other two. "You guys can wait here. We'll be back soon. I hope."

I followed Lainey up the rough terrain. She called for Glacier a few more times, then concentrated on the climb. We ascended higher than I'd expected. I offered my hand to help Lainey a couple of times, but she ignored me again. Was she still upset about the dream thing?

Glacier's head appeared above an outcropping just ahead of us. Before we could even say anything, she ducked back down again. Stupid cat. Why were we doing this? If we had just turned and gone back to the truck, Glacier would have eventually joined us. I didn't say this out loud, though. I figured I'd better watch my words with Lainey just now.

I stopped and let her go on ahead the last bit. I wouldn't be able to do much with Glacier, anyway. The cat never listened to me. I wiped sweat from my brow. It wasn't too hot for mountain climbing at this time of year, but the exertion made me warm enough. Plus, I think all that energy inside me generated its own heat.

Lainey climbed over the last rock in her way, griping out loud about turning Glacier into a fur coat. She stopped, standing atop the rock, staring down where the cat had disappeared.

"Beryl! You need to see this!"

What now? Did the cat get hurt or something? I climbed up after her. "Is Glacier all right?" I asked, hoping I sounded genuinely concerned. Lainey didn't answer, waiting for me to get to her. I pulled myself up on the rock and stood, looking down.

Glacier looked up at me from about thirty feet down, then bounded off to my left. I turned… and almost fell off the rock at what I saw.

Glacier had found an enormous cave entrance, hidden from our sight except from this particular angle. It cut into the rock of the mountain, sloping down into darkness.

"That… that's big enough…" I stammered.

"For a dragon," Lainey finished.

"What's going on?" Jaden called from below.

I waved to him and Scamandrius Green. "Come up here!" I called. "We found it!"

"Found what?"

I turned back. Lainey moved her head back and forth as she studied the descent below us. "Have you figured out a way down?" I asked.

"There's no easy way that I can see. Of course, Glacier can go just about anywhere."

I looked down. "I could jump down just fine, but we need to find a way for you and Jaden."

"Do we have a rope?"

I closed my eyes and mentally slapped myself. "We do. It's back at the truck." I opened my eyes and turned to go. "I'll run back. I can get there quickly."

"Flashlights too," Lainey called as I sent boosts to my legs and took off.

Boosting my legs and going downhill meant I was soon traveling at a very fast rate. I leapt from rock to rock like Glacier when needed and ran straight across the flat areas. It took only a few minutes to get back to the truck. Stopping without slamming into it proved a little more difficult, and I ended up a few dozen feet past the truck and had to jog back.

I found the rope in the back of the truck. I knew flashlights were in my bag, along with the claw launcher. That could definitely come in handy. I opened the bag, reached inside, then reconsidered. May as well take the entire thing, just in case. Who knew what we would find in the tunnel? As I zipped it shut, I caught a glimpse of Auric's electronic explosive device. I'd almost forgotten about it.

I sent a few more boosts into my legs and started back up. Ascending took longer, of course, but I was able to confirm my earlier thoughts: even knowing where the cave entrance existed, I couldn't see it. I angled off to the right, but it remained completely out of sight. Someone had done a fantastic job of camouflage.

When I got back to Lainey and Jaden, I discovered that Scamandrius Green had already climbed down. Big lizards with big claws can climb. Should have figured that.

I considered using the claw launcher, but the rope would be more practical for this spot. I tied it securely to a boulder and tossed the other end down. "Go ahead," I told the other two. "I'll untie it and climb down after you, so we can take the rope with us."

Lainey nodded and descended to the cave opening without difficulty. Jaden took a bit longer, but he made it as well. I untied the rope and tossed it down to the others. I considered doing just one jump down, but I would only be showing off. Instead, I boosted my legs for impact as I descended in a series of three quick jumps, bouncing off a couple of ledges. I landed next to the other two with a grunt.

"Show-off," Lainey muttered, turning away. Seriously? I'd been trying to avoid that!

Scamandrius Green called from further down. "The tunnel turns under the mountain down here!"

I handed flashlights to the other two. We made our way down to join the draconic. Glacier poked her head around the corner, then bounded over to join us also. Lainey scratched behind the cat's ears while grumbling at her.

"This is most definitely not a natural occurrence," the draconic announced.

"Someone dug this?" Jaden asked. "But it's huge!"

We walked into the passage, leaving the sunlight behind. Our flashlights barely reached the ceiling, and the width had to be at least the equal of the height. Again: big enough for a dragon to move through.

"Some places show evidence of tools, especially the floor," Scamandrius Green went on, "but a great deal of the rest does not. I am not entirely certain how this was accomplished."

"How do you dig without tools?" Jaden said.

I examined the walls, noticing how jagged and broken parts of them appeared. "Explosives?" I suggested.

"Conceivable," the draconic agreed, "but there is something more to it. Let us investigate further."

I stepped close to Lainey and spoke in a low voice. "Do you think this goes all the way through? To your home?"

"I don't know. How would I know?"

Everything about this tunnel screamed in my mind, telling me to turn back, leave while I still had the chance. No good could come of this. We knew the priests of Chroma, together with help from Onyx and Atramentous, were boring a tunnel through the mountains. Did we really need to know anything more?

I squared my shoulders and marched deeper into the tunnel.

42

The cave reminded me of the tunnels beneath Viridia and Auric… and yet they were all unique. Viridia's tunnel had appeared more natural, but the walls and floor had been worn smooth by centuries of the dragon's movements. The tunnel leading to Auric's chamber had been much smaller, clearly carved out by human hands. This one, though… In addition to Scamandrius Green's analysis, other things bothered me about it.

The smell did not become obvious until we'd walked for a few minutes. Glacier sniffed loudly several times before I noticed it. "What is that?"

"It is a… distinct odor," Scamandrius Green said.

"It doesn't smell quite natural," Lainey added.

"But it's—" I broke off.

"It's what?" Jaden asked.

"It's a little bit familiar." I frowned, trying to place it. My brain tried to make some kind of connection to burning, but that didn't seem right at all. I smelled no trace of ash or smoke. It was almost more of a metallic smell. I could taste it in the air as well.

The sun's light outside did not penetrate very far, and we soon left it far behind. Darkness descended around us, illuminated only by our flashlights. The tunnel stretched forward in a relatively straight line into the depths of the mountains, but sometimes jogged a little in either direction, adding to the jagged and broken impressions. It sloped down and up in equal measures, as far as I could tell.

Jaden wandered a little toward the left side of the tunnel, shining his light along its wall. "How far do you think this goes?"

"It could easily stretch five and a half to six miles or more," Scamandrius Green answered.

I turned toward the draconic, keeping my flashlight low to avoid shining in its face. "What makes you say that?"

"It's a simple matter of geometry, based on the height of the mountains and the angle of the exterior slopes. Anyone with even a modest grasp of mathematics could perform that calculation." The draconic's face looked expressionless, but I could see the condescension in its eyes.

"Are we going to walk through the whole thing?" Jaden wanted to know. "I know six miles isn't much of a hike for you, but…" He angled his flashlight directly up and followed it with his eyes. "I'm starting to think about how much of the mountain is above our heads."

"Don't think about it that way," I said. "We're just taking a hike at night in a rocky area." Great. Now that he'd said it, my mind couldn't help going there either. But instead of the oppressive force of thousands of tons of rock, I felt… something else. I tried to analyze it as I answered his question: "I don't know how far we'll walk. I'm just looking for some answers, I guess."

"What kind of answers?" Lainey asked.

"This place feels so wrong." I pointed my light ahead and watched it disappear into the darkness. "I get what Jaden's saying, but I feel something else. Not rock. Something… evil. Plus I want to know how they did this, and if it goes all the way through."

Now that I'd said it out loud, it did feel evil. I'm not sure how someone can "feel" something evil, but that's what I sensed: like some malevolent presence lurked above us in the darkness, watching, waiting… I shot my light to the ceiling again, just to be sure. Nothing but rock.

We walked on in silence for a while. Aside from the sounds we made, I heard nothing else. The air was still and cool. I noticed Lainey shiver. If I'd been wearing a jacket, I could have offered it to her.

"Missing your warmer clothing?" I asked.

She nodded. "Didn't expect to be going anywhere cold."

"Not as cold as the cave we first met in," I pointed out.

She smiled. Yes! I'd celebrate anything positive from her at this point. I didn't know how upset she still was about the dream thing, but I wasn't going to bring it up. "How long had you and your dad been up there before you found me?" I asked instead.

She glanced at me, her face full of shadows from the glow of our flashlights. "A few months. We'd come over the mountains through a narrow pass, and then worked our way around, observing the cities below. We traveled from Viridia around to Amaranth, at the least." She paused, shining her light on a bizarre chunk of rock that extended six feet out from the wall. It looked like it might break off at any moment. "We'd settled in that cave as our home of sorts just a few days before you crashed into the mountains."

"The walls are becoming more uneven. The floor as well," Scamandrius Green pointed out. "Perhaps they haven't performed as much work this far in."

"Who are 'they'?" Jaden asked.

"The zealots," I answered. "The purple robes. The priests of Chroma. One of them told us about this, and they're the ones who will gain from it."

"They wouldn't be doing it themselves," Lainey said. "They'd bring in other workers, maybe from one of the nearby cities: Caesious or Incarnadine."

"Since the black dragons rule them both now, it's likely," the draconic agreed. "They may bring teams of workers here, perhaps even from the cities' prisons."

"I thought you said this wasn't dug out," Jaden said.

"It wasn't. But I said someone worked here, smoothing things out, especially the floor. Here"—the draconic shined his light on the walls, highlighting rough spots—"they haven't done as much."

I noticed some crumbled rocks on the ground. We would need to watch our steps more carefully. At least we hadn't seen any holes or other tunnels so far.

I had no idea how far we'd walked, but more time passed before we came to a change. "Do you feel that?" Lainey asked. Glacier bounded ahead, leaving the range of our flashlights.

"Feel what?"

"The air… it's… a little bit clearer. Not as oppressive."

"Yeah," Jaden said. "It's almost fresher, like we were about to come outside."

"It's far too soon for that," Scamandrius Green said.

I shined my flashlight straight up. "I can't see the ceiling. We must have entered a larger space."

The others moved their lights around as well. "The walls both spread out from here," Lainey said. "And they look different. So does the floor." Ahead we could see pillars of stone rising from the floor, ranging in height from a couple of feet to far above our heads.

"This is a natural cavern," Scamandrius Green observed. "They must have broken through into it."

"How big is it?" Jaden wondered, playing his light across the various formations.

"We don't have enough light to tell," Lainey said.

"If everyone turns their lights off, I can see it," I said.

"You what?"

"I have night vision. Sort of. I discovered it back in Amaranth. Didn't I tell you that? After Bice and I had the accident...?"

Lainey narrowed her eyes. "Maybe."

Oops. I'd mentioned Amaranth.

"I can use my boosts to switch to a kind of night vision, but only if it's dark and I'm trying to do it," I explained. "If we all turn our flashlights off, I may be able to see how big this place is, and where it goes from here." I turned my own light off.

Lainey didn't say anything but turned hers off as well.

"Fascinating," Scamandrius Green murmured before its light went out.

"Don't take long," Jaden grumbled as he flipped his off.

I stared up into the darkness and sent a short boost to my eyes. The night vision should kick in within a few seconds... but I was nervous about what I would see. My hand tightened on my sword. Lainey said the air felt less oppressive, and maybe it did to her. But not to me. If anything, the sense of evil had grown when we entered this room. I shivered as a chill swept over my body. The feeling of standing at the brink of an enormous precipice filled my mind again, as if I were teetering on the edge, about to fall into endless darkness.

As my night vision kicked in, I remembered where I'd felt that before: when Troilus Green—or Viridia—turned his full attention on me. It was the feeling of being watched by a dragon.

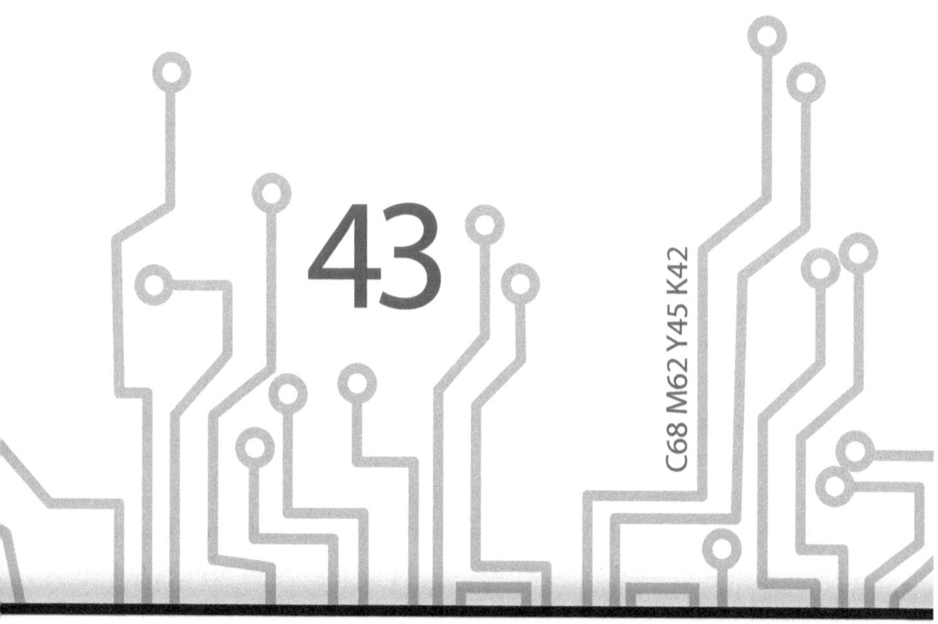

43

C68 M62 Y45 K42

I did not see a dragon. But neither did I see the full size of the cavern we'd entered. Apparently, my night vision had its limits as well. I wondered if I could combine it with my zoom vision somehow...

"Well?" Jaden's voice broke the silence. "What do you see?"

"It's enormous," I said, turning in a circle. "It reaches higher than I can see. But I can see the walls all the way around."

In the moments between their questions, I could hear something. It sounded like water dripping somewhere.

"Is it larger than Viridia's nest?" Scamandrius Green asked.

"Definitely. Larger than Auric's too." I peered across the chamber. "It does look like they've cleared the floor out somewhat all the way to the other side. I think I see another opening there." I also saw some odd shapes on the wall beside the opening. It was too far to make them out clearly. A white blur moved near them. Glacier.

"Then that's where we should investigate next," the draconic said, flicking on its flashlight.

I blinked rapidly, and my night vision disappeared. The rest of us turned on our lights as well.

"I thought I'd seen darkness before," Jaden said, "but that was dark. I mean, completely dark."

"I waved my hand in front of my face and couldn't see it," Lainey said.

"I'd heard of that before, but never, um, seen it. Or not seen it, I guess."

We started across the enormous chamber, our lights playing across odd formations, some whole and others broken. Something or someone had been here recently.

Scamandrius Green shined his light on a tall column broken off around twenty feet up. The shattered remains of it lay on the ground. "A dragon did that."

"You can tell?" Jaden's eyes grew wide in the flashlight glow.

I almost mentioned my feelings that a dragon was here, but changed my mind. Jaden was spooked enough; no need to really freak him out.

"Some of this is… beautiful," Lainey said.

I agreed. The formations, especially closer to the walls, were fascinating. My flashlight played across a short and wide column. The layers of flowing rock made it look like a short, squat little man with an enormous beard. Bizarre. And that was only one of many. Everywhere we looked, we saw pillars and even what looked like thin sheets of rock hanging from larger formations. A few columns stretched higher than our flashlights could reach. If it weren't for that nagging feeling, I would have enjoyed the tour.

Jaden stopped and stared at a shattered formation near our path. "It… makes me sad," he said. "Why did they have to destroy that one? It's not even in the way."

"It's in the dragons' nature to destroy," I said.

"So says the eyeblink who grew up in a world entirely created by dragons," the draconic said behind me.

I whirled around and glared at it. "And yet they could only do all that with the help of human slaves! What have they ever done alone?"

"Your arguments are pointless."

"Yeah, that's what you always say when you don't have an answer." I swung back into the path and kept moving. So much for admiring beauty.

At one point, we crossed what looked like a dried stream bed. A shallow impression crossed over our artificial path, running perpendicular to it. I bent to examine the ground.

"Liquid flowed through here," Scamandrius Green observed.

"Yeah. It's smooth, though. I kind of expected pebbles or something. That's what stream beds on the surface have."

"We're not on the surface. This world has a different set of rules."

World? Interesting choice of words. I panned my light left and right down the stream bed. I saw no sign of actual moisture in it, though we'd seen some on the pillars. Curious.

All together, it must have taken almost an hour to walk across the chamber. As we neared the other side, Glacier sat in the center of the path as if she'd been waiting. Lainey nudged her with a boot. "Move, you silly cat." Glacier got to her feet and sauntered ahead of us, tail high.

Scamandrius Green and Jaden reached the opening into the next tunnel and moved their lights back and forth around and into it. "It appears to continue in the same general direction as the previous tunnel," the draconic said. "Though I think it has more of a downward slope."

"Let's keep going then," Jaden said. "The sooner we reach the end, the sooner we can turn back and get out of here."

I let them lead the way. I paused at the entrance and looked off to the left. There were the odd shapes I'd noticed with my night vision. It looked like… crude stairs? I approached the first one and stepped up onto a short and rough platform. A few feet away, another platform rose a little higher. They appeared to continue on, higher and higher, spiraling up and around the chamber. My light couldn't find the end.

"Beryl?" Lainey called. "What are you doing?"

"Go on ahead. I'll be right there."

I waited until the others moved a little further down the tunnel. I turned off my own light and listened, standing alone in the darkness. Behind me, I heard a rock fall somewhere further down the tunnel. In the empty chamber, I heard the drips of water, but nothing else. I was about to turn to go, when one other sound caught my attention. Somewhere out there, a drip had been followed by a hiss. It wasn't a hiss from something living; more like the sizzle of something cooking on the stovetop. Bacon. We'd had some bacon back at Auric's underground base. I hoped the others didn't eat all of it before we got back.

"Beryl?"

"Coming now." I turned on my flashlight and hastened after the others.

This section of the tunnel turned out to be much rougher than what we'd traveled through so far. For the first twenty minutes of walking, it wasn't much different from the walk through the giant chamber. Someone had been busy clearing it out, but not to the degree they'd accomplished in the first half of the tunnel. After that, however, it became much rougher.

We could tell they'd worked on it a little bit, shoving chunks of rock aside to form somewhat of a path, but it wasn't much of one. The path wound its way through broken rocks and rubble, just barely wide enough for us to walk single file. Scamandrius Green led the way, followed by Jaden and Lainey, while I brought up the rear.

Glacier jumped from rock to rock, ignoring the path most of the time. Every so often, though, she'd lift her head and growl or hiss. The first time she did it, we all stopped and looked around, listening. We saw and heard nothing. Yet something bothered the cat, multiple times.

The walls and ceiling of this tunnel were uneven, shattered and brittle. We continued to theorize about the use of explosives to create this passage, as it showed clear signs of violence, but… it didn't explain everything. Some places were smooth. We found another spot where liquid had once flowed, which made no sense. How could there have been an underground stream in a tunnel newly carved out? Somewhere ahead, I heard dripping again. Another chamber maybe?

Only a few moments later, Glacier stopped again, growling louder than before. Having grown used to it, we continued on our way. "It'll be okay, Glacier," Lainey said.

The cat leaped from her current perch and shoved her way onto our path, in between Jaden and Lainey. She turned and blocked the path, staring up at Lainey.

"What is it?" Lainey asked. "What's the matter?"

"She doesn't want you to go any further," I said.

Jaden stopped too. "If it's spooking the giant cat with swords for teeth, I'm not going any further either!"

The dripping had grown much louder, and I heard more of it. It seemed a lot of things were wet ahead, dripping at various rates. And another sound too… the hissing or sizzling sound. I could hear more of it.

Scamandrius Green continued on for another dozen yards or so before stopping. "It is curious," the draconic observed. "I'm not sure what the creature senses. I don't—" It broke off, sniffing the air.

I sniffed too. That smell. I'd grown used to it as we walked, but now it became overwhelming.

"What is that?" Lainey wondered.

I knew it. It was right on the tip of my tongue. It was…

Scamandrius Green beat me to it: "It's acid."

I pushed past Glacier and shined my light ahead, paying closer attention to the walls and ceiling. Everywhere I looked, I saw dampness. Water
dripped from almost every surface. Except it wasn't water. It was acid, just
like the acid Onyx spat to burn my face. No wonder the smell had been
familiar.

"Good girl, Glacier," Lainey said behind me. The cat had saved her—
and the rest of us—from walking right into this mess. We could have all
been severely burned, at the least.

"This is how they did it," Scamandrius Green observed. "Acid from the
black dragons combined with explosives. After the initial blast, the acid
burns more away. And anywhere it finds soft rock, like limestone, it eats
completely away, opening up larger spaces, like the one we just left."

"It seems like a… very destructive method," Lainey said.

"Without question."

"I don't get it," Jaden said. "It seems like just using explosives would be
more efficient. Why bother with the acid?"

"As I said," Scamandrius Green answered, turning back from the dark
and dripping tunnel ahead, "the acid burns more away than the explosives
would. It breaks things down, and helps to find softer spots in the rock for
the placement of the next explosive."

"It's twisted and grotesque," I said. "Just the sort of thing that would appeal to Onyx." I waved my light around at the dripping rocks. "He probably laughs if a worker gets burned by this stuff when they're clearing things out, or planting the next explosive. And if anyone discovered this, they might run into it and get hurt themselves. Why just dig a tunnel to the other side when you can cause pain and violence while digging a tunnel to the other side? Just like a dragon!"

"You humans have such a limited perspective. You cannot comprehend the boredom of a god, or his children." The draconic started to move past me.

I shoved it back. "Don't give me that. You're saying you get to kill people because you're bored? Regardless of how long someone lives, it shouldn't change basic values. Hurting people, killing people: it doesn't become okay just because you've been around for hundreds of years."

"You are an eye blink. When you are gone—"

"How about when you're gone?" I put my hand on my sword hilt. "Viridia isn't around any more to make you come back. If you die now, you're dead forever."

The draconic growled and flexed its claws. "Do you wish to test me, human? Here in the dark? Amidst the acid and rocks? It would be a glorious battle, no doubt. One that would leave us both burned, broken, and probably dead." It took a step closer. "Our bodies would decay, eaten apart by the saliva of a god. Shall we?"

"Beryl," Lainey said. "We don't need to fight him. Not now. Think of Lovat."

She was right. I released my sword. "Not now," I repeated. "But a day will come, draconic."

"I look forward to it."

We stared at each other in the darkness.

"So…" Jaden broke in. "I'm guessing we're not going any further?"

Scamandrius Green glanced back at the tunnel ahead. "No. Since the acid still drips here, it must not continue much further. They will wait until this has subsided, and then set off a new explosion."

I considered our journey so far. "You said six miles or so. How far do you think we've come?"

"It's been over two hours. We walked fairly straight for most of that time." It looked around again. "We've traveled somewhere between four and six miles. It is difficult to say exactly."

"So they're not too far from completing this thing."

"It would appear so."

"Can we go now?" Jaden asked.

I nodded. "Yeah. Let's head back."

We turned back the way we came. Glacier, relieved by our actions, bounded on ahead. Behind me, as we started walking, I heard again the drip and sizzle of the acid. And I remembered.

I'd heard it back in the large cavern, where no acid remained.

It had to come from somewhere. Somewhere higher, where we couldn't see… in an enormous space large enough to hide…

I stopped walking. "There's a dragon hiding in the big room," I said aloud.

The others stopped and looked at me. "What makes you say that?" Scamandrius Green asked.

I explained the oppressive feelings I'd had earlier and the sound of acid. Jaden, as expected, freaked out. "What are we going to do? How can we get past it?"

"Your evidence is weak," the draconic said. "Some acid could have easily remained in a pocket, still dripping slowly."

"Draconics don't have a way of sensing dragons?" Lainey asked. "I seem to remember some of your brothers bragging about their senses."

That's right. "Troilus Green mocked me for only having five senses," I recalled.

Scamandrius Green's eyes narrowed. "I can detect the presence of my sire, and follow him. I have no connection to the others."

"That's sweet," Jaden said. "But beside the point. What are we going to do about this dragon?"

"There is no dragon!" the draconic snapped.

"Fine," I said. "You can go on ahead. We'll follow more carefully." I looked at Jaden and Lainey. "And we won't do anything until we're sure."

"We'll follow your lead," Lainey said. That was good to hear. Maybe she'd gotten over the dream thing.

Jaden shook his head. "You talked me into coming with you. You'd better not get me killed now."

"I'll do everything I can."

We headed back toward the giant cavern. Though it led the way, Sc-amandrius Green did not stomp on ahead, as I'd expected. Instead, the draconic stayed just in front of us, grumbling every so often. It would only be a few minutes. I tried to think through every possibility.

"Listen," I told Jaden and Lainey, "if I yell 'back,' then run back this way. If I just yell 'run,' then run across and head for the way out."

"What if you're not able to yell?" Jaden asked.

"Then do whatever Lainey says, Jaden. And if she's gone, then you'll have to make a decision for yourself." My words sounded much harsher than I intended.

"Just asking," he mumbled.

I felt the change in the air before we reached the chamber. I stopped, waiting. Scamandrius Green kept walking out into the open. After about fifty yard or so, the draconic stopped. The flashlight turned back toward us.

"You see? There is no dragon here!" it shouted.

A rumbling laughter echoed through the chamber. Jaden scrambled back several feet. Glacier hunched over, as if ready to pounce, growling.

"Oh, but there is, little green nephew. There is." The deep voice came from above, but echoed throughout the cavern. I shined my light up, but couldn't see anything more than the last time.

"It's Atramentous," I whispered. I removed the bag I'd been carrying and lowered it to the ground.

"How do you know?" Lainey hissed.

"I don't recognize the voice. And if it were Onyx, he'd have laughed at us when we first came through. He would recognize us and wouldn't be able to resist." I unzipped the bag and found Auric's device. I also grabbed the claw launcher and slung it on to my back.

Scamandrius Green stared up into the darkness. "What is happening here? Why are you making this tunnel?"

"Little green," the rumbling giant voice intoned, "you have such a… limited perspective."

"Hey, that's what it said to you," Jaden said.

"Quiet. Yes." I winced, not because Jaden had pointed out the obvious, but because of what it implied: the dragon had been listening to us through all our conversations. I turned off my flashlight, stood up, and inched a little bit into the open myself, trying to activate my night vision. Auric's device felt cool to my hand, even in the chill of the cavern.

"Are you seeking to reconnect with Chroma?" Scamandrius Green asked, straining to see anything. "With… her world?"

My night vision kicked in, despite the draconic's flashlight weaving around. I saw the crude stairs off to my right, spiraling upward, but no sign of the dragon. Was he that far above, further than I could see? Or was he right in front of me, using that disappearing act of his?

"Our actions are not subject to your questioning," the dragon declared. "Your sire is dead, and you serve an abomination."

"I serve Viridia alone!" Scamandrius Green shouted.

The enormous head of Atramentous the black dragon materialized right above the draconic, jaws wide.

"Back!" I screamed.

The jaws closed with a sickening crunch. Atramentous pulled back as more of his gigantic body became visible. The lower half of Scamandrius Green's body fell over onto the cavern floor.

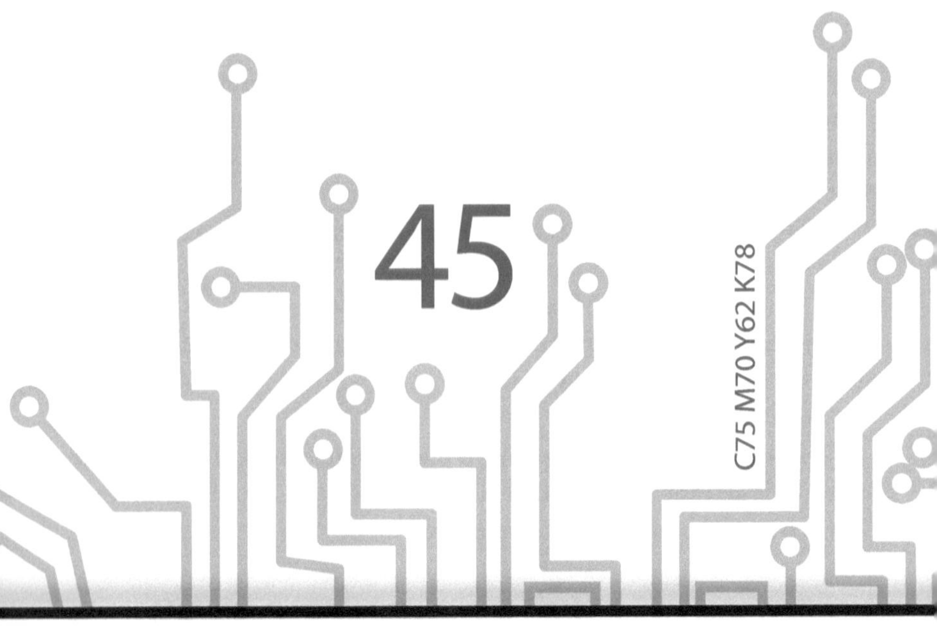

45

I didn't have time to make sure Lainey and Jaden obeyed my command. I boosted my legs with everything I could and bolted to the right.

"Glacier! Go with him!" Lainey shouted from further back.

I didn't want the cat chasing me around, but it was too late to argue. I leaped onto the first rocky platform, took another long step, and leaped to the second one. The stairs were far from even, either in length or height. Without enhancements, I would have climbed them with slow and careful movements. With my boosted speed and reflexes, I jumped from one to the next in moments, ascending rapidly. The claw launcher bumped against my sword as I ran.

Glacier bounded after me, staying a few steps behind. The cat's speed was impressive. I had the feeling that she could have passed me, even in my boosted state, if she'd wanted to.

The giant, clawed hand of the black dragon appeared on my left, reaching right toward me. With another boost, I managed to run fast enough that it slammed into the rock right behind me. Glacier, without stopping, leaped up and over it, kicking off one of the knuckles.

"Where are you going, little human?" Atramentous rumbled.

I had no idea. I only knew two things: first, if I were going to use this device against the dragon, I would need to get close. And second, I needed to keep him away from Lainey and Jaden. Ascending these steps as they wrapped around the chamber helped with the second, but not much with the first. If nothing else came to mind, I might have to jump on to the dragon and set it off there. I wouldn't survive, but if I saved Lainey, it would be worth it.

As I ran, I caught glimpses of the dragon. He seemed to be fading in and out, and not all of him at once, either. Parts of his body would be visible, while others weren't. Combined with the already strange view provided by my cybernetic night vision, my brain struggled with disorientation. I couldn't afford to lose my concentration. One wrong step, and the dragon would get me.

Twice more, his claws raked the cavern wall and stairs, tearing off enormous chunks of rock each time. Both times, I narrowly avoided him. Glacier leaped past me once and hung back the second time. She leaped over the resulting damage with ease and caught right back up.

"You are fast," the dragon observed. "Perhaps there is something different about you."

Seriously? He didn't recognize me? Then again, why would he? I'd never been to his city, and the one time our paths crossed, he'd been occupied with Auric. I'm sure Onyx would have told him all about me… or would he? I couldn't fathom the motivations any more. At the very least, Atramentous would have heard stories about the "rebel leader" with cybernetic enhancements. But I couldn't really stop and introduce myself.

How high did these makeshift stairs go? And why? I would soon be higher than the dragon, but that wouldn't make much difference. The cavern was big enough for him to take flight. As the thought popped into my mind, I also realized something else: somewhere up here, Atramentous had been hiding. With his ability, I suppose he could have been on the ground, but I didn't think so. Every time I'd sensed a dragon presence bearing down on me, it had come from above. He'd clearly descended from somewhere when he killed Scamandrius Green.

My leg muscles burned from the effort, but I could still feel an almost limitless well of energy within. Auric's last gift still empowered me, even as I kept the boosts flowing.

As I climbed higher and higher, the nature of the stairs slowly changed. At first, it had consisted of platforms extruding out from the wall. At greater heights, it transitioned more and more into the wall itself. In time, Glacier and I ran up through a shallow passageway carved into the rock.

Atramentous growled. I couldn't spare him a look. I had to concentrate on my steps or—

An enormous impact shook everything around me, and a wall of darkness swept toward me. I staggered and almost fell. I regained my balance and realized what had happened. The dragon leaped at my location, slamming all of his claws into the rock. He clung to it, hands and feet embedded somewhere on either side of my position. The wall of darkness pulled back, revealing itself as the dragon's chest and underbelly. As it moved, I saw the metallic "scales" covering his cybernetic implant. If I'd had the device ready, that would have been a perfect moment to set it off.

Atramentous pulled back enough to stare down at me. Glacier stopped beside me and crouched, growling back at the gigantic creature.

"Who are you?" the dragon wondered. "And why are you here in such unusual company?"

I really wished I had a speech of some kind for those kind of questions. But I didn't. "I'm, uh, Beryl." Wow. Anything would have been better than that.

"Your chromark." The dragon's face leaned in closer toward me, tilted so that one great eye could examine me. "How odd. Yet the original still shows through. You belong to Viridia."

"I belong to no dragon. I'm a free human being. And soon… every other one will be too." Okay, now that's better. Not a full-on speech, but… better.

"What a ridiculous sentiment." Atramentous snorted, sending twin jets of steam from his nostrils. "A free human has no more meaning than a free sheep or chicken. You belong to us. We determine your value. And those who cause problems are no longer valued."

With that, he reared back and opened his mouth. I knew what was coming. "Glacier! Run!" I boosted and charged up the stairs. Black, fiery acid sprayed the spot I'd just been standing and pursued me upward. Just ahead, I ducked under the dragon's left arm. The spray of acid stopped. Would it have damaged his own skin? Would have been nice to find out.

Glacier and I resumed our race up and around. Atramentous shot another burst of acid at us, but we outdistanced it. I still had no idea where this would lead, but maybe we had a chance to reach the top now. I glanced back at the big cat following me. "Not sure why you keep coming, cat, but thanks," I gasped.

By now, we had completed at least two circuits of the entire cavern. This didn't make much sense. Why would anyone build such a thing?

An enormous chunk of rock smashed into the cavern wall almost directly above us. The roof over the stairs collapsed right behind Glacier. I risked a quick look at the dragon and saw it tearing up another piece of rock from the floor of the cavern, destroying the beautiful formations.

The second throw impacted below the stairs a few yards ahead of me. I lifted my arms to deflect some of the shards that flew at my face. Parts of the next few steps were broken by the attack, requiring me to dodge left and right as I kept ascending. Glacier had no trouble at all.

The third throw smashed into the cavern wall only a foot or two behind me. A chunk of rock struck me in the back of the head and shoulders. My consciousness reeled. I fell forward, striking my knees on the stairs. More chunks of rock rained down around me. Glacier dodged past. I slid across the rock and blacked out for a second. When my vision cleared, I went over the edge. Desperately, I tried to boost my cyb hand and dug the fingers into the rock. I didn't feel a boost, but the metal tore into the stone anyway.

I swung out over the emptiness, only my cybernetic fingers keeping me from falling to my death. I almost dropped Auric's device. My shoulder wrenched as my weight jerked back. Even so, I fought to stay conscious. The back of my head hurt more than any recent memory of pain.

I threw Auric's device on to the stair and scrambled to reach something with my other arm. Glacier appeared, looking concerned. If the cat could take my hand somehow, that would help. Otherwise, she was no help. I got hold of something with my right hand and pulled. I tried to swing my foot up, but didn't make it.

"Well, well."

I turned my head—a painful act—and looked over my shoulder. The enormous head of Atramentous came toward me, mouth open, teeth dripping with black acid. I couldn't possibly get out of the way in time.

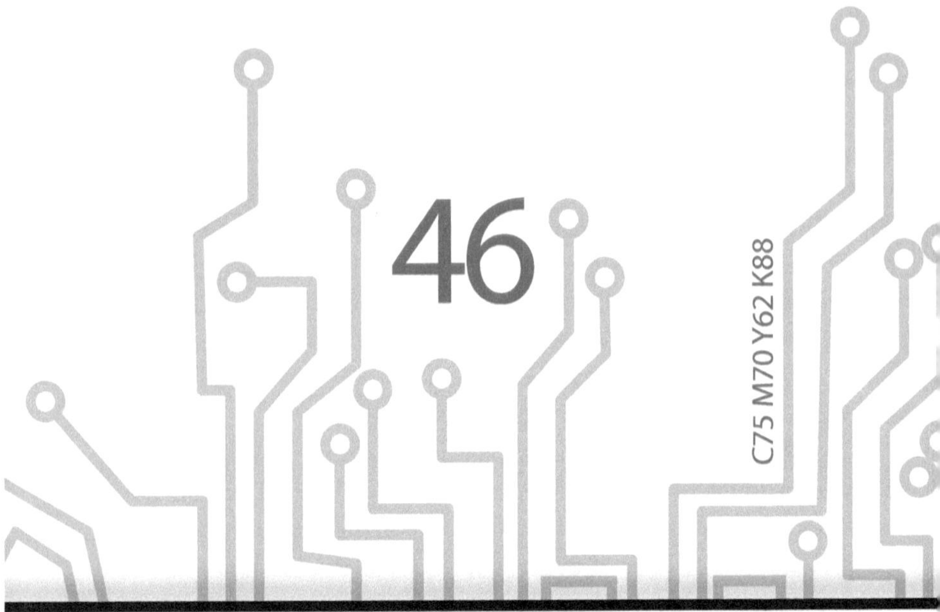

46

Glacier leaped over me with a roar. She landed on the dragon's nose, pushing his jaw down. His chin struck the rock right at my feet. I kicked off black scales and threw myself onto the stair. After I rolled away from the edge, I looked back.

Glacier scrambled up on to the top of the dragon's head, between his horns. Atramentous grabbed at her, but she kept moving. She bounded down his neck and between his wings. Atramentous twisted, trying to get at her. Glacier ran down the dragon's back, leaping along his ridged spine back and forth.

Atramentous pursued the cat with his claws, twisting and flailing furiously. But no matter what he did, he couldn't catch the swiftly moving blur of white fur.

My head swam, still struggling from the impact. I grabbed up Auric's device and pulled myself to my feet. As I did, I discovered pain in my left leg. Blood ran down from my knee. But I had to keep moving. Glacier had given me this chance; I shouldn't waste it. I tried to boost my legs, but nothing came. I couldn't concentrate. I moved anyway, limping along as fast as I could.

Down below, Glacier reached the dragon's tail. She ran along it until she reached the metal spike, then leaped to the ground. She timed the leap just as Atramentous snatched at her. The dragon's claws raked against his own tail. His growl of fury drowned out Glacier's own snarl of challenge. The cat roared up at the dragon, then turned and ran.

I paused long enough to watch Glacier dodge through several rock pillars and then dash into the tunnel that led to the surface. Atramentous pursued her, acid pouring from his mouth.

I couldn't keep watching. Glacier had been smart enough not to lead the dragon back toward Lainey. Maybe she actually knew what she was doing. I would have to trust her and keep going myself. I gritted my teeth and limped onward. Whatever happened with Glacier, the dragon would be back soon and trying to get to me. I had to get higher. And then…

I had no idea what I would do.

At least, if I were higher, the dragon would have to fly up to get to me. Or maybe I would find where these stairs led. But anything after that… I held Auric's device tighter. I had to find a way to use it, even if it killed me. Lainey and Jaden were depending on me.

My thoughts bounced around from Lainey's face as she turned and ran, to the way Scamandrius Green's lower body fell over, to Glacier running down the back of the black dragon. I wondered what Marcus and Cerise were doing back in Incarnadine. Or if Amaranth would show up in one of my dreams again. And what she would be wearing. Also acid. I remembered it hurt a lot when Rick spit some at me. Whatever happened to Mazarine Chalybe-something? Was he still back in the tower, moping? That tower had a lot of stairs in it. Like these. But smaller.

Why was my brain doing this? I stumbled and almost fell. Pain. The pain in the back of my head kept growing. A big rock hit it. Right. I closed my eyes and gritted my teeth. Concentrate. What was happening to me?

Back of the head. Hurt so much. Not good. Can't boost. Why? Because… my implant was in the back of my head. My eyes flew open. Had I damaged the implant? What would that mean? And why weren't there any bright colors in night vision? My shoes were brighter than that, weren't they? Like the bright colors on the buildings in the city of Auric. So much nicer than Viridia with all its concrete. Did they have concrete outside The Circle? I should ask Kelly. No, Lainey. Yes, Lainey would know.

Lainey was pretty. So was Kelly. And Olive. And Amaranth. Caedan called Amaranth "Amy." That was funny. I laughed.

What was happening to me? Somewhere in my brain, I screamed against these random thoughts. I needed to focus. I needed to do…

something. Something important. Somehow, at least I kept moving up the stairs.

The Flame in Incarnadine had a lot of stairs. But we destroyed it. No more stairs now. People would have to use the elevator.

Bacon. Why did our new headquarters have so much bacon, anyway? Did Auric store it there, or some of his men? Did the dragon hunt pigs to make bacon?

I stumbled and fell to my knees. The left one collapsed under me and I almost went down all the way. I stabilized myself on the right knee and my left hand. Why couldn't I clear my head? It hurt so much. And why did I have to carry two things on my back? Maybe I should get rid of one.

A cool breeze teased my hair. "Just a bit farther, apostate Beryl." The unnatural voice echoed around me.

I raised my eyes and saw one of the purple priests a few yards ahead. As if this whole situation wasn't messed up enough already…

"You have followed the winding path well. The end awaits you. Come." The priest stepped back and vanished, like they always did.

The cold air and the appearance of the enemy helped focus my thoughts, at least for the moment. I pulled myself to my feet with a grimace and resumed my climb.

The roar of Atramentous echoed through the cavern. Had he caught up to Glacier? Was he returning? It was impossible to tell from the sound as it bounced from wall to wall.

Light appeared above and across the cavern from me. I blinked multiple times to turn off my night vision. The light shone from another large cavern. The stairs appeared to be leading toward it. It also illuminated the actual ceiling of this enormous place. I had been starting to wonder if it stretched all the way up the inside of one of the mountains.

My feet moved a little faster, now that I had a goal in sight. Even so, it felt like heavy weights were attached to each foot. Every step was an effort. I could still feel Auric's gift roiling around inside me, but I couldn't access it.

Step by step, I drew closer to the light. It seemed to shimmer at times, with an odd quality to it. I think I saw some color mixed in, but it was hard to tell. At least my thoughts were focused now, though limited on the immediate desire to reach the end. The pain in my head hadn't diminished, though.

Another roar echoed through the cave, along with distant sounds of movement. If Atramentous wasn't back in the main room yet, he would be at any moment. And then he'd be coming up here. I tried to move even faster, but stumbled.

The illuminated cavern came more into my view. I saw figures moving about. More of the priests/zealots? It made sense for them to be involved in this venture, but I couldn't fathom a reason for this spiral stairway to another cave.

Did I hear the sound of dragon wings? No… just my brain imagining something again, and starting to wander… "stop it!" I said aloud. I stared at the lighted area and kept moving. Only a few more steps remained.

My head crested the floor of the illuminated cavern, and I stopped to stare. A trio of the purple-robed zealots stood not far from me, but I ignored them. The cave behind them might be near the size of Viridia's nest—huge, but dwarfed by the mammoth cavern below us. The directional lights all focused on a large object mounted on a stand about a hundred yards from the stairs. The reflections blinded me momentarily, making it difficult to make out the actual object. I squinted and tried to focus.

It was a dragon scale. A single, enormous scale, shimmering in the light, casting reflections in every direction.

It was also unmistakably purple.

"Welcome, apostate Beryl," one of the zealots intoned. "Welcome to the newest shrine to the almighty Chroma, mother of dragons."

A second one took a step closer. "It is here, bathed in her glorious light, that your rebellion comes to an end. It is here… you will die."

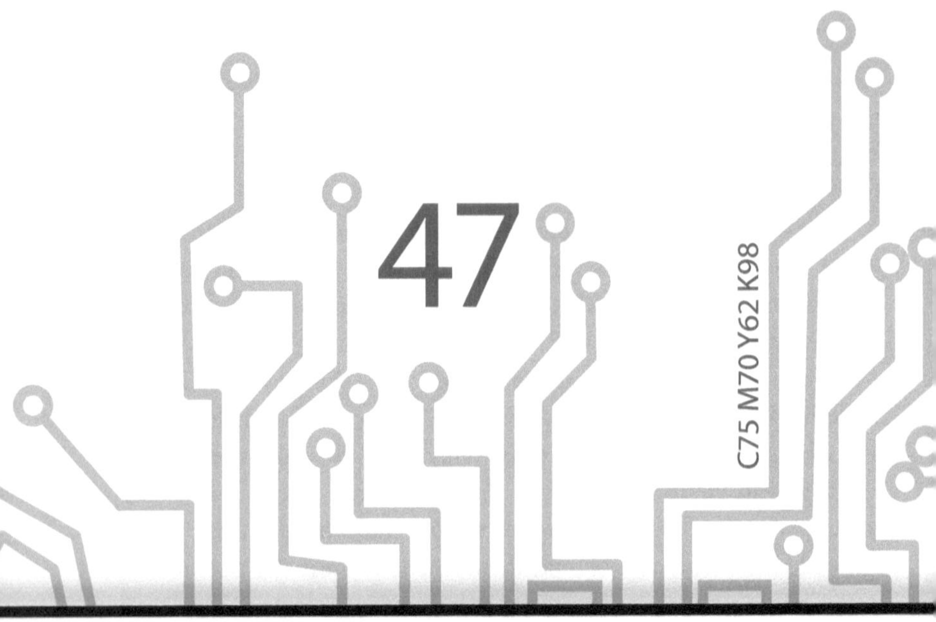

I wanted to respond with a brilliant quip, a thorough mockery, or at least my own threat. But my brain couldn't seem to feed the right words to my mouth.

"Chroma," I finally said. I'm not sure if I meant it as a curse or a question.

The zealot took it as the latter. "Surely by now, you have come to understand the truth about your world and the dragons."

I fingered Auric's device. I definitely heard sounds of movement from below. Atramentous was returning. "If I am to die," I said slowly, "enlighten me. I do not wish to die ignorant."

All three of the zealots placed their palms together in unison. Maybe Lainey was right about them being the same person. To my surprise, they began a kind of chant, each one of them reciting a single line. I let them carry on while I tried to focus on a way to escape this situation. With no boosts, my options seemed limited.

"Long ago, Chroma ruled all."

"Today, Chroma rules all."

"For ages to come, Chroma will rule all."

"In the process of time, Chroma bore children."

"Seven children were born to she who rules all."

"The seven grew to maturity and faced a decision."

"'Should we remain and serve our mother?' they asked."

"'Or should we set out and found our own kingdoms?'"

"Chroma wept when they decided to leave."

"The tears of a god are few but powerful."

"Yet Chroma, loving her children, let them go."

"The children sought their own place, but stayed together."

"In time, Chroma missed her children."

"She sent forth servants to locate them and inquire about their progress."

"At first, they seemed to be doing well with their own kingdoms."

"But they had forgotten their mother, the one true god above all."

"They proclaimed themselves gods and ignored her servants."

"Thus, Chroma removed her protection from them."

"And they began to die."

"Wait!" I held up my cyb hand. "What are you saying? That the dragons were immortal until Chroma… what? Let them die? That we just happened to start killing them when she allowed it?"

"They are gods," one of them answered. "Gods cannot die. Unless the higher god wills it."

"You have been her instrument," the second said, "her method to turn her recalcitrant children back to her."

"And thus it has succeeded," the third added. "Those who must die, have died. And the rest will serve her once again."

"For she is coming," they said in unison. "We but prepare her way."

"I am a free man!" I snapped. "I do not do the will of a dragon, no matter what dragon it is!"

"You have no choice in the matter," the middle one said. "All serve her, whether they choose it or not."

"That makes no sense. Then the dragons who rebelled against her would still be serving her through their rebellion. So why punish them?"

"You cannot understand a god's ways. You have served her, willingly or not. Until now."

"Now your service has come to an end," the first said. "She has no further use for you, and so your death will serve her more."

"No!" Atramentous roared behind and below me. "Wait!"

With a rush of wind from his wings, the black dragon soared up behind me. I staggered forward, closer to the zealots.

"This one has affronted me," the dragon bellowed. "His life is mine to take!"

"As you wish, child of Chroma."

If I were going down, I would at least take that monster with me. I turned the electromagnetic pulse device so my finger rested on the activation. I knew Auric had fixed a short timer, but I couldn't remember how long it took. I should wait until the last possible moment.

I still couldn't get any boosts going. And yet... my mind cleared enough to remind me: if the implant wasn't working at all, I wouldn't be able to walk. I wouldn't be able to use my cybernetic hand.

That was my only key. I didn't have one of the shocksticks. I didn't have boost energy. But the purple robes were vulnerable to my left hand.

With another beat of his wings, Atramentous drew closer to the shrine cave.

I let my shoulders sag and my head droop, the image of defeat. Two of the zealots stepped toward me on either side, reaching out gloved hands.

One little boost would come in handy right now. I pushed against the pain in my head, gritting my molars. A tiny trickle of warmth made its way down my back and into my legs. It wasn't much, but I'd take anything I could get.

I leaped to my left, seizing a big handful of the purple robe. I yanked as hard as I could.

The enormous head of Atramentous appeared in the light, only a few feet away.

"Stop him!" yelled the third zealot.

I flipped the activation switch on Auric's device with my right hand. With my left, I ripped the purple robe. I tore off part of the zealot's hood, revealing the same face I'd seen multiple times now.

"The light of Chroma will—"

I swung the device around and smacked him in the head with it. Auric hadn't said what it was made of, but it felt solid enough for this kind of trick. The zealot crumpled.

Atramentous roared. The force of his breath staggered me. And it smelled horrible.

The second zealot threw his arms around me from behind. "The child of Chroma will consume your flesh!" he cried as he pulled me toward the edge and the dragon's maw.

I seized a portion of his robe, whatever I could reach, and pulled, tearing a strip loose. The action was enough to make him loosen his grip on me, if only by a fraction. I screamed, mentally forcing a boost into my arms. I burst free and spun around.

I shoved the electromagnetic explosive into his outstretched arms. "You first." I pushed him backward.

The zealot fell into the open mouth of the black dragon. I collapsed onto my knees. I screamed from the pain, and kept sliding forward.

Atramentous jerked his head back a moment before I slid off the cliff edge. Maybe he was swallowing. I didn't want to think about it.

I fell into darkness.

Wind from the dragon's wings buffeted me, flipping me in mid-air. How long before that device went off? Would it shut me down before I hit the floor? It was a long way down.

I rolled back over to face down again. My sword on my back clanked against… the grapple launcher. I struggled to pull the strap over my shoulder as I continued to fall.

"Where is he?" Atramentous bellowed above.

My night vision kicked in and I saw everything in an instant. The dragon wasn't far, and I hadn't fallen completely past him yet. I aimed the grapple launcher at an enormous wing and pulled the trigger.

I couldn't tell whether the claw actually tore a hole in the wing, or whether it bounced and simply stuck. Either way, the dragon probably didn't feel it, and more importantly: it worked. The claw caught hold. I let the spool continue to spin as I plummeted. This wouldn't do any good unless…

There! I spotted the circling stairs on the cavern wall. I'd already fallen past one circuit, but the other was coming up fast. I held on to the launcher with both hands and activated the stop on the cable. I came to an abrupt halt, nearly yanking both of my shoulders out of their sockets. I couldn't stifle a scream.

The dragon whipped around in the air. How could something that big move so fast? His movements swept the cable in several directions, flinging me back and forth. I suspect it would have made me extremely dizzy if my head weren't already exploding in pain.

Atrementous roared, and his head twisted this way and that. Between the darkness and my constant motion, he probably had trouble seeing me.

Or at least I hoped so.

As the dragon spun around again, the cable took me toward the cavern wall. It wasn't exactly where I wanted to be, but I thought I could fall on to the stairs. I released more of the line and let it carry me almost to the wall itself. And then I let go.

At the same moment, I think Auric's device exploded.

48

I hit the wall with a jarring crash and fell. With no boosts to absorb the collision's force, I closed my eyes, rolled up as best I could, and waited.

I don't know what happened next. I guess I passed out from the impact, but it couldn't have been for more than a few seconds. The scream of the black dragon jerked me awake.

Pain filled my body. Everything could be broken; I couldn't tell. The pain in my head was still the worst. But I managed to turn and look out into the darkness.

Atramentous plummeted past me. His wings arrested his movement for perhaps a second or two, and then they went limp. The massive dragon plunged toward the cavern floor without another pause. When he struck the ground, everything shook. Smaller rocks fell around me. I heard the cracking of larger stone formations and secondary crashes as other things fell in the cacophony of echoes.

It worked. The electromagnetic explosive worked. "Thanks, Auric," I whispered, before the pain overwhelmed me again. I fell into a darkness greater than the cave around me.

"Beryl!"

The voice intruded on my consciousness with an insistency that annoyed me. Why couldn't they let me sleep? Or… whatever I had been doing.

"Beryl!"

All I knew now was pain. Everything hurt, but most of all my left knee and the back of my head.

Something pushed against my shoulder. I moaned.

"Beryl!" This time the voice sounded much closer and more frantic. I think I knew that voice.

Not that it mattered. I lost myself again.

The second time, I awoke to a cool dampness on my forehead. It might be the nicest feeling I'd experienced in months. The coolness calmed my pain ever so slightly. A few droplets of water ran down either side of my head. One of them trickled into my ear. Even that felt good.

Almost against my will, my eyes opened. I looked up into Lainey's anxious face, illuminated from the side by a flashlight being held by someone else.

"Beryl? Can you hear me?" I heard the words as her lips moved, but it took my brain a moment to connect the two.

I tried to answer, but my own lips didn't want to obey me.

"He's conscious," said another voice. Jaden, my brain finally told me. "Unless his bionic eyes are doing something weird, I guess."

"He's reacting. He can hear me," Lainey said. "Give him time. He's been through a lot."

Jaden's flashlight skipped away from Lainey. "Yeah. I still can't… I mean, I know he had the thing to kill the dragon, but still…" His light came back to our faces. "Hey, if his eyes are working, doesn't that mean it didn't affect him too?"

"I don't know, Jaden." Lainey sounded frustrated. "I don't know much of anything here. Just… be patient."

"Yeah, yeah."

Lainey reached up and adjusted the coolness on my forehead. A wet cloth. That had to be it. I felt pride for figuring that out. And then another part of my brain told me how pathetic that was.

"You'll be all right," Lainey said much quieter. "You have to be."

I had to be. I did. She needed me. Jaden needed me. Carl needed me.

Lovat needed me. And so many others. I never asked for it, but I had to be the one they needed. Focus, Beryl. Concentrate. Get moving again.

Something pushed against my shoulder again, this time with a soft growl. Glacier? She was alive? I couldn't help but smile at that.

"You're smiling," Lainey said. "I knew it. You're going to be all right."

I don't know how much longer we stayed there on the steps. It felt like hours before I could even begin to move. Lainey stayed by my side the entire time, while Jaden paced back and forth or sat up against the cavern wall. They kept only one flashlight on at a time, to preserve the batteries, but both were near-dying before I could get up.

It took both of them to help me to my feet, and then we started down together. Step by step, arms around each other, we descended.

"You're much heavier than you look," Jaden grumbled. "Must be all the metal inside you." Heh. Caedan said the same thing once.

"Can you tell us what happened up there?" Lainey asked. She'd already explained how the two of them stayed hidden until Atramentous fell and Glacier found them. I remained amazed that the cat had survived. Chased down a tunnel by a raging dragon, and it didn't look any worse for wear.

In slow words and sometimes incoherent sentences, I told them my story. When I talked about the blow to the back of my head, Lainey stopped us and examined it with her flashlight. "It's a bloody mess, but I can't tell how bad. We need to get you back to Hunter."

I agreed. I just wasn't sure how we were going to make it.

"Come on, Jaden," she instructed. "Let's keep moving."

"Bad leg here, remember?" he sighed. "Climbing these steps was bad enough. Give me another minute."

"My fault," I mumbled. I was the one who'd cut Jaden's leg, so long ago.

"We'll take it as slow as we need to," Lainey said, "for both of you."

And so we continued. It must have taken us hours to get down to the floor of the cavern again. A few times, I remembered to look up, but I saw no sign of the lights at the Chroma shrine. Why hadn't the remaining zealots come after us? Were they that shocked by the death of one of their number? Or the death of Atramentous?

On the floor, we had to work our way around the giant body of the black dragon. All of the beautiful formations I'd noticed before were destroyed now. Nothing remained but the dragon and shattered rock. We stopped frequently to rest; I simply could not keep going for long.

I'd been here before, of course, exhausted and wounded after a massive struggle, energy depleted, and needing lots of rest. Except this time... it was different. My energy, the power I used for my boosts, hadn't been used much at all. I could still feel the breath of Auric inside me. But I couldn't access it.

I don't remember much of anything else about our long, slow walk out of the cave. Pain, debilitating fatigue, and mental confusion pushed everything else away. Eventually, we reached the way out, but still found little light. Here we faced another serious problem. When we came down, I'd fully expected that I would climb back out afterward, taking the rope to the top of the descent, where I could help the others up.

I honestly don't know how Lainey did it. I think she got Glacier to take the rope to the top somehow, and then climbed up herself. However it was, Jaden helped loop the rope around me, then climbed up himself. Together, they pulled me to the top. I bumped injured parts of my body against the rocks multiple times, but what else could we do?

We rested for a long time after the ascent. As I lay on top of the rocks, looking up at the night sky, I tried to make sense of the passage of time. We'd entered the cave in mid-to-late morning. It took us somewhere between three to four hours to reach the acid at the end of the tunnel. The fight with Atramentous hadn't taken all that long, but I don't know how long I lay unconscious before the others found me. And of course, it took us hours to get back out.

"It's gotta be midnight, right?" Jaden voiced my thoughts.

"Maybe," Lainey said. She got back to her feet. "Let's get down to the truck before we sleep. I'll feel safer there, and ready to head out in the morning."

Once again, they helped me stand; once again, we walked with slow precision. Being out in the open air did improve my outlook a little. I doubted the zealots would come after us now that we'd left the cave, or maybe that was just wishful thinking.

It took us at least another hour to get to the truck. Once there, Lainey helped wash my wounds again before helping me into a sleeping bag. As my eyes closed, I heard Jaden muttering: "Five dragons dead. I never wound have believed it. What a crazy world we live in now."

wound have believed it. What a crazy world we live in now."

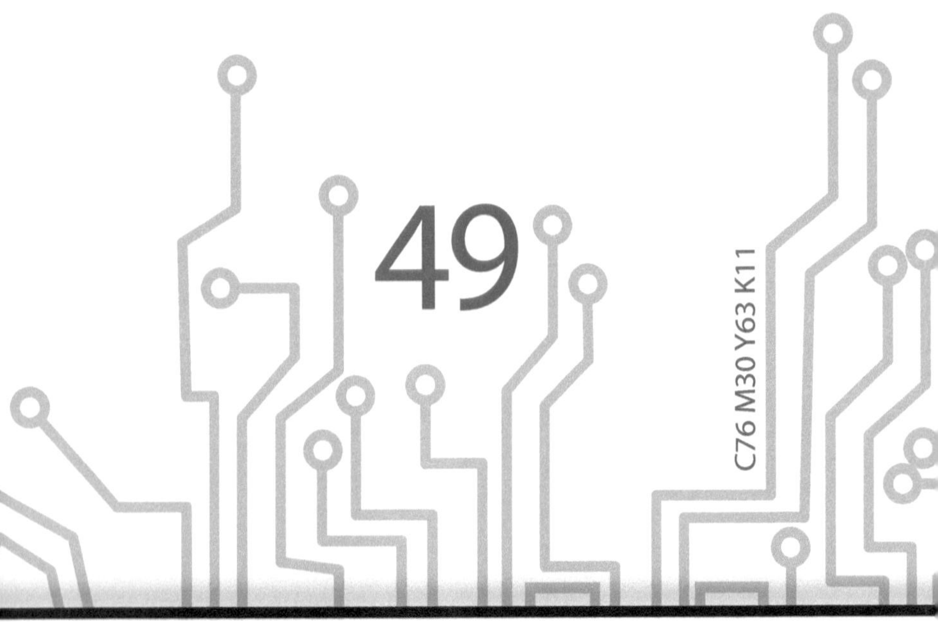

49

Jaden drove the truck back to the railroad. We met the next train at the loading station we'd used to get the truck off the last train. I guessed the crane was normally used for farm equipment, like tractors or something. At least it worked. Troilus Green might not appreciate it if we didn't bring the truck back. It would be upset enough that Scamandrius Green didn't return.

Without the draconic, we had to use the passes from Auric to convince the officials of our legitimacy. Even so, we were the target of some grumbling and quite a few suspicious looks. Inside the car, Lainey faced me while Jaden leaned over the next seat. "Before you rest, we need to talk," Lainey said. "What's the plan when we reach the city?"

"We tell Troilus Green what happened. We get our people. And we get out of there." I tried to project more confidence than I felt.

"And what if he won't let us?" Jaden asked.

"We're leaving Viridia," I repeated. "Maybe for good."

"No offense, Beryl, but… you said you can't access your boosts. You can't fight your way out." Jaden shifted on the seat and glanced over his shoulder at the train car door.

"Troilus Green doesn't know that."

"You're going to try to bluff him?" Lainey asked.

I nodded and winced. Moving my head in any way sent stabs of pain in the back. "We won't even acknowledge my injuries. I won't let Hunter check me out until we leave."

"I don't like that." Lainey frowned. "Something is seriously wrong, and the longer you go without treatment, the worse it could get."

"I'd rather risk myself than put everyone in Troilus Green's hands indefinitely." I stifled a yawn. "Just… wake me before we get there, in time to clean up and look like I know what I'm doing."

"You can barely walk!" Jaden protested.

"Let me rest. By the time we get there, I'll walk."

Jaden raised one eyebrow. He shrugged and turned to the window to watch for the city of Caesious.

"Glacier and I will have your back, if it comes down to it," Lainey said quietly.

"I know." I patted her leg. "I love you."

Her eyes widened a little. "That's… the first time you've said that."

Was it? I mean… I guess so. I don't know when I crossed the line of admitting that to myself.

Lainey leaned in a little closer. "Maybe it's just your weakened condition talking." She smiled. "But I'll take it. I love you too." She gave me a quick kiss. "Now get your rest. We're not out of danger yet."

Would we ever be? As I stretched out on the seat cushions, I wondered if that would ever happen. Maybe when Onyx was dead. And Chroma. And then we'd have to decide what to do with Amaranth. And…

Lainey said she loved me.

Wow.

I thought she did, but she actually said it. And so did I.

Wow.

I smiled, winced, and fell asleep.

Lainey woke me hours later, however long the train passage took. After I sat up and blinked a few times, I closed my eyes again and concentrated. I had to get a boost going. The rest had been good; I felt less like collapsing in a heap. But I needed to do more than just survive. I had to walk around and pretend everything was fine.

I think I felt a trickle of boost energy spreading through my body. It might have been my imagination. But I felt confident enough to grab the seat and pull myself up. I wavered a little and took my first steps.

"Are you going to be able to do this?" Jaden asked. "Or should we start running for our lives now?"

"We're not abandoning our people," I growled. I took a few more steps. "I can do this."

Going down the stairs from the train car was the worst. I gritted my teeth and held on to the railing. My knee almost buckled with each step. Fortunately, we didn't have to go far from there. Once the truck was unloaded, we took it back to the Emerald Ascendancy. Jaden parked right in front.

Unfortunately, that meant I had to ascend a long staircase. I kept trying to boost my legs, but even if I got a few trickles going, it didn't heal my knee. Each time I concentrated, the pain in my head grew. I had no choice, but to keep pushing on through. Even so, I had to resort to Lainey's help up the last few stairs. I hoped it didn't show too much weakness.

Troilus Green met us in the lobby of the Ascendancy, arms folded on its chest. "Where is Scamandrius Green?" came the expected demand.

"Atramentous bit him in half," I said. "Do you want to hear the rest, or shall we focus solely on that?"

"You went to scout a situation," the draconic growled. "You return without one of my last remaining draconics. I may have to forget my word to Auric."

"Scamandrius wouldn't listen to Beryl, and it got him killed!" Lainey snapped.

"Perhaps I should ask Atramentous what happened."

"You do that," I said. "You'll find his body where I left it, in the tunnel he was digging through the mountains."

Troilus Green stared at me, unmoving. After several moments, it finally spoke again: "Atramentous is dead?"

I nodded and stifled another wince of pain.

The draconic turned and looked out through the glass doors. "Then only Onyx and I remain of the children of Chroma."

I almost fell for it. I almost mentioned Amaranth. But I remembered Troilus Green had tried to get her whereabouts from me once already.

"Where are my people?" I asked instead.

The draconic gestured up. "Where you left them. I'm told the boy awakened."

Lovat? I needed to see him right away. Also, I didn't know how much longer I could stand still. "We'll go see them then." I took a step toward the elevator.

"Not yet." Troilus Green held out a hand. "Tell me the rest. What of this tunnel?"

I did owe him that much, I suppose. I explained everything we'd found. "So with Atramentous's body in there now, and without his acid, it's going to take much longer to make it a viable passageway," I concluded.

Troilus Green nodded. "Very well. I must consult with my advisors. See to your friends. We will speak more later." The draconic spun on its heel, robe twirling, and marched away.

"Not if I can help it," I muttered.

"Let's get to the elevator," Lainey said.

Inside the elevator, I let myself lean against the wall, but didn't go completely limp. I remembered the guard's reference to possible cameras in the elevator. Would those be like the cameras Auric used above The Circle to watch the cities? The concept of someone watching at any given time was disconcerting.

"Hunter's got to look at you," Lainey said. "He won't stand still until you let him."

"He can look at my knee. That injury is obvious. But not the head. We can't let on to Troilus Green that I might have lost my abilities. If he knows I'm weak, we're done for."

"We've got your back," Lainey reminded me, patting Glacier's head.

We exited the elevator on the medical floor. How long had we been gone anyway? I tried to figure it out: two days on the trains plus two days traveling in and around the tunnel. At least, I think I got it right. Some thoughts were still harder than others. I rubbed my eyes.

"You're back!" Caedan's voice burst on my thoughts. I looked up to see him and Kelly hurrying toward us down the hall.

"Beryl looks like he's been through a war," Kelly said, folding her arms. "As usual."

"But another dragon's dead," I answered. "It's worth it."

"Onyx?" Caedan asked.

"Atramentous." I glanced around to make sure no one else was near. "Listen, we need to make plans and fast. We should leave here as soon as we can."

Kelly moved nearer and noticed the blood on the back of my head. She reached a hand toward it, but didn't touch me. "Hunter needs to look at this."

"That's what I told him," Lainey said.

"Not yet," I said, gently pushing Kelly's hand away. "Listen to what I'm saying. We have to get out of this city before Troilus Green stops us."

"Beryl?"

I looked past my circle of friends. Lovat sat there in a wheelchair, pushed by Hunter. Stacy followed them, pulling a bag over her shoulder.

"If it is time to leave," Hunter said, "then let us waste no more time."

"Let's blow this place," Stacy added.

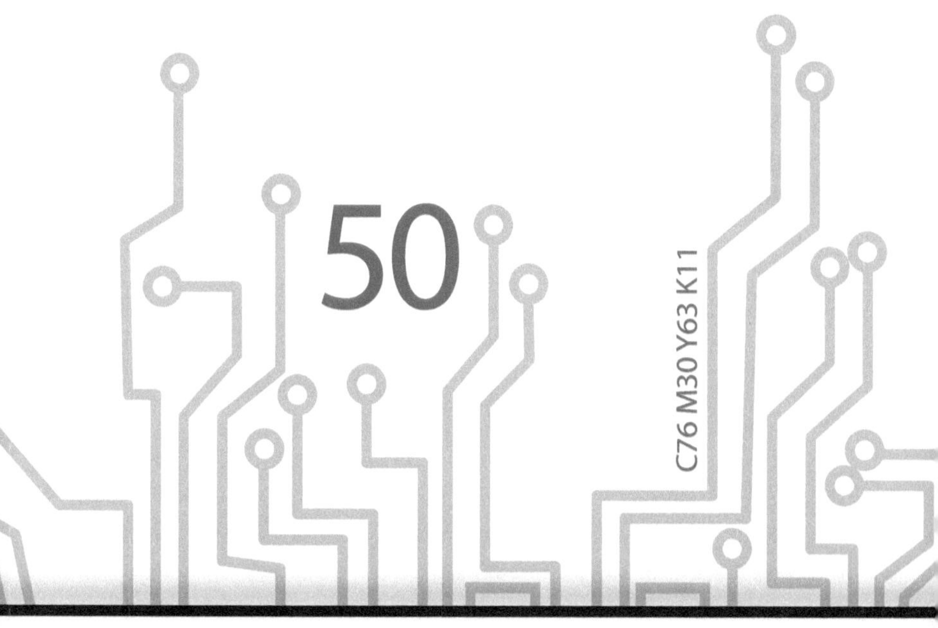

I swallowed the lump in my throat at seeing Lovat awake. I limped to his side and took his good hand, the one with a cast around only two fingers. The other, along with both legs and his neck, was completely encased in a cast. I would have knelt, if I could. "How you feeling, buddy?"

"I still hurt a lot," he said, his words slurring a little. "But Hunter says I'm going to be like you."

"At least a little bit." I tried to smile. "And I will be right beside you through it all, okay?"

"Okay."

Hunter looked me over. "We should—"

"Not yet." I cut him off and looked at everyone else. "Auric's passes can get some of us back on a train heading north, but we have other resources too."

"Cobalt and Turq are camped halfway between here and Atramentous," Caedan said.

"Right. I want you to meet up with them. And Lainey—"

"Glacier and I should pick up the three-wheeler from where we hid it and head north ourselves."

"Exactly. But don't leave us until we're on the train. We need Glacier's intimidation factor."

"Not mine?"

"Yours too. Whoever gets home first will need to hook up the trailer and bring it to the railroad. Lovat and I are in no condition to walk to home base."

"About that…" Stacy said, raising a finger. "I think I might head to one of the other cities. I told you I'm not so good at sleeping under the stars."

"We've upgraded our accommodations. Has no one told you?"

She shook her head.

"Well, come back with us, and then make up your mind." I looked around again. "Everyone good? Let's go."

We couldn't all fit in the elevator at once, not with Lovat's wheelchair and the giant saber-toothed cat. I took the first ride down with Hunter, Stacy, Kelly, and Lovat. We waited in the lobby for the others to join us, and then made our way to the doors.

The two Viridian Guards stationed there did not look pleased. "Where do you think you're going?" one of them demanded.

"We have work to do," I said. "If you cared about humanity, you'd join us. But since you don't, stay here and stay out of our way."

"I don't—" the other one began.

"Glacier, would you like to explain it to our friend here?" Lainey asked, patting the cat on the side. Glacier took a step forward and growled.

The guards stepped aside. "I'll have to notify Viridia of this," the first one warned.

I paused on the way out. "You do that. Tell him exactly how you let us go."

We descended the stairs much slower than I'd have liked, but that was mostly my fault. Caedan carried Lovat, and Hunter carried the wheelchair. At the bottom, we crowded into the truck.

"They aren't going to notice us taking this truck?" Kelly asked.

"Why? We parked it here." Jaden got behind the wheel and took off.

At the train station, Caedan split off from us. Once outside, he'd hitch a ride on a train toward Atramentous. He'd meet up with Cobalt and Turq within a couple of hours. As things turned out, we needed to wait at least that long before the next train left for Auric.

"This is crazy," Stacy said. "We're going to just sit here and wait for the Viridian Guard to come take us back?"

I sat down on a bench. Almost at once, Hunter knelt down beside me and began examining my knee. "We can't exactly force a train to leave early," I said. "I wouldn't know how to begin."

She smiled. "Let me see what I can do. Kelly, follow my lead." The two of them walked away.

"Heh." Jaden chuckled. "I should have known she was the one who could get away with not listening to you."

"Almost nobody listens to me."

"I do," Lovat said weakly.

"And look where that got you," I wanted to say, but didn't. I still hated myself for getting him hurt.

"Think it'll work?" Lainey asked.

"Stacy has a way of getting what she wants. Usually."

Sure enough, a few minutes later, the two women returned. "Train's leaving in ten minutes," Stacy reported. "Let's board."

"How did you do that?" Jaden wanted to know.

"Better not to ask," I said. "Hunter, can I walk?"

The doctor stood. "It would be so much better if you didn't." He glanced around and sighed. "But I suppose we have to get you on the train at least."

"Here comes trouble," Lainey said, taking her rifle from her shoulder.

I turned and watched a squad of Viridian Guard come toward us. No draconic at least. I swallowed and stood, ignoring the pain.

The leader of the squad stopped in front of us. "You are ordered to return with us to the Emerald Ascendancy," he announced.

"I don't believe that is going to happen," I answered, giving him a smile.

"It is the command of almighty Viridia!"

"We're getting on a train."

He lifted his shockspear. "You will come with us. We are authorized to use force."

I lifted my cyb hand and tapped at my chromark with one finger. "And I'm authorized to use force too. Maybe you've heard what I can do." I gestured back at the others. "Sure, you might hurt some of us. But I will take down half of you on my own. My girlfriend there will get the first kill with her projectile weapon. And then she'll let her cat loose." Glacier growled right on cue. "Those I don't take down will have to face her teeth and claws. Are you ready for that?"

The Guard members looked at each other. Several of them shifted uncomfortably.

"You don't even want to know what the others can do," I added.

The Guard leader glanced back at his squad. "I can't… I will be held responsible if I do not return with you."

"Give me your shockspear," I said, holding out my hand.

"What?"

"I'm going to do you a favor. Give it here."

Whether he intended to give it to me or not, he brought it close enough for me to seize it from his grasp. I snapped it in two with my cyb hand, easy enough to do without a boost. I dropped the pieces on the ground.

"Now you can tell Troilus Green that you tried to take me down, but I was too much for you." I looked past him at the others. "He really should have given you more backup."

"They're on their way," one of the other Guards volunteered.

"All the more reason for us to leave now," Stacy muttered.

"Head for the train," I said. "We're leaving."

Behind me, the others moved toward the train. I followed, keeping my eyes on the Viridian Guard.

"Do we stop them, sir?" one of the Guards asked.

"Let them go," the leader said.

"But—"

The leader turned on the other Guard with a furious look. A fierce argument erupted between them as we moved out of hearing range.

"I can't believe this is working," Jaden said.

"Just keep moving. We're not safe until the train leaves… and maybe not even then."

Despite my fears, the train left without incident. Lainey and Glacier waited until we were moving before running off toward the west to find the three-wheeler. I let myself relax and finally allowed Hunter to look at the back of my head. While he muttered to himself and cleaned the clotted blood out of the way, dozens of thoughts ran through my head:

Had Troilus Green really thought the one squad of Viridian Guard would be able to stop us? Or had it just been a show, to show us our departure was noticed? Our escape did relieve him of the problem of keeping his word to Auric any further. Also, how did Stacy get this train going early? What would the purple robes do with the black dragon's body? Where was

Onyx during all of this, anyway? And what about Basil? We hadn't seen him at all in Viridia, but he had to be the traitor, right?

"The bruising is significant," Hunter observed. "You say a rock hit you?"

"A very large rock."

"Clearly."

I heard scissors being used. "He has to cut away some of your hair," Kelly said from the side. I guess she was watching. "It's a mess, Beryl."

"Yes, it is," Hunter agreed. "Have you had difficulty thinking straight since this happened?"

"Sometimes. At first, my thoughts were bouncing around everywhere. I couldn't focus." I shifted a little bit in the seat. "And I still can't use my boosts. Much."

"Yet you are not incapacitated, so some of it must be working." Hunter sighed. "The physical effects I can understand. You have a serious concussion, and you are lucky to be alive. I do not understand how your implant may have affected that, or what it is doing now."

"Is it broken?" I asked.

"I do not know. Without Loden, or another cyberneticist, I do not know how we can know." He paused. "You may never regain its use again."

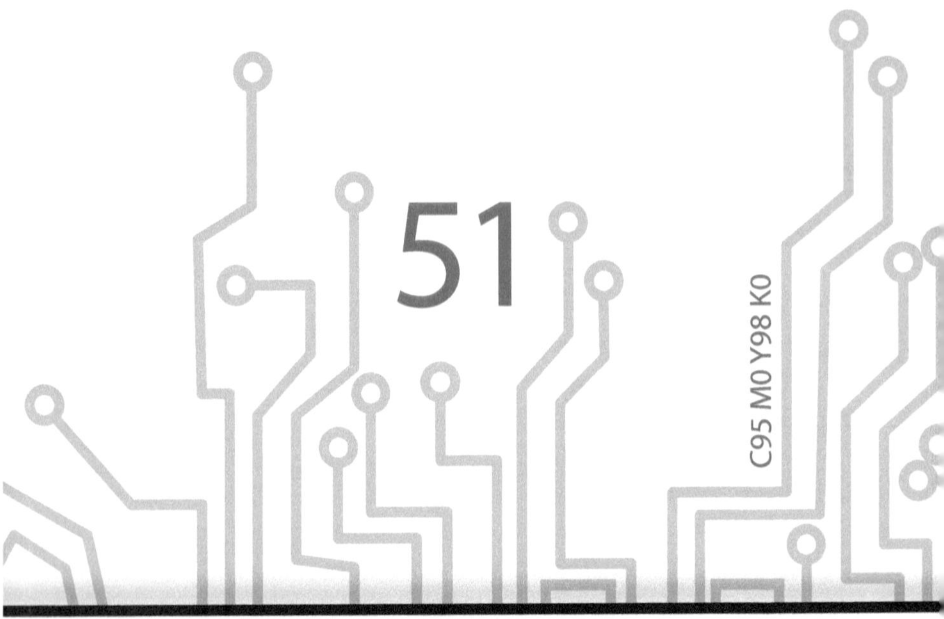

We disembarked from the train many hours later at a familiar spot near the city of Auric. Only then did I let Stacy know we'd have to sleep outside for a night or two waiting for transportation. She wasn't pleased.

We made our way out of sight from the railroad. Kelly assisted me most of the way. Once I found a seat, Hunter helped Lovat from the wheelchair and set him down next to me.

"You all right?" I asked him.

Lovat shrugged. "Weird. I can't feel my legs much. And I can't move much with these casts."

I leaned back to look behind his head. "And what about back there? Feel anything in your head?"

"I dunno." He reached his right hand to the base of his head. "Should I?"

"Maybe not. It might take a while." I swallowed. "Lovat… I'm so sorry this happened to you. It's all my fault."

"The drake hit me," he answered, wrinkling his brow. "Not you."

"But you wouldn't have been there if it weren't for me."

He wiggled his fingers and frowned at the cast covering two of them. "Itches." He brought his hand up to his mouth and tried to scratch parts of it with his mouth. I smiled and waited.

"If it weren't for you…" Lovat paused and tried to scratch at a spot on his leg. "If it weren't for you, I guess I'd still be on the streets of Viridia. Or in the pit. Or dead."

"Maybe," I acknowledged. "But—"

He turned his face to mine, and I winced at the bruises on it. "You saved me, Beryl. And now I get to be like you."

"A little bit like him," Hunter broke in. I didn't know he was listening. "You are not going to have the same abilities. This implant only connects to your back and legs."

"So I'll be able to run really fast, right?"

"If it works. And remember: it will be weeks before we even take these casts off."

"He keeps saying that," Lovat said to me.

"Because you need to understand what a very long and slow process this will be," Hunter said.

"He's right," I said. "I went through something like this. It took a very, very long time." I leaned in closer to him. "But I will be right beside you the entire time. I won't leave again until you are on your feet."

Lovat smiled. "Hue."

"I mean it. I will be there for you."

His smile got a little wider, right before Stacy exclaimed, "What in the name of all dragons of the world is that?"

"It's a, uh, grasshopper, Stacy," Kelly answered.

"Take me back to the city. Please."

Despite Stacy's protestations, we survived the night. The next day, we rested. Lovat and I were just fine with resting, though we would have preferred real beds. The others were restless. Kelly, especially, wanted to be on her way. "I've been away from Chance too long," she fretted. "What if something's gone wrong? What if he needs me?"

When Stacy tried to reassure her, Kelly politely told her to shut up if she didn't have any kids of her own. Stacy plopped down beside me in shock. "What happened to sweet Kelly?"

"She became a mom."

Kelly stomped over to us. "I'm going to start walking on my own," she announced.

"That won't help," I said. "You won't get there any faster than you will waiting here for the trailer."

"Ugh. I know, I know." She wandered off.

I reconsidered. "Actually, she might get there first," I admitted. "It just depends on how soon Caedan arrives."

"But you don't want her walking by herself, right?" Stacy whispered.

"Yeah. I can't help it."

"You're a good man, Beryl."

"So they tell me."

Caedan arrived with the trailer soon after dawn the next morning. I was impressed he made it that early. For the others, the ride back to the base was bumpy but uneventful. Lovat and I suffered, though. Every bump shook up every injury we possessed. By the time we reached the base, we were both extremely sore and tired.

The whole gang came out to meet us, even Lady Rust, Taizong Gold, and Captain Tawn. Seeing them reminded me of Auric's last words. Kelly jumped off the trailer and ran to meet Chance and Fern. Hunter helped Lovat into the wheelchair at the edge of the trailer, while the rest of us waited.

Don ran forward before any of the others. His normally stoic face showed an emotion I'd never seen on him before. "Lovat! Lovat! What happened to you?"

"Hey, Don! I'm going to be like Beryl now!"

Don whirled on me, eyes blazing. "Did you do this to him?"

"Troilus Green did it." I straightened up, in spite of the pain. "But it was my fault."

Don punched me. I never saw it coming. One moment, I was looking into his furious eyes, and the next, I was lying on the trailer, my head hurting more than ever.

Royal and Turq caught Don and held him back, while Bice talked him down. Hunter checked me out and helped me sit up on the edge of the trailer.

Don pulled free of the others and pointed at me. His finger shook, but he didn't say anything else. He spun and stalked away.

The rest of the group crowded around us, asking questions and talking over all the news. I let the others answer, as much as possible. The bumpy ride and Don's punch took a lot out of me.

Taizong Gold and Captain Tawn approached me. The others got out of the way of the draconic. I didn't blame them. Even though he'd been among us for a while, it wasn't easy to be friendly with a cybernetically-enhanced seven-foot tall lizard.

"We are returning to our city," Taizong Gold announced. "We waited for you to return as a courtesy."

"I understand," I said. "I was… horrified at Auric's death. I didn't…" I trailed off. I didn't know what to say.

"You said he had a message for me," Tawn said. "Contingency two, wasn't it?"

I glanced at Lady Rust. "Yes. Those were his last words."

He nodded. "I am to give you this, then." He held out a small electronic device.

"What is it?" I took it from his hands and looked over the rectangular object no larger than my hand. A series of buttons extruded from one of the narrow sides.

"It is an audio recording and playback device," he explained. "It has been set up to the appropriate location. You have only to press this button"—he pointed at it—"and it will play the message you are to receive."

I wrinkled my brow. "Is it from Auric?"

"You should listen to it alone." Captain Tawn straightened and saluted me. Then he and the draconic shouldered backpacks and started down the hill.

"Goodbye," I called. I wondered if we would ever see them again.

Lady Rust sidled up, arms folded. "And so you return again," she said. "And two more of my brothers are dead." She shook her head. "You are favored by some god somewhere, Beryl."

"If you say so." I took Hunter's hand and pulled myself up to my feet. "And stay out of my dreams."

She smiled with a tilt of her head, letting a lock of red hair fall across her face. "We'll see."

"Do you talk to the other dragons in their dreams?" I wondered. "Is that how you've communicated all these years?"

"On rare occasions," she answered. "Why?"

"Just wondering." I limped toward the base entrance, then paused. "Does Chroma ever appear in your dreams?"

"No," she said. "Not in hundreds of years, at least."

I'm not sure why I asked that, but it seemed significant, somehow.

"Are you going to be okay, Beryl?" Bice asked, coming up beside me.

"I could use a shoulder to lean on," I admitted.

"Always." He offered his own. "Where to?"

"I just need a bed right now," I said. "I'm in a lot of pain."

"Hunter told me some of it." He kept quiet until we reached the stairs going down. "How do you feel about your mission now? Five dragons are dead." He glanced over his shoulder. "And one is trapped with us."

"Only Onyx is left. We've never been closer to freedom for everyone," I said. "And yet... Ow!" I couldn't help reacting to the first step down.

"Can you do this?"

"I'll manage." I gritted my teeth and kept going.

"And yet, you're thinking outside The Circle now, aren't you?" Bice asked.

"I don't want to, but... yes. They're invading us." I stopped at the bottom of the stairs. "If we're going to be free, Bice... we have to stop the zealots too. We have to stop Chroma."

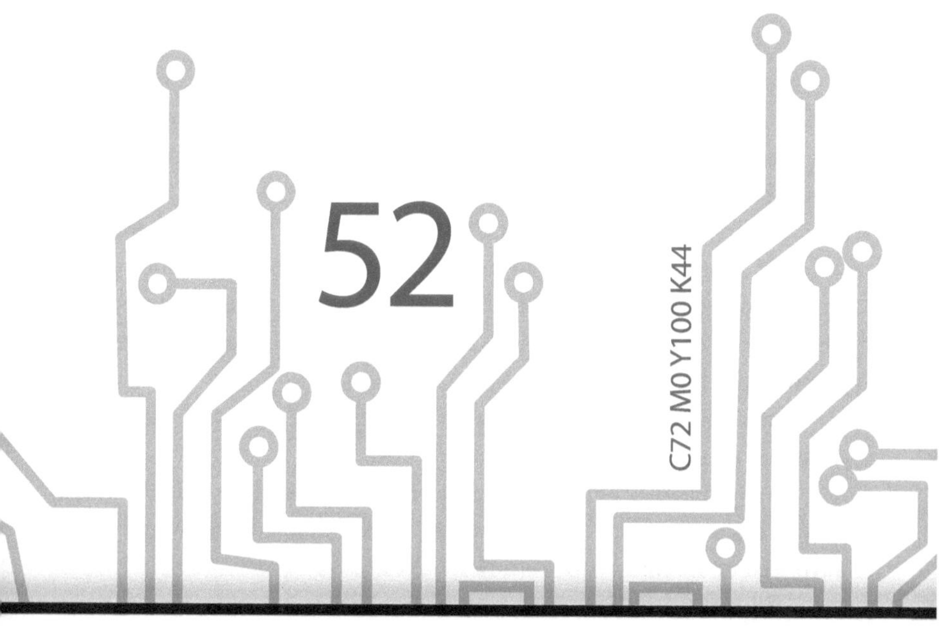

Alone at last in my room, I relaxed on the bed. Lovat would be here before long, but he was still talking with Don and the others for now. They might even get something to eat. I just couldn't take it right now.

I looked at the audio device and considered. I almost put it under the bed to wait for another time. Instead, I clicked the button Tawn had indicated.

At first, I heard only static and some rustling. "Is it on?" a voice asked.

I gasped and almost dropped the device. I knew that voice.

Loden.

"Yes," answered a second, deeper voice. "You may say what you wish, and it will be recorded."

I clicked another button to stop the playback. I trembled a little and swallowed hard. I knew the second voice too. It was Ciaru… Auric. He had known Loden. Why didn't he mention it? All this time, he had…

The patron. Hunter said Loden had a rich patron, someone who paid for much of his research and experimentation. It was Auric! Or rather, Ciaru. Had Loden known he was working for a dragon? And why?

I clicked the button again.

"Right, right," Loden said. "Let me see here." He muttered something else too quiet to be heard. I almost stopped it again. The emotion of hearing his voice again… my eyes welled up.

"Some time ago, I became aware of the true nature of The Circle," Loden said. "Lord Ciaru here was kind enough to educate me. With that knowledge, I also learned about a threat, an enormous threat, to everyone here." He paused. "Do I tell about that?"

"By the time anyone hears this, they will know," Ciaru answered.

"Of course. Anyway, I have turned my attentions from random experimentation to, ah, tools. Tools that will help against this threat. And the greatest tool of all is a young man I helped back in Viridia. He doesn't even know it yet, but he will. Someday."

The door to my room opened. I shut off the device and wiped a tear away before turning to see who had entered.

To my surprise, Chance stood there. He looked older, somehow, than when I'd last seen him, but still so small... for a draconic, anyway. I smiled, surprised to see him apart from Kelly already.

"What can I do for you, Chance?"

He closed the door behind him and stood near my bed. "Chance. The name my mother gave me," he said, his voice surprisingly mature. "You may continue to call me that."

I blinked. What?

"My true name, however, is Enlil Black, son of Onyx. I know that now." He lowered his snout to stare down at me. "We need to talk."

Beryl's story concludes in

Chroma

For more information on the Dragontek Lore series,
and other upcoming books,
visit timfrankovich.com

Joining the mailing list is the best way to stay informed,
plus you get free stories!
(including Rick's story before he arrived in Viridia!)

If you enjoyed this book, please post a review
on Amazon, B&N, Goodreads, etc.
There's no better way to spread the word.

Author's Notes

This book had a much longer path to publication than any of the previous books in the series, owing primarily to a serious hand injury. That same injury stalled a lot of things, and is still impacting things today. So… be patient with the final book. It's coming. I promise.

I've had the final scene of this series in my head since very early in the writing of Viridia. I'm very much looking forward to finally writing it.

Does anyone really read these notes? If you do, drop me a note on social media and let me know. I'm curious.

If you want to keep track of my progress on all my writing, you can connect on timfrankovich.com, my Facebook author page, X-Twitter, etc. But the best way, which keeps you informed and gives you exclusive previews, is to join the mailing list. Sign up on the website. (You'll get free stories too!)

Tim Frankovich has been exploring fantastic worlds since third grade, when he cut up a grocery sack and drew a Godzilla-meets-superheroes story. Since then, he's gotten a little bit better at the writing part (not so much with the drawing).

His goal as a writer is to transport readers to another world, make them care deeply about characters in dire situations, and guide them deeply into life itself.

At the moment, he is probably suitably conscious somewhere in Texas with his beloved wife, awesome four kids, and a fool of a pup named Pippin.

www.ingramcontent.com/pod-product-compliance
Lightning Source LLC
Chambersburg PA
CBHW020105310726
48970CB00002B/480